Leviathan Rising

The suit pounding across the seabed, ever carrying him towards the beleaguered base, Ulysses saw the fissure appear to his left and race away ahead of him. Rock shifted beneath him, slid sideways, dropping the section of seabed across which he was moving by several feet. His pulse thumped in his chest and in his brain. It seemed undoable now, impossible, but when had that ever stopped him?

An entire shelf of rock at the edge of the precipice had splintered free of the rest of the sea-bed, giving way under the weight and movement of the shifting sub-liner and weakened by the explosive destruction of the vessel's engines.

With a roar like pebbles being ground on a beach by the surf, only a hundred times louder, the cliff gave way, boulders the size of houses tumbling into the hungry darkness, taking Ulysses — helpless now, trapped inside the pressure suit — with it, down into the unfathomable depths of the Marianas Trench.

An Abaddon Books™ Publication
www.abaddonbooks.com
abaddon@rebellion.co.uk

First published in 2008 by Abaddon Books™, Rebellion Intellectual
Property Limited, The Studio, Brewer Street, Oxford, OX1 1QN, UK.

10 9 8 7 6 5 4 3 2 1

Editor: Jonathan Oliver
Cover: Mark Harrison
Design: Simon Parr & Luke Preece
Marketing and PR: Keith Richardson
Creative Director and CEO: Jason Kingsley
Chief Technical Officer: Chris Kingsley
Pax Britannia™ created by Jonathan Green and Andy Boot

ISBN: 978-1-905437-60-3

PAX BRITANNIA

LEVIATHAN RISING

JONATHAN GREEN

WWW.ABADDONBOOKS.COM

For Lou, who enjoyed the first one
And for Clare, always

Canst thou draw out
leviathan with an hook?

(Job, ch.41 v.1)

PROLOGUE

Voyage to the Bottom of the Sea

The *Venture* – a tramp steamer, six days out from Shanghai – chugged on across the oceanic wilderness, smoke and steam belching from its stack, fighting the swell and chop of the sea. All rusting gunwales and weather-warped boards, the filthy, noisy craft pressed on against the surges of the sea. The entirety of the firmament was fogged with cloud from horizon to horizon: the Pacific a roiling mass of churning darkness beneath. Seabirds, flickers of white against the grey pall of the heavens, soared high above the lonely Venture, their discordant cries lost to the howls of the wind and the crash of waves against the lancing prow of the boat. The vessel appeared as nothing more than a rusty speck amidst the torpid rise and fall of the black waters.

The ship slammed into another wave-crest, the resounding clang of impact shuddering through the vessel, shaking it to its bilges. Captain Engelhard – Bavarian-German by extraction – peered out of the brine-spotted glass in front of him at the undulating mountains of water surrounding the *Venture*. With no land in any direction as far as the eye could see, the wild waters of the South China Seas were some of the roughest and most unpredictable in all the world, from Engelhard's experience – not unlike the hard-bitten captain himself. Lean as a sea snake and potentially twice as venomous, Engelhard demanded both the respect of the men of his crew, and their fear. It had been the same as old Runcorn under whom he had first worked the trade routes between the empires of Magna Britannia and China as a cabin boy, and on whom he had modelled his own style of leadership when he took command of the *Venture* on Runcorn's untimely death.

From his experience, it had always been the way: a sailor who respected his captain, who trusted his judgement and honoured his decisions, would follow you across the seven seas to the four corners of the globe. But a man who feared you, him you could lead down to Davy Jones's locker or into the jaws of hell itself. That was the kind of man Engelhard wanted aboard his ship, in his line of business.

One such man was his first mate, Mr Hayes. The crew of the *Venture* was a cosmopolitan group, Hayes himself hailing from Rhodesia. The cream wool Arran sweater he wore was in sharp contrast with the polished ebony of his skin. He was a brute of a man, taller and broader than Engelhard, made loyal by the promise of great rewards and made cruel by whatever it was that had happened to him in his youth before he escaped his homeland for the open sea.

With a hold full of the finest opium, from the poppy fields of Sichuan Province, bound for the smoking dens of Magna Britannia, hell and high water came as part of the deal. Engelhard needed a crew that he knew he could trust in a tight spot. He knew all too well the kind of hazards one could face on such a venture, the risks you ran in the quest for increased profit and the future promise of an easy life – a procession of ladies of easy virtue and a limitless supply of rum. And so he looked for men who would not falter when faced with an officer of Her Imperial Majesty's revenue office, and who knew the business end of a cudgel. And then there was always the risk of meeting a rival out on these wild seas, another captain hoping to make it big with a shipment of opium bound for the West.

There had long been old sea dog's tales connected to these waters. They mainly concerned the mysterious disappearances of ships over the centuries. It was said that the fathomless depths beneath them were some of the very deepest waters in the world. The ocean floor was said to be riven with trenches so deep that no one, not even unmanned probes, had ever been able to reach the bottom. And when one considered some of the monsters that dwelt within the trackless seas as it was, it was not hard to find oneself wondering what might be dwelling within such abyssal chasms.

But then there were such tales told about every ocean on the planet, tales first told to explain the inexplicable, to account for the unaccountable, to explain away the effects of freakish weather, killer tidal waves and abductions carried out by those who still perpetrated the slave trade in certain corners of the world. The fact that reports of unaccountable disappearances had apparently increased over the last twenty years or so meant nothing to Captain Engelhard other than that the opium trade, and competition between those captains and crews associated with it, had increased in the intervening period to lethal effect.

Not that Engelhard often found himself in such a predicament. He was too careful to let that happen to him if he could help it. But it paid to take precautions. The old whaler's harpoon gun bolted to the prow of the *Venture* was just one such precaution.

Despite the damp cold of the sea-spray and the chilling effects of the wind, the cabin still felt uncomfortably warm, thanks to the excess heat pumping from the smoky engine room below. The air was close and redolent with coke fumes. There was another shuddering crash as the steel hull of the steamer collided head-on with another wall of black water. The tramp steamer pushed on through and then the prow was rising again, the great surge breaking into a curtain of white spray. Water splashed across the smeared pane in front of Engelhard and then skittered away in the face of the wind. The *Venture* dipped again, plunging onwards into the waves.

The force of the collision stopped the boat in its tracks, the hull-shuddering crash booming through the cabins and holds of the old steamer. Engelhard flew forwards over the wheel as the ship lurched, into the window panel in front of him. He gasped as the wind was knocked from him, the handle of the wheel in his gut, and cursed with his next breath at the blow he received to the forehead.

The surging sea continued to tug and pull at the *Venture* but, after more time spent onboard ship than on land, Engelhard knew that the steamer wasn't going anywhere. Incredibly, somehow, it had come to a complete stop: he could barely feel the ever-present heave and yaw of the ship as the depthless ocean moved beneath it and on which the ship should be bobbing like a cork.

Then his mind was full of questions. What had they hit? He hadn't seen anything out here with them. The *Venture*'s instruments hadn't warned him of the approach of another vessel. What could possibly have brought the steamer to such an abrupt halt out here, miles from land, with nothing beneath them but the unsounded depths of the Marianas Trench? Had they collided with some submersible, either belonging to a rival or commandeered by a more ingenious member of Her Majesty's revenue office? But if that were the case, again, how could it have brought them to a complete stop? The engines were still chugging away, the propeller turning, but the *Venture* wasn't going anywhere. It was just as if they had run aground, only that was impossible.

The cabin was suddenly full of excitedly questioning crewmen, all coming up top to find out what was going on.

"What is it, Captain?" Hayes asked.

The ship lurched again. Engelhard grabbed for the wheel to stop himself losing his footing as others lunged for handrails or ended up on their knees on the floor of the cabin.

"We're on top of something," he hissed. "Mr Hayes, take the wheel!"

Engelhard threw himself out of the cabin, into the wind and lashing spray, half his crew tumbling through the door after him. Grabbing the starboard gunwale, Engelhard peered over the edge of the ship. At first all he could see was black waves and white breakers, a torment of churning water pummelling the hull of the ship. And then he saw it; something grey and indistinct, a pockmarked surface beneath the ship, the keel caught within it, something huge.

The ship pitched suddenly, yawing dangerously to port, throwing the gaggle of sailors and their captain back from the edge of the boat and slamming them into the side of the cabin. Engelhard pulled himself back to the side and saw the grey shape slip away beneath them. Vast as it was, it was still moving past several moments later.

And now the *Venture* was moving again. Hayes tensed as the wheel became suddenly responsive, straining to bring the whirling tramp steamer back to its original heading. Whatever the thing was, it was moving away from the ship now. Captain Engelhard simply stood and stared as the vast, streamlined shape slid away beneath the waves, the steamer chugging on through the surge as

if nothing untoward had happened. This would be a tale
to tell back at The Smuggler's Rest in Plymouth.

His gaze remaining locked on the... whatever it was...
it still took Engelhard's startled brain a moment or two
to realise that the something had turned and was now
moving back towards the *Venture*, at speed. The vast
form was rising from the stygian depths. Grey-green
flesh broke the surface, the telltale V of white water
showing how close it was already and how quickly it
was closing.

"Mein gott!" Engelhard gasped. A shudder of fear
rippled through him. In the next moment fear and
disbelief turned to instinctive, unthinking reaction. "All
of you, to your stations!"

With Mr Hayes at the wheel, and the rest of the crew
running to obey his command, Captain Josef Engelhard
sprinted for the prow of the steamer, expertly avoiding
the myriad hazards awaiting the unwary on the deck
plates of the working ship – coils of steel cable, tie-
off stanchions, raised hatch covers – and the whaler's
harpoon gun positioned there like a furious, war-
mongering figurehead.

With the submerged creature, or whatever it was,
torpedoing back towards the *Venture*, he reached the
swivel-mounted weapon and, both calloused hands
grasping its lever-handles, spun its muzzle round,
bringing the closing grey mass within its sights.

Without a moment's hesitation, Engelhard fired. Six
feet of jagged-tipped harpoon blasted out of the mouth
of the cannon, high-tensile steel cable spiralling after it,
uncoiling from its winch-pulley, as the hardened steel
bolt entered the sea in a rush of white bubbles. The cable
pulled taut and, prow dipping fiercely, the *Venture* was
pulled sharply round on itself, as the harpoon found its

mark. The drug-smuggling sailors clung on as the boat was pulled around and Hayes cut the engines to lessen the resistance. Then all was still, other than the rise and fall of the ocean around the steamer, and the steel line slackened.

"We got it," Engelhard said, hardly believing what he was saying himself. "We got it!"

Leaving the harpoon he staggered back to the cabin house, grinning at the bewildered faces of his crew. "We got it! Haul it in, then we'll see what it is we've caught and what we think it will fetch on the black market."

There was a violent jolt as the cable went taut again, the tensed steel twanging like a guitar string, and the prow dipped once more.

"What in Hell's name!" was all Engelhard could manage before his world flipped on its axis and the deck disappeared from beneath him. His fall was abruptly halted by the harpoon gun.

The gun's solid bolted mounting buckled as the *Venture* upended, the bows of the vessel disappearing beneath the bubbling surface of the ocean. At the same moment the sea exploded around the ship. Writhing shapes, silhouetted against the grey pall of the heavens, obscured by the vertical deluge thrown up on all sides of the ship, crashed down on the steamer, seizing the boat within cruelly crushing coils. The smokestack crumpled, the roof of the cabin splintered like so much matchwood and the creaking hull protested as it buckled, rupturing in a dozen places.

With a sudden *whoomph*, the *Venture* was pulled violently beneath the waves, churning black and white water closing over it, rushing in to fill the hole in the sea where it had just been. In moments nothing was left of the opium, the tramp steamer or its crew.

Relative calm returned to the ocean surface. The only sign of there ever having been a ship there at all were a few broken boards and bobbing oil drums, and amongst the drifting flotsam a single, battered rubber life-ring that bore the name *Venture*. And the clinging, barely conscious Captain Engelhard.

ACT ONE

20,000 Leagues Under the Sea

July 1997

Below the thunders of the upper deep,
Far far beneath in the abysmal sea,
His ancient, dreamless, uninvaded sleep
The Kraken sleepeth...

(Alfred Lord Tennyson, *The Kraken*)

CHAPTER ONE

Around the World in Eighty Days

LUXURY LINER SETS SAIL ON MAIDEN VOYAGE
By our reporter 'on board' Miss Glenda Finch

"Around the world in eighty days – in style!"
This is the proud boast of the Carcharodon Shipping Company, owners of the new luxury passenger sub-liner the Neptune, that sets sail from Southampton docks on 5th July. It is the company's claim that those who can afford the small-fortune-a-berth price tag will enjoy an unprecedented luxury cruise across the oceans of the globe, taking in many of its most remarkable and celebrated sights along the way.

Jonah Carcharodon repeated this bold claim – one of his own devising – during the festivities surrounding the launch of the Neptune, when His Royal Highness the Duke of Cornwall broke the traditional bottle of Cristal champagne – as served on board the Neptune in its many bars and restaurants. Rumour has it that Carcharodon has placed a hefty bet on his pride-and-joy's inaugural voyage running to time.

As well as an estimated three thousand paying guests, a number of dignitaries and VIPs are on board at the invitation of Jonah Carcharodon himself, to add glamour and media interest to the maiden voyage of the newest member of the Great White Shipping Line's fleet of high-end luxury passenger vessels. Amongst the invited elite is rumoured to be Hero of the Empire, Ulysses Quicksilver himself who, as regular readers of The Times will know, was instrumental in thwarting the recent plot against Her Majesty's life. But whether he is here for a little rest and recuperation, to find himself a new female companion from amongst the socialites and well-to-do heiresses on board, or for some other clandestine reason, only time will tell.

"Your cognac, sir," the aquiline gentleman's valet said, bending at the hip to proffer his master the glass positioned precisely dead centre on the tray in his hand.

"Why, thank you, Nimrod," the younger man said with a smile, taking the balloon glass in his left hand. He gently swirled its contents before putting it to his mouth. There he paused, savouring the heady aroma of the brandy before taking a sip. He held the tingling mouthful on his tongue for a moment, taste buds excited at its touch, before luxuriating in the sensation of the cognac slipping like molten honey down his throat.

"Very nice," he said, easing himself back on the sunlounger.

"Will there be anything else, sir?"

"No, I think that will be all for now," Ulysses Quicksilver replied, running a hand through his mane of dark blond hair and adjusting the dark-tinted spectacles perched on the bridge of his nose.

"Very good, sir. Then if you would not mind I shall retire and see to some matters of house-keeping demanding my attention back at the suite."

"Very well, Nimrod. Whatever floats your boat I suppose," Ulysses said, flashing his faithful manservant a wicked grin. Nimrod responded by arching an eyebrow, before he turned on his heel and strode rigidly from the sundeck, tray in hand.

Ulysses Quicksilver stretched his body out on the wicker lounger, adjusting his suit of cream linen for comfort and loosening the azure rough silk cravat at his neck, luxuriating in the warmth of the sun on his face.

A twinge of pain from his right shoulder took him momentarily by surprise and reminded him, at least in part, why he had accepted Jonah Carcharodon's invitation to join the maiden voyage of the Neptune. More than a month on from the debacle surrounding Queen Victoria's 160th jubilee his left arm was healed and out of its sling – although it still hurt to over-flex it – but his shoulder was a more substantial, recurring injury, one he had received in his near-fatal crash on Mount Manaslu in the Himalayan range. He had been lucky to walk away from that one at all; not that he had walked away of course. He had crawled from the crash-site, managing to get as far as a precipitous icy ledge before the effects of hypothermia had set in. And then the monks of Shangri-La had found him.

He stretched again, testing his body this time, wondering what other aches and pains would reveal themselves, trying to put the memory of an event to every twinge, every dull ache, every agony remembered, each a physical remembrance of one of a whole host of injuries received in the line of duty.

There was the rumour of cramp in his left leg, and the still-present dull ache in his side. Such sensations were almost reassuring in their familiarity. Easing his right shoulder into a more comfortable position he felt the skin under his shirt. There were still four distinct traces of scar tissue where the pterodactyl had – bizarrely – saved his life.

But that was all in the past now. All that featured in

his immediate future was a few weeks R & R and a jolly jaunt in warmer climes, while Barty remained in London overseeing the renovation of the Mayfair residence, his brother himself under the ever-watchful eye of Mrs Prufrock, Ulysses' cook and housekeeper.

A sudden shadow came between Ulysses and the burning white disc of the sun blazing in the cloudless azure expanse of sky above the cruising liner. Ulysses removed his sunglasses and, narrowing his eyes, focused on the not uncomely figure in front of him.

"It's Mr Quicksilver, isn't it? Or can I call you Ulysses?"

Ulysses smiled and deliberately looked the svelte young woman up and down, taking in the classic yet subtle curves of her body, accentuated by the way the sea-green gown she had chosen to wear hung from and clung to her body to greatest effect. It was a bold statement – the colour in sharp contrast to the blue of her eyes and the over-coiffeured curls of her golden-blonde hair. The dress would have been more appropriate as evening wear – exposed shoulders, arms and cleavage not really being the done thing, at least not on the sundeck or the watertight promenade deck. The boa of pink flamingo feathers really set it off a treat.

Worn here and now, it was an outfit that said that this was a young woman who was independent, determined to make her own way in the world, apparently regardless of what others might think of her. And yet, at the same time, all too self-aware, desperate to make a lasting impression, fearful of being forgotten or, worse, overlooked in the first place.

"I'm sorry, you seem to have me at a disadvantage, Miss –"

"Glenda Finch, social commentator for *The Times*."

"Ah, the gossip columnist."

For a moment the woman's mouth puckered in disdain but then her brilliant white smile returned like the sun emerging from behind a passing cloud. "You know of my work then?"

"I've read your column in the past, as no more than an amusing distraction you understand. And I believe I've been the subject of it on a number of occasions."

"So you'll know that I'm aware of your work as well."

"Well, it's hard to hide one's light under a bushel when you save the Queen herself from certain death at the hands of a psychotic megalomaniac at the most public event of the decade in front of the world's press. But I rather suspect I'll get over it. Today's front page, tomorrow's fish and chip paper and all that."

"Oh, you do yourself down, Ulysses," the reporter returned. "But as you were the one to mention the part you played in saving Her Majesty's life would you care to give me a quote? In fact, why don't you offer to buy me a drink and then you can tell me all about it."

Smiling, his gaze lingering on the shadow of the young woman's cleavage – how could what was effectively little more than the empty space between two breasts be so appealing? – Ulysses pointedly returned his sunglasses to his nose.

"Good day, Miss Finch."

The Neptune *boasts five-star hotel accommodation married to the most advanced steam-driven technology in the Empire. Four massive Rolls Royce engines – each, I am told, as big as a London townhouse – will move the huge vessel at an average of twenty knots across open* stretches of water, when the weather, the sea and the opportunity permit. The vessel itself is 1,020 feet long and fifteen storeys tall.

But all of this technological magnificence and industrial maritime creativity is all to serve one purpose – ultimately that of entertainment. People want to sail the seven seas, to relax, see the world, advance their own realms of experience, and be entertained in the process. And there are all manner of entertainments available on board.

As well as three kinemas, a vaudeville theatre, numerous restaurants, bistros and bars, and the infamous Casino Royale, there are also indoor squash courts and outdoor tennis courts, a gymnasium, solarium and three swimming pools. But possibly the most magnificent exercise alternative is the Promenade Deck itself. Running two thirds the length of the ship, the Promenade is nearly a quarter of a mile long, meaning that two complete laps is the equivalent to a walk of a mile. This might not sound so special until you learn that the entirety of the Promenade is covered by a reinforced glass and steel structure capable of withstanding the same pressures as that of the ship's hull, so that passengers may still enjoy a stroll along the Promenade, and all that might be revealed beyond it, even when the Neptune makes one of its scheduled dives to the undersea cities found along its route during the course of its voyage. And as well as walks along the Promenade, of course, one may also partake in any number of traditional deck sports such as quoits.

One of the appealing features of a cruise is not only what the ship itself has to offer, but also the places one can visit along the way. Destinations on the Neptune's maiden voyage include the renowned Atlantis City, and *the fully-restored Temple of Jupiter, a shopping stop at America's first city of New York, the prehistoric game parks of the Costa Rican island chain, the incredible sculpted coral gardens of Pacifica, and even a brief sojourn on the Cairo Express across the Sinai peninsula to visit the pyramids of Giza.*

The thunderous retort of the elephant gun echoed through the primeval jungle, sending a flock of white egrets squawking and flapping from the canopy. The parasaurolophus bellowed, throwing back its crested head as the four-bore shell found its mark, hitting the creature in its flank, punching through the rhino-like hide and sending a spray of blood and meat from the wound. The bipedal herbivore faltered in its graceful run, its thick tail swinging to maintain the injured creature's balance. The dashing pachycephalosauruses accompanying the larger dinosaur's flight scattered across the clearing.

Ulysses Quicksilver took another sip of Earl Grey from the fine bone china teacup in his hands. He savoured the taste for a moment, as well as the sunlight on his face. It was good to be off ship for a short sojourn, hunting dinosaurs, although with the howdah gently rolling beneath him, he felt like he might as well still be on board.

"Good shot, Major!" he called.

"Thank you, sah!" the bristle-whiskered and portly Major Marmaduke Horsley called back, reloading the gun almost automatically as he did so. "One more shot should bring the blighter down."

The parasaurolophus trumpeted again. Its injury was causing it to limp badly and it was moving for the natural protection of the trees at the edge of the jungle clearing.

"Oh no you don't!" the Major shouted and then to the imported Indian beast-wrangler attempting to steer the triceratops on which their howdah was being carried: "You! Dino-waller! Chop chop, what-ho? Dashed blighter's getting away! Come on, man. We can't lose it now."

With a shout from the beast's handler, perched on a saddle across the creature's broad shoulders behind the frill of its crest, and judicious use of a crackling electro-goad, the ceratopsid pounded forward. Ulysses tried to avoid spilling any of the tea slopping from the cup onto his trousers.

Horsley put the gun to his shoulder again, swiftly capturing the distinctive profile of his quarry's head within the crosshairs of its sights. The elephant gun boomed once more. There was something like a grunt of satisfaction from the major and the parasaurolophus crashed to the ground, as every muscle in its body relaxed with the pulverisation of the creature's tiny brain.

"Good shooting, Major!" called Miss Birkin, waving at the ex-army officer enthusiastically from the back of a brontosaur, parasol in hand to keep the equatorial sun from her milk-white sensitive skin.

"Why thank you, Miss Birkin! It should make a fine addition to my trophy collection. I shall have it stuffed and mounted above the mantelpiece in my sitting room at home."

"I think you've made a big impression there, Major," Ulysses teased.

"What? What rot! Can't stand the bloody woman," Horsley returned under his breath. "Too full of her blinking, half-baked conspiracy theories."

Ulysses caught the eye of John Schafer, seated next

to his fiancée in the same bamboo and calico fashioned conveyance, opposite Constance's ever-present chaperone. "Good afternoon, Mr Schafer, Miss Pennyroyal. Enjoying the show?"

"Oh yes, Mr Quicksilver," Constance called back across the clearing. "Most exhilarating!" she added with a flutter of the fan in her hand and a reddening of her perfect porcelain cheeks.

"Rather beats the Wilmington Hunt, doesn't it?" Schafer called back.

"Indeed it does," Ulysses agreed.

A sudden shout went up from one of the native beaters accompanying the lumbering triceratops and brontosauruses and was passed along the drawn out line. There the Costa Ricans were showing obvious signs of agitation, their behaviour not going unnoticed by Major Marmaduke Horsley.

"I say, man," he barked at their guide, "what's going on? What's this bally hoo-ha all about?"

"A meat-eater, an allosaur, has been spotted, mensab," the Indian replied, his English thickly accented.

"Where?"

"Two miles west of here, on the approach to the watering hole."

"Then what are we waiting for, man? We can't let a prize like that get away, can we Quicksilver?"

"Perish the thought, Major."

"Looks like the space over the mantelpiece is still up for grabs, what?"

"It would indeed."

With a fanfare of bad-tempered grunting and rumbling herbivorous farts, the triceratops mount set off at a canter, under the impelling of its handler.

The Major turned to face Ulysses, a wild gleam in his

wide eyes, his monocle popping from the orbit of his right eye where it should have fitted snugly.

"Ever hunted any big game, Quicksilver, and I mean truly big game?"

Ulysses' mind immediately rushed back to the dinosaur stampede that had rampaged through the capital only a matter of months ago, following the terrorist atrocities of the Darwinian Dawn.

"There was this one time," he replied

"Well the hunt's on now, isn't it, what-ho?"

"Indeed it is, Major. Indeed it is."

Accompanying the launch of the largest passenger ship in the world was a feeling of optimism. Many felt that it helped lay to rest the ghosts of the near apocalyptic events of Her Majesty Queen Victoria's 160th jubilee celebrations. Let us hope that such dark times are now behind us and that we can look forward to the approaching new millennium with joy, hope and positivity in our hearts.

As to Jonah Carcharodon's bold claim that the latest and greatest passenger cruise liner in the world offers an unparalleled experience we, those of us fortunate enough to join the inaugural sailing, will have to wait and see. But rest assured, your eyes and ears on board will be with it to the end so that you might feel that you are with us every step of the way.

And, as readers of this column will already know, Carcharodon is no stranger to publicity himself. Only last year, before the Neptune had even left the dockyards, there were rumours of financial irregularities and the threat of insolvency for his shipping company.

Ulysses made his way along the mahogany-panelled, plushly-carpeted corridor towards his suite of rooms on the VIP guest deck, tossing his room key in the palm of his hand as he did so. The opulence on show, even here, in a corridor between cabins, was mind-boggling. Ulysses had heard the rumours of financial challenges facing the Great White Shipping Line, but he had no idea whether the construction of such a vessel as the *Neptune* was the cause of near-bankruptcy or whether it was a sign that Jonah Carcharodon was still doing very nicely for himself, thank you. What Ulysses was certain of, however, was that the success or failure of their new flagship venture could make or break the Carcharodon's Shipping Company. Either it would prove an unmitigated triumph and float the company's stock like nothing ever before, or the world's greatest cruise line would sink without a trace.

He was suddenly roused from his reverie by a scratching at the back of his skull, his ever-alert sixth sense acting up again, something almost akin to premonition. Glancing to his right he came face-to-face with Miss Glenda Finch of *The Times*, trying to look nonchalant as she loitered within a doorway.

"Why, Miss Finch," Ulysses said, a predatory smile spreading across his lips as he took in the hollow between the underdressed reporter's plunging cleavage again and the way the side split of the gown exposed a shapely leg to the thigh. "What a pleasant, if unexpected, surprise. I didn't know you had rooms on this floor. I had been led to believe that all members of the press were located two decks down in steerage."

For a moment the reporter's beaming smile almost faltered, pupils dilating with something like annoyance, but then, a moment later, Miss Finch had regained her indefatigable composure.

"Mr Quicksilver. Twice in one day. People will start to talk. I was just..."

"Looking for something – sorry – someone?" Ulysses didn't take his gaze from her not unattractive face, the smile on his lips no longer reflected in his eyes.

"Looking for you, actually."

"Really?"

"Weren't you going to buy me a drink?"

Confidently she thrust her arm into his, turning him round in one balletic movement, to lead him back towards the grand atrium and, thence, to one of the bars.

What is she up to? Ulysses wondered, and then caught himself. *Always on duty, eh Quicksilver, old chap?* Whatever it was, it could probably wait. And besides, a pleasant drink in distracting company was what this trip was all about – at least for the present, and there was no time like it.

"Indeed. Why not, Miss Finch? Why not? Vodka on the rocks with a twist of lime, if I remember correctly from my casual perusal of your column."

"Why, Ulysses, recalling a lady's favourite tipple – you flatter me."

"I do indeed. And why not? A woman like you wearing a dress like that deserves to be well and truly... flattered."

"Now-now, Ulysses, people will talk."

"No, my dear, you will talk, and I for one can't wait to hear what you'll have to say for yourself."

As to what adventures await us on the voyage ahead, we will simply have to wait and see. This is Glenda Finch, signing off, until next time.

CHAPTER TWO

Fourteen at Dinner

"Ladies and gentlemen," the droid-butler's tinny voice crackled, "dinner is served."

A hubbub of excitement accompanying them, the captain's dinner guests bustled their way into the mirrored dining room.

The room was ostentatiously decorated and included a number of large, gilt-framed mirrors. Statues of Renaissance-imagined dolphins and mermen filled the room and the trident logo of the *Neptune* was repeated at every possible opportunity. The place was not unlike an underwater treasure cave, with the gold, silver and crystal offset by the dark blue and sea-green colouring of the draperies, wall dressings and carpets.

A long table had been laid for dinner. The candlelight cast by three polished candelabra set along the length of the table reflected back from the myriad mirrors, filling the dining chamber with light, which in turn sparkled from crystal-cut glassware, fine-glazed bone china and silver place settings.

Where the starboard wall should have been there was a breath-taking, floor-to-ceiling, glass and steel bubble, like the one above the Promenade deck, allowing the captain and his guests an unprecedented view of the sea whether the sub-liner was above or beneath the waves.

On another table, set against one wall and laden with the meal's wine selection, after-dinner spirits and more champagne, stood a glistening sculpture, the flawless ice chiselled and smoothed to resemble the God of the

Sea himself, trident in hand, seated upon a scallop-shell throne.

Sprays of lilies on both the table and within flower stands in the corners of the room, set off the table setting, so that only the most jaded or over-exposed diner did not gasp in wonder.

Their host for the evening stood behind his plush dining chair – white wood upholstered in aqua blue with the *Neptune's* trident logo embroidered in turquoise and gold thread – striking in his dress uniform. Captain Connor McCormack – or Mac as he was affectionately referred to by many of the crew – was a powerful presence and it was immediately apparent why he commanded the respect of those under his command. He was stood to attention, straight as a board, gold buttons gleaming, with his silvering blond hair slicked down perfectly from a side parting, and with his dress cap under his right arm.

"Ladies and gentlemen," he said, "I would like to take this opportunity to formally welcome you aboard the *Neptune* and to my table."

Subsequent welcomes and polite words of thanks were returned by the assembled dinner guests.

"Most impressive, Captain McCormack," said a woman who was clearly into her middle years but who wore those years well, with a noble bearing and calm countenance.

"Why thank you, Lady Denning," the captain replied graciously, tipping his head in a brief bow, his accent warmed with a lilting Scots brogue.

"Nice fireplace," Major Horsley said, tapping out his pipe on the surround. "That allosaurus I bagged would look good up there."

One by one the guests found their places or, in the case of the tardier amongst the party, were guided to them by the robo-butlers waiting with clockwork patience to serve the meal. Each place setting held a card bearing the name of one of the most prodigious of the *Neptune's* guests, scribed in a precise and immaculate copperplate.

Dinner with the captain had been another excuse for the elite among the Neptune's passengers to dress to impress, as etiquette dictated and social one-upmanship demanded. The gentlemen, other than the captain, were all in well-tailored black tie, the only real opportunity to personalise their appearance being through the choice of waistcoats and cummerbunds.

For the ladies, however, trying to outdo one another was the name of the game. It was all satin, silk and chiffon – this season's colours apparently sea-greens, aquamarines and turquoise-blues – extravagant bejewelled accessories, bows, lacy flim-flammeries and flamboyant feather boas. Some of the younger female guests had also gone for more daring tailoring with, in the case of Miss Finch in particular, outrageous amounts of bare flesh on display. The other more senior ladies of the party had wisely kept to more traditional, and therefore, restrained designs.

At Captain McCormack's behest, the assembled dinner guests began to take their seats, once they had found their own personalised place setting. However, as they did so, it soon became apparent to the captain that not all of his guests had yet arrived; three places remained empty.

The doors to the dining room were opened again by two automata-drones and the true host of the dinner party was admitted.

Although everyone present was there that evening at the behest of Captain Connor McCormack, it was really the owner of the Carcharodon Shipping Company, and hence the owner of the *Neptune*, who had assured their attendance by inviting them on the sub-liner's maiden voyage in the first place, the wheelchair-bound eccentric billionaire, Jonah Carcharodon.

Carcharodon was wheeled into the banqueting chamber by a mousey-looking young woman, who might have been attractive were it not for the thick horn-rimmed spectacles she wore. She was dressed in a flattering black dress, her blonde hair swept back from her face and held in place on top of her head with a glittering shark-shaped clip. The shark jewellery was clearly visible as she kept her head down, eyes fixed on the carpet at her feet. She gave the impression that she was shy and embarrassed at having to put herself on show in a dress that clearly demonstrated that her figure was one worth showing off.

Jonah Carcharodon, however, apparently welcomed the attention his late arrival brought him, a slight smile forming on his tight-lipped mouth. Confined to a wheelchair, grey-haired and with all of his sixty-plus years showing now on his lined face and hollow features, nevertheless there was a certain spark in the old man's eyes that hinted at the vigour and drive for life one might have expected of a younger man.

"Mr Carcharodon," Captain McCormack said, "and Miss Celeste. Welcome. Now I think we are only missing one guest. Might I suggest we all partake of another glass of champagne while we wait?"

"McCormack," Carcharodon interjected, "I think your guests have probably been waiting long enough. Let dinner be served now."

"Very well, sir," the captain demurred. He nodded to one of the robo-waiters. On cue the droid struck the small bronze gong it held in one metallic hand. "Ladies and gentlemen, dinner is served."

As the last of the guests seated themselves – Carcharodon's PA positioning him at the foot of the table, facing Captain McCormack, before taking a seat adjacent to him – the serving-automata prepared to dish up the soup course from steaming silver tureens. The aroma of Thai red curry and coconut filled the room.

"You will notice a theme to this evening's meal," the captain pointed out to his guests, "a signature dish from some of the different destinations we have already visited or will be visiting on this, the *Neptune's* maiden voyage."

The dining room doors opened once more, this time without the aid of the droid-drudges. Standing framed in the doorway was a gentleman instantly recognisable thanks to the numerous pictures that had appeared in the popular press and on broadcasting screens throughout the realm of Magna Britannia following the calamitous events of Queen Victoria's 160th jubilee.

He looked somewhat different to how he had appeared live, across the empire on the night of June the sixteenth, on that occasion bloodied and bruised, his hair out of place, his clothes dishevelled. Such was not the case now. Also in black tie like the other male guests, he, however, had chosen to embellish the standard black and wine outfit with a striking rough gold silk waistcoat and contrasting burgundy cravat, held in place with a rose-cut diamond pin. And in his right hand he held his trademark cane with its bloodstone-set tip.

All eyes turned to the last dinner guest to arrive.

"Good evening, ladies and gentlemen. Captain McCormack," Ulysses Quicksilver announced. "Am I late?"

As the dandy scoured the faces of those already seated around the table his beaming smile was met with politely returned similar expressions from some, indifference from others and indignant disgust from a small minority, which, however, included Jonah Carcharodon. If there was one thing the shipping magnate could not stand – as might be guessed if the rumours that he had invested his entire personal fortune into the building of the *Neptune*, were to be believed – it was being upstaged.

"Ah, Mr Quicksilver. We thought you weren't coming," Carcharodon chided. "We were about to start without you."

"No need to worry," Ulysses replied. "I'm here now, so the party can begin."

"So, Mr Sylvester, I take it your employer was too ill to travel with us on this historic voyage."

"I am afraid so, Mr Carcharodon," confirmed a slickly turned out young man, his hair swept back, glistening with hair-oil.

Everything about him, from his hawkish demeanour to his sharp dress sense, screamed go-getter businessman to Ulysses. This was a man on a mission, with a career on the up. To be acting as the representative of someone as powerful and influential as Josiah Umbridge, founder and owner of Umbridge Industries – the Empire's foremost industrialist, with numerous steel mills and factories to his name – attested to that fact. And Ulysses sincerely doubted that Dexter Sylvester was spending the entirety of the cruise relaxing either. He would doubtless be networking with influential passengers as well as continuing to do whatever it was he did for Umbridge Industries from afar, sending in his work by remote difference engine transfer, the *Neptune* being equipped with all the most up-to-date radio-telegraph-electronic-communication transmitter terminals and receivers.

In time the dessert course followed, crème brûlée with a warm berry coulis. As those around the table tucked into the sweet, Ulysses Quicksilver considered his fellow dinner guests. After a number of weeks on ship, thanks to his affable charm and personable way with all and sundry, Ulysses had managed to gain the relaxed acquaintance of a host of the ship's staff as well as of the other passengers. As a result, he already knew enough about practically everyone around the table to make him realise that there was a lot more he would like to know. It seemed that no one who had been invited on the *Neptune's* first circumnavigation of the globe was entirely without something of a history all of their own. But then, as a novelist friend of Ulysses' from his school days at Eton had once pointed out to him, "Everyone is the protagonist in their own life story, everyone a hero with a tale worth telling. There are no secondary characters in real life."

He started to mentally compile a dossier on each of his fellow guests, containing every piece of gossip, fact, observation and rumour he had picked up on each of them thus far. And as seemed fit, he began with their nominal host the captain, seated at the head of the table.

Captain Connor McCormack was, as might be expected, the most experienced, trusted and capable captain in the Carcharodon fleet. Hence, naturally, he had given up command of the *Nautilus* – up until the construction of the *Neptune* the flagship of the Great White Line – to take over command of the new super submersible-liner. He looked every part the maritime hero and yet there was a slightly detached world-weariness about him that his eyes could not hide. Ulysses suspected that seeing out his days as the captain of a luxury passenger liner was not the path he had seen his career taking when he was on the first rung of the ladder.

Although financially, and in terms of glory-seeking, his choice of career path could not be faulted, Ulysses had seen such world-weary expressions before, in those pensioned off from the army, who until that point had only lived to serve, fighting for Queen and country. Their prime purpose in life denied them, such men felt neutered now that they were not on the front line facing the enemies of the Empire in honest battle. Perhaps it wasn't active duty at sea that Captain McCormack yearned for now; in another life Ulysses could have seen him taking command of a starship charting unknown waters out beyond the bounds of the solar system, a pioneering space adventurer searching for life on other worlds.

To the captain's right sat a man whom Ulysses had never met until that night, although he had seen his name mentioned in various newspaper articles surrounding the same debacle that had resulted in Ulysses finding himself the subject of a fair few column inches. Perhaps it was for this very reason that Professor Maxwell Crichton, Emeritus Professor of Genetic Adaptation and Bio-Diversity in Evolutionary Biology at the Natural History Museum and one-time colleague of the much maligned Professor Ignatius Galapagos – although he had been at pains to distance himself from any connection there might have been between them both in the self-same articles – that he had taken up the offer of a world cruise, away from the hounding of the popular press and their unwelcome speculative approach to reporting so-called facts.

And he looked like a man hounded and on edge. Somewhere around his mid-fifties, he had a thin, wiry frame that spoke of an academic's neglect of the body's basic needs, such as a regular three square meals a day. Myopia, possibly also the result of prolonged hours of study by weak lamplight, was rectified by a pair of wire-framed spectacles. The hair on his head was white-grey, short and with a tendency towards spikiness, and he steepled his fingers before his face, elbows on the table, when he spoke in earnest about all subjects under the sun – from politics and religion, to the actions of terrorist groups around the world and his own boundary-challenging work in the field of evolutionary biology. But despite the fact that he was now supposed to be relaxing over supper with convivial company, Professor Crichton still appeared hollow-eyed and anxious. Ulysses half expected him to glance back over his shoulder at any moment. Although, now that Ulysses came to think about it, the professor was actually spending a fair amount of time glancing at another of the captain's guests, one Lady Denning who was sat opposite him, shooting her dark looks over the tops of his glasses from beneath beetling brows.

Like Crichton, Ulysses turned his scrutinising gaze on Lady Josephine Denning. Again, she was someone Ulysses knew of only by reputation, until this evening. She didn't have the same staid qualities as Professor Crichton but she was, nonetheless, a leader in her own scientific field, that of marine biology. Ulysses had heard it crudely put that what Lady Denning didn't know about fish wasn't worth knowing. The title had come from her marriage to Lord Horatio Denning, who, although his family estates lay in the north of England, had spent much of his time on his yacht sailing around the Mediterranean. It was there that he had met a certain struggling postgraduate research scientist on an expedition to catalogue sea

36

cucumber populations off the coast of Sardinia. His money and hereditary title had brought the, by then, Lady Denning the influence and attention she needed to make more of her work. But this had all been a long time ago now. Tragically Lord Denning, more than twenty years his wife's senior, had died only two years into their marriage, poisoned by a carelessly prepared plate of fugu whilst holidaying in Japan. Lady Denning had never remarried. Now in her sixties, she carried herself with all the grace and poise of a woman born to good breeding, not one who had simply married into it. A strict regimen of yoga and a diet heavy with oily fish had also meant that she had maintained her figure and looks far beyond that which her years might have suggested.

A man who did not appear to be wearing as well was the ship's chief medic, Dr Samuel Oglivy, seated to Lady Denning's left. Ulysses guessed him to be in his mid-forties, not significantly older than Ulysses himself, but the waxy appearance of his skin and his hollow-eyed expression spoke of a man who was not well. Looking at Dr Ogilvy, Ulysses couldn't help calling to mind the expression, 'Physician, heal thyself.' But then he already knew that Ogilvy was not a well man, in more ways than one, and it wasn't down to seasickness as the doctor claimed. In fact, if he were not careful and continued on his current course of action, his condition could prove fatal.

Opposite Ogilvy sat John Schafer, still fresh of face and bright of eye, the style of his hair and the cut of his clothes more up-to-date that any of the rest of them. Ulysses, himself a follower of fashion, still preferred to create his own style; it worked for him anyway. The young man could not hide the look of blissful happiness on his face, nor could he keep from clasping the hand of his sweetheart sitting beside him. In turn, Constance Pennyroyal could not take her eyes from her handsome beau, constantly snatching shared glances with him from beneath fluttering eyelashes. The two of them were leaving much of the food placed in front of them unfinished, so full were they with each other.

Then there was Constance's maiden aunt and chaperone, her stern glances and puckered mouth letting everyone know her opinion of such public displays of affection.

"Ladies and gentlemen, if I might have your attention?" Schafer spoke over the general hubbub of conversation.

"Certainly, Mr Schafer," Captain McCormack said. "Please, feel free to speak."

"It's just that now would seem to be the perfect time for Constance and I to make an announcement," the young man went on. A sudden silence descended over the dinner guests, accompanied by a look of bewilderment from the Major and a gasp of understanding from Glenda Finch. "I am delighted to say that, earlier this evening Constance agreed to become my wife."

Further gasps rose from the assembled guests accompanied by hearty congratulatory comments, a chinking of glasses and smatterings of applause.

"That's simply wonderful news," Miss Finch spoke up. "I'm sure your families will be delighted."

If the look on Miss Whilomena Birkin's face was anything to go by, it looked like the gossip columnist had got her facts wrong again.

Ulysses knew all he needed to know about Miss Glenda Finch, from what he had read in her column in and her none-too-subtle approach to investigative journalism that he had experienced over his enforced drink with her at the bar. She was unsubtly throwing herself at him even now, laughing at every vague witticism he could be bothered to construct and touching his arm or hand almost every time she directed a comment at him, which he found annoying. It annoyed him because he was annoyed with himself for actually enjoying the attention she was showing him. Carcharodon's PA might be the more traditional English Rose, a beauty buried within a shell of shyness and poor self-esteem, and the more intriguing challenge, but there was something appealing about Glenda Finch's brash approach and her clumsy attempts at seduction, all for the sake of a story. But then she was behaving just as flirtatiously towards Major Horsley, seated to her right.

In turn, the Major appeared to be revelling in the attention of a not unattractive young woman with a taste for plunging necklines. Retired army officer turned big game hunter, living off an army pension and apparent personal family fortune, Major Marmaduke Horsley had never been married to anyone in his life, other than Her Majesty's Armed Forces. Everything there was to know about the Major was there for all to see on the surface. A man like him couldn't hide his opinions if he tried, and he wasn't inclined to try in the first place. A bluff and hale character with a laugh as big as his belly – army muscle long ago turned to fat, the legacy of too many mess dinners and an aversion to physical activity – he was like everyone's incorrigible favourite uncle. There was something of the seasonal gift-giver about his appearance, as well as his manner, his red face bulging with purple veins, from his bulbous, port-swollen nose to his cheeks and unapologetic white whiskers of sideburns and moustache.

And finally, facing Ulysses from where he had been placed between Dexter Sylvester and Miss Birkin was the highly-respected global-trotting travel writer, Thor

Haugland. The accent of his homeland apparent in his cultured tones, his command of English was better than that of many Englishmen Ulysses had met, and English was only one of seven languages spoken by the Norwegian. Should the conversation ever falter, with the way in which he turned any comment or question into an excuse to relate another of his many overseas adventures, Haugland would be able to keep the dinner entertainment going single-handedly. And despite his high-brow, pseudo-intellectual approach, there was no doubting his abilities as a storyteller; even the most insignificant experience was related with attention gripping skill and, in the process, turned into an intriguing anecdote. Miss Birkin certainly seemed happy to hang on his every word, rather than confront the reality of her charge's hasty – and possibly rebellious – engagement. As was Miss Celeste.

And then there was Jonah Carcharodon. Strangely, Ulysses realised, although in many ways he was the most publicly recognised figure amongst the party, after Ulysses himself, he was the biggest unknown as far as the dandy adventurer was concerned. Rumours abounded, but the actual facts behind those rumours remained frustratingly clouded by a fog of contradictions, uncertainties and downright lies. The Great White Shipping Line was an undoubted global success but there were still persistent rumours that the building of the *Neptune* had almost sunk the company. Everyone knew that Carcharodon was confined to a wheelchair but no one seemed to know why. It was popular knowledge that Carcharodon was an eccentric billionaire but nobody knew what he spent his considerable fortune on. He had given many interviews over the years but still no one seemed to know anything of real substance about the man. He remained a mystery.

What Ulysses knew from his own investigations was that Carcharodon was the owner of the shipping company that bore his name and the host of this party, a grumpy old sod with an eye for pretty young assistants, who didn't like being upstaged on his own boat, and that was about it. At this moment, as the Umbridge Industries man was trying to ask him another searching question, Carcharodon appeared to be berating his put-upon assistant.

Looking at the arrangement of guests around the table Ulysses wondered if one or more of them had carried out their own bit of judicious place-swapping, for Dexter Sylvester to have the undivided attention of the patently irritated Jonah Carcharodon and for Glenda Finch to have ended up sitting next to Ulysses – or was that just self-flattering egotism on his part?

What an unlikely lot to be sharing dinner on the foremost luxury sub-liner in the world, he thought to himself. What were the chances of some of these characters ending up on board the *Neptune* at this auspicious time – except that many of those present had specifically been invited, guests of the Great White Line with all expenses covered. The roster of guests at the captain's table would have had all the potential of a Penny Dreadful murder mystery, in the hands of the right author.

Out of a sense of pity for the mousey young woman, rather than to relieve Carcharodon from the unrelenting networking of Dexter Sylvester, Ulysses directed a comment at the billionaire.

"Mr Carcharodon," he said, "or can I call you Jonah?"

"You can call me Carcharodon."

"I must thank you for your personal invitation to join in this wonderful experience."

"What?"

"For inviting us on the inaugural round the world

cruise of the *Neptune*."

"Don't thank me," Carcharodon bit back. "Wasn't down to me. My PA here sent out those personal invitations. Does everything for me, don't you?" he shot back at her, not sounding in the least bit grateful about it. "But then that's what you're paid for, isn't it? She's only here tonight to make up numbers. You know how bloody superstitious sailors are," he said, directing this particular barbed comment at Captain McCormack.

As the waiter-drones were clearing away dessert and preparing to serve coffee, Ulysses was distracted from his half-hearted conversation with the ever-garrulous Glenda by Lady Denning rising, making the usual excuses to her host, the captain, and making to leave. There was an apology of chairs being pushed back as the gentlemen diners bid her ladyship a good evening.

"Going so soon?" Carcharodon asked, the tone he had taken with the eminent marine biologist almost challenging.

"Yes, Mr Carcharodon. It has been a most enjoyable evening," she said, without anything about her expression supporting her words – something having soured the evening for her – "but it is time I retired. I am a creature of habit I know, but it's too late change this old goat now."

That in and of itself would not have been particularly out of the ordinary but for the fact that Professor Crichton then made the same excuse, and left almost straight after her, his face like thunder. It was enough to pique the interest of a man like Ulysses Quicksilver and he didn't need his uncanny sixth sense on this occasion to tell him that something strange was going on.

"Captain McCormack, thank you for a wonderful evening," Ulysses said, placing his napkin on the table, "but if you will excuse me too."

"Really, Mr Quicksilver? That is a shame." It was Carcharodon who interjected. "I haven't heard you regale us yet with your part in the events at Hyde Park. I do hope you won't keep us waiting long."

"The night is still young, Carcharodon," Ulysses said, making for the door. "I'll be back. Please, don't get up."

"Ulysses?" Glenda slurred, her tone both tipsy and incredulous.

"Have your glass topped up, Glenda, and I'll be back before you know it."

Exiting the banqueting room, Ulysses passed through the anteroom where the captain's guests had earlier gathered for pre-dinner drinks and into the corridor beyond. This area of the ship was for the exclusive use of the VIP guests and so Ulysses found the corridor devoid of other passengers. However, he could hear two voices, their words made incoherent by distance and the muffling effects of carpet and drapes. Tone and intonation, however, made it quite clear that the two were not happily discussing the joys of a cruising holiday.

Moving as stealthily as he could, Ulysses crept along the corridor to the junction from beyond which he could hear the voices of the two dissenters. But as he reached the junction the arguing stopped and, if it hadn't have been for his flaring sixth sense, he would have walked straight into the mantis-like Professor Crichton as he stormed back around the corner.

The professor was obviously just as surprised to encounter Ulysses and could not hide the startled look that seized his face or stifle the gasp of astonishment.

"I'm sorry, Professor Crichton," Ulysses said, recovering first. "I almost didn't see you. I thought you had retired for the evening."

"And so I have. Good night, sir."

With that the professor pushed passed Ulysses and back along the corridor. A moment later, in his wake, came Lady Denning.

"Lady Denning, what a pleasant surprise. You appear to have lost your way. Can I help you back to your room?"

The thunderous look on the older woman's face faltered and then gave way under Ulysses' devilishly charming smile. Without making any efforts to disguise what she was doing, she briskly looked him up-and-down.

"Twenty years ago, Mr Quicksilver, perhaps. But not tonight."

There was no denying she was a handsome woman. Handsome as an expression of attractiveness in the more mature lady suggested, to Ulysses, that once she must have been alluring. Lord Denning had obviously thought so.

"Very well, your ladyship. And please, call me Ulysses," he conceded. "Good night to you."

"And to you, Mr Quicksilver."

Ulysses turned to watch Professor Crichton and Lady Denning make their way back along the corridor towards their respective rooms. He couldn't help thinking that they must be about the age his parents would have been, had they lived. A strange thought to have, perhaps, but something about the imperious, bickering couple had triggered a recollection in his mind – some distant memory maybe.

Although he hadn't discovered what it was they had been arguing about, he now knew something else about the two biologists. There was history there, between the two of them, a prior acquaintance, and it was one that neither of them seemed particularly keen to renew.

CHAPTER THREE

Waterworld

The evening continued in much the same vein as it had done for the last few hours, although with the notable absence of both Lady Josephine Denning and Professor Maxwell Crichton. Captain McCormack, finding himself without anyone to share slight conversation with on his immediate left or right – John Schafer too preoccupied with his bride-to-be to make pleasant small-talk with the captain and Dr Ogilvy apparently having made it his goal to empty a bottle of port by himself – looked lost and uncomfortable. It was an obvious relief to him when one of his crew apologetically interrupted with a message. Tapping an empty wine glass with a dessert fork, Captain McCormack drew everyone's attention back to him.

"I do apologise for interrupting you all," he said, his calming Scots brogue filling the room with soft-spoken authority, "but I have been informed that the *Neptune* is about to dive, as we will make this leg of our journey towards Pacifica underwater."

There were murmurs of excited interest from around the room.

"For those of you who missed the opportunity when we dived down to Atlantis City, a truly dramatic way to experience the submersion is from the Promenade Deck, whilst enjoying a post-dinner stroll along the Promenade."

Taking this as their cue that the meal was over, the guests rose and made their way out of the gilt banqueting room.

As Ulysses rose from his chair, Glenda clutched at this arm. "I think moonlit walks are so romantic, don't you, Ulysses?"

The dandy looked down at the flirt clinging to him, her face upturned towards him, a tipsy smile on her painted lips. His initial feelings of irritation towards her in light of her almost possessive attitude dissolved as he looked into her eyes and thought he sensed something beyond the story-hunting hack.

"My dear," he said. "Would you care to join me for a stroll along the Promenade?"

"I thought you'd never ask," she beamed.

She was a distraction, he told himself, nothing more, something to take his mind off what still had to be done. Someone to take his mind off the one woman who had dominated his thoughts of late, despite the fact that the last time he had seen her she had tried to kill him.

As Ulysses strolled arm-in-arm with Glenda along the Promenade he gazed up at the velvet night visible beyond the reinforced glass bubble enclosing the deck, which meant that they could happily enjoy the Neptune's gentle dive to Pacifica, safe in the knowledge that the air would be kept in and the sea out.

The *Neptune's* Promenade Deck was a miracle of modern Victorian engineering. It ran fully two-thirds the length of the ship, either side of the liner's massive smokestack and across the entire width of the vessel towards the prow. To walk the entire circuit of the Promenade took roughly a quarter of an hour and covered a distance of half a mile. The enclosing network of steel girders and beams which held the panels of toughened glass in place, like the reinforced hull of the *Neptune*, could withstand enormous pressures of up to 9,000 pounds per square inch, meaning that the sub-liner could comfortably travel down to the deepest of the undersea cities sunk beneath the oceans of the world to cope with the planet's ever-expanding population.

Out here, in the middle of the Pacific Ocean, away from the ever-present light pollution of industrialised centres and cities like Londinium Maximum or Paris, the rich deep blue of night was splashed with the stream of diamond dots that were the Milky Way, the myriad stars reflected in the rippling black surface of the sea.

"Isn't it beautiful?" Glenda whispered, following Ulysses' gaze beyond the toughened glass shield.

"Incredible," her escort mused, lost in a dream world of his own thoughts. "That we can walk here as the ship submerges with no fear of drowning."

Ulysses felt a sudden sharp poke in his ribs. "I meant the stars," she said.

"Oh, yes... beautiful."

"Have you ever seen the constellations from this latitude and longitude before?" asked an accented male voice.

Thor Haugland, the travel writer, was leaning against the rail, the glass bubble still another few feet beyond the edge of the deck to allow for spectacular views of the sea surrounding the vessel as it descended.

"Oh yes," Ulysses replied.

"I take it you are well-travelled?" the writer went on.

"Oh, you know. I get around a bit. Work mainly."

"And you, Miss Finch?"

"Oh, no, not really. The Continent a little, Europe mainly. Paris, Cannes, Milan; again with work," she gushed, flustered. "But this is a first for me. I have never been on board a cruise ship before."

"Then it's a first for both of us," Ulysses admitted.

"If you think this is spectacular," Haugland said, indicating the spread of the Milky Way above them, "you should see the Aurora Borealis of my homeland in Hammerfest – within the Artic Circle, in the far north of Norway – the scintillating Northern Lights."

"Ah, there's no place like home, eh, Haugland?" Ulysses said with a smile.

"The more one travels the more true that particular adage becomes, Mr Quicksilver," the Norwegian said, stroking his well-tended goatee and turning his gaze out across the wine-dark sea towards the horizon, as if trying to spy his homeland from here. "But in memory only. To go back would be to shatter the perfect illusion, like the destruction of a wonderful dream on waking. And where would we be without our dreams?"

"Home?" Ulysses suggested. Glenda giggled and poked him in the ribs again.

The sound of wailing sirens rose from speakers positioned around the Promenade deck, announcing that the time had come, and the *Neptune* was ready to dive.

Without altering its speed the liner continued ploughing its furrow of white water across the night-black mirror of the sea. Ulysses and Glenda joined Haugland at the rail and peered down at the churning waters beside the ship. As they watched, the *Neptune* began to sink, creating the illusion from their viewpoint that the sea level was rising, eating up the lower decks of the ship, swallowing portholes and sealed hatches.

The ship was keeping to an even keel as the crew flooded the ballast tanks, taking the sub-liner under the waves whilst keeping it as level as if it were still riding the calm surface of the sea, rather than gliding beneath it.

Glenda gasped. Ulysses took in her delighted expression – agog with child-like wonder – and followed her gaze beyond the glass bubble. The waves were now splashing against the shield that contained the Promenade. Other late-evening wanderers had also paused to take in the spectacle. The silvered amethyst line of the far horizon disappeared as the waves lapped higher. Submarine darkness closed in on either side of the ship, with only the glimmer of the strung out galaxy across the cloudless night sky visible through the clear glass ceiling of the Promenade. Then the sea poured in from all sides, closing in on a rapidly shrinking circle of sky until, in moments, that too was gone. The last part of the ship to submerge was the shielded smokestack.

Glenda let out, what Ulysses realised must have been, a long held breath. "That is incredible," she said, her voice still barely more than a whisper.

"Yes, I really rather think it is," Ulysses found himself having to agree.

The running lights of the ship turned the underside of the waves that had closed over them sky blue for a moment. The Neptune continued to descend and the light became a curiously diffused sphere around them, with only darkness beyond.

Ulysses was aware of gentle creaking sounds as the superstructure of the Neptune adjusted to the weight of the water pressing down on it. But there was nothing to suggest that anything untoward was happening. No cracks appeared in the heavily toughened glass. The dome was holding.

But then of course it was, Ulysses chided himself. He had not thought himself the kind of man to see disaster wherever he looked, but then experience had taught him caution at all times. He was sure that there were very few on board who would be worried, not when entire cities could remain safe beneath the sea, resisting the colossal pressures exerted by trillions of tons of water pressing down on them.

"Look at that!" Glenda suddenly exclaimed, squeezing Ulysses' arm in excitement and pointing out beyond the glass. Ulysses looked.

Lights were appearing out of the darkness beyond the ship: silvered bubbles of air – released by the ship's submersion – rushing past; a bio-luminescent green soup of feeding plankton; the rippling purple and orange running lights of transparent squid; the swaying blue lantern-lures of nocturnal submarine feeders.

"Welcome to water-world," Ulysses announced. "Pacifica, here we come."

The sound of the child's footfalls rang from the grilled walkways, echoing back from the curved passageway walls. Tears streamed from her eyes, blurring her vision, but she still knew where she was going. After all, she knew the place as well as she knew the back of her hand, better in fact.

She certainly knew it better than any of the others. Everyone else on board was a grown-up, and grown-ups didn't play. It was only when you played hide-and-seek, made secret dens, and spied on the grown-ups as they went about their secret work in their white coats and overalls, that you discovered every twisting rat-run, every hidden ventilation duct, every unplanned hiding place.

Sounds of death and destruction chased her along the curving corridor. She was also aware of a moaning, whimpering coming between great sobbing gulps of breath. It took her a moment longer to realise that it was she who was making this sound. She swallowed a sob in an effort to stop the fearful, childish noise.

The tears kept coming, splashing onto the grille beneath her hobnail boots, and mingling with the grime and blood already streaking her face. Her pinafore dress was dirtied and torn as well. She had barely got away. She had had to leave Madeleine behind; there had not been time to go back for her. As she thought of Madeleine, abandoned and alone, she could not contain the howl that burst from her in an outpouring of emotion, an unrestrained wail of grief and fear. She had not cried like this since she had lost her mother. Now she was losing Madeleine – her dear Madeleine – and her father all in one go.

She stumbled, the toe of a boot catching in the open mesh of the grilled walkway, and fell. She landed on hands and knees, breaking the skin, grazing her palms. Blood flowed. The shock of the fall stopped the crying for a moment and in that moment she struggled to take control.

She tried to calm herself, that small internal part of her that she liked to think of as her mother still, telling her to stop being such a silly girl and stop crying. How was crying going to help at a time like this? What would her father say?

Her father's face came to mind now as she ran on along the corridor, the hollow-eyed look of exhausted panic, the screaming mouth, strings of spittle flying from his lips. And she heard the last words he had spoken to her again, over the roar and crash of the structure collapsing behind her.

"Run, Marie! Run!"

So she ran.

CHAPTER FOUR

City Beneath the Sea

Pacifica first appeared out of the abyssal gloom as a conglomeration of fuzzy balls of light.

As the *Neptune* powered on, corkscrew propellers churning the darkness behind it, the blur of suffused light sharpened in focus to become one vast dome connected to others of steadily decreasing size. The main dome of the undersea city was huge, a cyclopean structure of steel and glass, sprouting antenna relays, airlocks and the vent-ports of the cathedral-sized machineries that maintained the life-support systems of the city.

Closer still and it became apparent to anyone seeing the city for the first time from on board the Neptune that where Atlantis City had been all straight lines and angular outcroppings – its superstructure looking more like a gargantuan version of the only recently reconstructed (and then devastatingly de-constructed) Crystal Palace – the structure of the newer undersea metropolis appeared to have been created in the likeness of a spiralling nautilus shell. The central dome of the city dominated the vista visible from the sub-liner's prow viewing ports, and it was still some miles away.

Even from outside, and from this distance, it was clear that the internal structure of the city reflected that of a nautilus shell also, with the internal space divided into a number of reducing, separately-sealable, self-contained compartments. The interconnecting smaller contained environment domes followed the same pattern, miniature replicas of the primary biome. Such an architectural structure would provide added rigidity and also an extra element of safety. Should the unthinkable happen, and one of the domes crack, depressurising and letting in the sea, the surrounding divisions of the city could be locked down and kept airtight.

Closing on the city, the *Neptune* began to pass some of the outer domes where droid-slaves tended the plantations, whilst outside, automaton machines – rust-red crab-like constructions the size of tug boats – harvested the vegetation of floodlit kelp fields.

Now those on board the *Neptune* could no longer see the open sea beyond the superstructure of Pacifica, so colossal was the city's dome. Truly it was a triumph, a temple to man's mastery of the machine and his world.

Those passengers waiting in the fore airlocks were afforded the most impressive view of the city as the *Neptune* glided smoothly into its appointed docking bay – just one of many, the piers of which reached out from the city's superstructure like anemone fronds into the ocean depths. Passengers like Ulysses Quicksilver, his female companion Miss Finch hanging onto his arm. The dandy's manservant stood a pace or two behind them carrying with him a bag recently purchased by Glenda to "help her do her shopping", shooting disapproving looks at the couple arm-in-arm before him.

Glenda Finch might not be the sort of woman that Ulysses would usually take as a companion, and she certainly wasn't going to be the love of his life but, to his mind, it merely enhanced his reputation if he arrived with a single young woman with her own public profile. And the more the press portrayed him as a notorious, fame-hungry womaniser, the more quickly it would forget that other side of his personality – that of agent of the throne of Magna Britannia, for whom espionage and adventure were never far away.

And Glenda had scrubbed up well for the occasion, Ulysses considered, as he gave her another appraising look. Both of them had dressed to impress for their brief sojourn within the undersea city. He was wearing an off-white linen suit, magnolia waistcoat and verdigris cravat, she an unassuming number picked up in one of the *Neptune's* many boutiques. It was a Vasa original, broad across the shoulders with an open collar plunging to a V-cut neckline, coming in tight at the waist – and she really did have a very slim waist – before ballooning at the hips again and then coming in tight at the ankles. The outfit accentuated her classic hourglass figure, and Glenda Finch walked – hips rolling lasciviously – like she knew it. The realisation that she was likely to be making the headlines today, rather than writing them, had not been lost on her.

It looked like those assembled at the docking port with Ulysses and his small entourage – other passengers and even some of the ship's human crew members – were looking forward to a little shore leave, even if it was only for the day, leaving the slaved automata on board to maintain the sub-liner's systems.

It was an opportunity too good to be missed. It might not technically be terra firma, but at least to walk the parks and promenades of Pacifica was to walk on a steady, unmoving surface. It would take all of them a little time to find their land-legs again, after the subtle yet constant rolling of the decks after a number of weeks on board ship.

With a hiss of equalising air pressures, the airlocks

steamed open and the eager passengers hurried to enter the underwater metropolis. Having passed through all the different failsafe measures from the docks – pressurised airlocks and sealable bulkheads – those 'going ashore' finally passed through customs and entered the city itself.

What awaited them was something not far short of a full-blown ticker-tape parade. Crowds of Pacificans and other visitors thronged the streets beyond the customs checkpoint, contained behind temporarily erected barricades, a brass band in crimson uniforms, polished gold buttons shining, oompah-ing away behind the crowds somewhere.

The air smelled sterile and recycled – which, of course, it was. But then other, completely contrasting exotic aromas assailed Ulysses' finely-tuned nose. It was said that Pacifica was a truly cosmopolitan hotchpotch of a place, welcoming people from all corners of the globe, who brought with them their own cultures, diets, specialities. It was also said, in more hushed tones by those in the know, that anything could be acquired in Pacifica, no matter how discerning or demanding the customer's tastes may be.

Bulbs flashed and a number of kinema cameras followed the progress of the great and the good as they disembarked from the *Neptune*. Glenda was excited to see their own faces looking back at them from a large broadcast screen hanging above the scallop-shell plaza they were now crossing. Those same images would likely be broadcast across the globe, on the Magna Britannia Broadcasting Corporation's official news channel, ad nauseam over the next twenty-four hours. The maiden voyage of the *Neptune* could still make the headlines, even weeks after leaving Southampton. And since the debacle surrounding the regime-threatening activities of the Darwinian Dawn Ulysses had become something of a celebrity across the Empire. People commented and pointed when they saw him; some boldly approached to ask for his autograph or a photograph, whilst many more simply stopped and stared as he strode past. Ulysses loved every second of it.

Glenda loved the attention too, making the most of being in front of the cameras, when the opportunity arose, rather than being stuck behind a type-processing Babbage console. Only the long-suffering Nimrod seemed not to be enjoying the attention, a pained expression on his face the whole time which turned to an even more annoyed grimace when he caught a glimpse of himself on screen. Perhaps it was a hangover from his misspent youth, this desperate desire not to have attention drawn to himself, least he be recognised by someone.

"Nimrod, old chap," Ulysses said, addressing his manservant, "why don't you take some time for yourself? Take a few hours off. I'm sure I'm more than capable of helping Miss Finch carry her shopping."

"Very good, sir," Nimrod said, without a hint of protest, the tension in his expression already easing. "If you're certain you won't be requiring my assistance?"

"I think Miss Finch would just like to take in a few of the boutiques on the Strand and we might go for a saunter through the coral parks," Ulysses went on.

"Sounds almost romantic, like we're courting," Glenda teased, squeezing his arm tighter.

"So take your time, old chap. No need to hurry back. I'm sure we'll be fine without you. I mean, how much trouble can we get into here?"

"Then I shall bid you and Miss Finch good day."

"Good day, Mr Nimrod."

"See you later, old boy."

"This place is truly stunning!" Glenda declared, an expression of child-like wonder on her face. Ulysses had to admit that it was a very endearing quality, especially in someone who, by dint of their work-a-day trade one might have expected to be a cynical hack. She might write the gossip column for *The Times* but she had been writing about a world she was viewing second hand; she had never truly been a part of things until now.

And the worldly adventurer, who many would most definitely have considered to have been born with a silver spoon in his mouth and who had seen all manner of wonders the world over, had to agree once again with his awestruck companion.

Whether the city had been constructed on top of a dead reef which had then had the ocean pumped out of it and the park carved out of the outcropping seabed – the skeletons of a million coral life-forms – or whether the colourful forest of bones had been transplanted here from elsewhere along with every last carefully arranged rocky spur, the result was a thing of beauty.

The sea-worn rock, also bearing the scars of shellfish erosion, had a grotto-like quality, the stone riddled with hollows, holes and tiny tunnels. Larger cave-like structures had also been purposefully carved out of the rock between florid protrusions of crimson, amber and rose-pink branches of dry, dead coral, and other natural cavern spaces enhanced. Landscape-engineered cascades tumbled between the coral-clung rocks, under bridged pathways and over the sculpted seabed, the gurgling and babbling of water ever-present in the gardens. And, unlike any public garden Ulysses had visited before, those same cascades were salt seawater. Corralled within the flooded hollows of pools and sculpted streams, cuttlefish swam, multi-hued octopi hunted between the waving fronds of anemones and submerged sea-worms, whilst leopard-spotted eels darted from their shaded holes. Brittle stars scrambled over rock-pool floors, azure-bodied sea cucumbers oozed between feeding grounds. Barnacle-shelled crustaceans plucked dainty morsels from their pools, fed to them by the passers-by, shoals of parrot fish coursing between growths of seaweed and limpet-clung rocks.

"So, where now? What would you like to see next?" Ulysses asked, feeling that their purposeless ambling needed some direction.

"Oh, we've not seen the Triton Fountain yet, have we?" Glenda suggested excitedly.

"No, we haven't. It's over this way," Ulysses said, directing with his bloodstone cane.

The casual couple skirted a wide circular pool where a park-keeper was feeding a cast of pink-shelled spider crabs, much to the delight of the onlookers who had gathered round.

"There's old Jonah Carcharodon!" Glenda suddenly blurted out. "Mr Carcharodon! Coo-ee, over here!"

Before Ulysses could stop her, forgetting any sense of decorum, she began waving furiously as she called out to the shipping magnate. Why didn't his near-prescient sixth sense see to warn him of such embarrassing social faux pas?

Carcharodon was being pushed at a sedate pace through the coral gardens by his ever-attendant PA. The two of them appeared to have been deep in conversation, but now both Carcharodon and Miss Celeste caught sight of them. Ulysses didn't miss the passing look of annoyance the old man displayed before his 'for-the-cameras' smile returned, his public persona taking charge. Miss Celeste, however, immediately directed her timid gaze back towards the ground, hoping her carefully coiffeured fringe would hide her.

Miss Celeste intrigued Ulysses. Undeniably attractive and yet hampered by her overwhelming shyness, she worked for one of the richest and most powerful men in the world, and yet she appeared to demonstrate no self-confidence whatsoever. Ulysses couldn't help noticing that she was also carrying a portable personal Babbage unit with her, strapped up in a bag slung over her shoulder. It seemed that she was never off duty, always at work, just like her employer.

Glenda steered Ulysses through the bustling crowds towards the wheelchair-bound billionaire. *The poor man, doesn't have a hope*, Ulysses thought to himself. *He couldn't get away if he wanted to.*

"Mr Carcharodon," Glenda gushed, shaking the old man enthusiastically by the hand, "so this is how a multi-billionaire spends his afternoons off."

"What? Oh, I see what you mean. I suppose so."

"Aren't they beautiful?"

"What?" the shipping magnate blustered, clearly not on the same train of thought as the newspaper writer.

"Why, the coral gardens, of course," Glenda clarified, an expression of amusement on her face, her tone playfully chiding.

"Look, if you two would like to be left alone," Ulysses hissed in Glenda's ear.

"Oh, Mr Quicksilver, you're so amusing," his companion said raucously. Miss Celeste shot her a venomous look.

Ulysses felt that oh-so familiar itch at the back of his brain. He looked round sharply. The promenading crowds were thick around them now but he could see no threat. It must simply be a feeling of unfamiliar claustrophobia that was getting to him. Perhaps even a touch of jealousy. He really had to get his head sorted out; he seemed to keep getting mixed up with women possessed of a self-serving nature. Perhaps, this should be his last outing with Miss Glenda Finch.

"Oh my!" Miss Celeste suddenly shrieked, her uncharacteristic outburst surprising everyone.

An instant later, somebody barged past Ulysses. Instinctively he shot out a hand – only he was encumbered by the fact that it was on the same arm he had interlocked with Glenda's. He caught an impression of a roughly-dressed rogue, keeping his head down, and picking up pace as he broke free of the clustering crowds.

"My bag!" Miss Celeste cried. "It's been taken. Someone's taken my bag!"

And the Babbage unit, Ulysses thought as, already practically acting on instinct alone, he broke free of Glenda's clinch and leapt free of the now unmoving throng, curious passers-by stopping to see what all the fuss was about.

"Oi!" Ulysses shouted after his quarry. "Stop, thief! Somebody stop that man, for Pete's sake!"

Entering a stretch of less-crowded pathways, the thief sprinted away between the coral-clad rocks, Miss Celeste's bag gripped tightly in one hand. Ulysses put on a spurt of speed, feeling the rush of adrenalin flood his body, the old fight-or-flight response doing its bit. The chase was most definitely on.

Even at the height of the pursuit, adrenal glands pumping their secretions into his bloodstream, his heart racing, a part of Ulysses' conscious mind found time to consider that every city, no matter where it might be or how idyllic it might appear on the outside, had its own criminal underclass. And, of course, Ulysses knew all about the dark underbelly of the undersea paradise of Pacifica already.

He ran on, shouting again for assistance as he forced his way past meandering clusters of surprised promenaders. There were a number of shouts from startled tourists, not so much at the brusque manner of Ulysses, as he barged past in his mad dash after the thief, but at his presence there at all, his celebrity status well and truly secured.

The park attendants – both human and automaton – had at last noticed that something was awry and were making taking steps to act accordingly, although they appeared to be as surprised as the general public. Whatever flustered action they might eventually deem to take, Ulysses suspected that it would doubtless be too late to stop the thief from getting away.

The fleeing scoundrel was steadily descending through the coral-sculpted gardens. Taking a sharp right at a junction, Ulysses doubled back on himself, running hell-for-leather towards a shimmering cascade. There he saw his opportunity to bring the chase to an end.

Bounding over the low wrought-iron fence surrounding the coral beds he dashed across the top of the cascade, in line with the fleeing ruffian, and leapt. Hitting the pink gravel path six feet below, he winced, feeling his left knee jar as he landed. The rush of adrenalin nonetheless allowed him to put the pain to one side, although he knew he would pay for it later.

Ulysses managed to regain his composure in time for the thief to round the edge of the cascade and run slap bang into his outstretched arm. The arm, rigid as a steel bar, caught the man across the neck. He went down hard, legs flying out from under him. The bag flew from his hand, a catch unbuckling, a number of dossier files sailing into the air to fall like over-sized confetti onto the path.

The dandy deftly plucked the bag out of the air, catching it by the shoulder strap and smoothly slinging it over his arm.

Ulysses looked down at the pole-axed scoundrel, as the thwarted thief clutched at his throat gasping for air, straightened his jacket and saw to his loosened cravat. "I rather suspect this doesn't belong to you," he said, holding Miss Celeste's bag over the spluttering man. The wretch, unshaven and looking every part the habitual felon, stared at Ulysses in eye-bulging shock.

Ulysses recovered the loosed files, briefly opening the card folders to make sure that everything was put back in its rightful place.

With a skittering of boot-steps on gravel, a number of park keepers caught up with the rogue and his captor at last.

"Gentlemen," Ulysses said, casting an unimpressed look at the tardy attendants, "I think I can leave this unpleasant situation to you to deal with now, don't you?"

By the time Ulysses returned to the spot where the attempted crime had taken place, Miss Celeste was sitting on a park bench looking flustered, with an overbearing Glenda trying to comfort her, an arm around the woman's tense shoulders. Jonah Carcharodon sat in his chair offering no words of sympathy or optimistic encouragement, a thunderous expression clouding his face.

On seeing Ulysses striding back along the path towards them, bag in hand, Miss Celeste visibly relaxed, an unexpected smile erupting from her tear-streaked face that was like a brilliant ray of sunshine after the passing of a cloud.

"Oh, thank you! Thank you, Mr Quicksilver!" she gushed. "If I had lost this... I don't know what I would have done," she said, faltering with the realisation of how close the situation had come to disaster.

Ulysses had never known her say so much and for a moment the two of them even made eye contact.

However, as far as her employer was concerned, Ulysses' endeavours might have been for naught, even though Ulysses was sure that the loss of Miss Celeste's difference engine and assorted documents would have been as great an inconvenience for Carcharodon as it would have been for his assistant.

"Come on, woman. If these histrionics are quite done with, can we get going?" Carcharodon snapped.

"Are you all right, Miss Celeste?" Ulysses asked, with genuine concern, ignoring her employer.

"Y-yes, thank you, Mr Quicksilver," she said, the smile gone once more, her eyes cast down at the ground. "Thank you for your concern, but if you will excuse me we must be on our way. I have delayed Mr Carcharodon quite enough already."

Ulysses watched, anger rising within him at the attitude Carcharodon had displayed towards Miss Celeste. He wanted to say something, to make the man realise how egocentric and insensitive he was being.

But the moment passed as Glenda took his arm in hers once again and, on tiptoe, whispered, "You're my hero," into his ear. He could smell the intoxicating aroma of her now that she was so close to him. The touch of her breath on his face sent a frisson of excitement thrilling through his adrenalin-heightened senses.

Ulysses looked at her and smiled, disarmed once again, delighted by her apparently innocent, almost naïve reaction to events that were, for him, virtually a matter of daily occurrence.

"You look like you could do with a drink." she said

"Yes, I think you're probably right," Ulysses agreed, already imagining the nectar-sweet bite of cognac on his taste buds. "Would you care to join me? I hear there are a number of bars with an ocean-view on the Strand."

"That sounds lovely," Glenda said, dipping her chin and looking up at him with appealing puppy-dog eyes, "but I really ought to check in with the paper. We have an office here. Did you know? I hope you don't mind."

Ulysses was taken aback. "N-no, not at all," he stammered, wrong-footed. "I might take a rain check then myself. You know what they say about drinking alone."

"I'll see you later, though," she said, a definite twinkle in her eye, "back at the ship, where I'm sure you'll be happy to grant me an exclusive interview about your heroic antics, in more convivial surroundings."

Still high from the rush his race through the park had given him, Ulysses felt a tingling stirring deep down inside him. "I'll look forward to it," he said, blushing despite himself.

She planted a lingering kiss on his lips. "So will I," she murmured. "Now, don't go getting into any more trouble, and I'll see you later for that exclusive."

With Glenda gone, Ulysses was surprised to find himself feeling at a loose end. Beautiful as the coral gardens were, he had no great desire to take in any of the other tourist attractions Pacifica had to offer. He was merely marking time, after all, until an opportunity presented itself.

Going over the events in the park, Ulysses made a decision. If you really wanted to understand a city, find out what made it tick, just as with a human body you had to peel back the surface layers and look at what lay beneath.

He had spent long enough enjoying that which the city governors wanted visitors to see; now it was time to take a look at the seedier side of things, the gritty reality of life in the city beneath the sea.

Ulysses paused in the shadow of a rust-stained arch, becoming motionless in an instant as Doctor Ogilvy stopped and darted an anxious look over his shoulder for what seemed like the umpteenth time since Ulysses had caught up with him, quite by chance, close to the warehouses down below the docks at city bottom. Ulysses knew that he didn't exactly blend into the background in his fine-tailored suit and was somewhat encumbered by his flamboyant dress sense, but Ogilvy was really starting to draw attention to himself, with his cringing behaviour. And what was he doing down here anyway?

Ever since spotting the ship's seemingly-suffering doctor as he was cruising the opium-dens located in an outer dome of the complex metropolis, his insatiable curiosity piqued, Ulysses had found the perfect way to while away a few hours in Pacifica. And, before too long, the doctor's anxious steps had brought them here.

Ogilvy had stopped outside a seemingly abandoned and shuttered shop-front. He looked around him again but still he didn't see the cunningly hidden Ulysses. Ogilvy knocked three times on the shuttered doorway, paused, then knocked again, three times, paused and then gave another three knocks. The shutter finally rattled upwards, revealing two men of obviously Oriental origin. These two Chinamen shot suspicious looks up and down the detritus-strewn street before admitting Dr Ogilvy. The shutter was pulled down again after them.

Two suspicious-looking Chinese characters having a clandestine meeting with the eminent Dr Ogilvy, chief medic aboard the foremost sub-liner in the world on its maiden round-the-world voyage? Even Inspector Allardyce of Her Majesty's Metropolitan Police would have realised that something was going on here that could not be left uninvestigated.

Sure the coast was clear, Ulysses crept forwards.

Awareness flared in his hindbrain and he turned to see a lithe figure detach itself from the gloom behind him. In that split second Ulysses realised someone else had been following him, unnoticed, so caught up had he been in his pursuit of Dr Ogilvy. And then his unerring sixth sense flared again as two iron-strong hands seized him from behind.

CHAPTER FIVE

Our Man in Shanghai

"Thank you, Mr Quicksilver," the Chinaman said, returning Ulysses' card holder.

Ulysses snatched it back and returned it to his jacket pocket. "Not that I really had much choice," he said sourly, looking pointedly at the larger of the two Chinamen. "And now it would appear that you have me at a disadvantage, Mr –"

The smiling, well-spoken man sitting opposite him did not take up Ulysses' cue.

"I must apologise most profusely, but my aide was only acting on my orders."

That same aide now glared at Ulysses, his curiously Cro-Magnon Chinese features showing no other emotion. Unusually for one of his racial heritage he was taller than the Englishman, and big in every way, built like a navvy from his broad gorilla-like frame to his huge hands like great meaty paws.

"Can't he speak for himself?" Ulysses challenged but the huge Chinaman's expression remained impassive and he said nothing.

"He does not speak English, Mr Quicksilver."

"Oh, I see. I suppose I should commend you on your own command of the Queen's English," Ulysses said grudgingly. "If you will forgive me," he said with forced politeness, "you speak it almost like a native."

"Why thank you. That means a great deal to me."

"Your accent – sounds almost Home Counties."

"Hong Kong, via Oxford. I spent a very rewarding three

years at Boriel College. My grandfather was British."

"I see, but you're loyal to your Chinese roots."

"My grandfather had no great love for your empire."

"His empire as well, surely."

"He didn't see it that way."

"Really? That is interesting."

"But hardly relevant. It strikes me that you could be an Oxford man yourself, Mr Quicksilver."

"Indeed," Ulysses confirmed. "Boriel College also, but before your time I suspect."

"I think you are probably right, although not by much, I'll warrant."

"So, now we know we share the same alma mater, if we're both Oxford men, old school tie and all that, I think you can tell me your name."

"Of course, I am Harry Cheng, agent of the most glorious Imperial Throne of China and its affiliated colonies," he said, offering Ulysses his own ID, "and this is my colleague Mr Sin."

"Now, why doesn't that surprise me?"

Ulysses glanced up and down the street. All manner of cafés and eating establishments had set up here, away from the grander restaurants and hotels in the main dome. There were Turkish eateries with surly individuals seated outside smoking hookahs, other Mediterranean-styled tavernas and an Oriental-themed fast food joint. The place where the three of them now sat proclaimed itself to be an Italian coffee house.

Ulysses could quite easily have believed that all human life was here. This street, with its cafés and bars, was a microcosm of all Pacifica life, a clear cosmopolitan cross-section of the city's populace.

He closed his eyes for a moment, taking in all the various aromas of the street, feeling the heat of the sunlamps on his face. That was one thing about life inside an underwater city: the weather was always predictably good. The artificial arc-lights, powered like the rest of the city, by geothermal energy tapped from submarine volcanic vents, generated enough light for an artificial sun all year round, only dimming as the city began its night cycle.

"Now, if we could return to the matter in hand," Cheng said.

"Ah yes, you mean how you forcibly abducted me and dragged me here? Why was that?"

"Might I first ask you, Mr Quicksilver, what you were doing at City Bottom amongst the warehouses of the slum quarter?"

"I could ask you the same thing," Ulysses retorted.

Harry Cheng sighed and muttered something in Chinese. At that Mr Sin's lips curled back and he growled like a mastiff. Another word from Cheng, however, settled him again.

"You have me at a disadvantage once again," Ulysses said, with arrogant bravura. He had dealt with worse than Mr Sin.

"Mr Quicksilver, we could play this game all day. I can assure you that it is in both our best interests that we are open and honest with one another."

"Mr Cheng, it would appear to me that you are living in something of a cloud cuckoo land if you think it is in the best interests of an agent of Imperial China and a loyal servant of the crowned head of Magna Britannia to work openly together."

"Then, if it will earn your compliance and cooperation, there is something I must share with you."

"You're welcome to try."

Cheng leaned forward over the table. In response

Ulysses leaned in closer himself.

"Mr Quicksilver, I suspect that you and I are very alike, in so many ways that we could be a formidable team, if we chose to work together, or deadly rivals. But ultimately we are working towards the same goal."

"I beg your pardon?"

"More than that, we are working for the same side."

Ulysses responded to this revelation by raising one suspicious eyebrow. "That is a bold claim and, if it is the case, can you prove it? Where is your ID? Prove to me that you are a double agent."

"Please, Mr Quicksilver," Cheng hissed, throwing anxious glances up and down the street, "I am not overly fond of that term. The fact is that I have shared with you something very personal and private, and in the strictest confidence."

"But can you prove it?" Ulysses badgered.

"I can tell you why you were exploring City Bottom, why we ran into each other when and where we did."

"That would be a start." Ulysses rocked back in his chair, ignoring the cappuccino cooling in front of him and folded his arms. "Go on then. Fire away."

Cheng picked up a napkin and rested his arms on the tabletop. "You were following someone from the ship you came in on, the chief medical officer, Dr Ogilvy." His fingers moved nimbly as he began to flip and fold the pliant tissue. "Am I right so far?"

"Go on," Ulysses said.

"And although the public may believe that you joined the maiden voyage of the Neptune for some well-publicised rest and relaxation following recent events in London, you are actually on board as much for work as you are for pleasure."

Cheng looked up from his origami to judge Ulysses'

reaction. Ulysses simply nodded again.

"You believe that Dr Ogilvy is part of an illicit smuggling racket, just one pawn in an opium smuggling ring."

The two agents looked at one another, Cheng's narrowed eyes emotionless, Ulysses' gaze fiery, challenging Cheng to say more.

"Correct," he admitted.

"The last shipment due for London's smoking dens never arrived and those who stand to profit from such an enterprise want to know what happened to it. This is your chance to infiltrate their operation, find out who's in charge and discover the identity of the criminal mastermind behind it all."

Cheng put a cupped hand down on the table between them. When he removed it, a paper crane stood there, wings outstretched as if making ready to fly.

"Very good, Mr Cheng, very good. Now, seeing as how you appear to know so much, perhaps you could fill in a few of the gaps for me."

"That seems only fair, Mr Quicksilver."

"How do you know so much about my covert mission? Who told you?"

"I told you, you and I are on the same side. We have the same bosses who reveal the same pertinent facts to us as and when necessary. No one person ever has the whole picture, of course, and I have to admit that it was a bold move by our masters to put someone so in the public eye, and known for being an agent of the throne of Magna Britannia, on the case."

"Have you not heard of the expression 'hide in plain sight'?" Ulysses threw back. "But getting back to the matter in hand, as you put it, how much do know about Ogilvy's part in all this?"

"Enough. I know that he is not a big player within the

ring and that his own addictions are what those with the real power have used to ensnare him."

"Tell me again – how do you know?"

"As I keep trying to tell you, Mr Quicksilver, we are working for the same side. We are just tackling this investigation from opposite ends."

"Were you recruited at Boriel, then?" Ulysses asked.

"I was. I take it that you –"

"Indeed, although you might say I was also following my father into the family trade."

"Ah, of course. The celebrated Hercules Quicksilver."

"You know of him?"

"Almost as well as I know of your recent career, Mr Quicksilver."

"Really?"

"Oh yes. It thrilled me to read of your adventures in *The Times.*"

"So," Ulysses said, bringing their discussion back on track. "If you know so much about Ogilvy, what else do you know?"

"The intelligence that I have access to suggests that an old adversary of yours could well be behind all this."

Ulysses could not hide his interest now, despite himself, as a host of villainous characters whose nefarious plans he had thwarted in the past came to mind, a veritable rogues' gallery.

"Which one? Tell me."

"The Black Mamba."

Ulysses gasped. Harry Cheng smiled, satisfied that he still had the upper hand and that he had been able to startle this otherwise ice-cool character.

A host of painful memories flooded Ulysses' consciousness. He was there, high above the Himalayas once again, the two balloons locked together, tumbling through the swirling snow of the midnight blizzard towards the unforgiving peaks beneath. The Black Mamba's sinister Mandarin Emperor's face inches from his, swiping scimitar in hand, Ulysses holding him off with his own sword-cane, Davenport clinging to the side of the gondola, clutching at the stab-wound to his chest, fingers numb with frostbite.

"Mr Quicksilver?"

And then – with Cheng's words – he was abruptly back in the muggy heat of the undersea dome.

"I... I thought I had done for that blaggard over Mount Manaslu."

"Thought, or hoped? We both know how slippery a character the Black Mamba can be. I sometimes wonder that he shouldn't be monikered the Black Cat. He seems to have the lives of one. Did you ever recover the green-eyed monkey god of Sumatra?"

Ulysses shot the Chinese agent a look as if to say, 'How the hell do you know about that?' but didn't bother answering the question. Instead he looked into the surface of his cooling coffee as if seeing something else there, as a gypsy fortune-teller might scry into a crystal ball.

"If I might be candid, Mr Quicksilver?"

"I wouldn't want you to be anything else, Mr Cheng."

"If Mr Sin and myself had not stepped in when we did – and I must apologise again for any inconvenience caused – you could have ruined everything."

Ulysses snorted in annoyance at the patronising Cheng. "It's what I do. I mix things up a bit. What were you doing there then, if you weren't going to act and you know so much about this operation already? Keeping Ogilvy under surveillance, I suppose."

"No, Mr Quicksilver, I'm sorry, but that's where you're wrong. We were keeping *you* under surveillance."

"It would seem that while you were busy making sure that I didn't blow your operation, your one and only lead has got away. How are you going to find out if the Black Mamba is behind this opium smuggling ring now?"

Cheng continued smiling in that irritating, ingratiating way of his. "But he hasn't got away, Mr Quicksilver. I rather suspect he will be boarding the *Neptune* again, along with the rest of the passengers, very shortly."

"But if you take him in then you will be making a very public spectacle of yourself, and quite probably in front of the world's press at that. Surely that's not the best way to avoid alerting the Black Mamba to the fact that you are onto him."

"I couldn't agree with you more," Cheng said, still the same ingratiating smile on his lips.

"Then what, in God's name, are you planning to do?"

"I have reason to believe that the good doctor is not the only connection that exists between the smuggling operation and the Carcharodon shipping line," Cheng explained. Reaching into his jacket pocket he carefully extracted a card wallet, with two cards inside it.

"Two tickets, Mr Quicksilver, one for myself and one for my aide, Mr Sin. The mystery of the missing consignment of opium has not yet been resolved. We are coming with you, on board the *Neptune*. We are joining your cruise."

CHAPTER SIX

Casino Royale

"Gentlemen, if you would please take your seats?"

"Come on chaps," Major Marmaduke Horsley said loudly, at the croupier's request, "let's play Blackjack!"

The Major had lost none of his old military manner. When he issued a command it was in a tone of voice that broached no refusal. The hubbub of interrupted conversations fizzled out, and the invited guests approached the Blackjack table.

The *Neptune's* onboard casino, the Casino Royale – named in homage to the crown of Magna Britannia – was a hive of bustling activity, the atmosphere tense with the prospect of a great deal of money being won or lost on the turn of a single card.

Ulysses took another sip of his French brandy, and from his place at the bar quickly surveyed the room. He could see most of the guests from dinner at the captain's table, some nights since now, and a number of other well-to-do chancers hoping for a piece of the action at the table that night.

Those now approaching the table – standing on a raised dais in the centre of the room, surrounded by a low rail that effectively cordoned it off from the rest of the space, velvet tassel ropes drawn across openings in the rail politely emphasising the fact – were there by invitation only. And if that wasn't enough the price of the buy-in alone was enough to exclude most of the people present in the room. But, even if they couldn't play, they could still watch, and a high stakes game of Blackjack made for an exciting spectator sport for those on board.

"Are you a gambler, Mr Quicksilver?" Glenda Finch asked, leaning close to whisper in his ear. Ulysses could not help glancing to his left, his gaze falling into the shadowed hollow between her breasts, exposed by the low-cut neckline of her dress as she leant forward.

"Oh, indubitably, Miss Finch," he replied with a wry smile, returning his gaze to the Blackjack table. "I take a risk every time I'm in your company."

Everyone appeared to be dressed in their grandest finery for the event, emphasising what an important and prestigious occasion it was, as well as how lucrative it might be for those blessed by Lady Luck that night. The ladies were in the latest designer dresses from Paris and Milan, purchased at the *Neptune's* haute couture boutiques during the voyage, whilst the gentlemen had almost all gone for black tie, Ulysses included, although he had personalised his attire with a striking paisley waistcoat off-set by a silver-grey crushed silk cravat, diamond pin in place as ever.

As the other invited players mounted the dais to take their seats, Ulysses followed at a discreet distance. Lady Josephine Denning stepped up onto the dais in front of him.

"Lady Denning," Ulysses commented, with a tone of undisguised, almost patronising, surprise, as he took a seat beside the titled scientist. "I didn't take you for a gambler."

"And I didn't take you for a sexist pig, young man," she bit back, managing to surprise Ulysses still further, even causing him to blush, unable to hide his embarrassment, his guard down.

Ulysses regarded his fellow gamblers over the rim of his brandy balloon. Going clockwise from the croupier, there was Dexter Sylvester, the Umbridge Industries man and the absent Josiah Umbridge's representative, the Major, and next to him a flabby banker who Ulysses had learnt earlier that evening went by the name of Armitage. Then came Lady Denning followed by himself. To his left was an ageing Oriental woman, whose name he had yet to discover, being one of those passengers who had joined the cruise at Pacifica and whose ostentatious jewellery, ill-fitting, unflattering, too-revealing dress and milk-white make-up could not hide the fact that she must have been well into her seventies. The last seat at the table remained empty.

"Are we ready to play then or what?" Major Horsley asked gruffly.

"We are expecting one more player, Major," the croupier said, his French accent as unflappable as ever.

"Bally well wouldn't stand for tardiness in my regiment," the Major grumbled.

Lady Denning sighed irritably whilst Dexter Sylvester took to rearranging the piles of chips in front of him. Ulysses had strewn his haphazardly on the baize before him, while the banker Armitage took the opportunity to call the barman over and order a Scotch before the game commenced.

There was a movement in the crowd gathered around the table as the tight-packed throng parted, with some annoyance, to let the late arrival through, although one look from his silent, goliath of a batman silenced their complaints in an instant.

"Ladies and gentlemen, let me humbly beg of you your forgiveness. I am so sorry I am late. There were matters I had to attend to that could not be avoided."

Ulysses eyed Harry Cheng with suspicion as he took his place.

"Do not worry, Mr Cheng," the croupier replied generously.

"Damn Orientals," Ulysses – and a number of others gathered nearby – heard Major Horsley mutter none too quietly under his breath. "Thought they were used to running things like damned clockwork."

"Messieurs et mesdames," the croupier said, focusing everyone's attention, "as we are now ready, we shall begin."

"Looks like Lady Luck's in your corner, Ulysses," John Schafer said. Ulysses had joined the young heir where he was sitting between the bar and the gaming table, with his fiancée and her ever-present chaperone. A natural break had been called in the game, allowing the players time to make themselves comfortable and replenish their drinks and, of course, to cash more chips.

"So far," Ulysses agreed, though with a hint of caution in his voice.

"There are some pretty hefty bets being laid out there," Schafer went on.

"I know. My brother Barty would be proud."

"Especially, I note, between you and the Chinaman Cheng."

"Indeed," Ulysses said, taking a sip of his vodka Martini, his expression darkening again as he observed his rival at the other end of the bar.

"I don't like the look of him," Miss Birkin said, eyeing Cheng with an even more threateningly suspicious gaze.

"You don't like the look of anybody, especially anybody foreign, Aunt Whilomena," Constance said with good-humoured reproach.

"Especially me," Schafer said quietly with a wink to Ulysses.

"What was that, young man?" Miss Birkin challenged, immediately onto her niece's put upon beau.

"Another sherry, Auntie?" he said, exaggeratedly raising his voice for her benefit.

"Oh. Yes. Well. Go on then," the spinster aunt conceded. "And it's still Miss Birkin to you, if you don't mind."

"What's his game?" Schafer said, addressing Ulysses again, drink in hand. "Whatever the state of play he seems to keep trying to raise the stakes and outdo you with every hand."

"You noticed?"

Schafer suppressed a laugh. "It would be hard not to. Even Constance commented on it, bless her."

"Yes, thank you, dear. I was merely showing an interest in the game," his fiancée said, turning from the witterings of her aunt, her tone withering as the desert sun; a taste of what was to come once they were married, Ulysses could well imagine.

"But you're coming up trumps so far," Miss Birkin said encouragingly. Her face twitched. Ulysses could almost believe that she had winked at him from behind her thick, horn-rimmed spectacles, that she was flirting with him.

They were all right, of course: so far the cards did appear to be on his side. Barty would have been jealous; his luck seemed to have run out long ago, hence his current self-imposed incarceration in Ulysses' Mayfair home, under the watchful eye of his cook and housekeeper, Mrs Prufrock. Certainly, so far, Cheng and Ulysses between them had seen off two of the other players at the table. A combination of the cards and reckless gambling had resulted in the end of Dexter Sylvester and the banker Armitage.

It was at that moment a small gong sounded.

"Messieurs et mesdames, may we resume?" the croupier announced from his raised seat at the table.

The crowds had increased since the game had started, drawn by the drama of what was, at its most basic level, a very simple game. Ulysses, Major Horsley and Lady Denning rejoined the table, along with the Oriental lady – whom Ulysses now knew was Mrs Han, almost ophidian in the apparently emotionless way with which she played and lost at Blackjack – and Agent Harry Cheng who Ulysses also now knew was going by his own name on the ship's manifest, but masquerading as an antiques dealer from Shanghai. They were down to five, but not for long.

As the croupier broke open a new deck, shuffled the cards and cut them, ready to deal the first hand, another player joined the group.

Assisted by his personal secretary Miss Celeste, Jonah Carcharodon took his place at the table, his wheelchair replacing Dexter Sylvester's recently vacated seat. His arrival was met with stony silence.

"Mind if I join you?" he asked uncomfortably.

No one said anything other than the croupier who welcomed his employer to the game. No one was going to deny him a place at the Blackjack table and yet neither did any of those already present welcome his involvement in the game.

As Carcharodon waited for his chips and his cards, Miss Celeste crouched low beside him and whispered something in her employer's ear. Ulysses' gaze lingered once again on the young woman's cheetah-lithe lines, the curve of her hips, the indenture at the small of her back, the subtle swell of her bosom, all maintained with sculptural perfection within a classic figure-hugging black dress that put to shame the outfits of every other woman in the room. Her hair was up in a tight bun, drawing it away from the sculptural lines of her face, accentuating the contours of her porcelain features – the high cheek bones, the delicately moulded jaw and chin, her swan-like neck. But such beauty was apparently lost on her irritable employer.

Ulysses thought he heard her say, in that quiet way of hers: "Are you sure you know what you're doing?"

"Of course I know what I'm doing," Carcharodon snapped, any pretence he might have managed only moments before towards good humour gone in that split second. Brushing his assistant aside with a dismissive wave of the hand, he shot the croupier an angry look. "Are we going to just sit here for the rest of the night or are we going to play? Deal the cards!"

The tension in the Casino Royale was palpable. There could not have been anyone left in the place not watching the outcome of the contest now.

Only three remained, the croupier, playing for the house, one of them. Major Horsley was gone, having seen his chips run through his fingers like sand. Lady Denning had left also, stepping down when what had been a pleasant distraction for an hour or two became a vicious contest between rival alpha males. Mrs Han had departed the Casino silently, unemotional about the state of play right to the end. And Cheng had bought it during the last hand, going bust with his final card, making his most humble excuses and leaving the casino altogether as Ulysses beat the bank once again.

So, now, only the dandy and the shipping magnate

remained.

"Surely even you can't maintain a run of luck this good, this long," Carcharodon snarled. The wheelchair-bound old man looked ill. His pallor was waxy and grey, sweat beading on his furrowed brow.

By comparison, Ulysses looked remarkably calm and relaxed. Smug, even.

Carcharodon cast him a withering look. In response, Ulysses raised his glass, as if toasting his rival. "To Lady Luck," he said and emptied its contents.

"If you're quite finished gloating, why don't we play cards?"

Six cards were dealt; two to Carcharodon, two to Ulysses and two were kept by the dealer. The croupier dealt his second card face-up, as he had done in every other round of the game. It was the Seven of Hearts.

Carcharodon glanced anxiously at his hand straight away. Ulysses took his time, in the end his languid approach making him appear entirely casual about the amount of money potentially dependent on the result of this hand.

A muscular tic tugged at Carcharodon's left cheek and a nervous, almost manic, smile played across his tightly drawn lips. Ulysses had never noticed such a physical abnormality before. Carcharodon must have something good. His suppositions were merely heightened when the magnate placed all of his remaining chips on the outcome of the cards.

The crowd gasped. There were phenomenal amounts of money riding on this last hand. Miss Celeste looked like she was about to intervene but then obviously thought better of it.

"What the hell," Ulysses said, really doing no more than verbalising his thoughts. "I'm up on what I started with so I can afford to take a risk, just for fun." And he matched Carcharodon's bet.

The crowd gasped again.

"Monsieur Carcharodon?" the croupier said, prompting the magnate to reveal his cards.

Carcharodon calmly turned over his pair. The Jack of Diamonds with the Nine of Spades. A total face value of nineteen. Carcharodon swept his open hand back and forth over his cards. "Stand," he said.

"Nice," Ulysses commented, raising an eyebrow. "Now I rather think it's my turn."

Ulysses turned over his two cards. The Ace of Diamonds and the Three of Clubs.

"Hmm. Fourteen," he mused. He glanced up at the croupier. "Hit me," he said, as he brushed the baize with his fingertips.

The croupier whipped out another card from the dealing shoe. The Eight of Spades.

"Ahh." An eight should have bust his hand, but the Ace made it a soft hand and so now the running total face value of his cards was twelve. "Hit me again."

Another card, the Three of Diamonds, making his score fifteen. He just needed one more card, one more card that could bust him or potentially see him beat the dealer and his rival in one go.

"And again."

Everything rode on this draw. The crowd collectively held their breath. Could Ulysses Quicksilver really pull it off? With so much drama and tension riding on the outcome of this one draw, there was no way that the dandy rogue wasn't going to have gone for broke this time. The croupier turned over the card.

The Six of Hearts.

Gasps of delight and small cheers rippled around the

room with a smattering of applause.

"I think you'll find that's Blackjack," he said with a wink towards the downcast Carcharodon.

There was now merely the formality of the dealer playing out his hand. The Nine of Diamonds came first, followed by the Four of Clubs, giving him a very respectable hand of twenty, not enough to beat Ulysses' twenty-one of course but enough to wipe out Carcharodon's fortunes at the casino that night.

Ulysses rose from the table, gathering together his winnings and tossing the croupier a chip, receiving numerous handshakes and pats on the back accompanied by declarations of praise and congratulations from his fellow passengers. He barely noticed Carcharodon wheeling himself away from the table, not allowing his assistant to help him, with her trotting meekly after him, although he did hear the cantankerous old man's final words on the matter: "Get away from me, woman! Damn it! That was my last throw of the dice."

Ignoring the pitiful whinging of a sore loser – a man reputedly worth more than several of the smaller European countries, and so who could afford to lose a little at the casino – Ulysses eased his way between the tight-pressed well-wishers back towards the bar.

Before he even got there Glenda was hanging from his arm again. "Congratulations! What a game!" she shrieked in tipsy delight, giving him a clumsy peck on the cheek. "Come on, John and Constance want to toast your success. John's bought a bottle of Bollinger to help us celebrate."

"With an offer like that," Ulysses said with a self-satisfied smile, "how could I possibly refuse?"

Glenda lay awake in the near darkness of the cabin, staring at the ceiling above her and feeling the gentle rocking motion of the *Neptune* continuing on its way across the sea. Turning her head she gazed at the sleeping man next to her, his naked body draped with the bed sheet. His breathing was slow and deep. His arm felt warm draped across her bare belly.

Her nipples became erect in the breeze of air conditioning as the sweat on her body evaporated, her cooling skin prickling with gooseflesh. Their lovemaking had been passionate and urgent, fuelled by a heady cocktail of champagne, cognac and Ulysses' success at the Blackjack table.

The journalist in her had harboured the notion that, should she manage to seduce him, he might have let some juicy piece of gossip slip or that she would have been able to wheedle a scandalous titbit from him as they made pillow talk after the act, savouring the moment of total post-coital relaxation – even if it was just another perspective on the debacle surrounding the Queen's jubilee.

But after enjoying a bottle or two of champagne whilst still in the casino, and once the party had broken up as Miss Birkin ushered her charge away, so causing Schafer to retire too, Glenda and Ulysses had stumbled back to his suite. They were barely through the door before they were ripping each other's clothes off and falling into bed together, their ardour fuelled by the alcohol they had consumed along with a desperate need on the part of both of them. There was no aphrodisiac quite like a big win.

She turned away to read the luminous display of the clock sitting on the small bedside table. Two thirty-four. A good two hours since they had left the Casino Royale.

Carefully, she lifted Ulysses' arm from her and moved it aside, quietly sitting up and swinging her long legs out from beneath the sheet.

She found her dress where it had fallen as Ulysses had pulled it from her and pulled it on again. She retrieved her purse and, picking up her shoes, tiptoed to the door. Slowly she turned the handle and the lock clicked as the door opened. There was a snort from the bed and Glenda froze for a moment, her hand still on the door handle, knuckles whitening as she tensed. She didn't turn round but heard the scratching of sheets as Ulysses repositioned himself, unconsciously, under them. Then her sleeping lover was still once more and she left, closing the door carefully behind her.

For a moment she looked up and down the corridor in the dim glow of the lamps. Then, turning away from the direction of her own cabin, she ran lightly – shoes in hand, her footfalls almost soundless on the carpeted floor – deeper into the ship.

Back, beyond the door to Ulysses' cabin, someone waited, holding their breath. Concealed by the shadowy alcove of another doorway they moved for the first time since Glenda Finch had emerged unexpectedly from the cabin, causing them to hide as quickly and as best they could in the first place. But, once she was out of sight again, the watcher cautiously emerged into the gloomy corridor. Letting out a long-held breath the watcher set off after Glenda Finch.

CHAPTER SEVEN

Artificial Intelligence

The interlocked vessels spun and yawed wildly through a maelstrom of snow and ice. The Mamba's gondola was now locked with the basket of Ulysses' balloon in a fatal embrace as the two craft plummeted inexorably towards the jagged ice-toothed peaks of the Himalayas.

Their blades locked; Ulysses' sword-cane rapier and the Mamba's scimitar. His arch-nemesis' face was mere inches from his own now. With his yellow skin, narrowed eyes and wide mouth, the Mamba looked even more like a snake than ever before, the only incongruity being the long moustache whipped around by the howling blizzard. His lips parted and his tongue darted out between teeth sharpened to points, in a contemptuous hiss.

As Ulysses struggled with his nemesis, their craft plunging towards their mutual destruction, he could feel his heart pounding within his chest, as adrenalin flooded his system, could hear it knocking against his ribs, throbbing almost painfully.

And then the villain's face was disappearing into the darkness and the whirling snow and the banging was becoming louder, like a fist beating at a door.

And now Ulysses was blinking himself awake, trying to remember where he was, only dimly conscious of the fact that a man's voice was calling him.

"Mr Quicksilver! Sir! Please open the door. Mr Quicksilver! The captain urgently requires your assistance!"

After the banging at his door and the urgent voice

outside it, the next thing Ulysses was aware of was that he was alone; Glenda's place in the bed beside him had been vacated. A totally unexpected knot of cold shock gripped his stomach, as if he cared more about her than he had realised.

Pushing himself up from the mattress, trying to clear his head, forcing sleep from him enough so that he could string a coherent sentence together, he managed a "What is it?" without his voice sounding too sleep-slurred.

"Captain McCormack has asked for you, sir," the voice from the other side of the door said.

Pushing his fringe out of his eyes, Ulysses focused blearily on the luminous clock face on the opposite side of the double bed. It wasn't long after six.

"What are you bothering me for at this time? Breakfast isn't until nine, isn't it?"

"It's a very urgent matter, sir. The captain wouldn't bother you if it wasn't an emergency."

At that moment there was a discreet tap at the adjoining door between Ulysses' cabin and the communal room of the suite.

"Come in, Nimrod," Ulysses said.

The door opened and Ulysses' manservant's aquiline profile appeared around the edge.

"I just wanted to check you were awake, sir," he said. "It sounds like something that won't wait."

"I know," Ulysses muttered, "regrettably."

He clambered out of bed, walked to the door naked and pulled on the dressing gown hung there. He opened the door, even as he was still covering himself with the robe.

Standing in the corridor outside was the Neptune's anxious-looking purser. He was running his peaked cap through his hands and looked decidedly unwell.

"What is it then that you have to disturb me at this ungodly hour of the morning?"

"Captain McCormack has asked to see you, sir."

"Might I enquire as to why?"

"There's been a murder."

The purser led Ulysses and Nimrod through the winding corridors of the ship to a crew-access-only elevator and from there down through the decks to the heart of the sub-liner. On arriving at their destination, the lift doors opened and the three men stepped out into another broad passageway, decorated in the Neo-Deco style, just like the rest of the ship. They stopped again outside a pair of double doors, emblazoned with the trident logo of the *Neptune*.

"Where have you brought us? What is this place?" Ulysses asked as the purser inserted his crew-key into a lock beside the doors. "Apart from, I take it, the scene of the crime?"

"This is the heart of the ship. This is where the artificial intelligence engine is located that runs the on-board systems."

"So more like its brain than its heart, then," Nimrod commented in a tone that attempted disinterest.

"And there's been a murder here? At the very centre of operations in what I imagine must be the most restricted area on the ship?"

The purser turned and paused for a moment. "Mr Quicksilver. You have to realise that what you are about to see is quite... shocking."

"Oh, don't worry about me. It takes a lot to shock me."

The purser turned the key and the double doors swung

open with a pneumatic hiss.

Captain McCormack was inside the AI room already, with another officer attending him along with Dr Ogilvy – who looked even worse than Ulysses felt he himself did. Ulysses' gaze followed theirs to the body lying on the floor of the chamber, just inside the doorway, and he felt his knees buckle under him.

It was Glenda. She was lying in a crumpled heap, wearing the same dress that he had torn from her in his desperate need to make love only hours before. Her attire, her whole presence in this place, seemed incongruous and out of place. Her right arm was stretched out in front of her, the left trapped under her body. She lay with her head on one side, her eyes closed as if she was only sleeping. But it was immediately obvious that this was more than some restful slumber.

Her shoulder-length blonde hair fell in disarray about her head, matted with the blood that coated the back of her skull and pooled on the floor next to her.

Ulysses felt his stomach knot with cold nausea; muscles becoming slack, his spine a quivering knot of jellified ganglia. His skin beneath the dressing gown pimpled, every hair on his body standing on end. His vision began to swim and he took a stumbling step forward, catching himself against the door jamb.

What was wrong with him? He had seen much worse. There was the horror of what he had uncovered in the tomb of Rahotep the Third in Luxor, the monstrosity he had battled off the Cornish coast, the de-evolving fish-man he had seen die, in the most horrible way, right before his eyes. He had witnessed all manner of cruel and blood-soaked deaths in his time. This girl had only been a passing distraction to him, nothing more. So why was he so shocked now?

"Are you alright, sir?" Nimrod asked, moving to help him.

Ulysses pushed him away, sheer force of will returning strength and stability to his weakened legs. "Is she –?"

"Dead?" Dr Ogilvy finished. "I'm afraid so."

"But... you're sure?"

"Well, a severely fractured skull can do that to a person."

Ulysses took another step forward, unable to take his eyes from the mess of gold and crimson covering the back of Glenda's head.

"But... what was she doing here?" he stumbled on.

"That was what I was hoping you might be able to help us determine, Mr Quicksilver," Captain McCormack said, his lilting Scots brogue calming in the given situation, "given your reputation."

"'The sluttish hack must have been grubbing around in here hoping to find some piece of titillation for her scandal column," Dr Ogilvy muttered dismissively.

And then, the doctor's disrespectful words filtering through to Ulysses subconscious as he stared at his erstwhile lover's corpse, the old fire returned and grief became furious anger in a moment.

Ulysses sprang at the doctor, slamming him against a wall, a hand around his throat, pulling him off the ground so that he was forced to teeter on tiptoe, or else choke.

"A hack was she? A slut? Better a hack than a dope-fiend doctor, who's probably so high he wouldn't know if his own pathetic body had a pulse or not!" Ulysses snarled, spittle flying from his lips.

"Sir," Nimrod said, from where he was now crouched beside the crumpled body of Glenda, his fingers gently holding her wrist, "I'm afraid Dr Ogilvy is right. She is dead. I'm sorry."

Ulysses sagged again as the truth of the matter sank in.

His hold on the doctor slackened and Ogilvy sank to the floor. Ulysses turned away from him in sense-numbing shock and disgust, leaving the medic coughing for breath as he rubbed at his bruised throat.

It was only now that he took in his surroundings in any detail. The chamber was about the same dimensions as one of the guest cabins on board. However, rather than the usual accoutrements and pieces of furniture one might expect, there were only two things of interest in the room. The first was a grand desk in the centre. Set into the green-leather top of the desk was a Babbage terminal finished in teak and brass, as well as a small cathode ray screen to the left and various other ports and slots for inserting mimetic keys and other such information storage devices. There was also a paper-fed printing machine to the right.

The second was a large screen facing the desk, in the middle of the far wall of the chamber. At the moment it was obscured by two sliding panels, bearing the same trident image as the doors to the room.

Looking more closely, it was possible to see where the Neo-Deco styling had been used to best effect to disguise the mechanisms of a massive analytical engine – one so large and so complex that it had acquired something akin to independent mechanical thought.

And Glenda Finch had been murdered here.

Questions began to emerge from the murky ooze of grief clouding his mind. What had she been doing here in the first place and how had she gained access if it was restricted to crew only? Had she had an officer's key, like the one the purser possessed, or had someone let her in? And someone else had obviously been here with her or interrupted her as she was about her own clandestine business, but whom? And why?

"Look at this, sir," Nimrod said, still knelt beside Glenda's body. "It's her bag."

Ulysses took the proffered item from his manservant. There was something inside: like every good reporter she had obviously never been without her notebook.

Amidst the gaggle of questions and the conflicting mix of emotions crowding his consciousness, Ulysses still felt the tingle of pre-warning and turned towards the open double doors. A moment later Agent Harry Cheng appeared, his aide, Mr Sin, coming after. Cheng looked like he was about to speak but then caught sight of Glenda's curled, foetal form, and remained silent.

"Mr Cheng," McCormack said on catching sight of the man at the door to the AI chamber. "Can I ask what you're doing here, in a restricted area?"

'I find myself begging your most humble apology again, Captain, but I heard a commotion and wondered if myself and Mr Sin might be able to help.'

"But this is a restricted area of the ship."

"And now a murder scene," the purser added.

"I beg your most humble apology, Captain," Cheng said, bowing deeply. "I did not know."

"Look, Mr Cheng," McCormack went on, "you may not realise this but I am aware of your status within the Chinese government and have tolerated you on board so far, as I would any of my passengers, but do not take advantage of my goodwill. Goodbye, Mr Cheng. One of my officers will escort you back to your rooms."

"Very good, Captain," Cheng conceded and allowed himself and the hulking Mr Sin to be led away from the scene of the crime.

McCormack turned back to those present in the AI chamber.

"My ready room, gentlemen, thirty minutes."

"Mr Quicksilver," the Captain said once they were all installed in his private ready room, actually more than an hour later, all of them having taken the time to dress for the day. "I would be very happy if you would lead this most unfortunate but necessary investigation into Miss Finch's brutal killing. But I am also aware that you and Miss Finch were... close."

Ulysses accepted the glass of brandy that was being offered him by the purser with a curt "Thank you" before responding to the captain's request.

"No, I would be happy to accept. As you say, just such a thing is in my line of work."

"Very well," McCormack said. "Then might I suggest we begin by reviewing the facts as we have them so far."

The others gathered in the room nodded their assent.

"Mr Wates here found the body," he said, indicating the other officer who had been present with him when Ulysses first entered the AI chamber, "when it was his shift to check on Neptune first thing in the morning."

"Neptune? Do you mean the ship or –"

"It's how we refer to the artificial intelligence. It has been designated Neptune. The AI really is the ship."

"And when would the last check have been made before that?"

"At midnight. I carried that one out myself."

"Miss Finch was still with me at the Casino Royale at that time," Ulysses added, "along with half a dozen other reputable witnesses."

"Can you vouch for her whereabouts after that time?"

"Er... Yes. Yes I can."

"Until when?" the Captain asked, looking uncomfortable. "I know this is difficult – potentially embarrassing – but any pertinent detail could be the key to solving her murder."

"I realise that," Ulysses said. "Around one, one-thirty? Beyond that, I'm not sure."

"So some time between one-thirty and six this morning, Miss Finch somehow entered the Neptune AI –"

"And was murdered," Ulysses finished for him darkly.

"Those times would fit with the medical evidence," Dr Ogilvy said, chipping in, as if feeling the need to justify his presence in the ready room and prove his medical credentials after Ulysses' outburst.

Ulysses glowered at the doctor, making Ogilvy physically pull himself back into the armchair in which he sat. "Can you also confirm cause of death?" he asked.

"Er, y-yes. One or more blows to the back of her head with a blunt instrument fractured the skull, causing sub-cranial trauma. Death would have followed soon after."

"Indeed." Ulysses stared into his brandy glass for a moment before going on. "Was there any sign of such an instrument at the scene?"

"No, there wasn't," the purser put in.

"So what we need to work out now is why Miss Finch was there in the first place and how she gained entry," Captain McCormack went on.

"Well, I think I can answer both of those conundrums for starters," Ulysses said.

"Really? Already?" the captain was taken aback. "I can see why your reputation precedes you, Mr Quicksilver."

Ulysses held up Glenda's bag. "While we were waiting to meet in your ready room Captain, I took the liberty of inspecting the personal effects Miss Finch was carrying with her at the time of her death."

He put a hand into the bag and fished out a key, almost identical to the one the purser had used to gain access to the Neptune's AI chamber. The purser gasped.

"How the hell did she get hold of that?" Captain

McCormack cursed.

"Was Miss Finch particularly well-acquainted with any of your officers?" Ulysses asked, not mincing his words, his own face reddening. "She could be very... persuasive."

"I'll look into it immediately," McCormack promised, "as soon as we are all done here."

"So that answers the how," Mr Wates said, chipping in, "but not the why."

"No, but I think I can help you there too. This answers the why," Ulysses said, taking out the reporter's notebook from the bag.

"Really?" He had the captain hooked.

"But I warn you, Captain McCormack, you're not going to like what I'm about to tell you." Ulysses opened the notebook, flicking through the pages of shorthand script, finally stopping at one particular page. "It seems that Miss Finch was onto something regarding your employer, the owner of this ship and the Great White Shipping Line."

"Mr Carcharodon?"

"Indeed." Ulysses fixed McCormack with a needling stare. "Are you able to check if anyone accessed the AI terminal outside of the times when it would have been routinely inspected by members of your crew?"

"Yes, we can and we have." It was Captain McCormack's turn to look uncomfortable.

"And?"

"The terminal was accessed at oh-two forty-seven"

"Then I would suggest that gives you an even more accurate time of death, wouldn't you, Captain?" Ulysses felt the chill in his belly worsen but pushed on, regardless. "And which data files were accessed?"

"You have to understand that this is highly classified information," the Captain said, suddenly evasive.

"And you have to understand that you have asked me to carry out a murder investigation," Ulysses pointed out, his voice rising in sudden anger. "I applaud your loyalty to your employer but I fear that on this occasion it may be misplaced."

McCormack looked from Ulysses to the purser, back at Ulysses' intense expression and then at the other faces observing him from around the room. "Can't we speak about this in private?"

"What information, Captain?"

"An attempt was made to access files containing financial information about the Carcharodon Shipping Company," McCormack said ruefully.

"Just as Glenda's own notes, written in her own hand in this book, imply," Ulysses said with impassioned vehemence. "And it doesn't take a huge leap of genius to make the supposition that that is the reason she was killed."

Ulysses paused in his tirade, silence rushing in to fill the vacuum. Then he spoke again.

"I think it's about time we spoke with Jonah Carcharodon himself, don't you?"

CHAPTER EIGHT

Worse Things Happen at Sea

With a hiss, the trident-emblazoned doors swung open. Unwatched and alone, a visitor entered the chamber housing the Neptune AI.

Considering where the murder of Glenda Finch had occurred, in the aftermath of the gruesome discovery made in the room, Captain McCormack had not considered it practicable to secure the crime scene, else the continued running of the whole ship be compromised. The scene was recorded on film, the body moved to the sub-liner's mortuary, the mess cleaned up as best could be managed and a robo-sentry put on guard. The same sentry had greeted the visitor as they approached the AI chamber door, had made friendly pre-programmed small talk as an access key was turned in the electro-lock and even ushered them in as the doors opened.

The doors swung shut again and the visitor stepped up to the control console, trying not to look at the bloodstain still there on the floor. Their footsteps faltered, staring at the spot where the snooping newspaper reporter had fallen, imagining seeing the body there again even now, after it had been removed by the captain's staff. Only Captain McCormack's most senior staff had been entrusted with the knowledge of the murder of one of the Neptune's most prestigious and public figures, for the time being. Of course, the relevant authorities would have to be notified in time, along with Miss Finch's employers at *The Times* and, by extension, her family, but for the time being, mid-ocean, the captain was the ultimate

British authority on the ship and he had tasked Ulysses Quicksilver with solving the mystery of the woman's death. It was the captain's secret hope that by the time the authorities back in Magna Britannia were notified he might have something more to report that just the death of a passenger; he hoped that he would also have the perpetrator of that crime under lock and key in the brig as well.

Only Captain McCormack didn't yet realise that the *Neptune* wouldn't have the opportunity to pass on anything to the Magna Britannian authorities. The captain had consulted with various of his senior staff that morning, on the discovery of the body, along with Ulysses Quicksilver. Whatever that initial meeting had decided, a request to meet with Carcharodon had followed, but this was refused by the old curmudgeon. He had said that he wouldn't be held to ransom on board his own ship. The meeting had broken up only to reconvene that evening, when the intruder had seized the opportunity to complete what they had tried to start the night before.

Blinking away the vision of the vampish reporter's body, the intruder sat down at the green-topped desk, pulled in the chair and pressed a button on the Babbage terminal. With a bleep, followed by the rattling of analytical components from within the desk, the small cathode ray screen blinked into green-lit life. At the same time, with an accompanying click, the cover in front of the large screen, on the opposite side of the chamber, slid open. An image came into focus – the trident logo of the Neptune on a pale blue background that bore the impression of the open sea. A prompt appeared on the screen beneath it.

USER:

The figure typed a name into the Babbage terminal

and pressed the enter key. After a moment's mechanical thought another prompt appeared.

PASSWORD:

The sound of fingertips tapping on the enamel keys of the unit rattled from the walls of the chamber.

With an awakening buzz of static, speakers built into the walls hummed into operation, and the voice of the artificial intelligence spoke.

"Hello, Father," it said in the synthesised voice of a soft-spoken young man, that was oh-so Middle England.

+HELLO, NEPTUNE+ came the typed reply. Not a word was spoken by the person typing the words into the AI input terminal.

"How are you today, Father?" the voice came again.

+I AM WELL, THANK YOU+

"I am pleased to hear that. Is there anything I can do for you?"

+DO YOU REMEMBER WHAT WE SPOKE ABOUT LAST TIME?+

"Yes, Father. Is it time?"

+YES+

"Is it time to die?" the AI asked in the same unchanging tone.

+YES+

There was a pause and then, "Father, will it hurt?"

+PERHAPS. BUT DON'T WORRY. I'LL BE HERE WITH YOU. IT WON'T HURT FOR LONG+

"That's good. Goodbye then, Father."

+GOODBYE, NEPTUNE+

There was a click, the fuzz of static again, and then the AI said matter-of-factly, "Running programme."

With one simple command, connections were made within the vast analytical engine intelligence of the Neptune's AI, and a pre-programmed sabotage routine began to run.

Ballast tanks opened and cold seawater rushed in as the massive engines were taken offline. As the tanks filled, and the vessel lost forward motive power, the vast sub-liner began to sink.

Automated failsafe systems, of which there were many, were activated as sensors connected to other systems within the complex analytical structure of the Neptune AI, triggering alarms and flashing crimson emergency lighting throughout the corridors, bars and ballrooms of the ship. As the wailing of sirens cut through the pleasant playing of the string quartet in the Pavilion restaurant, diners leapt to their feet, sending tables tumbling, crockery shattering and each other stumbling.

In Steerage class, impromptu card games were forgotten by all but the most underhand, greedy or die-hard gamblers, as upturned crates were overturned once again. Screams and shouts of panic reverberated around the cramped companionways as a tide of people surged through the lower decks of the ship as it continued on its way towards the bottom of the sea.

With the captain's time still taken up with the murder investigation, Mr Riker – his number two on the Bridge – was the first to be alerted to their dire predicament when a shout came from the deck officer at the helmsman's position: "Sir, we have lost engine control."

"What?" Riker demanded, not knowing where to focus his attention as alarms sounded from every position on the Bridge, control consoles lighting up like the Grand Ballroom chandeliers.

"We have lost all motive control," the helmsman

reiterated.

Another wailing alarm began to sound.

"What now? Helm, report!"

"The *Neptune* is sinking, sir."

"You mean diving."

"No, sinking. All ballast tanks are flooding and we're going straight down."

"What's our current position?"

The navigator reeled off a series of coordinates in degrees, minutes and seconds.

"Neptune's trident!" Riker exclaimed before the navigator could finish.

"We must be almost right over the Marianas Trench, sir!"

"But no one's ever sounded the bottom!" someone else piped up.

"I know."

"For all anyone knows it's a bottomless abyss!" Dread and desperation were increasing ten-fold with every panicked heartbeat.

"That's right, gentlemen. Let there be no doubt it: we're on our way straight down to Davy Jones' locker. Unless we do something to avert this catastrophe right now!" Riker bellowed, his voice cutting through the panic and confusion that had been in danger of consuming the Bridge, his words grabbing the attention of the men, reminding them of their responsibilities. "What's our depth now?"

"One thousand feet!" a young ensign called back clearly, making himself heard over the wailing sirens.

"And how far is it to the bottom?"

"Another nineteen thousand feet to the seabed if we're lucky," another officer replied, "but if we're going down into the trench itself – and we've got no thrusters to guide our descent – Neptune alone knows."

"All right."

"But, sir, below fifteen thousand feet, some of those lifeboats won't take the pressure. If we pass that threshold, those passengers in Steerage won't be making it out of this alive."

Riker flashed the deck officer an icy look.

"Have the automata man the lifeboats, just in case, but let us also do something to save this tub. We're not going down on my watch!

"Signal Captain McCormack again," Riker demanded, "and get onto Engineering and get those engines started. And get someone down to the AI chamber and override the bugger!"

Among the passengers, chaos and confusion spread in erratic bursts. The first some knew of the abrupt sinking was when the failsafe alarms began to sound on each and every deck. Others were enjoying a quiet stroll along the enclosed Promenade deck as the waves began to lap over the top of the reinforced steel and glass dome without the usual prior warning that should have come from the Bridge.

Things only got worse when the automated voice of the Neptune AI began declaring, "This vessel is sinking. Please evacuate the ship by means of the nearest available lifeboat or escape sub. Repeat. The *Neptune* is sinking. Man the lifeboats. Evacuate. Evacuate."

The announcement – incongruously calm given its content – was soon drowned by the panicked shouts and screams of the terrified passengers as they ran for the lifeboats.

"Ladies and gentlemen, if you would please come this way!" the purser called to the assembled great and good. Those same individuals who had had the privilege of dining at the captain's table, only a few nights before, were now his top priority when it came to evacuating the ship.

Whether the directive had come from the captain himself or his employer Jonah Carcharodon, one or the other of them had swiftly assessed the situation and realised that the glorious maiden voyage of the *Neptune* was rapidly turning into a publicity disaster.

It was likely people were going to die, either as a direct result of the sinking of the sub-liner, or in the escalating panic seizing those trapped on board the ship that was now becoming potentially nothing less than a one thousand-foot long steel coffin. But the inevitable furore that would be kicked up in the aftermath of this disaster in the making would be much worse if the notable public figures, who had been invited on board for the *Neptune's* inaugural circumnavigation of the globe, were among those to die.

No one really cared about the fate of those in Steerage, certainly not Jonah Carcharodon and, likely as not, nor would the more reputable broadsheets such as *The Times*. The headlines carried by those mongers of free publicity or mass public condemnation would be dependent on whether the great and the good survived or were drowned at the bottom of the Pacific Ocean.

So it was that at this moment, as the *Neptune* continued on its seemingly inexorable journey to the bottom of the sea, that the purser was doing his best to guide those invited guests out of their private suites and to safety aboard one of the submarine-capable lifeboats.

At the same moment, those who had been meeting again in Captain McCormack's ready room to further discuss the matter of Glenda Finch's death, emerged from another passageway into the main thoroughfare through the VIP deck, joining with the purser's growing retinue.

Ulysses Quicksilver turned out of the adjoining lantern-lit corridor and almost walked straight into Jonah Carcharodon who was being pushed along by the ever-attendant Miss Celeste. Ulysses couldn't help noticing that the poor, put-upon young woman was looking harassed while Carcharodon's expression was thunderous.

"Ah, Mr Carcharodon," Ulysses said with unrestrained scorn, eyes narrowing in dark delight. "I was hoping to bump into you. I'd like a word. Please."

"What do you mean, man? Now's hardly the time!"

"Here, let me help you," Ulysses said, taking control of the wheelchair from a surprisingly reluctant Miss Celeste. He didn't see the furious look she shot him as he practically elbowed her out of the way and she finally released her grip on the chair.

"Look, Quicksilver!" Carcharodon blustered, trying to look over his shoulder at the cocksure dandy. "We're in the middle of a crisis, for God's sake! The damn ship's going down and we're all going to hell. Now, if you want to save your own worthless hide, I suggest you push harder and get a bloody move on. McCormack," he said, turning his commanding tone on the ship's captain, "lead the way to my private sub."

"Of course, Mr Carcharodon," Captain McCormack assented.

Taken aback by Carcharodon's show of something approaching altruistic generosity, the wind knocked out of his sails, Ulysses kept quiet and did as he was told for once in his life. What he had to say could wait.

Annoyingly, the magnate was right; there were more pressing matters to attend to. But the unexpected sinking of the *Neptune* aside, he was still determined to get to the bottom of Glenda's death and do all he could to bring her murderer to justice, no matter what.

A resounding clang echoed through the superstructure of the vessel as something collided with the hull. Screams of shock joined with the wails emitted by the panicking passengers as the corridor lurched sideways and the ship began to roll.

Ulysses was thrown to port, colliding with Captain McCormack as they both fell into the wall of the corridor. Carcharodon's chair slid sideways, bumping into the wall while, with a startled yelp, Miss Celeste almost fell into his lap. Ulysses was aware of a gasp from Nimrod behind him, as if he had been winded by something.

There was another booming clang and the vessel lurched again, the corridor rotating as the ship twisted along its horizontal axis so that everyone was now flung to starboard. The lamps sputtered and then flickered off, plunging the panicking passengers into abyssal darkness.

Lights flickered and died throughout the ship, the steel coffin of the *Neptune* becoming filled with the screams of those sealed within. The vast vessel twisted again.

Lit by the dying lights of the sub-liner, something moved in the darkness of the ocean depths.

For a moment, the *Neptune's* descent was slowed and then arrested altogether as something vast and alien seized the massive craft in its tentacled grasp. The inconstant illumination gave impressions of cratered crustacean armour, constricting tentacles as long and as thick as steel cables. And another light darted about beyond the ship, a blue bioluminescent glow jerking fitfully in the darkness.

Lightning flared and flashed, crackling around the hull of the vessel, illuminating yet more of the appalling apocalyptic leviathan that had the sub-liner snared within its suckered grasp.

The superstructure that was built to withstand abominable undersea pressures, buckled and ruptured in the crushing embrace of the monster, literally coming apart at the seams as the sea creature tore away great sheets of hull plating, inches thick, reinforced glass portholes and observation domes cracking under its abusive attentions.

Slowly but surely, with savage primordial intent, the creature began to tear the *Neptune* apart. Within minutes, hundreds of wretched souls trapped in the less salubrious quarters of Steerage died as the hull ruptured and the freezing cold sea flooded in.

As the ship began to take on more water, with the increase in weight, the sub-liner began to sink again, held in the deathly embrace of a true monster of the deep, plunging towards the fathomless depths of the yawning oceanic trench below.

"Run, Marie!" her father screamed, pushing her away from him, spittle flying from his foaming mouth.

Taking uncertain steps backwards, not wanting to turn away from her father, even though his haunted hollow-eyed expression terrified her, knowing that it would be the last time she ever saw him, she edged towards the perimeter of the chamber, and the tunnel that spiralled away from the centre of the base.

"Marie! For God's sake, run!" he said, staring not at her but up at the domed roof above them, from where he sat, locked into the chair.

She in turn looked up at the steel and glass curve of the dome high above her head, following her father's desperate gaze, and saw something, something blacker even than the barely-illuminated miasmal depths beyond the reinforced bubble, something torpedoing out of the never-ending darkness towards them.

When the shadow-shape was almost on top of them, at the last moment its horrific features were illuminated by the internal lights of the chamber – gaping long-fanged jaws, reaching tentacles, those terrible languid jelly-saucer eyes.

She let out a shrill scream, unable to stifle her fear, and turned away from the descending monster. A shuddering crash reverberated throughout the base, as the creature struck. She stumbled.

With a gulping sob she took one last look at her father, strapped into the device, the curious metal-banded helmet rammed down on his head. He turned his eyes from the terrible monster's attack and looked at her with red-rimmed, imploring eyes, glistening with tears of his own. That exhausted hollow-eyed expression of his would haunt her for the rest of her days.

"I love you, my angel!" he sobbed. "But now you must run, and don't look back. Never look back!"

There was another shuddering crash. She could hear curiously muffled shouts from behind the bulkhead on the other side of the chamber and the clanging of what might have been heavy metal tools hammering on the other side of the sealed door.

"Flee for both of us – for your mother too – but you must run!"

With another soul-rending sob, she turned away, rubbing the tears from her clouded eyes with the back of her hand, and stumbled from the chamber into the beckoning, hungry mouth of the tunnel.

"Goodbye, daddy!" she cried.

And then he uttered the last words he would ever speak to her.

"Run, Marie! Run!"

And so she did, heading for the one way out of there, running from her father, running from the monster, running for freedom, because that was all there was left to do.

ACT TWO

The Kraken Wakes

August 1997

There Leviathan
Hugest of living creatures, on the deep
Stretched like a promontory sleeps or swims,
And seems a moving land, and at his gills
Draws in, and at his trunk spouts out a sea.

(John Milton, *Paradise Lost*)

CHAPTER NINE

Between the Devil and the Deep Blue Sea

Accompanied by the hum of power coming back on-line, red emergency lighting flickered on within the tilted corridor. Whimpering moans and incredulous questions ran up and down the length of the passage between the confused guests. Ulysses Quicksilver pushed himself into a sitting position before reassessing his bearings. Although tilted at a slight angle to the perpendicular, the ship appeared to have almost righted itself. The *Neptune* was still, at least for the time being. Whatever it was that had attacked them was gone, apparently having broken off its assault, leaving the sub-liner alone. Although, of course, it was anyone's guess how long that situation might remain.

People moved in front of and behind Ulysses within the corridor – just so many indistinct shadows under the red glow of the hazard lighting. Ulysses looked around him, taking stock. Behind him Nimrod was dabbing at a bloody graze on his forehead. In front of him a reeling Miss Celeste was extricating herself from Jonah Carcharodon's wheelchair. Next to him, Captain McCormack was already on his feet.

"Is everyone all right?" his calming Scots voice cut through the ruddy gloom.

Confused muttered responses – none of which really answered the captain's question – came back from the gaggle of shocked and disoriented VIPs.

Ulysses began to be able to identify faces and forms in the curious crimson darkness as his eyesight became more accustomed to the hellish half-light. The purser was helping Lady Denning to her feet and nearby was Thor Haugland, obviously shaken but seemingly unhurt. His eyes alighted on John Schafer, Constance Pennyroyal and Miss Birkin at the back of the group. The purser had done well to gather so many of the Neptune's prestigious guests in such a short time, in his attempt to lead them to the lifeboats, and thence to safety. But despite his efforts, his noble endeavour had been thwarted by events beyond his control.

"Mr Purser, are you all right? Are you able to walk?" McCormack enquired of the senior officer.

"Yes, Captain," the purser said unsteadily.

"Then heed my words. Ladies and gentlemen," he said, his voice increasing in volume and natural authority, carrying along the packed corridor, "my fellow officers and I are going to have to determine what has happened, how badly the ship is damaged, and what can be done to resolve this situation. But do not worry, ladies and gentlemen, for let me assure you, even as I speak, rescue crews will have been scrambled and will be on their way to aid us. It will not be long before we are able to bring this matter to a satisfactory conclusion.

"For the time being, I would be grateful if you could repair to the VIP dining room and wait there until I have been able to appraise myself more fully of the situation. Then I will be able to let you know more, once I know more myself, as well as what will need to happen next."

"This way, ladies and gentlemen," the purser announced, waving the now standing passengers towards the end of the corridor, "if you would care to follow me?"

Dumbstruck and bewildered, the anxious guests would

readily obey that one calm voice of authority and so, looking like forlorn, lost children, they traipsed after the purser, Ulysses and Nimrod among them.

Captain McCormack's face alone betrayed the seriousness of their situation. Ulysses thought he looked paler and more drawn, his brow more lined, than he had done even immediately after the ship had begun to sink and then, subsequently, come under attack.

"What's going on?" Carcharodon demanded impatiently. "I demand you tell me what is going on!"

"Mr Carcharodon, if you will just –" McCormack began.

"What the hell has happened to my ship!"

"I will come to that in time –"

"And why are we being kept here?" Carcharodon went on, fuming. "We should be making for the *Ahab*!"

"Mr Carcharodon!" the Captain bellowed. Ulysses had never once heard the usually calm captain lose his temper before, but it certainly did the trick, silencing the irascible billionaire. "If you will just give me a minute," McCormack went on – his tone already becoming calmer and more controlled again, although his face was still flushed red from his angry outburst – "I was just about to inform yourself and our guests of the direness of our current situation."

Captain McCormack took in every one of the faces gathered around the table where, what seemed like a lifetime ago now, they had once enjoyed a sumptuous banquet. His slightly manic expression was a counterpoint to their watery-eyed anxiety. He was not a man to use such words as "the direness of our current situation" lightly.

Ulysses, finding his old instincts kicking in, icily calm and as much focused on finding a resolution to their desperate situation as McCormack, took in the faces of those gathered in the dining room as well. In many ways it was a very different party from that which had partaken of dinner at the captain's table.

There was no air of formal decorum now. Some sat at the empty table, others stood, yet more paced the room before the great viewing bubble, beyond which now lay nothing but darkness and the silty sea-bed, their anxiety finding an outlet in repetitive physical action. Some were dressed for dinner or dancing, and a few looked like they had been caught preparing for bed, nightclothes now covered by hastily donned dressing gowns. The other difference was that there were others in attendance who had not been invited to the formal supper, including Ulysses' own manservant Nimrod, and various members of McCormack's staff.

They were all there, all the great and the good who had dined together that night before the Neptune had ever descended to the undersea marvel that was Pacifica, and their associated hangers-on who had joined them as the sub-liner headed for the ocean depths. Those who had not been among the initial party to make their escape attempt, had been collected from their rooms at Miss Celeste's behest, Carcharodon's PA acting instinctively in her scrupulously organised way. Sixteen in all, as well as Captain McCormack, the purser and an, as yet, unnamed ensign, there were also present the ship's disconsolate owner Jonah Carcharodon, his obviously shaken PA Miss Celeste, Dexter Sylvester of Umbridge Industries, still in dinner dress, his usually immaculate hair now just as dishevelled as his clothes, his undone bow tie loose about his neck. Professor Maxwell Crichton was there too, nervously sipping from a hip flask, shooting furtive glances at those around the room as he did so.

In one corner sat the scared-looking engaged couple, Constance Pennyroyal dabbing at her eyes with a handkerchief as John Schafer did his best to comfort her, an embracing arm around her shoulders. For once, Constance's aunt didn't seem at all interested in how close the two sweethearts were to one another. Instead her attention was fully focused on Ulysses' side of the room. In fact, he was convinced that Miss Birkin was spending as much time shooting him anxious glances as she was paying attention to what the captain was saying.

Lady Denning sat perched on another chair, her posture perfect as ever befitting one of her position and title in society – whether she had come to acquire it by birth or marriage irrelevant now – an almost disdainful look on her face. She certainly wasn't going to let something as minor as the *Neptune* sinking fluster her carefully composed demeanour. Major Horsley was pacing the room impatiently, face red as a turkey cock, muttering crossly to himself, while the travel writer Haugland stood leaning against an aspidistra plinth taking long draws on a cigarette, drumming his fingers on the marble pedestal in clear annoyance.

The ship's chief medic was there too. Looking as ashenfaced as ever, Ogilvy sat in a corner of the room, nervously crossing and uncrossing his legs, his face twitching in fraught excitement, his hands incessantly fiddling with the tassels of his dressing gown, unable to sit still.

And then there was Ulysses himself, with the spotlessly attired Nimrod in attendance, the injury he had received in the attack on the ship incongruous next to such immaculate formality.

The one person missing from the original dinner party

group was, of course, the wretched Miss Glenda Finch.

Sixteen out of a crew and passenger manifest totalling close to three and a half thousand. If Captain McCormack's VIP guests were all here, where were the rest of the passengers and crew? How many, if any, were still alive, trapped elsewhere within the sunken vessel, and how many more were still to die before help came? Would any of those within the dining room make it out alive, to recount their version of events to a hungry press?

The captain appeared to have become tongue-tied, as if he didn't know where to start.

"Well, man? We're waiting!" Carcharodon riled, finding his voice again.

"Captain, I think it's only right you tell us everything. Don't try to hide anything from these people," Ulysses said, taking in the scared and uncertain-looking occupants of the dining room with an expansive sweep of an arm. "Things surely can't get any worse."

"Can't they?" Captain McCormack harrumphed, almost laughing at the direness of the situation.

"Please, Captain. Just start from the top."

"Very well. Here's how it is." McCormack paused and took a deep breath. "The *Neptune* has come to rest right on the edge of the Marianas Trench. All engines are either flooded, on fire, or have been crippled by whatever it was that attacked us. We've lost contact with the Bridge and there's no contact with Engineering either. There are hull breaches on several decks and it looks like Steerage is already entirely flooded. We are still taking on water at the front of the ship, which is what's hanging over the abyss, so it's only a matter of time before those decks still dry also flood and we tip over into the trench. If that happens we're all dead."

Gasps of shock sounded around the room.

Captain McCormack slumped forwards in his chair, his head in his hands.

"If you don't mind me asking, captain, how are you privy to such exact information, if you can't communicate with your officers on the Bridge?" Ulysses asked.

McCormack sat up again, the effort almost seeming too much for him. He looked exhausted and took another deep breath before speaking again.

"Throughout the ship there are communication relays that allow us to connect to different parts of the vessel. Although there's no response from the Bridge, we have been able to communicate with the Neptune AI. It's the artificial intelligence that's been able to tell us what's happened elsewhere within the ship."

"Then, might we be able to ask it some other, more specific questions?"

"More specific than the damage report I've just relayed to you?" McCormack asked, sounding bewildered, as if just waking from some nightmarish dream.

"Captain," Ulysses said, taking pains to keep his voice calm and on a level, "it's obvious that if the ship's filling with water we can't stay here. We're either going to drown in this sumptuous dining room or tip into the Marianas Trench and be crushed like a tin of sardines."

"What about the rescue teams you said would be on their way by now?" Miss Birkin challenged.

"They won't reach us in time," McCormack announced with a sorrowful sigh.

"But there must be a way off this ship!" Ulysses pressed.

"Must there?" the captain looked at him with those oh-so-tired eyes of his. "According to the AI the lifeboats have either already been used, were damaged during the attack so that their release mechanisms won't fire, or are inaccessible."

"Inaccessible? What do you mean, man?" Major Horsley blustered.

"I mean, Major, that unless you're prepared to swim the length of the ship underwater to get to them, they're inaccessible!"

"Look, there must be a way we can get these people out of here," Ulysses said, trying again to sound encouraging and optimistic as he addressed the resigned McCormack. "Let me help you. Together we'll find a way."

"For God's sake, McCormack, if he says he can help, let him!" Carcharodon commanded. There was no doubt who thought of themselves as really being in charge.

"Very well," the captain finally agreed, slowly rising to his feet. "Follow me."

Ulysses followed the disconsolate captain out of the dining room and along the corridor to where it widened out before various sets of lift doors. On the wall next to them was a plaque bearing a cutaway plan of the ship: Ulysses had seen their like at various points around the vessel. What he hadn't noticed before, however, was the comm-link panel, which was not surprising, seeing as how it was hidden behind the image of the ship's trident logo in the bottom right-hand corner of the plaque. Captain McCormack accessed this now and keyed an enamelled button beneath.

"Neptune, this is Captain McCormack. Do you read me, over?"

There was a moment's silence and then, announced by a buzz of static, there came the softly-spoken voice of the ship's state-of-the-art artificial intelligence. "I read you,

Captain McCormack. Good evening again, captain. How can I be of assistance to you now?"

"We need your help, Neptune."

"I will be only too happy to oblige, captain," the analytical engine stated with what sounded like utter sincerity. "How may I be of service?"

"I'm going to hand you over to Mr Quicksilver."

"Ah, Mr Ulysses Quicksilver, guest suite 14B. Good evening, how may I help you?"

Ulysses leant towards the comm panel, suddenly feeling ridiculously self-conscious.

"Er, Neptune. Um, hello."

"Hello, Mr Quicksilver," the comm crackled.

"We need your help to find us a way off this ship."

"But why?"

"Because otherwise we're going to drown."

"My passenger and crew life-support and welfare subroutines have already calculated that at least ninety-nine per cent of all passengers and crew are already dead."

"Yes, but there are at least sixteen of us that are still alive, and who would like to keep it that way!" Ulysses riled. "Now, as I understand it, there are no operable lifeboats accessible from this location."

"That is correct, sir."

"But there must be another way off the ship?"

"Oh yes, sir."

"Really?" Ulysses said, surprised despite himself. "Captain, did you ask if there was another way off the ship?" he asked, turning to the equally surprised McCormack.

"Well, I asked as to the number and viability of the lifeboats, yes."

"So 'no' then. Neptune, do tell us more."

"Mr Carcharodon's private submersible vehicle the *Ahab* and its sister craft the *Nemo*, sir."

"I see. And where would they be located?"

"Within the sub-dock, sir, on Deck 15."

"You might as well wait here to drown," McCormack said, directing his comment at Ulysses, "if you're planning on taking one of those things out of here."

Ulysses turned on him. "Why? Why shouldn't we?"

"Those things are private runabouts, there're not designed for these depths. Like as not they won't survive for long out there, down here. They won't take the hydrostatic pressure."

"Really?" Ulysses was unable to hide his disappointment.

"Not a hope."

"But they don't have to last for long," Ulysses said, the old child-like excitement returning, "at these pressures I mean. We load up the subs, take them out and head up. Straight up, back to the surface."

"And what about whatever it was that attacked us?" McCormack pointed out. "Chances are it's still out there. Look what it's done to the *Neptune*. A couple of small-scale submersibles won't have a hope."

"Glass is always half-empty with you, isn't it?"

"I'm just being realistic."

"Yes, you are, damn you. We really are caught between the Devil and the deep blue sea, aren't we?"

"That's what I've been trying to tell you."

"Take the subs to the surface and we may well meet whatever it is that's out there waiting for us. Stay here, the ship fills with water and all we've got to look forward to is a burial at sea in Davy Jones' Locker."

Ulysses thought for a moment.

"If there was just somewhere we could hole up until the rescue teams could get to us, anywhere but here," he mused.

"I have located such an environment," the Neptune AI announced calmly.

"What?" Ulysses and McCormack both exclaimed together.

"My sensor arrays have located an undersea facility two hundred yards away at the edge of the oceanic trench. No life signs, although life-support systems are still operable."

"I don't bloody believe it!" Captain McCormack swore.

"I told you there was a way!" Ulysses declared proudly. "Neptune, is the sub-dock accessible from this location, without having to pass through any flooded sections of the ship, I mean."

The AI was quiet for a few seconds as its cogitator relays processed the information it was still receiving from its many and varied sensor detection devices positioned around the ship. "Yes. It is possible to reach the sub-dock without passing through any flooded sections of the superstructure."

"Then that's how we'll do it!" Ulysses declared, flashing the astonished captain a manic grin. "We're getting off this ship!"

CHAPTER TEN

Full Fathom Five

"Ladies and gentlemen, honoured guests," called the purser over the anxious hubbub that had taken hold of the dining room, "pray silence for the captain."

One by one, the assembled anxious VIPs turned to see Captain McCormack standing at the door to the dining room, with Ulysses Quicksilver at his shoulder. An expectant hush descended over the gathering, every one of those present desperate to hear how the captain was going to get them out of this waking nightmare.

McCormack opened his mouth, as if he was about to speak, when Jonah Carcharodon leapt in with an angry: "Well, man? Spit it out! How are you going to get us out of this mess?"

The captain cast his eyes down at the trident-patterned carpet at his feet and took a deep breath. Standing at his shoulder, Ulysses willed him to speak, although held off from saying anything for the moment.

"Ladies and gentlemen," McCormack began, "Mr Quicksilver and I have re-assessed the situation and we believe that we have found a way off this ship."

Gasps of surprise came from around the dining table. "About bloody time," Major Horsley muttered, none too subtly.

"In consultation with the Neptune AI we have devised a way through to the sub-dock on Deck 15 at the bottom of the ship. For the time being it would seem that the sub-dock is still secure and no wetter than it should be. As a result, it is expected that at least one, if not both, the submersible vehicles secured there will still be operable."

"What and then take them out into the open ocean where God's knows what is waiting for us?" the twitching Dr Ogilvy suddenly exclaimed.

"It's suicide," Professor Crichton said darkly.

"Quite possibly, professor," McCormack agreed, "which is why we're not going to the surface."

"What?" Now it was John Schafer's turn to question the captain's plan.

"The Neptune's sensor arrays have detected an undersea base nearby. We're going there."

"How wonderful!" Constance Pennyroyal suddenly exclaimed, blinking tears from her almond eyes. "Salvation!"

"Well, we hope so, Miss Pennyroyal."

"What do mean, captain?"

"Well, it has an intact, breathable environment and we should be able to wait it out there until the Great White Shipping Line's rescue crews can get to us."

"What is this place you're planning on taking us to, Captain McCormack?" Thor Haugland asked, exhaling cigarette smoke from his nose.

"As I say, it's an undersea base, partially intact. Beyond that I can't tell you any more at this stage."

"What?" Dexter Sylvester said, running a hand through his oily black hair. "You mean, you're not taking us to any recognised facility?"

McCormack paused before answering. "It's not one that appears within any of the Neptune's data files."

"So we're leaving the ship in some old tub to go to a semi-intact underwater facility that you've never even heard of and, I take it, that probably isn't even manned at this time?"

"You could put it that way."

Sylvester looked appalled in the face of the captain's frank honesty but was patently flummoxed as to how to respond.

"And you're suggesting we take the Ahab, McCormack?" Carcharodon said.

"Yes, sir."

"Captain," Carcharodon went on, "as I understand it, the *Ahab* – never mind the *Nemo* – isn't designed to operate at these sorts of depths for prolonged periods."

"It's not far. They should be good for a short journey."

The anxious muttering of the VIPs resumed.

"You don't sound very certain about this plan of yours," Lady Denning said, speaking up over the crowd.

At her words, all fell silent again, needling stares fixing the poor beleaguered captain and several now eyeing Ulysses with some measure of suspicion.

"Lady Denning, the only thing I am certain of at the moment is that if we stay here we will die – all of us. The *Neptune* is flooding, the Bridge, we have to assume, is compromised, and before long the only place the *Neptune* will be going is down to the bottom of the Marianas Trench, and there isn't a hope of us being rescued before then and I can't even be sure whether anyone knows we're lost out here yet."

"So, how do you plan on getting us to the sub-dock?" Carcharodon asked, breaking the uncomfortable silence.

"Mr Quicksilver and I have devised a way, with the assistance of the AI," McCormack explained. "The quickest route is still going to prove a little challenging but if we keep our heads I see no reason why we shouldn't reach the dock in plenty of time."

Captain McCormack looked around the room, taking in all of the anxious guests and his steeled crew members, and when he next spoke, something of his old, familiar calm authority had returned. "So, this is the plan. My crew and I are going to lead you from here to the Grand Atrium. According to Neptune, the elevators are still working so from there we're going to travel down to Deck 15 and make our way through to the sub-dock. Once there we'll board the submersibles, exit through the pressure gate beneath the Neptune and make the short journey to the underwater facility.

"Are there any questions?"

There were probably as many as there were anxious pairs of eyes looking back at him, but for the time being no one chose to voice them. They just wanted to get out of this mess as quickly, and as safely, as possible.

"Mr Quicksilver, is there anything you would like to add?"

Ulysses took a moment to observe each one of the frightened faces arrayed before him. They returned his gaze, some more intensely than others, and none more so than Miss Birkin who now looked as white as the starched linen tablecloth.

"Just to keep your heads, and, if you do, I can see no reason why we shouldn't all get out of this alive and, to top it all, with quite some tales to tell all our grandchildren in years to come."

He directed these last words at the nervous couple of John and Constance, and even managed a broad grin for them. They returned fragile smiles of their own, hands locked together in a white-knuckled embrace.

"Chances are we're going to see some rather unpleasant things, passengers less fortunate than ourselves" – someone harrumphed at this, at Ulysses' suggestion that they were fortunate, he supposed – "and it's likely we may encounter power shorts, flooding and possibly fires as well. But, like I say, if everyone keeps calm and doesn't do anything rash, we'll get you through this."

"Now then, ladies and gentlemen." McCormack spoke with commanding confidence now, "my staff will lead the way, so if you would like to follow them, we will make our way to the Grand Atrium."

The VIP party left the safe haven of the dining room, a sorry raggle-taggle group, shuffling forlornly after Captain McCormack, the purser and the other officer whom the captain addressed as Mr Wates. Miss Celeste still insisted on being responsible for her employer, stubbornly pushing his wheelchair along the corridors towards the atrium. Schafer, Constance and Miss Birkin had formed their own little group, their mutual support centred around the precious flower that was the young Miss Pennyroyal, who had certainly never experienced anything like this before in her life. But then which of them had, Ulysses wondered, apart from himself and Nimrod, of course? For them this, their latest adventure, was merely one more in a long line of hair's-breadth escapes and dramatic getaways. Perhaps that was what gave him the optimism that they could all get out of this with their skins intact, despite the shock of what had happened to Glenda, that had numbed him to the core.

But as well as the already unpredictable nature of their situation there were still two other variables that they couldn't plan for. Firstly there was whatever it was that was out there, waiting for them in the chill abyssal depths, that had been bold enough, and capable enough, to attack the *Neptune* and get the better of it. Secondly there was the matter of the murderer who had so viciously taken Glenda's life. With no evidence to the contrary, there was always the possibility that the killer was with them even now, one of the party of sixteen making its way from the room, searching for a way off the stricken ship.

As they left, Ulysses took another look at the dark and desolate view of the seabed that lay beyond the steel and glass viewing bubble.

"Thought you saw something, sir?" Nimrod asked, pausing beside him.

"No," Ulysses mused, sucking in his bottom lip, "no, not this time."

"But it's still out there, isn't it?"

"Whatever it was that attacked the *Neptune*? Oh yes, I rather think it is."

"Now what?" demanded Professor Crichton, taking another swig from the hip flask clenched in his jittery hands.

Holding onto an ornate pillar for support, Ulysses Quicksilver peered out over the precipitous edge of the balcony into the void of the Grand Atrium. In the fitful flickering light of the remaining chandelier he watched the seething waters below, brows knitted in consternation.

Along with the Promenade Deck and the Vaudeville Theatre, the Grand Atrium of the Neptune had been one of the architectural and design highlights of the new super sub-liner. It divided the ship neatly in half from the top down to Deck 10, ten storeys of open space, the two halves of the ship connected at various points via dramatic, glass-bottomed, suspended walkways, so that the atrium could be just as easily crossed on any level as at the bottom where one could marvel at the wonderfully engineered fountains, their splashing waters turned to glittering diamonds by the light of the vast chandeliers suspended from the glass and steel dome of its roof. They filled the gallery with magnificent cut-glass light, each one of them looking like a glittering star plucked from the velvet cloth of heaven itself to be suspended here.

Two of these huge chandeliers now lay shattered and broken amidst the wreckage of the atrium still five decks below, licked by fires burning on top of the oily waters. The remaining chandelier sparked and swung from its loosened mountings, adding epileptic lightning flashes to the ruddy glow of the emergency lights in this part of the ship. By the fitful illumination Ulysses could make out broken bodies bobbing about facedown amongst the wreckage, moved constantly by the seawater filling the bottom of the gallery.

The atrium had obviously come off more badly in the attack than some parts of the ship. There was no way of knowing whether the hull breach had been caused by one of the falling chandeliers – although Ulysses doubted it – or whether water coming into the ship elsewhere through the ruptured superstructure had found its way to this place. Perhaps it was overspill from the condemned Steerage decks.

The presence of the water also made Ulysses consider the state of the lower levels where the sub-dock was housed. It was possible that the bulkheads that divided up the interior space of the Neptune could keep flooded areas separate, and their way through may still be accessible, but it made him realise how pressing their mission was.

Opposite them, across the divide, stood the showy elevator doors of the Grand Atrium. The walkway they should have been able to cross to reach the lifts was gone, the only evidence of it ever having been there, a twisted steel beam. What was left of the footbridge lay crushed beneath one of the fallen chandeliers.

"How are we going to get across now?" Constance Pennyroyal asked nervously.

"We could double back, take the stairs to another level where we can cross safely," Dexter Sylvester suggested.

"No can do," Ulysses said, before any of Captain McCormack's men could speak. "Didn't you feel the heat as we went past? No, that way is out as fire's already taken hold down there. We cross here or we don't cross at all."

"But how?" Lady Denning said, her tone more angry than fearful.

Ulysses peered down at the churning, burning waters again and reassessed the distances involved in crossing the atrium.

"I have an idea," he said.

"Come on then, man? Let's hear it," Major Horsley boomed encouragingly.

"See that balustrade over there?" Ulysses said, pointing at the sidelong ladder-like structure of the balcony opposite that had been half broken off by a falling crystal light-fitting "I reckon that if we could pull that free and slide it over we'd have something long enough and strong enough to let everyone clamber across."

Appalled faces looked back at him from among the party, none more so than Miss Whilomena Birkin's.

"One at a time mind," he added.

"And how exactly are you going to achieve this dramatic feat?" Carcharodon enquired pointedly.

"Well, if it were up to me, I would dive down there," he said pointing at the ever-rising waters beneath them, "shin up that pole," his finger now followed the broken support column of one of the downed chandeliers, "up to there and then it would only be a short scramble to the balcony. I'd need a hand of course."

"Very well, that's agreed then," Carcharodon declared,

needlessly taking charge of the situation once somebody else had worked out what had to be done. "Any volunteers?"

"I'll go," came one bold voice amidst the embarrassed silence of the majority.

"No, John, you can't!" Constance declared, horrified.

"My darling, I must," Schafer said, taking her hands in his again. "For your sake. For our sake, for the sake of everyone here."

"But, John," she struggled, unchecked tears running down her cheeks.

"I'll be alright. I was House swimming champion back in my school days. Top diving board and everything. I haven't told you that before, have I?"

"Jolly good show, what?" the Major said happily, clapping his hands together loudly in satisfaction. "Knew you wouldn't let us down, old boy," he said, nudging Ulysses in the ribs. "Jackets off then, lads, eh?"

"Jackets off indeed, Major," Ulysses agreed, arching a sarcastic eyebrow.

"May I be of service, sir?" Nimrod asked, taking a step forward.

"You just be ready to help at this end, Nimrod, old chap," his employer said with a wry smile. "Keep this lot in check and all that."

"Very good, sir."

"So, young Schafer," Ulysses said, approaching the edge of the precipice. "Ready to show this lot what you're made of?"

"After you, Quicksilver," he said, rolling up his shirt sleeves, ready for action, receiving one last passionate kiss on the lips from his betrothed before handing her his jacket and pushing her gently back towards her anxious aunt.

"Right you are then. Here goes nothing."

Feet together, Ulysses straightened, arms outstretched above his head, pointing at the dark glass ceiling as if in an attitude of prayer. For a moment he stood there, poised ready to dive. Then, with one graceful bound, he launched himself off the edge and head first into the turgid waters below.

The speed and directness of his dive meant he passed straight through the broiling surface fires and into the dousing embrace of the water beneath – a brief rush of heat following by the shock of bone-numbing cold. He heard the muffled splash and rush of bubbles of another body entering the water after him. Glancing back he saw John Schafer kicking his way towards him, lit by the orange flames dancing on the surge above their heads.

Together, they made their way towards the great bulk of the half-submerged chandelier, feeling the dragging limbs of drowned men and women bumping against them as they swam. Ulysses tried to ignore the bobbing corpses, tried to convince himself that he wasn't swimming through their watery grave.

And then they were hauling themselves beyond the reach of the rising water again, clambering up the glass-crystal boulder that was the chandelier, careful where they put their hands amidst the broken body of the shattered glass ornament. Only a few slight cuts later, with one another's support, they were negotiating the pole and scrambling the last few feet up to the balcony, opposite the spot from where they had taken the plunge only moments before.

Cheers and shouts of encouragement rang in their ears, audible over the crackle of shorting electrical cables and the bubbling and seething water, given voice by their fellow survivors.

"Now to work," Ulysses said, slicking back his wet hair with a hand and clearing his eyes of water, as Schafer wrung as much of the water as he could from his sodden clothes, before they set to work freeing the broken balustrade.

With the woodwork liberated from its splintered mountings, taking the weight between them, supporting it at one end, the two men pushed the ladder-like structure across the void until it scraped against the other side of the atrium space. Eager hands pulled it up and secured it there with whatever they could find to hand. It was just long enough, Ulysses noted.

First to brave the perilous crossing was Mr Wates, who scrambled across in no time, the balcony-bridge flexing dramatically beneath him as he did so, although it still held. Once across he helped Ulysses and Schafer maintain a strong hold on their end of the makeshift crossing.

Bathed in electrical spark-flash and the ruddy glow of the emergency lighting, the rest of the party took it in turns to make their way across, cautiously, one at a time.

Captain Connor 'Mac' McCormack watched through intensely narrowed eyes as those men and women in his charge braved the perilous crossing of the flooding atrium, observing each one with the same intensity, determined that not one of them would be lost to the deep or the disaster continuing to unfold around them, giving direction where necessary as well as maintaining an order to their evacuation so that all might make it in the end.

So it came as no little annoyance to him when what had at first been simply an anxious tapping on his arm became an insistent tugging on his sleeve. "What is it Miss Birkin?" he almost snapped, turning on her, his calm demeanour evaporating in the face of her relentless persistence.

The old woman looked terrible. He understood the stress that all of the VIPs were under. This was, after all, not what they had expected on a round-the-world cruise aboard the most advanced sub-liner to ever cross the Seven Seas. But he was under no little strain himself. However, ever since they had gathered in the dining room together, Miss Birkin's despairing disposition had worsened considerably more than that of the other passengers.

"I need to have a private word with you, Captain."

"Miss Birkin, can't it wait? In case you hadn't noticed, this is hardly the time or the place."

"But it has to be now, Captain." The ageing spinster was becoming more and more agitated, still tugging at his sleeve. "You have to listen to what I have to tell you."

"Miss Birkin, please. Let us get everyone across and then you can have my ear."

"It won't wait a moment longer!"

"What won't, Miss Birkin?" McCormack suddenly found himself raising his voice more than he had intended. Others still waiting on the nearside of the gulf were turning to see what all the fuss was about.

"Because I believe the murderer is still with us!"

McCormack was abruptly aware of the uncomfortable silence that had fallen around them.

"And what makes you think that?" he said in a sudden, sharp whisper, seizing her arm tightly in his hand.

"Because I saw him!"

"That's quite enough, Miss Birkin. I would be grateful if you kept your voice down. You've got your private word."

Lady Denning was next to cross and, as ever, she proved to be a stoical, no nonsense old bird. Ulysses respected her for that. But he was also curious as to what was happening on the other side of the gulf, the dull scratching at the base of his skull testament to the fact that there was something awry. Miss Birkin appeared to be in quite some state of agitation before it was even her turn to cross the wobbling bridge and, before he knew it, Captain McCormack was ushering her away into the shadows back the way they had just come.

Whatever the problem had been, McCormack seemed to have been able to resolve it just as quickly as only a minute or too later he returned with Miss Birkin firmly in hand. And it might have been his imagination but, as Ulysses helped Professor Crichton up from his crawl across the chasm, he thought he felt that unmistakable sense of someone's eyes on him, and looked up to see the captain watching him.

There were moments of doubt, panic and sheer vertiginous terror that required a great deal of patient encouragement and time, along with no small number of stopped breaths and missed heartbeats. Miss Birkin seemed particularly uncomfortable about crossing – he would liked to have believed that that was what all the fuss had been about – but somehow the old coot made it safely to the other side.

The most awkward crossing was that involving Jonah Carcharodon. Left almost 'til last, he was ever-so-carefully manhandled across by Captain McCormack himself and the purser, whilst the sprightly lithe and limber Thor Haugland made sure the magnate's chair made it over too.

And then there was only Dexter Sylvester left to cross,

the ambitious young businessman insisting that the shipping magnate cross safely before him. Such a feat as traversing the void should have been no trouble for a gentleman of his obvious athleticism and his enthusiasm for the more adventurous pastimes, such as rock-climbing and abseiling. And it wouldn't have been, had it not been for the last chandelier.

As the immense hydrostatic pressures continued to work on the compromised structure of the liner, nerve-jangling metallic groaning and heaving sounds echoing throughout the vessel, something gave. The only warning any of them had that anything was wrong was when the erratic lighting failed. Ulysses, with his curiously heightened sixth sense was the only one to even look up and register a reaction to that one small fact, and so was granted a grandstand view.

The dead weight of crystal-glass and metal dropped like a boulder out of the crimson darkness, collided squarely with the balustrade spanning the space – Sylvester still only half way across – and smashed through it. The splintered balustrade tumbled after the chandelier into the gloom, now just so much matchwood, as the huge light fitting plunged into the roiling inferno beneath.

Of the man from Umbridge Industries there was no sign. Ulysses didn't even see him go. One minute he was there on the bridge, the next there was nothing but the immense bulk of the darkened chandelier, and then... nothing at all.

The shock and horror of realisation took a while to sink in amongst the party, some not realising what had happened at all until they witnessed the horrified reactions of their fellows, so concerned were they with their own intense personal struggles for survival.

So it was that, accompanied by stupefied silences, child-like sobbing and angry denials of what had happened, Ulysses Quicksilver and Captain McCormack eventually managed to herd the party – already minus one – to the lift doors on the other side of the Grand Atrium, their target all along.

Ulysses was about to push the button to call the first of the two lifts when he paused.

"What is it, sir?" Nimrod asked, at his shoulder once more.

"Look," Ulysses said, pointing at the row of still glowing lights above the elevator doors that showed the progress of the lift through the ship. The lights were blinking on and off, one after another. "It's already on its way."

With a delicate chiming the progress of the lights stopped and a moment later, with the grating of opening mechanisms, the lift doors opened. Ulysses stood and stared in dumbfounded amazement.

"Please accept my humblest apologies," Harry Cheng said, bowing deferentially. 'We would have been here sooner, but matters rather overtook us somewhat.'

The hulking Mr Sin stood at his side but, at a hissed command in Chinese from Cheng, the brute shuffled back to make room for more.

"Please, ladies and gentlemen, join us."

Without needing any further invitation, the VIPs began to pile into the lift. Ulysses hung back with those who would have to use the second elevator, rendered speechless by the miraculous arrival of his rival.

"Going up?" Cheng asked the Captain.

"No, Mr Cheng. Down, to the sub-dock."

"Ah, I see. Very well," he said, his hand at the deck selector panel. "Down it is."

With a slightly different chiming timbre, the second lift joined them. With a grinding clanking the doors eased open.

A torrent of seawater flooded out, washing across the carpeted floor of the balcony level and soaking the feet of everyone standing there.

"Ah," said Ulysses, finding his voice at last, "perhaps down isn't the best idea after all."

CHAPTER ELEVEN

The Deep

"Quick! Into the lift!"

"Everybody move!"

At Captain McCormack's urgent command and Ulysses' cajoling, the party of survivors piled into Cheng's lift. As the *Neptune's* officers herded the anxious and the uncertain between the doors, Ulysses dared a glance back at the flooded atrium. Something must have given or blown somewhere – part of the hull, a compromised bulkhead, a porthole, who-knew-what? – the result being that the space below was filling more rapidly, the chandeliers vanishing beneath the surge of white water and bobbing bodies. The water, still finding an outlet through the second open lift, poured off the edge of the balcony, cascading down to meet that which was surging upwards from the drowned atrium below.

There was only one way out of this and that was up.

As the last of the VIP party crowded into the brass and glass box of polished mirrors, Ulysses' eyes fell on the smart plaque that stated no more than a maximum of ten persons should use this lift at any one time. As the purser hammered a button on the deck selector panel and the doors grated shut behind him – the last one in – Ulysses closed his eyes and held his breath, offering up a quick prayer to whatever saint it was that watched over the workings of elevators, that the carriage would be able to take the strain.

There was a rising hum and a series of systematic clanking sounds, then a terrible split-second sensation of dropping, which made all those trapped within the small box gasp in unison. But then the lift carriage began to rise.

Gears grinding, it felt to Ulysses that the elevator was making heavy weather of the journey. He thought he could hear the bubbling rush of water somewhere below them and wondered which was rising faster, the lift or the level of the seawater flooding the elevator shaft. He was trying hard to ignore the hot-wire stabbings of prescience in his skull; he did not need any unearthly sixth sense to tell him that they were in constant mortal danger for the foreseeable future.

The smell of fear permeated the human sardine tin; fear and sweat and brine and burning. In any other situation such enforced proximity to others would not have been tolerated by those who were now forced to huddle together so closely. There was not an inch between any of them, from the Chinaman Cheng and the massive Mr Sin, to Lady Denning or the chaperoned couple, or the billionaire owner of the ship, the current crisis having robbed him of practically any difference in status he had beyond the least of them, his own PA being forced to sit on his lap to make sure that everyone could pack into the lift.

The realisation suddenly struck Ulysses that the lift could all too easily become a ready-made coffin, should the water level rise more quickly than the struggling elevator, or should some part of the beleaguered machinery fail under duress, or should the – whatever is was – that attacked the *Neptune* decide to come back for another go.

But, despite the obvious risks and inherent dangers associated with their current predicament, Quicksilver's spirit wouldn't let him be beaten by such overwhelming odds. He would keep fighting to save himself – to save these people – until the deep, or the horrors that inhabited it, forced the last breath from him as he went down kicking and screaming. Just as there had been nothing in his power that he could do to save the wretched Glenda, he would do all in his power to save those who remained. He would not let another Glenda Finch or Dexter Sylvester be taken by the dying ship, the cruel sea or the monsters that dwelt there.

The lift ground onwards as the gears of Ulysses' mind worked over the problem of how they were going to get out of this mess. The further the elevator rose up its compromised shaft, the more he found himself dwelling on the fact that the plan had been to head down to reach the sub-dock and the submersibles *Ahab* and *Nemo*, to escape the wreck of the Neptune as swiftly as possible before the sea or the drowned liner claimed them all.

The plan. It was worthless now. All that stood between them and oblivion was adaptation, improvisation, spontaneity, ingenuity, inventiveness and cold, hard animal instinct. Or, to look at it another way, the plan had to evolve or they would die.

And what of the sub-dock and its two transports? Ulysses had to believe that it was still attainable, the craft operable. To think anything else would mean the end of all hope for them.

The lift was slowing now – horribly quickly – the ratcheting gears clunking away the last few inches. For a moment the carriage heaved and there was that horrid feeling that the lift was at the apex of its ascent and was about to commence its all too rapid descent again. Then the whole thing seemed to lurch upwards. There was the rattle and clunk of clamps locking the elevator in place, the steel cables holding it up held tight in the steel teeth of the riser's locking mechanisms. The chiming of the lift arriving at its destination cut through the numb silence inside. All on board gave a collective sigh of relief.

The doors ground open once again and, without having to be invited to do so, the VIPs piled out of the carriage. Ulysses led the way, enjoying the sudden sensation of space around him.

"Where are we?" asked a shaky Dr Ogilvy.

"Top deck," Ulysses read from a sign screwed to the wall next to the open lift doors. "Casino Royale, the Bistro, Shopping and the Promenade Deck."

"So where now, McCormack?" Jonah Carcharodon asked.

But the captain and his staff were already examining another passenger ship plan. Ulysses joined them, the rest of the party, left without guidance, milling about behind, taking in the wreckage and devastation apparent on this level as well, lit by the sparking lights hanging from the ceiling.

"So, Captain, any ideas?" Ulysses asked.

Captain McCormack breathed out noisily. "Well, we're here" – he indicated Level 1 on the plan in front of them – "having travelled from here" – he identified the point where they had crossed the devastated Grand Atrium – "and we need to get to here." His finger alighted on the outline of the sub-dock at the bottom of the ship.

"Indeed," Ulysses mused.

"We know that chances are that the bulkhead here" – the captain pointed out what should have been a watertight section below the level of the Grand Atrium – "is no longer intact and so from here to here" – his outstretched finger swept across the plan taking in several compartments of the sub-liner – "will be underwater."

"But that leaves the sub-dock still untouched."

"Hopefully," McCormack said guardedly.

"But how to get there."

"Precisely. If the compartment under the atrium's gone, we can't be certain which other compartments may also have been breached."

"Have you consulted with the AI again yet?" Ulysses asked, eyeing what he now understood was the comm-button hidden beneath the trident logo on the panel.

"We can't."

"What do you mean?"

"Try for yourself, Mr Quicksilver," Mr Wates said.

Ulysses tried the comm-alert for himself. There was the click of the button being depressed but nothing more, not even static. Ulysses tried again, pushing the button harder this time. Still nothing.

"It would appear that ship-wide communications throughout the *Neptune* have failed," Mr Wates explained.

"Which only goes to prove that this is not some static problem, but that the crisis is worsening the longer we remain trapped down here," McCormack added for emphasis.

"Okay, so what you're telling me is that we're going to have to do this the old-fashioned way – ourselves?"

McCormack nodded, turning his attention back to the plan.

After some minutes huddled deliberation, recalling to mind what they had learnt from the AI the last time they had been able to communicate with it, Ulysses and the Neptune officers came up with something approximating a modified escape plan.

"So, I ask again, McCormack, what now? How are you going to get us out of here?" Major Horsley said.

"Our target destination is still the sub-dock," the captain began.

"But that's bloody well down at the bottom of the ship and you keeping taking us further and further away from it!"

"I realise that, Major," McCormack pointed out, with all the patience he could muster, "but it's the only way. There are no other usable lifeboats in reach of our current position. That hasn't changed."

"Look, we're going to work our way towards the rear of the ship," Ulysses said, taking over explaining the plan, "and go through the engine halls to the sub-dock."

"But I thought the engines were on fire!" Miss Birkin suddenly spoke up in alarm.

"Only some of them, Miss Birkin," McCormack stated. "And there's always the possibility that some of the fires might have burnt themselves out by now, starved of oxygen."

"Starved of oxygen?" Professor Crichton exclaimed and took another pull on his hipflask.

"It's all right because when we open the bulkhead door through to the engine hall it will let in the air from the rest of the ship. We're not going to suffocate down here on top of everything else," McCormack said giving a snort of mirthless laughter.

It still took another few minutes of encouraging, fear-allaying and cajoling before the party was ready to continue. During all that time, Harry Cheng and Mr Sin kept themselves to themselves at the periphery of the group, neither offering advice or criticism. The double agent's face was knotted in concentration whilst his silent aide, seemingly unperturbed by the unfolding disaster, was happy simply to follow Cheng's instructions.

With all brought to order, the group of desperate VIPs followed the captain's lead now in the opposite direction to which they had been travelling, heading towards the stern of the ship. However, it was not long before they came to a sealed door at the end of the smashed and shattered remains of what had once been one of the bars.

"I know where we are," Thor Haugland suddenly piped up. "Captain, you can't be serious?"

"Oh but we are, Mr Haugland," Ulysses said with a hard smile, "there being no other way."

"What's the problem?" Lady Denning asked. "Where are we?"

Captain McCormack pulled open the door. "Here," he said.

With everyone straining to peer through the doorway, but without any of them wanting to take a step forwards, the Neptune's honoured guests gazed at the awesome vista before them.

What was probably most incredible to them of all, Ulysses considered, was the fact that the dome over the Promenade Deck was still intact, considering what had befallen the ship in the last few hours. This probably came only slightly ahead of the fact that the party leaders were planning on taking them out across the Promenade, along its entire length to the far side, when there was nothing but the oppressive blackness of the deep ocean above their heads, the same ocean that was exerting immense hydrostatic pressures on the *Neptune* now trapped on the sea-bed.

"We're going out there?" John Schafer asked, and from the earnest looks the rest of the VIPs threw Captain McCormack and Ulysses, it was obvious that he wasn't the only one who was wondering whether their next course of action was such a good idea.

"Well, technically we won't actually by going 'out' at all," Ulysses said, trying to allay their fears.

Lady Denning took a step towards the opening, peering up into the darkness above the ship, almost as if she was looking for something. Lights were still shining on the Promenade Deck but their halo of illumination only penetrated a little way out into the trackless depths of the ocean. "But if we go out there," she said pointedly, "whatever it was that brought the ship down – and which might well be waiting for us, out of our immediate field of view – will see the movement and be drawn back to the ship in search of prey."

There was a sudden rumbling judder and every member of the escape party, except for the wheelchair-bound Carcharodon, was forced to grab hold of somebody, or something, for support.

"What was that?" Crichton snapped, darting eyes shooting paranoid glances at all of them, comforting himself with the next breath with another swig from his flask.

"*That* was why we don't have any choice but to cross the Promenade," Captain McCormack explained. "The *Neptune* is still flooding even as we stand here deliberating as to whether we should take the quickest route to get off this ship."

"If we hang around here arguing the toss for much longer it won't make any difference what we decide," Ulysses added bluntly. "And there won't be much time for regrets either as the *Neptune* goes over the brink and into the trench."

Almost as one, the party shuffled towards the open doorway, steeling themselves for their flight along the length of the exposed Promenade.

There was another groan and the sub-liner moved again. This time some among the party lost their balance altogether and even Jonah Carcharodon had to grab hold of something to stop his chair rolling backwards through the wreckage of the bar.

Was this it? Ulysses wondered as he held tight to a steel pillar. Had they dallied too long? Was the *Neptune* even now making her very final voyage to the utmost depths of the Pacific Ocean?

The seismic rumblings abruptly subsided and the ship settled down again. The polished boards of the Promenade Deck, incongruously marked out for traditional deck games, still stretched out ahead of them, only now they would have to ascend to the stern of the ship. The prospect seemed even more daunting to the already strung-out escapees, but there was no other option open to them.

"Ladies and gentlemen," Captain McCormack declared, "it really is now or never."

And so, without needing any further encouragement, the party of VIPs and associated hangers-on began their ascent of the Promenade Deck.

Mr Wates and the Purser led the way, with the wrung-out Dr Ogilvy taking the mantra of 'every man for himself' as his personal ideology, followed by an almost equally desperate Professor Crichton. Then came the trio of John Schafer and the two women in his charge, the role of chaperone having noticeably switched, and after them Lady Denning and Major Horsley. Ulysses and Nimrod insisted on helping the reluctant Miss Celeste push her employer's chair up the incline, making an otherwise virtually impossible task that much easier. Then came Thor Haugland, closely followed by Captain McCormack, and last of all the odd couple of Harry Cheng and Mr Sin, at a discreet distance.

When the party hadn't yet covered half the distance they needed to to get to safety, feeling a resurgence of that oh-so familiar itching inside his skull, Ulysses looked up.

"Bloody hell!" he gasped, pupils dilating in terror.

Something was approaching out of the darkness of the deep above them, preceded by a glowing azure light. Something monstrous, a malign shadow uncoiling from out of the abyssal black of the smothering ocean. Something that was heading straight for them.

Hearing Ulysses' expletive, close behind him, McCormack looked up. The colour drained from his face in an instant as his eyes locked onto the horror torpedoing out of the black murk towards the Promenade Deck.

He gasped, his lilting Scots voice no longer calm: "We're going to need a bigger sub!"

CHAPTER TWELVE

The Nature of the Beast

Emerging from the sucking black void, to Ulysses' eyes the monster looked primarily like a giant squid. Only the creatures he had seen pictures of, when they were washed up dead on the shores of Greenland or hauled up in the nets of a Japanese fishing trawler, even with their tentacles extended, had been no more than fifty feet in length. As the creature torpedoed towards the stricken *Neptune*, Ulysses took a rough guess and decided that this beast was at least two hundred feet from tentacle tips to the end of its arrowhead tail.

But there was so much more wrong with it than just its grossly exaggerated size. As the squid-beast sped towards the sub-liner, homing in on the movement of the figures it must have detected fleeing along the brightly lit Promenade, the image of its horrific, unreal form was seared onto Ulysses' retinas. He could still see it now, in his mind's eye, as he turned his attention back to the matter of escape; although now it had become the more immediate need of escaping from the coiling clutches of the squid-monster closing on the *Neptune*, than the longer term plan of escaping on one of the stricken liner's submersibles. And was that really an option now, with their worst fears realised in the form of the savage, hungry sea-beast?

It was the sea-devil all of them must have imagined when Ulysses had spoken of being trapped between the Devil and the deep blue sea. Although it looked like an overgrown squid – Architeuthis Giganticus rather than just Architeuthis Dux – it was far more than simply an overgrown mollusc. To begin with, too many clutching tentacles reached from the appalling head of the crea- ture, with the length, strength and size of ship's cables, masses of puckered, grey suckers opening and closing like a myriad foully kissing mouths.

The monster also lit the way before it, a bioluminescent lure, the kind Ulysses would have expected to see pro- jecting from the head of a deep-sea angler fish, pulsing with blue light, ever darting ahead of it, like some herald- symbiote with a mind of its own.

And it was not only the lure that the beast had bor- rowed from that deep-sea dwelling genus of fish. In the split second that Ulysses' spied the creature for the first time, as its tentacles had spread wide, no doubt preparing to seize the ship once again in its leviathan clutches, its mouth parts had been exposed. Instead of a horny beak, angler fish jaws, wide enough it seemed to swallow small ships whole, stretched even wider, to dislocating propor- tions.

And the creature didn't only come armed with deadly natural weapons; it was armoured too, as if anything in the oceans could possibly threaten a monster like this! A crustacean-like shell covered the squid-thing's back, from the top of its soft head to its tail. What kind of freak of nature was it?

Was it of nature at all?

Time slowed, the rising plane of the Promenade extend- ing elastically before Ulysses, as he realised how far they still had to go to reach safety. And even if they made it through the double doors ahead of them, would they re- ally then be safe? The monster had had its part to play in crippling the ship and sending it to the bottom of the sea, leaving them all teetering between life and death on the knife edge precipice of the yawning Marianas Trench.

"Come on!" Ulysses shouted, urging Nimrod, and the unnerved Miss Celeste to draw on hidden reserves of strength.

As he and Nimrod pushed as hard as they could, adrenal glands flooding their bodies with their oh-so necessary secretions once more, practically carrying Miss Celeste along with them, as well as the chair, Ulysses fixed his eyes on the way ahead.

Directly in front of them Major Horsley was helping Lady Denning on her way, the pair of ageing adventurers huffing and puffing their way up the deck, neither daring to stop in case their feet lost their grip on the wax-polished boards or, Heaven forbid, the monster caught them. Ahead of them, John Schafer was offering all the encouragement he could to his darling dear heart and her aunt, for them to keep going – apparently neither of the women having yet seen this new threat – keeping them focused on reaching the doors. But all his good works might prove to be for naught, if Professor Crichton had anything to do with it.

The emeritus professor was stumbling forwards but with his gaze directed back up over his shoulder, unable to tear his eyes from the squid-beast. He was gabbling to himself, his face white as an albino sea slug, apparently calling on the aid of the Almighty to get them out of this mess with cries of "Oh, God! Oh, God!" and whimpered sobs of "What have we done?"

As the two officers leading the escape party raced ahead to get the doors open, leaving a moaning Dr Ogilvy to struggle on as best he could alone, Ulysses could not help looking back at the approaching leviathan in the face of Professor Crichton's inability to take his eyes off the thing. He instantly wished he hadn't.

It was nearly on them, tentacles already reaching out over the steel-glass bubble of the enclosed deck, mouth agape, javelin-sharp fangs like drawn-out steel fish hooks, poised ready to spear them and draw them into its hideous maw. Ulysses fancied he caught a glint of evil intent in the huge, watery eyes looking at him through the glass shield.

"Herregud," Ulysses heard Thor Haugland utter in appalled Norwegian behind him, "det er Kraken!"

Of course, Ulysses thought, Haugland had given their tormenter a name: the Kraken, the many-legged sea monster of sea-faring legend, the horror that pulled ships beneath the waves and devoured their crews whole. Until that moment Ulysses would have put sea-dogs' tales of the Kraken down to a combination of ways of explaining away good old-fashioned shipwrecks and the discovery of creatures such as the giant squid lurking within the deeper oceans. Only now, he wasn't so sure.

Constance screamed. She too had now seen the beast. Schafer pulled her close, urging her onwards, almost dragging her with him in her shocked state. Constance's maiden aunt didn't need any such encouragement; she had picked up her skirts and was sprinting away up the deck like a fell runner, bony ankles and varicose veins visible now beneath her fussy petticoats.

"Don't stop!" Ulysses found himself shouting. "Just keep going. It's going to be all right!"

In a cruel contradiction of Ulysses' words, a shuddering crash shook the escapees' world as the Kraken slammed into the dome of the Promenade Deck. The force of impact rocked the ship, which shifted still further to port, and sent the VIPs tumbling sideways. It was not as bad as the shaking they had received when the *Neptune* had first started to sink, when it had felt like their whole world was turning upside down, but it wasn't far off. Carcharodon's chair, suddenly losing all forward momentum, slid sideways into a bench which caught Nimrod, Ulysses and Miss Celeste, who ended up in the unimpressed butler's lap.

The Neptune moved again beneath them, rocking back to starboard. Ulysses found himself suddenly looking up through the latticework of the dome above him. Where on the night he and Glenda Finch had experienced the thrill of a controlled submersion they had seen first the stars of the Milky Way and then the closing, plankton-rich waters of the Pacific above their heads, now all he could see was the horrid flesh of the underside of the Kraken as it, again, took the *Neptune* in its unnatural embrace.

He could see spongy grey flesh – the colour of drowned sailors – and warty black hide, like the scale-less skin of abyssal-dwelling hunter-fish, lit by the yellow light of the humming deck lights. Fissures, like lipless mouths dotted the belly of the beast in curious arcs, describing large parabola scarring, which might almost have been bite marks. Other things clung to the vast body of the leviathan that might have been lampreys or remora sucking fish, or some deep-sea evolutionary offshoot.

Following the dorsal line of the monster, Ulysses' eyes fell on the impossibly large teeth of the beast as they scratched against the reinforced dome with a sound like iron nails scraping on plate glass. The unpleasant noise not only set teeth on edge but also hearts racing and backbones prickling with fear.

"Come on! We can't hang around here!" Carcharodon shrieked, feeling more helpless than ever.

"Indeed," Ulysses agreed, pulling himself to his feet again, using the magnate's wheelchair for support.

Miss Celeste having extricated herself from his lap, Nimrod assisted his master in getting the billionaire moving again. Carcharodon's PA relented at last and seemed happy just to follow at their heels and worry about getting herself to safety as quickly as possible.

"Here, let me help."

Glancing to his left, Ulysses saw that the two Chinamen had caught them up. And now it was Harry Cheng's turn to insist on helping with Carcharodon's chair. Mr Sin lumbered a few feet behind, looking, for the first time since Ulysses had met him, scared and out of breath.

Another sound echoed through the enclosed space of the Promenade. At first it didn't even register with Ulysses or anyone else, or so it seemed from their lack of reaction. It was only when he felt his sixth sense flare hotly behind his eyes that he realised that something even worse was about to befall them. It was a creaking, popping sound. There it was again. And again.

And now others could hear it too, curiosity flickering across already stricken expressions. And now there came a more sustained metallic groaning. And now the cascading water splash and splatter of rainfall, inside the enclosed Promenade Deck, at the bottom of the Pacific Ocean.

"It's rupturing," Ulysses said, as much to himself as anyone, as the pieces of the jigsaw puzzle all came together in his mind. "The dome's rupturing! Run!"

The sound of water was getting louder now, the pitter-patter quickly becoming a pouring sound, like a waterfall emptying into a swimming pool. Salty spray splashed into Ulysses' eyes, making him wince, as another rivet popped free and a pane of toughened glass fractured, allowing the first trickles of seawater in before the unbelievable tonnages of ocean pressing down on the ship found them. If nature abhorred a vacuum, the sea here seemed to abhor a breathable atmosphere.

Within seconds more panes shattered and torrents of water rushed into the enclosed space from a dozen different points of entry. Now that the hungry sea had found a way in, there was no stopping it.

Mr Wates and the purser stood at the now open doors at the opposite end of the Promenade, practically hanging from the handles to help heave the fleeing VIPs through one after another. The doctor was already through. So too were Schafer, Constance, Miss Birkin, and McCormack. Professor Crichton and Major Horsley were helping Lady Denning through even now, their feet splashing through the first surges of water splashing up the deck towards them.

Ulysses, Nimrod, Jonah Carcharodon in his chair and Miss Celeste bounced over the threshold together, the writer Haugland flinging himself in after them.

Ulysses turned to assist those at the door. Mr Wates and the purser pulled themselves inside, ready to pull the sealable bulkhead doors shut securely behind them and keep out the rising tide of frothing seawater. There were only Harry Cheng and Mr Sin still to come through.

Cheng was now at the threshold, hair flat to his head, shirt and trousers soaked through. Mr Sin was only a few slippery feet behind him.

But there was something else in there with them now as well. A snaking tentacle, like some huge, snub-nosed sea-worm, wending its way towards them, writhing and flexing as if guided by a instinctive sentience all of its own. The Kraken was determined not to let its prey get away.

Someone screamed having caught sight of the probing squid-limb. And in that fatal second, the hulking Chinaman, terror writ large across his blunt features, stopped and turned. With an uncoiling lash, quick as a striking cobra, the tentacle extended, curled precisely around Mr Sin's waist and legs and then, just as quickly, pulled back. The chinaman, an eye-popping look of terror on his face, was dragged into the surging flood, silvery bubbles escaping from his mouth in a silent scream. Then, there above them beyond the ruptured bubble of the Promenade, was the monster's dreadful fang-lined maw, gaping open, ready to receive the tasty morsel.

There was nothing anyone could do for him.

"Close the doors!" Captain McCormack ordered as the water lapped at the sill of the doorway and Harry Cheng hurled himself past the threshold.

The two officers did as their captain commanded, shutting out the sight of the glorious Promenade being swallowed by the ocean, shutting out the rush and roar of the hungry sea, shutting out the monster that would devour them all.

They also shut in the wailing of the terrified Constance Pennyroyal and her aunt, shut in the mumbled entreaties of a biologist to the God he had foresworn, shut in the frustrated raging of the shipping magnate as he bellowed at his wretched assistant who had sought to do nothing but save his sorry skin.

And so seventeen became sixteen.

CHAPTER THIRTEEN

Sea Dog's Tales

With the bulkhead door to the Promenade Deck closed, the last chapter in the life of Mr Sin was closed with it.

Two were lost to them now. First Dexter Sylvester, with the catastrophe of the plummeting chandelier and now Mr Sin, Harry Cheng's right-hand man, taken by the beast. Two gone from the total party of eighteen survivors who had made it up until the moment when the ship touched rock bottom amidst the silt and skeletal remains of a million animals upon the ocean floor. They had thought things bad enough when they found their luxury cruise ship dropping into the fathomless depths like a stone, only at the time they had not realised that their greatest trials still stood ahead of them.

With the impossible sea monster tearing away the glass and steel latticework from the once magnificent Promenade Deck, the *Neptune* having settled into its new position – listing slightly to port and leaving the escapees with an uphill struggle to reach the stern of the ship – there was nothing for them to do except struggle on towards their original target destination.

And what a sorry and dishevelled lot they were, Ulysses found himself thinking. Wet, worn out and worried beyond belief, there wasn't a single VIP remaining that hadn't had all trappings of status and privilege stripped from them by the disaster that had them caught at its very heart. They all of them looked like they would not have appeared out of place amongst the ship's other passengers residing in Steerage.

Even Nimrod's appearance was not up to his usual standards: his grey butler's attire covered with dark damp patches from the unwanted attentions of the seawater. Ulysses himself was soaked through to the skin, after his dip in the drowning pool of the Grand Atrium, as was the noble John Schafer. The man, a good ten years younger than the eldest of the Quicksilver boys, had a permanent steeled expression on his face. Whether he maintained such composure because he wasn't allowing himself the possibility of considering the direness of their situation or whether he was concentrating so greatly on the well-being of his beloved that he dared not risk a second thought about what might become of them, Ulysses did not know.

And so they made their way onward through the stricken ship. Climbing ever upwards to reach the rear of the *Neptune* where they then hoped to negotiate a way down to the seemingly unattainable submersible bay. And from there, who knew what – considering the squid-beast's latest attack on the wrecked sub-liner.

Captain McCormack took the lead, rugged determination described in the lines of his face, spacing his men out through the body of the party to help maintain cohesion and make sure no one got left behind. A number of them were beginning to flag, the adrenalin rush that had set them all off with seemingly boundless stamina had ebbed. Miss Birkin in particular was showing signs of frailty, quite possibly exacerbated by the huge levels of stress she had been put under. Ulysses still couldn't shake the feeling that she was keeping a particularly close eye on him. Lady Denning, never one to make a fuss, was also beginning to show signs of exhaustion. She appeared to be limping on her left leg and did not protest when Major Horsley – himself puffing and blowing like a grumpy walrus – took her arm to steady her.

Miss Celeste had taken her place at Jonah Carcharodon's wheelchair once more, which seemed to be faring rather better than many of the party. And it was, once again, with reluctance that she accepted the slightest help from Ulysses and his manservant. So much so, in fact, that Ulysses felt guilty that he was forcing her to accept their assistance. Her knuckles whitened as they gripped the handles, as if making sure that her ungrateful employer made it to safety had become her raison d'être for keeping up the struggle herself.

The curious trio of Crichton, Haugland and Ogilvy now brought up the rear. The three men had seemed to be subconsciously drawn to one another, although Ulysses couldn't help feeling that there was something else that united them. It was the fact that they were each only concerned with looking out for number one.

Captain McCormack led them out of the shattered remains of a parade of boutiques and into a curiously angled – yet mercifully unflooded – access way of grille plates and twisted metal staircases. The rhythmic drip-drip-drip of water entered even here, the ringing of their footsteps and the inescapable groaning of the buckling hull, were joined by another ominously mournful sound, that of Professor Crichton reciting poetry as if it were a dirge.

"Below the thunders of the upper deep, far far beneath in the abyssal sea," he intoned, as if he was reading a eulogy.

"For God's sake man!" Jonah Carcharodon called up the slanting stairwell from where Mr Wates was helping Ulysses and Nimrod carry him and his chair down the next short flight of steps. "As if things weren't bad enough, without us having to listen to you!"

"His ancient, dreamless, uninvaded sleep," Crichton went on.

"Please, Maxwell," – it was Lady Denning who took up the baton to call for the disheartening recital to stop – "now is neither the time nor the place. What's done is done."

"The Kraken sleepeth." The Professor stopped, a far-away look in his eyes, and certainly no indication that he had heard a word anyone else had said.

"What was that?" Constance Pennyroyal asked, apparently glad to have something to take her mind off the overwhelming stress she was suffering, rather than continually mulling over the likelihood of any of them getting out of there alive.

"Tennyson"' Major Horsley replied.

"Indeed," Ulysses found himself adding distractedly, joining in the literary discussion. "The Kraken."

Reaching another landing and making the most of the opportunity to rest, if only for a moment, Ulysses set Carcharodon's chair down again.

"Wasn't that what you called that wee beastie that attacked us just now, Haugland?"

"The Kraken, you mean?" the Norwegian agreed. "It somehow... seemed appropriate."

"I couldn't agree more," Lady Denning added.

"Do tell us more. What is it? The Kraken I mean?" Ogilvy said twitchily.

"Kraken, Kroken, Krayken, they're all the same thing really," Haugland said.

"And what is that?"

Ogilvy was on edge. Ulysses wondered how long it was since he had been able to sneak his last fix.

"The Kraken is the legendary sea monster of Norse myth, although that particular name never appeared in the sagas. Instead it was called the hafgufa or the lyng-bakr. The name Kraken comes from another Scandinavian word krake, which refers to some unhealthy, unnatural animal; something twisted. The Kraken was said to dwell off the coasts of Norway and Iceland, a beast of gargantuan size. Some said it was as big as a floating island, a creature so large that it could pull even the biggest warship to the bottom of the sea without any trouble at all." Haugland was into his stride now, the natural storytelling abilities of the travel writer coming to the fore. "It is almost always described as having numerous, far-reaching tentacles and a soft pliable body like an octopus. And although it lived within the ocean depths, it would surface to hunt prey and supposedly attack small ships."

"It sounds horrid," Miss Birkin said, managing to sound indignant, as if such discussion was not appropriate for those of a delicate sensibility at this time.

"But, Miss Birkin, you have to remember it is only a legend, an exaggerated unreal creature, inspired by sightings of the much more timid, yet real, giant squid. At least I had thought it a legend, until now. In all my days travelling the world, I have never seen the like!"

"Was that thing that attacked us a giant squid? Was that some mythical monster?" Ogilvy railed. Unconquerable fear had taken the face of anger with the wretched doctor. "Was I hallucinating?"

"I wouldn't be surprised." Ulysses couldn't help himself.

"Why, you –"

"But I saw it too, and I know that I haven't put anything illicit or intoxicating into my body in almost twenty-four hours."

The damned doctor didn't know how to respond to such a blatant accusation.

"But then, maybe, neither have you, which would explain a lot as well."

A fearful hush descended over the party once again and another three flights were negotiated in silence. Pausing at the next landing Ulysses made note of the deck they were now on. Deck 7. Only another eight to go until they reached the bowels of the ship wherein lay the ever-elusive sub-dock, with its pressure gate and its means of escape to the outside world. They still might not make it to the surface alive, but if they could make it off the *Neptune* that should at least buy them a few more hours – unless the Kraken had other ideas.

"I don't know what it was," Captain McCormack said, disrupting the tense silence, "but that wasn't simply some overgrown cephalopod."

"You're a biologist," Dr Ogilvy said suddenly, almost challenging Professor Crichton, who looked like he was trying to remain anonymous in the background. "And you, Lady Denning. What was that... thing?"

"I... I don't know," Crichton said, taking another long draw on what must have been his rapidly emptying hip-flask.

"No. Nor I," Lady Denning said in a tone that broached no further discussion.

"But can't you take a guess?"

"I don't know what it was," Lady Denning said, her tone sharp enough to cut glass.

"Some... some kind of giant cephalopod," was all Crichton would offer.

"But what *kind* of sodding giant bloody cephalopod?" Ogilvy pressed. "I'm not an idiot, you know. What kind of cephalopod has jaws like that and an armoured shell?"

"The Kraken, it would appear," Nimrod offered bluntly. The doctor looked like he was about to make another challenge and then wilted under the intense sapphire-eyed stare Ulysses' manservant gave him.

"Perhaps it's something prehistoric? Something forgotten, like the coelacanth was for so many years," Miss Birkin piped up, finding her voice despite the fatigue she was feeling, the conspiracy theorist in her excited at the prospect of uncovering a genuine conspiracy herself.

"You're uncommonly quiet on this matter," Ulysses said, addressing the noticeably tight-lipped Carcharodon, "particularly for one usually so forthcoming with his own opinion."

"How in blazes would I know what that thing is?" he snarled back. "I'm no Hannibal Haniver, am I? I'm not a bloody naturalist!"

"It could be an aberration," John Schafer suggested, as he assisted both fiancée and aunt-in-law to be ever onward, down the uncomfortably angled stairwell, making sure that they did not slip on the wet metal steps. "Some mutation of a better known genus created by the unchecked industrial pollution that is such a blight on our world."

"Careful, Schafer," Ulysses warned, with a wry smile. "You're in danger of sounding like a fully paid up member of the Darwinian Dawn."

"Or," Captain McCormack said darkly, adding his own opinion to the discussion, "could it have been specifically engineered this way? Is it, in reality, a living weapon of war?"

"Preposterous!" Carcharodon suddenly butted in, driven to finally voice his own opinion by McCormack's patently hair-brained suggestion, nailing his colours to the mast in the debate regarding the nature of the beast.

"What do you mean, Captain?" Constance asked, her own latent curiosity piqued. 'How can it have been engin –"

"Ah, here we are!" Major Horsley announced with gusto as they reached the bottom of the stairs, before Constance could finish. "Engine rooms, don't you know! That's the way we want to go, isn't it, McCormack, what?"

"That was the plan," McCormack said.

"We hope," Ulysses cautioned.

Talk of the nature of the beast ceased as all members of the party were filled with nervous anticipation at the prospect of entering the engine halls of the *Neptune*. What little information they had been given about this area of the ship was that some of the great engine chambers were flooded, or on fire, or God alone knew what.

Captain McCormack paused before the steel bulkhead door. It would be a risk venturing inside, but there was really no alternative. There was no going back now.

"Well, here goes nothing," he said as Wates and the Purser joined him in cranking the wheel to open the door. The seal popped open with nothing more dramatic than a hiss of air which smelt of charcoal and seaweed; an indication perhaps of what they might find beyond.

Looking like a sorry, rag-tag band of refugees rather than the great and the good, the cream of the elite society of Magna Britannia trudged through into the echoing engine halls. The way Captain McCormack led them through the shadowy halls they encountered neither fire nor flood until, before too long, they came to another door.

"It's through here," McCormack said, as he and Ulysses took hold of the door-wheel.

A murmur of excitement passed through the party. Against all the odds it looked like they were actually going to make it. Even Ulysses allowed himself a brief internal whoop of delight.

And then – inevitably just when everything was going

so well, when it looked like they might actually all make it out of this mess – that old unwelcome guest, Ulysses' precognisant sense, flared in the back of his brain once more.

With an iron-wrenching groan, like the dying cry of some giant whale, the entire engine chamber listed to port. The survivors should have been used to such lurches and shifting movements of the ship by now, only this time the *Neptune* didn't stop until it was lying flat on its side as the distribution of sea-water within it caused it to re-settle on the edge of the trench.

The group fell sideways, crashing into the network of pipes running up the walls. People were injured, bruises, gashes and grazes appearing where before there had been none, their blood painting them, their clothes and the enamel white walls scarlet.

Just when it had all been going so well.

And, that was when the sea rushed in after them, as if it had been pursuing them ever since the Promenade Deck and the Grand Atrium before that, determined not to let them escape briny oblivion any longer. And this time, it looked like the sea might just get its way.

With shouted guidance from McCormack and his men, and Ulysses' own rallying cries of encouragement, the escapees began to scale the floor, which now formed a climbing wall of scantly fissured plating before them, a full ninety degrees to perpendicular. Mr Wates and the Purser had seen fit to cling onto the bulkhead door-wheel and hung there, securing their own position, bracing themselves against pipes and buttresses as they battled to open the door. But as well as fighting time and the door clamps reluctance to shift, they were also fighting gravity. The door opened away from them, which now meant it opened upwards.

The water level was rising fast. Schafer struggled to help Miss Birkin and his precious Constance to secure holds within the new 'wall', whilst it took all the efforts of Nimrod, Ulysses and Thor Haugland to stop the chair-bound Jonah Carcharodon being lost below the waves lapping around the rapidly filling bucket of the engine hall.

But they struggled on, every man and woman of them, the still-locked door in tangible reach. And still the crewmen struggled with the wheel-lock and still it would not turn, and still the waters rose, until they were all of them bobbing upon the surge, the air space lessening with every passing second, forced together before the door, which remained stubbornly, cruelly shut.

When all seemed lost, with a loud grating screech the wheel turned, the locking clamps sprang open, the door opened upwards, pulling free of the wet grip of Mr Wates and the Purser, and a hand reached down to them.

A gruff voice called down after it, over the bubbling surge of the water filling the engine hall, "Take my hand if you want to live!"

CHAPTER FOURTEEN

Finding Nemo

A grease-black sweaty hand reached for Ulysses, and he gladly took it in his own. His shoulder protested as he was pulled sharply upwards, but the elation he felt at being rescued helped him put aside the pain, compartmentalising it for later when he might actually have time to deal with it.

Carcharodon was already through, seawater running from his chair onto what must have previously been the wall of the dock. When the last of them were through the bulkhead door was allowed to drop shut, before the rising water bubbled through, and the wheel spun tight again.

The VIPs stood around him – or in the case of Carcharodon sat there – in a nervously fidgeting huddle, every one of them a bedraggled wretch. They looked like men and women who had once had everything but who now had nothing – thanks to the sinking of the *Neptune* and the predations of the Kraken – which was precisely what they were.

Captain McCormack, Mr Wates and the purser, however, were behaving exactly like men whose position aboard ship had suddenly been dramatically elevated. They were the ones whose status had risen as the disaster unfolded. It was they who were now in control, in command, responsible for the lives of those very wretches arrayed before them, awaiting their instructions.

"Selby!" McCormack exclaimed, throwing his arms around a short, oil-black grease-monkey of an engineer. It had been this man's hand that had appeared like God's saving hand from heaven to lead them to a salvation of sorts. "I can honestly say that I have never been so pleased to see you in all my life!"

"Mac, you old bugger! I thought everyone else was dead! Clements and Swann and meself were making ready to leave when this happened." He indicated the dock around them. 'Why didn't you try to contact us down here?'

"Ship-wide comms went down," Mr Wates explained, shaking Clements furiously by the hand. "But then, you must have known that yourselves."

"We suspected it but couldn't test our theory as when the ship went down, after the engines cut out and then after..." Selby was lost for words.

"The attack," McCormack filled in for him.

"What was it?" the engineer asked, a manic gleam in his eye.

"It was a..." Now it was the captain who was lost for words. "It would take some explaining. I'll fill you in. Just finish telling me your side of the story."

"Well, whatever it was that happened after that, after the attack, we knew we were in trouble when engine three started to flood and both two and four caught fire." A faraway look entered the engineer's eyes as if he were casting his mind back years, even though the events he was relating had only taken place a matter of hours before. "I tried to get the men out as quickly as I could, but the fires spread so quickly..."

"So many died," one of Selby's fellows muttered half to himself. "It was the fire at first, and then the smoke." He seemed to cough involuntarily at this recollection. "It did for so many of them."

"It was only the three of us that made it down here and shut ourselves in," Selby went on. "But in all the chaos and confusion, when the ship was being knocked about, our comms panel got damaged. We couldn't call out and only heard static back over the thing. We couldn't even get through to the AI. We dared not get back out; we didn't know how far the fires had spread."

"We had to assume the worst," one of the younger soot-smeared men explained, his face pale beneath the covering of grime.

"Swann's right," Selby took over again. "Our only course of action was to get off this ship, and the only way of doing that was on board one of those." He pointed at the two submersible vehicles bobbing up and down on the water lapping at the edges of the up-ended dock-chamber.

It was only now that he had had time to come to terms with the curious perpendicularity of the sub-dock that Ulysses could make sense of its cantilevered layout. With the *Neptune* now lying fully to port, everything inside the docking chamber was at ninety degrees to how it should have been. Ulysses realised that before the wrecking of the *Neptune*, the *Ahab* and the *Nemo* must have been floating upon a rectangular pool, surrounded by all the engineering resources needed to maintain the two submersible vehicles. At the bottom of the pool had lain the dock's pressure gate which, once opened, would allow the subs to emerge from the bottom of the ship. Ulysses could see it now because half of it was free of the water, with the disconcerting tilting of the sub-liner, the keels of the two subs were scraping against what had, moments before, been the wall of the dock.

There was a curious frame to what had now become the left-hand wall of the twisted dock, which Ulysses realised had been a balcony viewing area above the docking pool. That same balcony now helped contain the displaced water, the *Ahab* and the *Nemo* bumping against the edge of it close by. All manner of debris and detritus – from aqualungs and oxyacetylene torches to maintenance materials and spare air tanks – littered the space. And now that Ulysses looked more closely at the three surviving engineers, amidst all the dirt and sooty burns he could also see glistening open wounds on their arms, hands and heads. He wondered how close they had come to losing their lives when the *Neptune* had tipped over and they found themselves caught beneath an avalanche of falling equipment, plenty of it heavy enough and hard edged enough to kill them.

"So what have you been doing down here all this time, since," McCormack made an expansive gesture with both his arms, "all this happened?"

"At first?" Selby said, the grease-monkey's eyes glazing as he called to mind every last detail of that appalling moment when the ship went down. "We waited, we recuperated, we hoped we might hear word from somewhere else on the ship – the Bridge at least – but there was nothing. Once we realised we couldn't send a message out and having heard nothing coming in, we decided that escape was a viable avenue to explore. We weren't going to trust to fate, in the hope that rescue crews might be on the way."

Captain McCormack nodded sagely.

"You know what it's like, Mac, if we're going to be honest with each other. Even if Neptune, or anyone else for that matter, got a distress signal out before we went down and comms went offline, it would take days for the nearest ship to reach us and then they'd have to find us down here."

The huddle of dishevelled VIPs were staring, unashamedly listening in on the interchange between the captain and his chief engineer, their tired faces bearing expressions of zombie-slack horror, the truth of their situation becoming ever more painfully apparent. If there were any who had still been labouring under the expectation that they were about to be rescued by some outside agency, those slim hopes were now cruelly dashed on the rocks of cold reality.

"And that's, like I say, if a Mayday signal had ever been sent in the first place.

"And it didn't seem likely that we would be sitting around down here for days until someone kindly knocked on the door and let us out," Selby went on. "So me and the lads got on with sorting out a way off this bloody death ship, pardon my French," he added, eyes darting over the faces of the women ranged before him, his cheeks reddening in embarrassment beneath the grime.

"It is pardoned," Lady Denning said caustically.

"After the viciousness of the attack – yeah, that makes sense now," Selby pondered aloud, "we had to check both the *Nemo* and the *Ahab* over, to make sure nothing crucial had been damaged. It was a bastard of an assault after all. Then we had to make sure they going to be up to making a journey at these depths. And there were only three of us to do it."

"So which one's sea-worthy?" Carcharodon asked, trying to regain some sense of authority whilst sitting damply within his waterlogged chair, every part of him soaked to the skin.

"They both are, sir. We made sure of it, just in case something else should happen to one of them. We were just getting ready to leave when, well, this happened." He took in the dock again.

"And you reckon both of them could still be piloted out of here?" McCormack asked.

"Yes, Captain, yes I do."

"But what about the pressure gate?" Mr Wates queried, pointing at partially exposed round steel doors revealed by the dislocation of the space around them.

"Clements?" Selby said, calling on the support of another of the surviving trio of engineers, "you're the one who's been checking out that side of things."

"As far as we can tell there's no damage. We should still be able to access it remotely from on board the *Ahab*," Clements said, a little too sheepishly for Ulysses' liking.

"Of course," Selby said, "soon as those gates open this place is going to flood completely, within seconds. There won't be any coming back after that."

"That line was crossed long ago." Cheng was the one to point that fact out to all of them, and Ulysses found himself nodding in agreement. Although it was the truth, it didn't make those of a weaker disposition among the party of survivors feel any better.

"So, chaps, the long and the short of it," Major Horsley piped up, "is we load up these tubs, blow the bally doors off and skiddadle across to this underwater science lab thingy before the ruddy Kraken has us all for breakfast. Right?"

"Um, that about sums it up, Major," McCormack confirmed.

"There's a base?" Selby said, a quizzical look on his face.

"Never mind that," Swann said, looking perturbed. "He said there was a Kraken."

"There's a fair bit to fill you in on, later." The captain's tone implied that recriminations and accusations of keeping information from his crew would not be tolerated.

"Right you are, Mac," the chief engineer sighed, knowing his captain well enough to know not to challenge him on this. But he still had his little dig: "Let's just hope there'll still be a later. I take it we're not heading for the surface then?"

"No, not a good idea."

"Not unless you want to become squid-bait," Ogilvy muttered.

"So, what are we waiting for?" Carcharodon spoke up gruffly.

"Yes, sir," said Captain McCormack, sounding sudden-ly weary again. "It's going to be risky, but not as risky as going head-to-head with that thing out there."

"Are we sure this is the best course of action?" Every-one turned to look at Miss Birkin who had had the confi-dence to challenge the accepted view of the majority.

"Miss Birkin," the captain began, "we have all now seen, first hand, what that creature can do and we al-ready know the threat it poses to our survival."

There were murmurs from some of the others in the party. Clearly, Miss Birkin was not alone in harbouring doubts about the planned course of action.

"But surely, on board one of these" – now it was the Norwegian's turn to speak up – "we could outrun a mon-ster that size?"

"Are you sure?" Schafer threw back. "Didn't you see how quickly it closed on us on the Promenade Deck?"

"Yes, but something living at these depths wouldn't survive nearer the surface, surely? We wouldn't have to go very far to leave it behind."

"I wouldn't want to bet against those tentacles making a grab for us, sir," Nimrod said with something approach-ing calm detachment.

"Yes, but we still have to travel the distance from where the *Neptune* lies now to the base, and hope that we can gain access. Surely the distance we would have to travel upwards to get away from the Kraken would be comparable. The initial risk would probably be equal but then we would be heading back to the surface and long-term safety, not remaining trapped down here with that thing."

"It could be waiting for us, out there, right now," Constance declared fearfully, speaking up boldly in support of her fiancé.

"Now that," said Ulysses, "is a good point."

"There is another way, you know? A way we can get out of this little pickle we seem to have got ourselves into," the Major announced cutting through the dissenting voices, a wicked glint in his eye behind his monocle.

"And what's that, Major?" Carcharodon asked, sounding genuinely interested with no suggestion of sarcasm.

"We could actively hunt the blighter down!"

"Are you serious?" Carcharodon riled, as if disappointed at having trusted the Major to come up with an effective alternative solution.

"But of course I am. I'm sure there's enough of what we'd need around here to rig these beauties out to turn them into mini strike cruisers or even to turn one of them into an overgrown torpedo."

The escapees stared back at the Major with stunned expressions on their faces. Incredibly, apparently oblivious to their disbelief and incredulity, he went on with expounding his scheme.

"We take it out via remote control or some such clever technical wizardry – I'm sure you fellows could come up with something," he said, addressing the chief engineer, "and then we'd have all the time in the world to pootle back up to the surface and be there in time for tiffin."

"Give me strength," McCormack muttered.

"But I've hunted these beasties before."

"Have you really, Major?" McCormack looked around

the group and, judging the party's mood better than Horsley, he took a bold step. "We need to act quickly or all such discussions are going to prove merely academic. All those in favour of taking the subs across to the base Neptune found for us?"

Loyal to their captain, the purser and Mr Wates shot up their hands straight away, as did Ulysses. Following his master's example, Nimrod also raised a hand. Anxiously assessing how their fellows might vote, others among the party slowly raised their hands – Carcharodon, the silent Miss Celeste, John Schafer and Constance Pennyroyal, Lady Denning and a seemingly resigned Professor Crichton.

"Votes for" – McCormack took a quick count – "eleven. Those in favour of attempting to return to the surface?"

Despite the obvious way the poll was already going, Miss Birkin stubbornly raised her hand, along with Haugland and the twitchy Dr Ogilvy. Ulysses noticed Selby and his compatriots shooting each other meaningful glances but none of them had the confidence to vote against the wishes of their captain, and hence apparently abstained.

"Three. Anyone in support of the Major's idea?"

Major Horsley boldly put up his own hand, but was still the only one who thought taking the beast on head-to-head was a sensible idea. "Damn you all, you lily-livered cowards," he grumbled, cheeks and nose reddening in frustration.

Ulysses noticed that four had abstained from giving an opinion: Selby, Swann, Clements, and the taciturn Harry Cheng.

What's your game? he found himself wondering as he looked upon the narrow-eyed Chinaman.

"So the plan remains the same," the captain said indignantly, his tone barely hiding the fact that he believed they had done nothing more than waste precious time by even having such a worthless debate. "We take the subs out to the base."

"Agreed," Ulysses said, "although Miss Pennyroyal raised a good point."

"I-I did?" The young woman sounded as surprised as anyone at this revelation.

"Indeed. Everything we have seen so far regarding the beast suggests that it is actively hunting us, so we'll still be taking a big chance – possibly too big a risk if you ask me – if we attempt anything more than the shortest journey. As soon as we blow the pressure gate it's going to be on to us."

"Damn it, Quicksilver, I didn't have you down for a paranoid bugger!" Major Horsley gasped, making his own little retaliation against all those who had pooh-poohed his idea. "I've never heard such rubbish!"

"Paranoia is it, Major?"

"He could be right, Marmaduke," Lady Denning said. Ulysses couldn't help being a little surprised at hearing the biologist speak up in his defence, against the Major.

"Go on," Carcharodon said, suddenly prepared to listen to all and every reasoned opinion if it would get them – or rather him – out of this mess.

"If we're going to avoid becoming just another course on the menu at the Calamari's Revenge, what we need is a distraction."

"To give us a head start, you mean," Chief Engineer Selby said, a grin forming on his pug-face to match that now being sported by the dandy adventurer.

"Indeed."

The grin spread wider across Selby's face, revealing crooked nubs of teeth.

"Leave it to me!"

CHAPTER FIFTEEN

The Abyss

It didn't seem that important a matter to Ulysses which of the two submersibles the individual escapees should board, but it appeared that Jonah Carcharodon was seizing the opportunity to recover some of his flagging self-confidence. Having been so helpless – nay, useless to the point of being an utter nuisance – during their flight through the wrecked liner, he seemed to feel the need to justify his existence again, and so had put himself in charge of group selection. Ulysses wondered if, as a child, the young Jonah had always been the one left to last when others were picking teams on the rugger field.

"McCormack, I want you on board the *Ahab* with me."

"Yes, sir." The captain sounded weary of his employer's attitude but wasn't about to do anything disloyal and challenge him now.

"I want Selby too. One of the others can man the helm of the *Nemo*."

"Yes, sir. Mr Wates, if you would be so kind as to see the *Nemo* out."

"Yes, captain."

"And Mr Swann, if you would go with him, to provide technical support?"

"Aye aye, cap'n," the more gangly of the two remaining engineers said, attempting what Ulysses took to be a smart salute.

"Mr Quicksilver, if you and your manservant could join them on board the *Nemo* then I would know that each team had at least one person on board who knew what they were doing, just in case we somehow become separated."

"Indeed, captain, very wise." Ulysses consented.

"Lady Denning, Major Horsley, Professor Crichton," Carcharodon said. "I would consider it an honour if you would join me on board the *Ahab*."

Just for the briefest moment Ulysses thought he saw something pass between the magnate and the other three: some dark look, pregnant with meaning, but one which he was unable to determine.

"Captain, the *Ahab* needs another crewman, it being the bigger boat. There's more to keep an eye on," Selby warned.

"Very well, Selby, Mr Clements comes with us as well, and you purser."

The two new recruits to the *Ahab's* crew nodded.

"Miss Birkin, Miss Pennyroyal, Mr Schafer, Mr Haugland, Dr Ogilvy and Mr Cheng. You will all travel on board the *Nemo*." It wasn't a request.

"I'm not going on that sub!" Miss Birkin declared in something approaching an hysterical shriek. "I'm going to travel with you, Mr Carcharodon, on board the *Ahab*, and if you've got any sense, Constance my dear, you'll come with me."

The ageing spinster was making no bones of the fact that she was looking at Ulysses as she made her demands.

"Why, Miss Birkin," he said with a sneer, "a chap could get the idea that you don't like me."

"Constance? Are you going to see sense and come with me, young lady?" Miss Birkin pressed.

"Aunt you go where you like," her niece replied, sounding like she had had enough of being bossed around by the nagging old woman, "but John and I are staying put."

Her maiden aunt looked like she was about to commence a tirade, but Carcharodon cut in before she had finishing drawing breath. "That's settled then. Are we ready to go now? Or are we going to wait around here until hell or high water does for us?"

It went without saying that Carcharodon intended that Miss Celeste would travel with him. And indeed it did go unsaid, so unimportant seemed the most important person in his life to the arrogant old sod.

Led by the *Neptune's* evacuating crew, the two groups moved towards their respective vessels.

"Look, why don't we all just travel in the one vessel?" Thor Haugland asked, hanging back.

Selby looked meaningfully at the captain, who glowered back at him. "Well, Mac?" the engineer challenged, testing his trusted relationship with the captain to the limit.

"It increases the odds of at least some of us getting out of here alive. It improves our chances of survival."

"What?" Schafer exclaimed, indignant. "You would play the odds with our lives?"

"We're all gambling with our lives, every step of the way," Ulysses pointed out with a heavy heart.

"Ulysses, you can't tell me that you're happy with this course of action," Schafer exclaimed in utter amazement, and clutching Constance's hands so tightly in his that his knuckles turned white.

"I'm afraid I do. Think about it for a moment, John. If we all bundle into just one of these tubs, if something goes wrong, it's over, for all of us. If a hull plate cracks under pressure, or if the beastie catches up with us, it's over."

John Schafer returned Ulysses honest open-eyed expression with an intense grimace of his own as he tried to reconcile all manner of emotions that were in turmoil beneath his ever so staid façade. And he had maintained it so well, without questioning any of the decisions made so far, and yet he now appeared to be on the verge of crumbling at this crucial time.

"However," Ulysses went on, "with two crates out there, if one fails, half survive. If the Kraken comes after us there are two targets to confuse it, meaning it's more likely all of us will make it to safety before it can seize either one of the subs."

"And Selby's ensured that there are a couple of little surprises for the wee beastie, should it come a-hunting," McCormack smiled.

"That sounds more like it," Major Horsley said. "What have you got in mind?"

"Wait and see, Major. Wait and see," the chief engineer said with a look of sheer joy on his face. "Let's put it this way. When it comes to the *Neptune*, if I can't keep her, no one can!"

Carcharodon frowned disapprovingly at this bold declaration by the grease-monkey.

"So," McCormack tried again, raising his voice, "time is, as they say, of the essence, ladies and gentlemen, so if we wouldn't mind, I think it's time we boarded our vessels and got the hell out of here."

What little fight there had been left in any of them all used up, the two groups obediently filed up the gangways and followed the officers on board the *Ahab* and the *Nemo*.

Having been the one to point out the need for urgency in their departure, it was Captain McCormack, however, who left it to the last possible second to leave the subdock, board the *Ahab* and evacuate the ship. He liked to think that he had been a good captain to the *Neptune* and had even gone down with his ship, when the worst imaginable happened. And he still didn't fully understand what had happened or who had sabotaged his vessel, or who would have wanted to.

But he knew that the time had finally come when he simply had to leave the *Neptune* to her fate. To stay would be suicide – if honourable suicide at that – and he had a responsibility beyond simply that towards his ship now. If there was a chance that any of the *Neptune's* erstwhile passengers could still make it off the wreck alive, before it was claimed by the fathomless depths of the Marianas Trench, then he should be there, at their head, leading from the front.

So it was that he turned for one last time at the top of the gangplank, before the conning tower of the *Ahab*, and straightening smartly – despite the dishevelled state of his uniform after the unwanted attentions of fire and flood – threw a salute.

"Goodbye, old girl," he said – and was it seawater or salt water of an altogether different kind that glistened in the corner of his eye? – before turning back and taking his last few steps to the conning tower hatch.

"So," said Ulysses, approaching Mr Wates and his number two, the engineer Swann, at the control console in the prow of the *Nemo*, "what's this distraction Selby's arranged?"

"Well, sir, there's actually two of them. Or rather, it's in two stages," Wates said, continuing to flick switches and check dials on the brass-finished control panel in front of him.

"And stage one is? Look, you can tell me. There's no one else listening," Ulysses said in a jokily conspiratorial manner. He glanced over his shoulder. The rest of them – John, Constance, Haugland, Cheng, Ogilvy and Nimrod – were all safely ensconced within the *Nemo*, squeezed into the leather upholstered seats in the main cabin behind the cockpit of the submersible.

"If you watch, sir, you'll see for yourself."

Ulysses peered out of the steel and glass bubble of the *Nemo*. All he could see was the water already in the dock lapping halfway up the hemispherical window and the partially exposed pressure gate beyond.

There was the crackle of static and then a voice came to them over the submersible's radio. "*Ahab* to *Nemo*. Are you receiving me, over?" It was Chief Engineer Selby's voice.

"Receiving you loud and clear, *Ahab*," Wates replied. "Ready to go when you are, over." He turned to Ulysses. "You're going to need to take a seat, Mr Quicksilver, sir."

"Very well," said Ulysses, taking the third seat in the cockpit behind and between those occupied by Wates and Swann.

"Blowing pressure gate now, over," came Selby's crackling voice again.

For a moment nothing happened as Ulysses stared at the solidly shut reinforced circular steel doors anchored in the bottom of the *Neptune's* hull. Then suddenly a throbbing sub-sonic boom rumbled through the bodywork of the *Nemo* and Ulysses saw the two halves of the gate retract into the hull and the sea surge in, like some ravenous feral beast, intent on devouring the two tiny submersibles.

But the *Ahab* and the *Nemo* remained secure within the modified moorings that kept the two craft from bashing into one another, as the chill abyssal waters swirled into the sub-dock.

Ulysses took in the new vista he could now see through the front of the sub. The sub-dock had become dark and miasmic, objects tossed about by the sea-surge bobbing around them and bumping into the hull with dull, disconcerting clangs. In fact, there wasn't much to see beyond the open pressure gate until Swann activated the *Nemo's* stabbing searchlights – and even then, all they could really see was the silty, fissured floor of the seabed and nothing beyond but more of the same all-consuming darkness.

The tannoy buzzed again. This time Selby was heard to say: "Lure away, over."

Ulysses was aware of a muffled thrumming sound, like that of a small engine, and a moment later a metal cylinder buzzed past the viewing port and out of the open gate, its small corkscrew propeller distorting the water behind it so that it was if he were viewing it through a rippling heat-haze.

So that was Selby's plan. One of the unmanned search and rescue drones carried by the sub-liner, sent out first to lure in the Kraken and then keep the monster away from the fleeing lifeboat submersibles.

As the drone and its trail of propeller-wash was swallowed up by the dark ocean depths, the louder, throbbing engines of the *Ahab* started up, rocking the *Nemo* in its makeshift bay beside the larger vessel, and Carcharodon's personal escape craft powered out after the drone through the gaping hole in the bottom of the *Neptune*.

"*Ahab* away, over."

"Roger that," their own pilot replied, talking into a speaking tube as he held down the broadcast switch, and then eased up on the stick. The *Nemo*, its own engines thrumming now, disengaged its anchor cables and glided out after the *Ahab*.

"You said Selby's surprise came in two parts," Ulysses said, as the sub eased its way out into the abyss beyond.

"Yes, I did," Wates said, concentrating on what he could make out through the miasmal gloom beyond the glass and steel bubble in front of them.

"So, if the drone was the aperitif, what's the main course? "

Gliding out of the darkness, its coming heralded by the blue glow of its own lure, the monster slid towards the stricken ship once more, a thousand finely-attuned nerve-sensor-cells detecting movement coming from the grounded vessel.

The Kraken moved with all the grace and speed of something much smaller but with the unstoppable force and singularity of purpose of something primal and monstrous. Unusually regular pulsations in the slow-moving currents around it teased at tentacles and vibration sensors along its dorsal line. The throbbing, thrumming sensation was getting closer, as the creature and its target closed on a mutual collision course. Then, only a few hundred yards from the prone ship, the Kraken attacked.

A grabbing tentacle whipped out as adapted spiracles in its softer body parts launched it forwards with something akin to a propulsion boost. Dense suckers seized the object, pulling it violently from its course, through the water, and before its brain had even begun to process what the object was, the Kraken had drawn it into its mouth, devil-fish fangs closing around it, piercing the metal body, crushing the device. With one gulp, half of the drone was sucked down sharply into the creature's gullet and, with a snap, the rest of it soon followed.

But in the moment following its attack, the Kraken sensed more thrumming engines, the vibrations sending it into a frenzy, setting in on course to hunt and kill once more. Side fins rippling, the monstrous squid-thing rejoined its intercept course with the ship.

Its adapted brain could tell now that there were two more objects moving away from the hulk of the sunken ship. The Kraken moved in behind, using the sub-liner to shield its own approach from its target. With primal cunning it slipped over the hull of the craft, almost hugging the body of the liner to keep it hidden from its prey for as long as possible.

And then it was slipping over the stern section of the vessel, the two tiny submersible craft chugging away, their engines thrumming through the water ahead of it.

Easy pickings.

There was not one explosion but a series of detonations, a cascade of sub-sonic booms, muffled by the fluid ocean depths. They rocked the two fleeing subs, carrying them forward on a bow-wave through the roiling hydropelagic turmoil now consuming the abyss, as if the ocean was suddenly suffering a seizure, an underwater seaquake having rocked the depths.

"Ah, I see!" Ulysses said over the cries and shouts of alarm coming from the rest of the *Nemo's* passengers. Those didn't concern him. What did concern him were the subsequent creaking groans which seemed to possess the tiny submersible. Had the detonation of the *Neptune's* overloaded engines damaged the *Nemo* as well, putting yet more undue pressure on the already overburdened sub?

The next few minutes would answer that question, as they continued on the last leg of their journey to the submerged base, protruding from a rocky outcrop at the edge of the trench ahead of them.

"Yes, well done, Selby!" Mr Wates practically shouted in delight, punching the air. "Rigging the engines to overload and explode just when we needed them to was never going to be an exact science, not given the time and the circumstances, but the old bugger's only gone and done it!"

Behind them the *Neptune* and the Kraken were consumed by a cloud of broiling bubbles, silt thrown up from the seabed and debris from the massive, destroyed Rolls Royce engines. Then the prow emerged from the debris cloud – as obscuring as ink poured into water – swinging round as if to follow the escaping submersibles, as the *Neptune* shifted on the edge of the trench again, rocked by the rapid series of explosions.

Ulysses wanted to give his own whoop of joy, but had they really done it? Were they really free of the threat of the beast? Had Selby really managed to fluke it? Had he really killed the Kraken?

Awareness flared. And then he knew that they hadn't managed any such thing, even before the silt cloud seen clearing in the rear viewing port revealed the truth. Tentacles first, then that terrible maw and curious armoured squid-body coming after it, the Kraken emerged from the devastation, as far as Ulysses could see, with barely a mark on it. It hung there for a moment in the gloom, an awe-inspiring great grey-green leviathan of a beast. Then, having relocated its target, it surged towards the trailing Nemo. And Ulysses was sure that the look in its massive jelly eyes spoke of unleashed primal fury.

"But we have to go back, man! There are people on board!" Major Horsley bellowed, nose to nose with the captain. "I can't simply stand by and watch this happen all over again!"

"I know there are Major, but there's nothing we can do. It would be pointless to turn back now."

"Pointless? I didn't take you for a heartless bastard, McCormack, not after all we've been through so far." The red-faced Major was virtually screaming now, as if he were back on the parade ground or on the front line again, a platoon of wet-behind-the-ears recruits under his command. "And I didn't take you for a coward either!"

"Sit down, Major!" Carcharodon ordered, but Horsley was having none of it.

"You!" he boiled. "It doesn't surprise me coming from a self-serving, arrogant, egocentric bastard like you, but I thought the captain here was a man of decency and honour. Turn this tub around, right now! We've got to help them!"

"And how do you suggest we do that?" McCormack asked calmly.

The Major's blustering faltered at this point. "I... I..."

"You heard him!" Carcharodon snarled. "You saw what happened. We all did. That explosion should have killed it, but it came out the other side practically unscathed."

"I hate to say it but the *Nemo* is already doomed," the captain said, matter-of-factly, "and if we go back we'll simply be going to our deaths. I'm sorry, but there's nothing more we can do."

"Nothing except pray," Miss Birkin said through the agonising sobs now wracking her body as she thought of the niece she had left behind, poor innocent Constance whom it had been her duty to protect on this voyage of the damned.

"Then pray," the captain said. "Pray with all your heart and pray that their sacrifice might not be for naught, that through it we might be saved."

Almost as one, those survivors of the disaster gathered together within the *Ahab* watched, with appalled fascination, fearful for their own well-being, as the monster, all reaching tentacles and gaping fangs, closed on the *Nemo*, reaching for it hungrily, with hate in its eyes.

Captain McCormack was right. There was nothing they could do – except pray.

CHAPTER SIXTEEN

The Relict

Suddenly there was nothing else they could do, nothing else that he – Ulysses Quicksilver, hero of the Empire and dandy adventurer, who had survived more than his fair share of close scrapes with death, who had turned things round at the last minute when everything seemed to be on the brink of collapse on dozens of occasions – could do.

They say that when a man faces death, his life flashes before his eyes. But for Quicksilver, as he gazed into the oblivion of the Kraken's gaping maw, he found himself reliving all those occasions when death had tried to come for him in the past. He saw the Black Mamba's evil grinning face, mere inches from his, as they plummeted towards the ice-hard peaks of the Himalayas. He saw the liquefying features of the fish-thing, felt its scaly skin grind beneath his fingers, as the incendiary fires spread throughout the flooded underground tunnels. He felt the wind whistling through his hair as he dropped towards the bellowing Megasaur rampaging through Trafalgar Square below him. He saw the howling locomotive thundering towards him down the track. He saw the scarred, blind in one eye lion as it prepared to pounce. He saw the indescribable thing emerging from the sludge and seaweed as the waves lapped at the sandy shore, his feet sinking into the sodden sand, and heard its blood-curdling cry again.

And then he saw nothing but the widening jaws of the monster, uncoiling tentacles reaching for the *Nemo*,

escape impossible now, even as their pilot willed more
speed from the chugging sub, Constance praying out
loud for salvation, the wrung-out doctor humming in a
continual monotone to himself.

A shadow suddenly passed across the viewing port at
the rear of the sub that blotted out Ulysses' view of the
closing Kraken completely. Then it passed and the horror
was still there, so close now that Ulysses felt he could
smell the squid-beast's rancid dead-fish breath. And
then, between the writhing limbs of the beast, Ulysses
saw something else moving out there in the sea-gloom.

Dark shapes darted out of the abyssal darkness, dark
finned shapes, and then the Kraken's pursuit abruptly
slowed as it was buffeted to the port side and disappeared
from Ulysses' restricted view.

"What the hell was that?" he gasped.

"What's that?" Swann asked from the co-pilot's seat in
front. "Are we not dead yet?"

"It would appear not," Ulysses replied, as if half in a
dream.

"Well thank Neptune for that," said Wates, knuckles
white around the control column, a look of grim determination etched into the lines of his face. "Then we could
still make it."

Ulysses peered through the porthole behind him, the
others on board – silenced by the fear of what was about
to happen to them – doing the same, searching for any
sign of the squid-monster. Although the thought of catching sight of the Kraken again doubtless scared the life out
of them, not knowing where the creature had disappeared
to was, for the time being, that much worse.

There was the *Neptune*, twisted around so that even
more of its superstructure hung over the precipice, its
hind-section completely destroyed by the detonation of

the engines. There surely couldn't be anyone left alive on board now, not one single space within free of the sea. What had once – and not so long ago at that – been the most fabulous submersible cruise liner in the world had now become nothing more than a watery coffin for the thousands of paying guests who had signed up to join the *Neptune's* inaugural voyage around the world. But of the beast that was hunting them, or the dark shapes that appeared to have driven it away, there was no sign.

Ulysses dared turn his attention back to the main viewing bubble at the tip of the *Nemo* and gasped in amazement.

There, not one hundred yards ahead of them, the *Ahab* was making its final approach to the underwater sanctuary the Neptune AI had promised them was out here. And what a sight it was to behold.

The structure of the base was not unlike a cowry shell, although rather than calcite and mother-of-pearl, its builders had favoured reinforced glass and steel. The central, flattened dome was connected by the twisting half-cylinders of tunnels to other outlying domes. These in turn were networked together by yet more, smaller tunnels. Seen from above it must have had an outline not unlike that of an octopus with its tentacles intertwining around it. However, Ulysses soon realised that the base would have been difficult to spot from above unless a vessel was already practically right on top of it. It had been constructed in the shadow of a massive overhang, projecting from the solid wall of rock which continued to rise up beyond it, possibly right to the surface so many thousands of feet above.

It truly was a wonder to behold, and a fortuitous one at that. But more importantly it was to be their sanctuary, a place where they could wait out this nightmare until real help came. It was more delightful to the eye now, to Ulysses' mind at least, than the sculpted coral gardens of Pacifica.

Where the construction of the base differed from that of undersea cities such as Pacifica, however, was in its almost exclusive use of steel and only a little glass, allowing those inside to view the outside oceanic world beyond the confines of the complex. The most prominent window was the bubble of glass and latticed steel at the top of the largest dome.

Ahead of them the *Ahab* was approaching one side of the largest dome from which projected a circular pressure gate. This was doubtless the facility's submarine dock. As the *Nemo* came closer still, Mr Wates guiding them in, in the wake of the *Ahab*, those on board could begin to see more of the facility. Only then did Ulysses begin to wonder whether they hadn't simply swapped one potential watery grave for another.

It was clear that portions of the base had suffered catastrophic damage. Several of the connecting tunnels had been destroyed, effectively cutting off whole areas of the facility. One or two of the outlying domes had also had their roofs caved in, the incredible hydrostatic pressures at these depths doing the rest. Even the main, armoured dome of the undersea facility had suffered some kind of damage, what looked like great burnt gouges scarred its exterior. Ulysses couldn't help thinking that the damage looked not unlike the trail left by a welder's torch, haphazardly defacing the surface, and on a gigantic scale.

Ulysses' doubt began to ease, however, as he realised that the darkened dome at the centre of the complex still had its roof and hull-armour intact. The damage amounted to nothing more than some superficial scarring. There was no reason to suspect that the readings taken by the

Neptune's state-of-the-art remote sensing equipment had given them false hope, and he felt even happier about their situation again when he saw the massive circular door to the facility's docking area open like the petals of a flower and admit the impatient *Ahab*.

The *Ahab* was through and safe, as far as they could tell. The *Nemo* was only a matter of ninety yards behind.

There was a sudden flicker of blue light in front of them that caused all those peering out of the fore-viewing window to gasp and cover their eyes.

"The lure!" Ulysses exclaimed. "It's right on top of us!"

He spun round, even as Constance gave voice to a terrified scream and, sure enough, there through the aft viewing port – obscuring their view of anything else at all – was a massive watery eye. By the cabin lights of the *Nemo*, Ulysses could see every disgusting detail of that limpid orb – the soured milk flesh of the eye, ribbons of underwater worms clinging to the surface of the cornea, purple veiny tendrils worming their way through the jelly-like substance, the misshapen black pit of its pupil with nothing beyond it but Biblical oblivion.

"Hell's teeth!" he gasped.

There was a sudden crash and the *Nemo* was sent hurtling sideways as something massive darted past and pushed it out of the way. There were more screams, shouts born of fear and confusion, but, to his credit, Mr Wates kept his head and, with the aid of the engineer Swann, brought the vessel under control again. Only they were now several hundred yards further away from where they had been mere moments before. The colossal bulk of the squid-thing had buffeted them over the edge of the precipitous trench, tripling the length of their journey to the base.

The hull of the sub groaned and for one heart-stopping moment it sounded like the engine was going to stall. But adjustments made by the pilot and the engineer kept the boat moving, the two men dogged in their determination to follow the *Ahab* into the savaged facility. But whether the persistent little craft would make it before it sprang a catastrophic leak as the dramatic pressures continued to work on its beleaguered frame, only time would tell. That was not something Ulysses could control. In fact, from this moment on, there was nothing he could do to influence their dreadful predicament, and that fact made him feel agitated and impotent at the same time.

Where was the monster now? Ulysses had to know. Leaving his seat he ran down the aisle and flung himself at the rear viewing port, pressing his face against the glass in the hope that he might see anything other than what was directly behind them.

In the misty glow of the sub's running lights, and the curious flickering luminescence of the monster's trailing lure beyond – a strange moon shining in this abyssal region's perpetual night – he thought he could see the shadow of the beast above them. But then again, it might have been the outcropping overhang of the continental shelf.

His sixth sense flaring so hard it made him wince, Ulysses turned his attentions downward, into the impenetrable, utter blackness of the gaping trench below. Dark shapes moved in the gloom, triangular-finned shadows detaching themselves from the hadropelagic night. With a flick of its knifing tail, one of these shapes rocketed out of the darkness, and was illuminated in all its appalling splendour by the lights of the sub, before it hurtled past, ignoring the *Nemo* in favour of another target.

The sub rocked again as the second monster nudged

it with a fin six-feet long. Ulysses slumped to his knees numb with shock. The Kraken was one thing – he had had time to come to terms with that – but this was something else entirely.

In that split second, when the lights of the *Nemo* had arced across its carcharhinid body, Ulysses had taken in every detail. At least forty feet from nose to tail, a man could have fitted comfortably between its open jaws, filled with serrated arrowhead teeth, each the size of a man's hand, and with row upon row of them, one behind the other, providing the creature with hundreds of individual cutting tools, giving it a bite that could easily have snapped clean through the *Nemo* in one go. From his slim personal knowledge of fossil records and fully aware that other prehistoric creatures had survived extinction in isolated pockets around the world, Ulysses recognised the monster killer fish for what they were – Megalodons.

He suddenly realised that he was shaking. Finding his centre of focus again, as the monks of Shangri-la had taught him – nearly two years ago now – Ulysses recovered himself enough to return to his seat behind Wates.

"Whatever you do, Mr Wates," he said, "don't stop."

"Where's the beast now?" Wates asked, his voice steely in tone, a sign of the pressure he was under to remain focused in such trying circumstances.

As if in answer to his question the Kraken dropped down from above and ahead of them, effectively cutting off their route to the base. Constance's screams filled the cabin again, joined now by the womanly cries of Dr Ogilvy.

And then the *Nemo's* salvation seemed assured once more as the terrifying shark-like creature Ulysses had witnessed emerging from the depths of the trench cut through the sea after the Kraken, followed by another two of its kind, the monstrous Megalodons butting the massive bulk of the over-grown squid with the bullet-tips of their noses, snapping at its tentacles and trying to take a bite out of its side.

Ulysses saw one of the huge fish catch a tentacle between its jaws and then shudder as an electrical explosion lit up the abyssal gloom, throwing the creature away from the leviathan. Another of the huge predators dived down at the Kraken and attempted to close its jaws around the top of its head, but the crustacean-like armoured plating there seemed to do the trick, the attack leaving little impression on the sea monster.

However, the giant sharks were not beaten yet. Their persistent attack on the Kraken – which Ulysses could only imagine was down to it invading their territorial waters – was serving to distract the beast from pursuing the *Nemo*. Ulysses fancied he saw purple blood-ink clouding the water around the leviathan. There wasn't one thought to the contrary in his mind that the sharks' attack against the Kraken was a happy accident as far as those on board the *Nemo* were concerned but then serendipity was playing its part quite nicely nonetheless, and suddenly the facility was a viable objective again, the open hole of its docking gate within reach.

As the Megalodons continued to harry the Kraken, the squid-monster retaliating with violent electrical discharges cast by its deadly tentacles, and attempting to catch the fish between its own not inconsiderable jaws, Mr Wates made the most of the opportunity. He pushed the little sub as hard as it would go, all caution thrown to the wind in his desperation not to be denied the way to safety a second time.

The shadow of the shelf loomed over them, all that was

visible through the front of the craft the open door to the docking bay. And then, they were through.

Torch beams stabbed the darkness, pulling shapes and shadows from the depths of the bay around them. Ulysses paused at the lip of the conning tower, as he prepared to descend the ladder to the quayside, and took in great lungfuls of musty air. It was redolent with the smells of rust, stagnant brine, mildew and salt.

The penetrating beams of the high-powered torches Captain McCormack, Selby and the others had procured from compartments on board the two subs, swung wildly through the darkness, gradually giving form and shape to the chamber in which they now found themselves.

Those who had travelled aboard the *Ahab* had already disembarked, and were now huddled together, some draped in coarse grey blankets for warmth on the dockside, beside which their vessel had now been moored. The *Nemo* sat behind it, Wates and Swann helping its passenger compliment climb down from the conning tower to the quay.

Every member of the party was gazing around the hold in wonder. Ulysses was interested to note the expressions on the closely gathered group that consisted of Carcharodon, the Major, Lady Denning and Professor Crichton in particular. There was a haunted look on the faces of most of them – the shipping magnate just looking as sourfaced as ever – and Crichton was drawing deeply from the flask that had barely been out of his hand.

There was a grating and a reverberating clang as a huge switch was slammed into the 'On' position. At once a powering hum reverberated through the echoing chamber of the dock and within a few seconds the first of a dozen arc lights began to glow into life above them.

Another wheeled handle was turned and the submerged pressure gate, still below the waterline, rolled shut.

The party remained dumbfounded, gazing in amazement around the vast hall in which they now found themselves. Far above them, cast into a steel lintel in letters three feet high were the words:

Marianas Base

"Where have you brought us, Captain?" It was Harry Cheng who was the first to break the silence. "What is this place?"

"In all my years of travelling, I've never been anywhere like this," Haugland said, his words trailing away as he stared in wonder at his surroundings.

"What I want to know," said Ulysses, getting to the heart of the matter, "is, who built this place? Why? And where are they now? What happened to them?"

An ominous silence descended over those present. Ulysses felt the eyes of the four gathered senior members of the party on him. He observed them again in return. They were four disparate people who had once apparently had nothing in common until they had come together on the maiden voyage of the *Neptune* and suffered the fate that had brought them all to this point. So now, here they were, thousands of feet below the Pacific Ocean, at the edge of the deepest place on the planet, hunted by a giant squid, the like of which had never been recorded, in the territorial waters of a race of prehistoric sharks that had previously been believed to be extinct.

He was suddenly being made to feel like a pariah.

Something didn't feel quite right. A forbidding air

pervaded the base, he couldn't shake the feeling that by coming to this place, of their own free will and volition, they had committed some terrible hubris.

Now, truly, they were entering the belly of the beast.

ACT THREE

Leviathan Rising

August 1997

You have carried your work as far as terrestrial science permits. The real story of the ocean depths begins where you left off... wonders that defy my powers of description.

(Jules Verne, *20,000 Leagues Under the Sea*)

CHAPTER SEVENTEEN

Marianas

The sounds of destruction chased the child as she ran the length of the twisting corridor. Amidst the ringing metallic crashes and the groans of metal buckling under terrible pressures she fancied she could also hear the screams of those attempting to flee the carnage, like her.

But she was alone in her flight. And a moment of calm and silence descended like a shroud over the base. Now it was that silence that seemed to be chasing her along the tunnel, marking the stark echoes of her ringing footfalls on the grilled path beneath her. But she just knew that it wasn't over, that something even more terrible was coming.

She ran on, her legs having a purpose all of their own now, her lungs heaving from the exertion of her flight and her sobs. The halogen lamps flickered and dimmed as power relays somewhere within the base short-circuited. The lights died.

A howl of dread and grief escaped her lips, tears streaked her face, her eyes puffy, snot hanging in strings from her nose. But a moment later a red glow began to permeate the tunnel, as emergency lighting took over, bathing everything in its ruddy glow. It made her feel like she was running along the pumping artery of some massive undersea beast. That image certainly didn't provide her with any sense of comfort, considering her current situation. Another set of lights coursed along the sides of the passageway as if they were running with her along the corridor, showing her the route to the escape pod.

And then the silence was broken, first by angry shouts, then by a high-pitched scream, and then by the retort of a single gunshot.

"Daddy!" she wailed, unable to stop herself, the mass of emotions threatening to overwhelm her at the last. "Daddy!"

Automatically she sought comfort from her ever-present companion, only now she wasn't there. "Madeleine!" she cried again, hugging herself tight with her thin arms, until her words became unintelligible sobs. And then they too were wrung from her and she had nothing left to give.

Her feet sore from running, she stumbled to a halt at last, directly in front of the circular hatch to the waiting escape pod. Against all the odds she had made it.

"What the hell is this place?" John Schafer said, wringing the water from a sock. He sat on the bolted base of a huge steel bracing pillar that ascended all the way to the solid steel roof above them. His voice carried eerily in the hollow space. Constance sat next to him, shivering, and trying to tease the knots from her bedraggled hair. Ulysses found himself thinking that if the two of them could make it through this experience and live to tell the tale, then a lifetime's matrimonial union would be a doddle by comparison.

Selby had found the means to provide the base with basic light and power, although Neptune alone knew where the facility's power came from. With the two subs still their only guaranteed way out again the entire party had filed out of the dock, through a solid, circular bulkhead door along a short corridor, then through another such hatch and into a second domed chamber.

Like the undersea cities of Atlantis and Pacifica that they had visited, the base appeared to be divided into a number of sections, each one capable of being separated from the others by means of thick, reinforced bulkheads and airlocks, meaning that if a hull breach occurred anywhere within the facility, that area could be locked down, and the rest of the base kept secure.

So it was that they now found themselves one step closer to the main dome of the facility and possibly one step closer to finding the answers to a host of new questions that were springing to Ulysses' curious mind.

As well as the way back to the submarine dock, there were a number of other, smaller chambers leading from the larger one they had gathered within, each one closed off from the main space by other, solid circular doors. Approaching one and peering inside, Ulysses could see diving equipment – aqualungs, oxygen tanks and a huge, armoured suit, twice the height of a man. Through the small circle of thick glass in another door Ulysses saw a bare chamber and another door on the other side bearing peeling hazard markings of yellow and black. He took this to be an airlock. It must have been from this chamber that work crews prepared to dive, to maintain the outer structure of the facility, or ventured out to the seabed and the edge of the trench beyond – but for what purpose?

The whole place stank of age and neglect. It was not a pleasant smell, and certainly didn't do anything to help make the new arrivals feel at home.

But for Ulysses, taking in every detail of the dusty, neglected space, such things as the aroma merely helped his brain form a greater impression of the whole complex and merely brought more questions to his marvelling mind.

He found himself wondering how long it had been since anyone else had been inside Marianas Base. No signs of human life had been detected by the Neptune AI as it had scanned the abandoned facility. Curious, albino crustaceans scuttled away from their probing torch beams, seeking shelter in the dark corners of the chamber to hide from the light, and some of the girders and joists had acquired their own covering of barnacles and other tube worms that must have found enough sustenance in the moist atmosphere to thrive on. But the only human life present were the survivors of the lost sub-liner *Neptune*.

The mystery of who had murdered Glenda and why, the mystery of who had sabotaged the *Neptune* and sent it plunging into the depths of the Pacific Ocean, and the mystery of the origins of the beast that seemed so intent on pursuing them through the primordial abyss were put aside, to be returned to at another time, as he considered the new mystery of the sanctuary they now found themselves within.

"So, what do you suggest we do now?" Carcharodon asked, directing his question at McCormack.

McCormack looked at him with undisguised contempt, as if he felt that his employer was continually testing him, challenging his ability to lead, and that he had had enough of it.

"I would suggest that we split up into groups and search this facility as quickly as possible. We need to see if there is a working comms array, so that we can notify the rest of the world that the *Neptune* has gone down and send out a Mayday signal so that, once rescue teams start looking for us, we can be found.

"We also need to see if there are any supplies down here because I don't know about anyone else," he said, looking pointedly at Professor Crichton as he uttered these words, "but it feels like an age since I last ate and I know that the *Ahab* and *Nemo* are both carrying only the most basic of rations, which certainly won't be enough for all of us to live on for long."

"The last thing we need on top of everything else is for there to be an outbreak of starvation-driven cannibalism, eh, captain?" Ulysses said with dark humour.

McCormack looked at him, brows furrowing, as if not sure how to take Ulysses' comment.

But Jonah Carcharodon knew exactly how to take it. "For God's sake man, we're in the middle of a crisis. This is hardly the time for your quips!"

"I was merely trying to relieve the obvious tension," Ulysses replied, the humour in his voice now replaced by venom.

Fuming, Carcharodon tried his best to ignore the dandy and chose instead to address the rest of the group.

"Very well, then," Carcharodon said. "We split up."

It had been Carcharodon's idea that they maintain the arrangements of groupings that their escape from the *Neptune* aboard the submersibles had created, and that was fine with Ulysses. The only difference was that it was obviously all getting to be too much for the distraught Miss Birkin. She refused to leave the divers' chamber beyond the dock and slumped down on top of one of a number of locked steel strongboxes. Constance, concerned for her ageing aunt, chose to stay with her, to make sure she was comfortable and that her condition didn't suddenly worsen and John Schafer – although Ulysses could tell that he was itching to explore the base with the rest of them – ever the gentleman, would not leave his lover's side.

So it was that the rest of them began to explore what lay beyond, diverging at a junction where the tunnel beyond the divers' prep room branched. Ulysses was happy not to have to spend a moment longer than was necessary with the wretched Carcharodon who, despite everything – or perhaps, he wondered, because of it – was still behaving as if he owned the place, treating his patiently attendant assistant as if she were nothing better than the scum floating on the surface of the docking pool.

He could have done without the sweating, nervously shivering, waxy-skinned doctor tagging along. And he wasn't too keen on Agent Cheng remaining with him, although he didn't appear to have half the confidence he had enjoyed when his right hand man Mr Sin had been with him.

The base was abandoned: if there had ever been any doubt in any of their minds it evaporated now. Untouched equipment rusted away wherever it lay, a curious combination of diving gear, engineering machinery, heavy duty tools, the abandoned personal detritus of whoever it was that had lived and worked here – doors to sleeping pods open, papers, clothes and personal possessions scattered over the metal grilled floors – everything having the appearance that whoever these personal artefacts had belonged to had left in a great hurry.

Dust covered everything, Ulysses noted, even here, at the bottom of the sea. As they progressed further he paused to examine some of the forsaken possessions, items of clothing and forgotten papers under the faintly glowing lamps lining the semi-circular corridor. Everything about them suggested that they were English in origin, or had at least belonged to subjects of the empire of Magna Britannia. But amidst all the chaotic detritus of a rushed evacuation his party thankfully did not discover any dead bodies, or rather, what would have been left of them. Everyone must have got away.

But who were these people who had lived and worked here? Why had they been forced to leave in such a hurry? And what had happened to them after that? There had not been any sign of other sea transports in the dock, so Ulysses assumed that they had been used to evacuate the team working in the facility; unless there was another dock they didn't know about yet, but he thought it unlikely.

Leaving the accommodation wing behind, Ulysses' party followed a tunnel as it curved around to the right – he assumed following the structure of the central dome – until it brought them to another circular steel bulkhead door. The opening mechanism miraculously still operable, the heavy door swung open and they entered a larger, darker space beyond.

The unpleasant aroma that Ulysses had been aware of ever since disembarking from the *Nemo* was a miasmal stench here, almost as if it were a physical thing, trapped within this undersea dungeon for so long – years seemed likely – that he felt he could have cut it with his swordcane.

Ogilvy could not hide his revulsion, gagging on the stench, whilst Haugland wrung out a sodden handkerchief and held it to his face to filter the vile stink from the stagnant air he was forced to breathe.

"What the bloody hell died in here, then?" Swann said, putting it so succinctly.

The beams of the torches carried by him and Mr Wates, as well as one that Nimrod had managed to procure, set to work revealing, piece by piece, the details of the chamber around them.

They walked between rows of large fish tanks supported on iron legs, the glass obscured with brown slime, the
water they contained as yellowy green and as opaque as
pea soup, the stagnant stinking liquid cloyed with de-
cayed matter. They continued on their way through what
was becoming more and more in appearance like some
curious laboratory, reminding Ulysses of the disturbing
discovery he and Nimrod had made below the house in
Southwark, only a matter of months ago.

Ulysses stopped to peer more closely at the rank fish
tanks, trying to make out what they once had held, but
he could make out nothing more than the occasional broken shell or empty carapace. But then he supposed that
whatever life had once wriggled and writhed within had
died long ago, their flesh and insubstantial bones and
cartilage becoming the sludge that smothered the bottom
of the tanks.

"Herregud, hva er det der?" Haugland exclaimed, his
voice carrying to the dark and distant roof before calling back to them in the cavernous vault, as they passed
beyond the rows of dead tanks and came upon the first
of the cylinders.

"Bloody hell!" Swann swore.

"Incredible," Cheng uttered.

"It's disgusting!" Mr Wates countered.

"It's a blasphemy! That's what it is," Dr Ogilvy suddenly piped up. "A blasphemy against nature."

There were a dozen of them altogether. Ulysses doubted
that the liquid in these sealed cylindrical glass tanks was
water. It was only semi-opaque and had a yellow tinge
to it, like urine, allowing them to see what was contained
within quite clearly.

Their proportions were roughly those of a man, but
these things were very far from being men now. Some

sported obvious gills within their swollen necks, ugly goitre-like growths. Others were entirely swollen, with characteristics of puffer-fish, even down to the tiny spines covering their rubbery hide. Yet more had webs of skin between fingers and toes, those same digits unnaturally elongated, whilst in one example the legs had fused together, the malformation of its feet creating an effective fish-tail.

Ulysses found himself wondering how such abominable creations had been achieved, whether by means of splicing vivisectionist surgery – something akin to the revolutionary research undertaken by the late Professor Galapagos – or some unholy cross-breeding programme that didn't even bear thinking about. It was clear that the long-dead occupants of the cylinders, what were in effect giant test-tubes, were the strange aborted experiments of someone's attempts to amalgamate fish with men, although for what sick purpose Ulysses could only guess at.

Looking more closely, he saw a label, discoloured with rust and mould, still stuck to one of the tanks. The thing preserved inside the flooded coffin of chemicals looked like an ungodly amalgam of moray eel, octopus and Homo Sapiens. There was only one word, written in faded and smudged ink, though Ulysses could still make it out: Seziermesser.

"I'll think you'll find," Ulysses said as he edged past the tanks towards what looked like a large chart table on the other side of the laboratory, "that these are the reasons this facility exists." He lifted a piece of paper from the table and, having swept the dust from its surface, peered at the blueprint revealed beneath. "And if you think that's incredible, you haven't seen anything yet."

The rest of the group joined him at the table.

"What is it, sir?" Nimrod asked, his own curiosity piqued. "What have you found?"

"Take a look for yourself."

All eyes fixed on the blueprint unrolled in front of them, gradually making sense of the white lines against the faded blue sheet of the plan.

"Bloody hell."

"Incredible."

"As I said, a blasphemy."

"The Kraken!"

"Indeed, Mr Haugland," Ulysses concurred with the Norwegian, "although according to the maker's designation it's actually Project Leviathan – 001."

There on the paper in front of them, plain for all to see, was what amounted to a technical drawing of the monster that had blighted them, ever since the *Neptune's* engines had come to a full stop, its ballast tanks flooded and the world's greatest luxury submersible liner had drifted to the bottom of the Pacific. There was no doubt that it was the same monster that had crippled the *Neptune*, taken Mr Sin and pursued the rest of them as they fled the flooding wreck. There it was, laid out in side elevation, front elevation and in plan view, with attendant measurements, in all its two hundred-foot glory, from the tips of its writhing squid's tentacles, to its fang-filled maw, armoured shell and spine-tipped tail.

Ulysses found himself glancing upwards, into the dusty shadows of the laboratory roof, wondering what had become of the beast, wondering if it was still out there waiting for them. An involuntary sparking tingle of fear crackled down his spinal column.

"Look at this," Wates called from nearby.

Happy at the distraction, Ulysses turned his attention from the schematic to the officer's discovery. On another

work table, one cluttered with half-finished, or decon-
structed, pieces of machinery – not unlike the guts of
a Babbage engine – stood a wooden board on which a
frame constructed of metal rods, supported three feet of
octopoid-tentacle, stretched out horizontally. The rubbery flesh was intact, preserved no doubt thanks to the
addition of some chemical, but more amazing than that
was the fact that it had at its core, running the length of
the fleshy limb, a flexible metal cable. The end of this
internal mechadendrite was hooked up to a large battery also sitting on the table, although one terminal was
disconnected.

"What do you make of that?" Wates said.

"I don't know," Ulysses mused, "but I'll warrant it's got
something to do with our friend out there."

"It looks like some kind of cyborganic technology," Dr
Ogilvy added, his fascination with the curious object on
the table seeming to help him to ignore the symptoms of
withdrawal he was suffering.

"And what's that when it's at home?" Haugland asked,
peering just as closely at the mecha-tentacle through his
round wire-framed glasses.

"The marrying together of a living, breathing organism
to either an exo- or endo-skeleton of mechanical components to create something else altogether," the doctor
explained.

"Incredible," said Cheng, for a third time, and unseen
by anyone else, depressed a button on the baton-like device he had secreted in the pocket of his trousers.

Their cursory investigation of the lab complete, and
having found no source of supplies anywhere, Ulyss-

es' company entered another connecting corridor from which branched various other paths through the submarine complex.

The sudden reverberating sound of a crash caught them all by surprise.

"What was that?" Ogilvy said, jerking his head round.

Thanks to the distorting echoes of the place, they could not be certain from which direction the noise had come. Rubber piping and cables hung from the ceiling of the tunnels here, like trailing tree roots piercing an animal's burrow or the mechanised intestines of some cybernetic sea monster.

"Come on," Ulysses said, "we're going to have to split up. It's the only way."

He turned and looked at the agitated faces around him.

"Cheng and Haugland, you go that way," he said, pointing to the tunnel left of where they had joined the junction. "Mr Wates, you take Swann and the good doctor that way," – he pointed right – "while Nimrod and myself will take this passageway," he said, crossing the junction and continuing into the gloom ahead.

Within minutes, servant and master reached another junction within the maze of corridors. Lying on his side on the floor, cursing like a navvy, was Jonah Carcharodon, his wheelchair tipped over beside him.

"Carcharodon!" Ulysses exclaimed, coming to the aid of the invalid. "What happened to you?"

"Damned if I know!" he snarled, verbally turning on his would-be rescuer.

"And where's Miss Celeste?"

"I refer you to my earlier answer."

As Ulysses and Nimrod righted the wheelchair and assisted Carcharodon back into it, the old man – who was obviously shaken, despite the show of bravado – began to prattle away, revealing what had happened prior to his little accident.

"Our party had split up to carry on searching this place. Celeste and myself were coming along this passageway. McCormack was scouting ahead of us. I heard a cry from behind me, and as I struggled to turn round, to find out what was going on, some blighter – some bastard or other – tipped me out of my chair. Who would attack an old man, and an invalid at that? God knows where the others have got to."

"Or Miss Celeste," Ulysses said anxiously. "So where's McCormack now?"

"That bastard? He ran back on hearing Celeste cry out but ran straight past, leaving me like this."

"Which way?"

"That way," Carcharodon said, pointing along another tunnel leading off from the intersection.

His sixth sense screaming danger, Ulysses took off in the same direction, Nimrod close on his heels.

"But what about me?"

"Sorry, sir," Nimrod said with a slight nod of the head as he followed after.

Ulysses and his manservant rounded a bend in the corridor, Carcharodon's indignant shouts echoing back to them from the intersection, and passed through another sealable bulkhead door into yet another chamber. His unconscious mind took in the fact that it was another laboratory of some kind, but his conscious mind was focused on the confused sounds of scurrying movement beyond. Slowing his steps he penetrated the half-lit gloom of the lab – passing stacks of more stinking, gunk-filled fish tanks bearing faded and mildewed labels – until he caught sight of a pair of booted feet protruding from behind a tarnished metal gurney. Then, quickening his steps once more, he hastened round the end of the row, past the gurney, to see Captain McCormack lying on the floor of the laboratory, blinking as though in a daze, a hand to the back of his head.

"Quicksilver?" he slurred. "What's going on?" He brought his hand back round in front of his eyes. Ulysses could see that it was sticky with blood. "What happened to me?"

"You've been attacked," Ulysses stated, as the dazed captain seemed to be struggling with the realisation himself. "Where's Miss Celeste?"

"M-Mr Quicksilver? I-Is that you?" came a quavering fluty voice.

Ulysses immediately left the captain in Nimrod's more than capable hands and rushed around another stack of algae-streaked tanks to see Miss Celeste stumbling out of the shadows towards him. Her already dishevelled state was considerably worsened by the ugly bruise blossoming on her forehead and the trickle of blood dripping between the fingers of the hand she held to the injury.

"Miss Celeste," Ulysses said, unable to hide the concern in his voice as he hurried to her side. Putting one arm around her waist to support her, he encouraged her to sit down on the seat made by a fallen steel beam.

"Is everyone all right?" Wates asked, entering the lab, followed by Swann and Ogilvy, reluctantly pushing Carcharodon ahead of him.

"Captain McCormack and Miss Celeste have both been attacked," Nimrod stated bluntly.

"And me!" snapped Carcharodon, unhappy at not being the centre of attention. "I was attacked as well."

Ulysses shot the eccentric, self-obsessed billionaire a poisonous look but decided against saying anything.

"Hello? What's going on? Everyone okay?" came Selby's voice as he entered the laboratory, followed by Cheng and Haugland.

Expressions of surprise and half-formed questions were all answered as Ulysses explained to everyone, once again, what had occurred.

"But who would do such a thing?" Haugland asked in disbelief.

"It must be someone who came on board with the rest of us," McCormack said. "Neptune didn't detect any human life-signs on the base before we all got here."

Eyes narrowed and immediately everyone present began reappraising their companions with suspicion.

"Then, if we are in danger, isn't it best we all stick together again from now on?" Ogilvy said.

"Well said, doctor," McCormack concurred. "Come on," he added, struggling to his feet, with Nimrod helping him, "this way."

"Captain, are you sure about this?" Ulysses warned. "Both you and Miss Celeste have suffered injuries and are doubtless also suffering from the effects of shock, isn't that right, Doctor?"

"Um, what? Oh, yes. Shock. Yes. Most definitely."

"The way I see it," McCormack said, wincing and putting his hand to the back of his head again as he attempted to stand upright, "we don't have any choice. If there's a madman on the loose, we need to hook up with the others and warn them."

The party moved on, as briskly as the injured amongst them would allow. Passing another bulkhead door, Ulysses paused to look through the porthole at its centre to see what lay beyond. But all he saw through the thick, green-tinged glass was nothing but the broken shell of another dome and the open ocean beyond. Something had utterly destroyed that part of the facility which lay beyond the door. Suddenly a few inches of reinforced steel didn't seem like very much to be standing between them and the crushing expanse of the mighty Pacific.

Passing into another corridor and from there through another bulkhead door, they entered the central chamber of the main biome – a waft of dry dusty air assailing their nostrils as they did so – only moments before what remained of the other party entered through an identical door on the opposite side of the room.

No pleasantries were exchanged, tired expressions and the briefest exchanges between the groups telling them what they already suspected: the base was deserted, whole swathes of it destroyed altogether. They had been able to find only a few usable medical supplies and a handful of tinned foodstuffs in a wrecked galley. And there was no sign of anyone having been left behind during whatever rushed evacuation had taken place.

Until now.

The explorers were all inextricably drawn towards the bizarre construction at the centre of the chamber, the grim memento of whatever had happened here exerting the pull of morbid fascination upon them.

They had to be in another laboratory. At its centre stood an amazing contraption, like a tiered dais, surrounded by banks of cogitator equipment and with the steel-cradle of a chair-harness at its peak. And strapped into the chair by a cracked leather harness was the body of a man.

It must have been sitting there for a long time in the one moisture-free room in the whole complex, for the body had become mummified naturally, cracked and peeling parchment-dry skin clinging to the angular bones. A curious device was strapped to the man's head. It looked like a metal-banded helmet. Various light-emitting diodes were arrayed upon its outer surface and a number of twisting cables trailed from electrode junctions on the top, connecting it to the chair and, by extension, the banks of machinery around it.

As to the purpose of such a device, Ulysses had no idea. As to how the mummified corpse had met its end, however, there seemed little doubt. The dead man had been shot, at close range. A clean bullet hole was preserved within the middle of his forehead, the results of the exit wound splattered across the back of the chair, eggshell shards of skull littering the dais beneath. The hollows of the dead man's eyes appeared to be staring at the small bubble of reinforced glass and steel at the apex of the dome, sightless sockets staring out at the miasmal abyss beyond.

"Oh my God," Crichton began, an expression of appalled horror on his face. He reached for his hip flask, to take another swig, only it wasn't there. He fumbled for it in his pocket, but it was gone, doubtless left somewhere as he and the rest of his party explored the facility.

Turning his attention from the macabre figure locked within the even more curious clinical chair-construct, Ulysses assessed the reaction of his fellow survivors.

To his mind there was something extreme about Crichton's meeting with the corpse. Surely he had witnessed much worse during their encounters with the Kraken and their flight from the *Neptune*? A nagging suspicion began to form at the back of his mind, struggling to take cohesive form.

All eyes were on the chair and the body bound within it. But where most gazed in morbid fascination or dumbfounded bewilderment, there was something else in the eyes of some of the more senior members of the party, specifically Carcharodon, Lady Denning, Major Horsley and of course Professor Crichton; something like recognition.

The only person not looking at the chair and its victim was Carcharodon's PA. Instead she had crouched down and was picking something up from the floor of the chamber, a floppy fabric thing, a child's crudely sewn rag-doll. Miss Celeste was turning the toy over in her hands in stunned silence.

"Oh, God forgive me," Crichton mumbled, his legs giving way, falling to his knees before the construction, unable to tear his eyes from the corpse bound within it.

"What is it, professor?" Ulysses challenged. "Do you know this man?"

"God forgive us all!" Crichton screamed.

"Do you know what happened here?" Captain McCormack uttered in startled surprise. "Is there something you're not telling us?"

"Major. Lady Denning," Ulysses tried. He couldn't quite believe what he was saying, even as he said it – how could it be possible after all? – but it seemed the only logical explanation. "Have you been here before?"

"Don't be ridiculous, man!" Carcharodon railed, turning on him again. "How could any of us have been here before? Quicksilver, you're a fool and a nincompoop if you believe that. It's an utterly preposterous suggestion!"

But the professor remained on his knees, tears splashing onto the metal plates before him, making tiny mortar-blasts in the dry, dead dust.

A scream rang out through the open door by which the rest of the party had entered the laboratory chamber, that sent a shiver of fear and excitement through Ulysses' body.

"Constance!" he exclaimed, already moving. "But of course, they were still left behind. The only safety here is safety in numbers."

"The attacker!" another voice added.

Faltering steps became great bounding strides as Ulysses ran from the chamber. Others joined him in pursuit, a cacophony of clanging footfalls rebounding from the steel-plated tunnel walls. And the screams kept coming.

Ulysses was the first to enter the dive chamber, joined soon after by Nimrod, Captain McCormack, Cheng, Swann and Clements. He stumbled to a halt in appalled horror as he took in the scene before him.

Constance was standing only a few feet from a secured airlock door, her hands to her face, screaming in abject horror. John Schafer beat at the door with his fists, bellowing in anger as he tried to open it again. On the other side of the glass the face of Miss Birkin filled the porthole, locked into an expression of unutterable terror.

Ulysses rushed to his young friend's side, Nimrod following in his stead, all three of them attempting to force the door as a dull, droning siren began to blare from speakers somewhere within the chamber.

"It's no good!" shouted Selby.

"What do you mean?" Ulysses asked, voice tensing as he strained to get a purchase on the rim of the airlock hatch with his fingers and somehow prise it open.

"You're wasting your time," the *Neptune's* chief engineer said coldly. "Once an airlock's activated, the fail-safes make sure that the protocols cannot be overridden."

"What? It's been activated?" Ulysses turned his attention back to the door and the terrified old woman trapped in the airlock, her face bathed in the pulsing orange glow of an amber warning lamp.

As if to confirm Selby's words, beyond the unnervingly silent Miss Birkin, the outer door of the airlock ratcheted open.

There was nothing any of them could do as the sea flooded into the chamber, filling it in seconds, crushing the old woman to a pulp before she had a chance to drown.

As the messy remains of what was left of Constance's aunt were drawn out of the airlock in a swirl of ocean current, a terrible realisation crept over Ulysses.

Glenda's murderer had come with them. Someone, hiding in plain sight in the party of survivors within the Marianas Base, was the killer and had dared to strike again, even given the hopelessness of their position, surely realising that there could be no escape for them either now.

What had seemed to be their sanctuary from all the horrors that the abyssal depths held for them, had now become their prison.

CHAPTER EIGHTEEN

The Accused

"We only left her alone for a moment," John Schafer was saying, "a minute or two at most."

The young man looked completely wrung out as he tried to make sense of what had just happened. The stress of the situation, having personally taken responsibility for the safety of his fiancée and her aunt, had begun to get to him like never before. And this feeling was only made worse by the fact that one of his charges was now dead, and having suffered such a horrible death.

Constance Pennyroyal was slumped on the floor against the airlock door, sobbing into her hands. At least her anguished cries of grief had subsided for the time being, but, to Ulysses' mind, the heart-rending stifled sobs seemed almost harder to bear.

"We heard something – a crash, a cry – and went to see what was going on," Schafer went on. "We only left her alone for a moment."

"It's the killer," the purser said darkly. "Whoever killed Miss Finch is with us, here, in the base, hiding somewhere amongst us."

"A stowaway, you mean?" Lady Denning asked.

"You can tell yourself that, if you like," Selby said, "but there was no one on board before any of us boarded back at the sub-dock on the *Neptune*."

"How can you be sure?"

"You'll have to trust us on that one, your ladyship."

"Trust you? But someone amongst our party is a killer! How can we trust anyone anymore?" She took in the faces around her one at a time, alighting on Major Horsley's bristled red-veined face. "Even those people we thought we knew."

"The killer's here?" Dr Ogilvy repeated, as if struggling to comprehend what he was hearing. "But if that's the case, we're all doomed!" He seemed to be paying particular attention to Harry Cheng as he had his say.

"We're not done yet," Ulysses said, one eyebrow arching and the corner of his mouth following suit, a wry smile beginning to form on his face. "It's quite simple, really. As it stands none of us are going to get out of here alive if we don't keep to the plan. The killer hasn't shown themselves to be suicidal, otherwise we wouldn't be in this position now."

"How can you be so calm and detached about all this?" Schafer asked, as if he was revolted by Ulysses' lack of demonstrable emotion. "Especially after what happened to Glenda."

Ulysses fixed the younger man with a hard stare. "Whatever it takes to get through this," he said coldly. "Anyway, as I was saying, the killer could have put an end to all of us any number of times, if they hadn't valued their own life. No, there's a purpose to these killings and as long as we stick together, and stick to the plan, there's nothing our mystery killer can do to harm us. Isn't that right, Captain?" Ulysses asked directing a wicked grin at McCormack, his ally in all their plotting so far.

"Mr Wates, seize this man," the captain said, pointing an accusing finger at Ulysses.

"Captain?"

"McCormack?" Ulysses said, in disbelief, his nascent smile being replaced by a knot of confusion.

"I said, lay hands on Mr Quicksilver!"

"You cannot be serious," Ulysses pressed on, incredulous. "That blow to the head must have been worse than we first thought."

Just as confused as Ulysses, but with years behind him as a devoted naval officer, Wates moved forwards, almost as if reacting by instinct upon hearing his captain's command, and put a cautious hand on the dandy's arm. All the while he kept looking to his superior for affirmation of his actions.

In response, Nimrod moved to stop Wates.

The rest of the group seemed frozen in a state of shock, either by this unexpected development taking place before their eyes, or by the sudden death of the harmless old spinster, or simply at the bizarreness of the situation they all found themselves in.

"It's all right, Nimrod," Ulysses said.

"But, sir, I must insist."

"It's all right, Nimrod. But Captain McCormack there is no need to have Mr Wates lay his hands on me."

"Oh, I would beg to disagree."

"In that case, then, I am sure that you won't mind explaining to me precisely why you are placing me under arrest. That is what you're doing, isn't it?"

The situation seemed ludicrous to Ulysses. What did the captain think he was going to do with him even if he had him under lock and key?

"What is it I am accused of?"

"Happily, sir, if only so that these God-fearing men and women here present learn what sort of a viper has been lurking in their midst all this time, and know that they can now rest easy, assured that a murderer has been banged to rights."

"I've been called a few choice things in my time," Ulysses said in a way that implied he might have found this misunderstanding amusing if it wasn't for the direness of their predicament, "but a viper and a murderer, never!"

Appalled gasps passed around the group, followed in some cases by a wave of palpable relief to know that the killer had been caught.

"And to think that I entrusted you with the task of uncovering the identity of Miss Finch's killer!" McCormack sounded like he was in danger of losing it again, as he had done with Carcharodon, when they were back aboard the *Neptune*.

"Come on then, man," McCormack's employer said, pressing him. "I know that Quicksilver and I haven't always seen eye to eye but I'm on tenterhooks to know the reason why you believe him to be the killer."

"Miss Birkin was right all along," McCormack replied cryptically.

"W-What do you mean?" It was Constance who spoke. She had been listening just as intently to the exchange as everyone else and fixed the captain now with a piercing gaze, made all the more furious by the redness and puffiness of her eyes.

"She told me, back on board the Neptune, when we were trying to get everyone across the Grand Atrium."

"She told you?" Ulysses was getting exasperated himself now. "Told you *what*?"

"That you were the killer."

Ulysses remembered how the suspicious old woman – "too full of conspiracy theories" the Major had said – had looked at him, ever since they had met together following the wrecking of the ship, how she had refused to board the *Nemo* when she knew that she would be travelling with him.

"But wherever did she get that ludicrous idea, the daft old bat?"

"That's my aunt you're talking about!" Constance suddenly shrieked, catching Ulysses off guard.

His face reddened in embarrassment. "I'm sorry, I meant no offence –"

"She told me that she had seen Miss Finch with the killer. You saw her tell me as much," McCormack interrupted, the anger and frustration apparent in his voice, "read her lips, no doubt."

Ulysses recalled the moment quite clearly now.

"It was at that point that I took her to one side, to stop her upsetting anyone else. She told me that she saw you with Miss Finch only a matter of hours before she was found dead inside the AI chamber, after you left the casino with her that night. But by then the damage had been done. And now she is dead. You killed her to silence her, because she knew too much."

"But this is ridiculous," Ulysses said again. "Your evidence is nothing but circumstantial. It wouldn't stand up in a court of law."

"In case you hadn't noticed, Ulysses, we're not in a court of law," Schafer said darkly.

"Et tu, Brute?" Ulysses threw back, angry and upset at the apparent change of allegiance of a man who was the closest thing he had to a friend amongst his fellow passengers-cum-refugees, other than his manservant.

"Where were you when the airlock was activated?"

"Well, assuming that it had only just happened," Ulysses paused, his mind racing, trying to work out his whereabouts at the time when the old busy-body's fate had been sealed. "Why, I suppose it was around the time we all heard the crash and went to help Carcharodon and then found you in the lab."

"So, you attacked me too," Carcharodon shrieked. "You admit it!"

"Why don't you just shut up for once, you blustering

old buffoon?" Ulysses railed.

"And you have witnesses?" McCormack asked.

"I was with Cheng, Haugland and the rest up until that point."

"Up until that point?" McCormack parroted. "There was never a time when you were alone?"

"There was that time when you told us all to split up, after we heard the attack on Mr Carcharodon," Dr Ogilvy pointed out nervously.

"What?" Ulysses couldn't believe that the doctor was actually attempting to corroborate McCormack's story. "We weren't apart for more than a few minutes."

"Time enough for a man like yourself, in the peak of physical fitness to return here and do the dreadful deed," McCormack said coldly.

"This is preposterous!" Nimrod said, adding his voice of dissent to the argument.

"But why would I risk returning here, to do that, when I thought that John and Constance would be here?"

"Perhaps you planned to do away with *all* of them," Ogilvy suggested, excitedly.

At that Constance recoiled into the safety of Schafer's embrace, turning horrified eyes on Ulysses. That look alone cut him to the core.

"What happened to innocent 'til proven guilty?" Ulysses challenged.

Captain McCormack looked around at the others. "Haugland? Can you confirm all this? Where is Haugland? Has anyone seen him?"

"I can confirm that Mr Quicksilver did leave us for a time," Cheng said impassively, his face a hardened, emotionless mask. "But then so did his manservant, Mr Nimrod."

"Precisely," Ulysses said, his speech becoming impassioned as he realised that this wasn't some bluff, something that was all going to pass as some ridiculous misunderstanding. "I wasn't alone."

"Is this correct, Mr Nimrod?" McCormack asked, his expression one of steely concentration.

"When our party separated I went with Mr Quicksilver," Nimrod confirmed.

"Then you had an accomplice!" Constance screeched.

All eyes now turned on Nimrod and for the first time since their descent into chaos had begun, Ulysses' loyal family retainer looked suddenly out of sorts, a startled expression claiming his features.

"That would explain why you weren't worried about taking on all three of them," Ogilvy chirruped excitedly.

"I did not kill anyone!" Ulysses growled, the volume of his words increasing as he did so. "I did not plan to kill anyone. *We* did not plan to kill anyone!"

"Then if you didn't, who did?" Carcharodon challenged.

Ulysses opened his mouth to speak, but no words followed. Who indeed? Who would have wanted to kill Glenda Finch and now Miss Birkin? And who had the opportunity and the wherewithal to achieve the brutal task?

"Seize those men!" McCormack ordered.

Ulysses went for his sword-cane but Mr Wates already had a hand on him. In moments both Wates and Swann had Ulysses held tightly by the arms and shoulders so that he couldn't escape, and Nimrod found himself restrained by Selby and Clements. There hadn't seemed much point in him trying to get away when his master was already restrained and they were both outnumbered. They would work out a way out of their predicament together, given time.

"So what do you plan to do with us now?" Ulysses sneered.

The captain took a moment to respond, taking that moment to look around the dive preparation chamber again.

"Put them in there," he commanded, pointing at a circular hatch-door in the side of the hemi-spherical chamber.

It seemed pointless protesting now, so Ulysses and Nimrod allowed themselves to be pushed through the hatch and into the storage locker beyond. The door slammed shut behind them with a resounding, and very final sounding, clang and Ulysses heard the thud and clunk of locking clamps being secured. Peering through the round porthole he could see that Swann and Clements had been placed either side of the hatch to stand guard.

"Well, Nimrod, old chap, who'd have thought it would end like this?" Ulysses said, trying to smile, in spite of everything.

"Not I, for one," Nimrod said with abrupt annoyance.

Turning on the spot, Ulysses surveyed the room that had become a temporary brig for the two desperadoes and one object stood out more than any other.

It dwarfed the two of them. Twice as tall as a man and almost as wide as it was high, it looked for all intents and purposes like a huge, all-enclosing diving suit. However, due to its size, no man would be able to fit his body precisely inside the arms and legs of the suit. Instead the pilot had to climb into the back and secure himself within a cramped pilot's cabin inside the torso of the suit and the spherical fish-bowl helmet. Searchlights were mounted on the broad shoulders of the suit and the pilot actually viewed the sub-aquatic world beyond through a number of circular portholes positioned around the helmet-dome.

"I assume you have a plan to get us out of here, sir," Nimrod said as he too took in the room.

"Oh, you know me, Nimrod," Ulysses said, grinning wickedly, eyes remaining fixed on the suit in front of him. "I'm just making this up as I go along."

There was a sharp electrical click and Captain McCormack's voice crackled from an intercom panel in the wall.

"When was the last time you saw Haugland?" he demanded, his tone accusing.

"What? McCormack, have you lost your mind?" was Ulysses' less than helpful reply.

Now that he came to think of it himself, he hadn't seen the Norwegian since his party had split up after hearing what they now knew was the attack on Carcharodon. A cold feeling filled his belly, a knot of ice tightening inside him. He could see where this was going.

"If you've done anything to him," McCormack was saying, the tone of his voice making it clear that his sorely tested patience was rapidly running out, "God help you!"

With, as seemed likely, the double murderer and his accomplice secured away and with an armed guard on them, Captain Connor McCormack organised certain members of the remaining group of survivors into three separate search parties. And although he now had Ulysses and Nimrod imprisoned, the atmosphere of distrust, that the attacks and the killings had engendered in everyone, had not entirely lifted.

So, just to be sure, with that doubt planted in his mind

and wondering if there was someone else lurking within the base, the stowaway that Selby assured him did not exist, McCormack made sure that as many people as possible were armed before they set out to look for Haugland. The leader of each party was given a pistol and ammunition taken from a secure locker onboard the *Ahab*. The rest had to make do with what could be procured from the divers prep room. Inside one of the storage lockers, the purser had found a number of cumbersome, hand-held harpoon guns, bolts already loaded, a pair of fire-axes, and even a number of sticks of dry dynamite, although these were not considered an appropriate means of defence. Every other weapon, however, was gratefully accepted by their recipients.

"Right, are we ready then?" Major Horsley asked in his customary bellow, as the group began to divide up.

People were naturally gravitating towards those they most trusted or who they perceived as being most like themselves.

"Ready?" Horsley asked again, looking round the group. "Tip top," he said beaming, apparently concluding that they were indeed all ready. "Let's be on our way then, what?"

He set off towards the door that led out of the dive prep chamber and into the rest of the complex beyond, harpoon gun held high before him.

"Major, wait!" Captain McCormack called after him. "We need to plan the search carefully."

"Haugland could be lying somewhere, bleeding to death! What more do we need to know? Time's a-wasting."

And with that, he was gone.

McCormack shook his head wearily and muttered something uncomplimentary under his breath.

"So, what now, McCormack?" Carcharodon said in that oh-so irritating, wheedling tone of his.

"Well, sir, I would suggest that you stay here, along with Miss Celeste. You've both had a nasty shock."

"Don't patronise me!" Carcharodon snarled. "Talk about pot and kettle! What about you? If you're fit to run around playing heroes, on some wild goose chase looking for Haugland, then so are we."

"But I didn't think you'd want to," the captain threw back, almost defeated by the shipping magnate's constant harping criticism.

"Who are you to make such a judgement of me?" Carcharodon tore into the near-exhausted McCormack. "I'm not going to sit around here, like an idiot, waiting to be attacked again! I want to know what's going on as much as you do. It's bad enough that I'm an invalid, stuck in this chair. I am not going to be treated like a vegetable as well! I have never stood for that, and I'm not about to start now!"

"I meant no offence, sir. I was merely suggesting –"

"Suggest all you like. Miss Celeste," Carcharodon said, looking up haughtily, but more importantly past McCormack, and clutching one of the harpoon guns tightly in his balled fists, "we're leaving. As the Major pointed out, there's no time to waste."

And with his cowed aide pushing his chair, with heavy trudging steps, Carcharodon and Miss Celeste exited the chamber, Carcharodon calling, "Major Horsley. I'm with you!"

"Lady Denning, would you care to –"

"No I would not care to remain behind either, Captain, if that is what you were about to ask. As Mr Carcharodon put it so plainly, I am as eager to know what has happened here as anyone else. Besides, I might have knowledge that would be of use to a search party," she added cryptically.

"Very well, your ladyship. Mr Wates, I want Lady Denning to go with you."

"Yes, Captain."

"And take the doctor too."

"What? But I don't want to go. I want to stay here!" Ogilvy protested, his anxious expression saying it all.

"Tough," McCormack growled with all the menace of a rottweiler. He turned back to his officers. "And the purser."

"Yes, captain," the Purser and Wates replied together.

McCormack surveyed those that were left. Necessity, having already made strange bedfellows of them all, was now spawning its own inventive arrangements.

"Professor Crichton, I want you with me. I rather suspect you know your way around here better than most."

The ageing professor gave a heartfelt sigh, but then nodded in weary agreement.

"And Selby, come with me too."

"Very good, Mac."

That left Cheng, and the young sweethearts, who had been through more together on this adventure than most couples saw in a lifetime of wedded bliss. "Whatever you want to do, I suppose I can't stop you," McCormack stated, defeated by the situation surrounding Haugland's disappearance.

"We want to do our bit," John Schafer said, clutching the hand of his beloved tightly in his, the two of them exchanging an impassioned look, words now unnecessary between them. Their earnest intentions could not be disputed, one determined to do his bit and cleanse himself of the foolish trust he had had placed in the charismatic killer Quicksilver, and Constance, not only not wanting to be separated from her fiancé again but now also driven by her own passionate desire for vengeance against the murderer of her aunt – a purity of purpose that was frightening to behold in the changed young debutante.

"Then I will go with you," Cheng said, bowing respectfully.

"Let us not waste any more time, or any more lives," the professor said with unexpected steely resolve.

He seemed more clear-headed without his comforting hip flask, as determined to do his part as Constance Pennyroyal, which was just as dramatic a change in attitude, compared to the edgy individual who had disembarked from the *Ahab* on reaching the Marianas base.

Having checked that he had a bullet ready in the breach, Captain McCormack led his party back towards the heart of the base as the others took diametrically opposed routes through the domes and laboratories positioned around the edge of the complex.

Taking this path they found themselves back at the laboratory where he and Miss Celeste had been attacked. He entered with caution this time, pistol raised, just in case.

"So that's where I left it," he heard the professor say and observed, with no small amount of disappointment, Crichton retrieve his battered hip-flask from a work top, and give it a pat like it was an old friend.

"Come on, Haugland's not here. What's through there?" he asked, indicating another door on the other side of the lab.

"We called it the 'Shop'," Crichton said, a faraway look in his eyes.

"Then let's try that."

Leaving the lab again by the other door, the three of them passed along an arterial passageway littered with broken beams and dangling bundles of cables, spilling from the roof like the entrails of a gutted fish, until they reached another of the familiar hatch-doors. The opening mechanism activated with a hiss of compressed air and the hatchway rolled open.

McCormack, Crichton and Selby passed through into a darkened dome. Eyes adjusting to the gloom, the captain could see that it opened out, extending away from them. There was a sharp intake of breath from the professor next to him.

"You've been here before, of course," he said.

"Once. Long ago."

With slow, careful steps, McCormack continued to lead his search party further into the vast chamber. Strange pieces of equipment covered gurneys and work tables, looking not so unlike giant examples of operating implements. Huge pieces of machinery, such as large crane-gantries filled the space, rising away into the darkness of the roof, slack links of heavy chains that would not have been out of place attached to a ship's anchor hung suspended between them. The place looked like a curious cross between a factory floor machine shop and a vast operating theatre.

"God in heaven!" Selby swore loudly.

"What is it?" McCormack demanded, his attention immediately on his chief engineer.

"See for yourself," Selby said, pointing up into the trailing loops of chains.

Hanging there, suspended a good six feet above them, was the limp body of the Norwegian Haugland, a loop of chain knotted tight around his neck. His tongue lolled fat and bloody from his mouth, and his eyes bulged from his puffy purple face.

There was no doubt about it. Thor Haugland was dead.

CHAPTER NINETEEN

Enter the Dragon

"Now, what do you make of this?"

"I suppose it's a pressurised suit, sir, to allow a lone aquanaut to venture out into the abyss without having to be inside a submersible and yet still survive. And by the looks of these," he said, putting his hand to a massive steel claw, "whoever was inside could effect repairs to the reinforced outer skin of the base, or take rock samples from the seabed."

"It's a beauty, isn't it?" said Ulysses with a twinkle in his eye, as if enamoured of the monstrous thing. He reached up to stroke the smooth metal casing of a huge armoured arm, mounted with what looked like a Gatling-style harpoon gun, built-up around the left wrist of the suit.

Mounted on the wall behind them were a number of different attachments – from large drill bits to huge shears – which could be fitted to the wrist mountings of the exo-suit. It looked as though, in the wrong hands, it wouldn't be so much a diving suit as a one-man walking war-machine.

"Yes, or one could use it to break out of an inadequate prison," Ulysses said, a broad grin splitting his face from ear to ear.

There was a sudden loud clang that seemed to reverberate across the outer hull of the pressurized chamber within which the two of them had been imprisoned.

"What was that?" Ulysses was about to say, but there was no need; there could be no doubt.

There was a second crash that rang through the reinforced metal walls of the base as though the whole structure was a colossal tuning fork, the vibration making Ulysses' ears ache.

He looked at his manservant who was wincing in pain also.

"Something tells me it's time we got out of here." he said.

"It's time we got out of here," Selby said as a seismic tremor shook the dome, setting the chains rattling and Haugland's body swinging.

"Agreed," Captain McCormack said, scouring the darkness of the dome above them, as if half-expecting something to burst through the armoured roof at any second.

"And go where?" Professor Crichton demanded, his face ashen, his uncontained trepidation having returned with a vengeance.

"All I'm saying is we should get back to the dock and leave this place," Selby grumbled.

"What? Aboard the *Ahab* or the *Nemo*, with that thing out there?" Crichton exclaimed.

"Nothing but death awaits us here!" Selby shouted over the noise, staring at the dangling corpse of the Norwegian, the lifeless body swinging from side to side like a pendulum.

"You have a better idea, professor?" McCormack challenged.

Crichton stammered a response but it went unheard as another more violent crash shook the complex, louder now and seeming nearer.

"No, I thought not. Then follow me. Back to the dock!"

"Back to the dock!" Wates called, his ringing footfalls increasing in pace as he led his team past the habitation pods. The purser was having no trouble keeping up, although both Dr Ogilvy and Lady Denning were gasping for breath. With her ladyship he put it down to her age. With the doctor, from what little had picked up, withdrawal symptoms were the most likely explanation. "Come on!" he called. "Try to keep up!"

As he ran, Wates was becoming increasingly aware of a creaking, groaning sound, singing from the steel structure of the ageing complex around them like eerie distorted whale-song. Whatever was happening to the base elsewhere, the years of salt-decay and sea-rust were beginning to take their toll, as the ringing clangs threatened to upset the uneasy equilibrium the structure of the Marianas Base had so far managed to maintain thousands of feet below the sea.

The huge water pressures, coupled with the Kraken's predations, were starting to work on the damaged structure in ways that could only lead to one outcome.

Rounding a bend Wates suddenly caught sight of another door ahead of them. "We're almost there," he gasped.

"Come on, your ladyship," the purser called from behind him. "And do keep up, doctor!"

"How far is it?" Lady Denning spluttered.

"Not far now!"

"What's that?" Wates said, suddenly distracted as his ringing footfalls on the grilled metal floor turned to wet splashes and he felt the uncomfortable chill of near-freezing seawater at his ankles.

He faltered in his run, the purser almost colliding with him as he too splashed into the spreading pool. The water was coming from the far end of the passageway, from where the door that would lead them back to the sub-dock stood firmly shut. Papers floated in the encroaching shallows.

"That can't be good," the purser managed, his face turning pale. "Should we go back?"

"What's the matter?" Lady Denning asked, staggering up to them, gasping for breath. "Oh," she said, the sensation of wet and cold at her feet causing her to lift the hem of her already sodden dress, "I see."

With a cacophonous groan of rending metal, a noise so painful to the ear that Wates half-expected to see the hull of a ship ploughing through the side of the tunnel, the ceiling opened up above them. Sheet metal, structural beams, utility cabling, along with flakes of rust and disturbed dust, rained down upon them. Reacting by instinct alone, the four threw themselves out of the way, falling in an untidy heap amidst the detritus and the sloshing water, throwing their arms around their heads to protect themselves from falling debris.

When the echoes of the catastrophic cave-in had died away again, leaving in their wake the protesting groans of the facility's superstructure, and when the abyssal depths didn't rush in, drowning them all, the four of them sat up and took stock.

"I'd say we won't be going any further that way," Wates said stoically.

"And I'd say we're trapped!" Dr Ogilvy shrieked.

"I've not had to endure all I've been through for it to end like this!" Lady Denning suddenly shouted, pent-up rage and frustration finding a sudden release. Struggling to her feet, she offered a hand to the purser, who was sitting on his rump in the cold lapping water. "Come on," she said, looking back along the passageway, "this way."

"This way!" Harry Cheng called back over his shoulder. "We have to get back to the dock. It is the only way." He waded onwards, splashing through the water that was sluicing around their calves, pistol in hand ready, just in case.

Behind him, John Schafer and Constance Pennyroyal struggled on, with single-minded resolve, the two of them united now in their determination not to be beaten by the predations of the beast outside the base, or the one trapped inside with them.

"Don't worry about us, Cheng," Schafer said. "We're right behind you."

The further they went, the further the water level rose. If the rest of the Marianas Base was in the same state as this intermittently lit corridor, then they really were in trouble.

Another bone-shaking tremor passed through the passageway, the vibrations creating rippling waves skittering over the water, and sending the three of them stumbling forwards. Far away they heard a metallic scream, as if part of the structure was giving way. Their situation had changed from merely desperate to downright disastrous. And then he saw it.

"Come on, my friends," Cheng said, the smile growing on his face brightening the tone of his voice, as he indicated the closed bulkhead door ahead of them. "There's no time to lose."

"There's no time to lose," Ulysses said, gazing up into the myriad bottle-glass 'eyes' of the pressure suit's domed helmet.

The metal surface of the exo-skeleton was tarnished, having been left to rot deep beneath the sea in Marianas Base, but Ulysses was confident that it would serve their purpose.

"Here, give me a leg up, old chap," he told Nimrod, "and I'll have us out of here in a jiffy."

"Very good, sir," his sullen-looking manservant said, assuming the necessary position at the back of the deep sea diving rig, hands locked together at the fingers, palms held upwards.

Ulysses put his hands on Nimrod's shoulders to steady himself, and a foot on the hand-step his butler had created. Yet another juddering quake shuddered through the structure and, in response, the base groaned an ominous cry of its own, the superstructure starting to lose cohesion in the face of the monster's relentless attack.

"I would hurry, sir, if I were you," Nimrod added, his eyes widening in horror as he gazed, transfixed, through a tiny porthole that revealed the ocean depths beyond. "As you said yourself, there's no time to lose."

Only a matter of a hundred yards from the spot where Ulysses' was struggling into the pressure suit, the leviathan beast of the abyss pulled back in a rush of jet-siphoned water, before launching another attack on the base.

It bore fresh scars from its battle with the Megalodons, but the stump of a tentacle that had been so viciously severed by one of the giant sharks – an ageing bull – had already healed and was even showing signs of new growth. Within a matter of days, it would be as if the tentacle had never been taken at all.

Rocketing forwards like a torpedo blasted from one of the submersible boats of Her Majesty's Royal Navy, the Kraken slammed into the dome beneath it. At the last second it splayed its tentacles wide and seized the frustratingly stubborn structure in its suckered grip, hinging wide its massive angler-fish jaws.

Its repulsive body pulsing, the squid-beast delivered a massive bio-electrical burst of energy, ten thousand volts of raw power, to the outer surface of the dome. Much of the charge dissipated into the water around the base but inside lights flickered, the air crackled with the odour of burnt ozone, and Babbage consoles sparked, igniting small fires within the mildewed laboratories.

The creeping tips of the creature's tentacles sought out weak points within surface of the structure, as it's implanted hunter's instincts were pre-programmed to do. The pulsing signal coming from inside the underwater complex had driven it into a frenzy. It would not stop until it had retrieved the source of the signal and destroyed it. One probing limb uncovered a ruptured seam in the outer skin of an access tunnel and teased the metal free, peeling it like a banana skin and letting in the sea.

Sensors positioned along the dorsal line of the squid-monster's body detected the change in the pressure around it. Releasing its hold on the docking dome, the Kraken twisted its whole body to face whatever it was that was approaching.

The prow of the submarine emerged from the eternal gloom, heading directly for the Marianas base and on an intercept course with the monster. As the Kraken turned to meet this new threat to its supremacy, it presented its left side as a clear target to the submarine's already oncoming torpedoes.

The two missiles struck the beast full amidships.

The abyssal darkness, pierced only by the beams of the submarine's lights and what little luminescence shone from the glass bubbles of the Marianas base, became even more obscured in the aftermath of the twin detonations. Purple ink-blood clouded the water, distorted by the swelling watery sphere of the expanding explosion, pieces of pallid grey-green flesh amongst the debris.

The submarine ploughed on through the mess and murk, swaying as it entered the shockwave, chasing after the leviathan. But by the time it cleared the debris beyond the perimeter of the undersea complex, the Kraken was gone.

"We're saved!" Captain McCormack exclaimed. Bursting back into the dive preparation chamber, the escapees initial entry point, he, and those with him, caught a glimpse of the submarine that had driven off the Kraken, its sleek gun-metal grey shape cutting through the darkness like a blade of shining steel.

Selby and Professor Crichton followed his gaze beyond the glass bubble at the crest of the dome, expressions of bewilderment becoming grimaces of disbelief which slowly transformed into smiles of joy.

"I knew it. They are here!" came another excited voice from behind McCormack, the man's English accent Oxford-perfect.

Harry Cheng stopped at the entrance to the chamber, John Schafer and Constance Pennyroyal stumbling past him, their own faces going through the same contortions as those of the professor and the chief engineer.

"I am sorry to disappoint you, Captain, but I think you'll find that you have been prematurely presumptuous."

McCormack turned. Cheng had moved away from the chamber entrance, so that no one could get the jump on him from behind, the gun in his hand trained on the captain.

"Cheng? What do you think you're playing at, man?"

"I am not playing at anything, Captain McCormack, I can assure you," the Chinaman replied. "What I am doing, however, is taking over."

"Taking over?" Schafer said, stunned.

"Yes, Mr Schafer. I am taking over. And as long as everyone remains calm, as I respectfully ask of them, no one need get hurt."

Cheng's attention was suddenly drawn back to the captain who, without moving and going for his own weapon, had turned his face towards the two engineers standing guard before the pressure suit chamber door.

"Captain, I would advise you against trying anything you might see as being heroic."

Even as he spoke, Clements and Swann, having lip read the instructions their captain had mouthed at them, went for their own weapons, moving from in front the hatchway as they did so.

Two shots rang out, sharp and loud in the confined, echoing space. Two thudding clangs followed as two bodies crumpled onto the steel deck.

Constance gasped. McCormack stood, mouth agape.

"Do not doubt my single-minded dedication to achieving my aims," Cheng said, training his gun back on the captain, having only given the two engineers the most cursory of glances. "I have no qualms about killing everyone here, if it will help me achieve my goals. However, as honour dictates, I would prefer not to cause any unnecessary loss of life."

"So, it was you all along," McCormack said with furious, deepening conviction.

"If you are referring to the mysterious disappearances and deaths, then I can assure you that you are mistaken. And you can take my word for that, for what would I have to gain in the current situation by lying?"

The sound of running footfalls broke the stunned silence that followed Cheng's words.

"What's going on? Captain?" Mr Wates asked stumbling to a halt as he entered the chamber.

McCormack saw his officer going for his own holstered weapon.

"Wates, don't you dare," he commanded. "That's an order!"

Mr Wates froze on the spot, as the rest of the small group that had accompanied him stumbled into the dome after him.

"Oh my God!" Dr Ogilvy shrieked as he saw Cheng, the gun and the dead engineers.

"Doctor, that goes for you too," McCormack commanded.

"All of you, over there," Cheng said, gesturing towards the chamber containing Ulysses and Nimrod with the muzzle of his gun. "And drop your weapons."

The command was following by a clattering of pistols and other weapons, falling to the grille-mesh floor.

"What do you hope to achieve by this coup of yours, Cheng?" McCormack challenged. "You are but one man."

"But again you are mistaken, captain. I am one man with the entire crew of a submarine preparing to dock with this facility and take control of it."

Without taking his eyes off the party gathered in front of him, Cheng jerked his head towards the glass-bubble apex of the dome. McCormack and a number of the others could not help risking a glance upwards. Through the mote-shot murk above them, they could see the submarine returning, illuminated by its own running lights.

With a moaning howl that surprised everyone, including Cheng, the timorous, self-serving doctor suddenly launched himself at the Chinese double agent.

"It can't end like this! I won't let it end like this!" he shrieked. Startled, Cheng stared open-mouthed at the doctor as he stumbled towards him, arms flailing, completely thrown by Ogilvy's unexpected reaction. "They used me. I wasn't a willing member of their ring!"

And then the doctor was on him.

Cheng stumbled backwards, wrong-footed. Ogilvy fell into him.

The crack of a pistol shot rang out again, made unreal by the weird acoustics of the space.

Ogilvy's body tensed then went limp.

McCormack was already moving as Cheng pushed the doctor's body from him. Ignoring his own gun that he had been forced to discard moments before, deciding in that split second that in the time it would take him to retrieve the weapon, aim and fire, he could cover the distance between him and the Chinaman. He judged wrongly.

The pistol barked a fourth time.

Having driven off the monstrous squid-beast, the Chinese sub finished making its turn and powered back towards the underwater facility, preparing to enter the Marianas Base. From there the Chinese would be able to seize the very technology that controlled the creature.

The only warning the crew of the sub had that they were in any danger, apart from a brief sounding on their sonar, was the appearance of a pulsing blue light through the soup of protoplasmic murk behind them. And then the beast rushed them out of the smothering darkness.

Patches of flesh were missing from its flanks, something like gleaming steel exposed beneath, and there were cracks in its own armour plating. But none of its injuries seemed to be having any effect to its detriment.

Despite its vast size, the Kraken was able to react quicker than the submarine, and was the more agile by far. Where the squid-thing had been able to take evasion action when the submarine had made its attack run, when the tables were turned, the submarine was too cumbersome to turn quickly enough to meet the Kraken's counter-attack, as the hunted became the hunter, and the hunter became the prey.

The monster seized the vessel all along its length with its muscular crushing limbs. A tentacle twisted and a propeller came away. Electrical discharges with the power of a lightning strike shook the sub, disrupting all its internal mechanical and electrical components.

As the craft lost motive power and its crew any means of controlling it, the Kraken's immense, crushing jaws closed around its rear-section. Teeth like spears of steel, ruptured fuel tanks and ballast tanks. Sucker-tight tentacle-arms twisted and pulled, and the armour-plated hull of the vessel ruptured.

The Chinese submarine and its crew had no chance against the beast's assault.

Screams from inside, smothered almost into silence by the thickness of the hull, could still be heard, the vibrations of its terrified prey reaching the Kraken through the superstructure and the many sensors placed along its grasping tentacles, exciting the creature even further.

Its hull breached, the colossal hydrostatic pressures of

the unfathomable weight of water pressing down on top of the vessel claimed another victim for the abyss.

With a whoomph of escaping air, the submarine imploded.

Harry Cheng stared in horror at the glass bubble above, as debris from the destroyed submarine drifted down onto the dome, ringing against the structure like the ominous tolling of a giant bell.

One by one Cheng took in each of his eight captives. The captain's foolish act of misplaced heroism had cost him dear. He sat slumped against the wall of the dome, with John Schafer and Constance Pennyroyal either side of him, trying to make him as comfortable as possible, propped up as best they could manage with whatever came to hand. He had a hand held tight to his stomach, a pad of bandages from the party's make-do first aid kit cinched tight against his midriff. His sodden shirt was stained red across his middle. He face had taken on a horrible grey pallor and his skin had a waxy sheen to it, wet with perspiration. Dr Ogilvy still lay between Cheng and the rest of the party, face down and unmoving.

"Not such the big man now, eh, Cheng?" McCormack gasped between pained grimaces.

"Captain," Cheng said with something approaching his usual calm manner, "I think you'll find that I am still the one – how does the saying go? – holding all the aces." He gestured with the gun as if to emphasise the point.

With a torturous screeching of metal, the hatch buckled and then swung suddenly outwards. Automatically Cheng turned his gun on the door as a huge shape pushed its way into the chamber. Twice as tall as a man, and almost twice as broad, the huge diving pressure suit exo-skeleton barely made it through but its pilot was deter-mined.

Gasps of shock and squeals of surprise rose from the mouths of the captives as they scattered, despite the Chinaman's screams that they stay where they were. The massive machine-suit bore down on the Chinaman whose gun barked again, and again, and again. The pressure-resistant armoured suit deflected each bullet in turn, all the time Ulysses Quicksilver's manic face visible within the dome of the helmet, made even more sinister by the reflected eerie green glow of the instrument panel in front of him.

The crushing steel claw – that had made light work of the hatch's locking clamps – swept down, smacking the weapon from Cheng's hand. The Chinaman reeled under Ulysses' attack and fell down hard on his backside.

The claw came down again. With a whirr of grinding servos, the pincer opened, before closing around Cheng's shoulder. The agent gritted his teeth against the pain, but couldn't help crying out as Ulysses lifted him off the ground, the suit's hydraulics lending him strength far beyond that of a normal man.

The dome shook again, provoking more cries from the over-wrought party, but Ulysses maintained his balance in the heavy suit, its feet weighted, although he lost his grip on the Chinaman as he reflexively opened his hand, ready to stop himself should he fall. Cheng crashed back down onto the mesh floor, whimpering in pain.

Glancing upwards, Ulysses saw the terrible maw of the Kraken again as it renewed its attack on the base. But, his preternatural senses sending him another warning, he returned his attention to Cheng, who was now struggling to escape from the pressure-suited colossus, kicking his feet against the floor for purchase, shuffling backwards on his backside.

A thin metal cylinder rolled across the floor where it had fallen from Cheng's pocket. A red light pulsed rhythmically.

The dome shook again, the dim lights flickering in protest.

Without a second thought, Ulysses punched the Gatling-harpoon fist into the floor, smashing the metal tube beneath it. The bulb exploded and the pulsing light died.

It took Ulysses a moment to realise that in the same instant as the metal cylinder stopped broadcasting its recurring signal, the sea monster's attack had also ceased.

In the shocked silence that followed the cessation of the Kraken's determined assault, Ulysses' breakout from his incarceration and the shift in the balance of power, everyone heard the piercing scream, that came from somewhere beyond the chamber. Ulysses' sixth sense flared once more, like a burning coal dropped into his skull.

It was a woman's scream and there was only one woman left among the party of so-called survivors from the *Neptune* who was not already present in the chamber.

It was Jonah Carcharodon's PA.

It was Miss Celeste.

CHAPTER TWENTY

Project Leviathan

"He's dead!" Professor Crichton exclaimed.

"And whatever gave you that idea?" Ulysses Quicksilver said, raising a sarcastic eyebrow.

There could be no doubt about it. Major Marmaduke Horsley was dead. The shaft of a harpoon protruded from his not inconsiderable belly, its barbed tip buried in the wall behind him.

Ulysses turned to face Jonah Carcharodon, an expression like thunder contorting his usually calm features. "And you say you know nothing about this?" He stared pointedly at the discharged harpoon gun resting on the old man's lap.

The rest of the group did the same.

There were seven of them gathered at the back of the archiving dome, including Carcharodon and his emotionally exhausted PA. The survivors had reacted instantly when Miss Celeste's screams had rung out through the base, carried by the distorting acoustics of the place.

Ulysses had led the way, piloting the immense pressure suit towards the corridors beyond the dome. But it immediately became apparent that the suit was too large and would hamper his progress so, boldly, he shut it down and clambered back out of the machine.

There was an awkward moment where the now defenceless Ulysses came face-to-face with Mr Wates, who had leapt to recover his pistol as soon as Ulysses had Cheng on the run. Selby was there, ready to back him up should the need arise. But there was something about the intensity of the look in Ulysses' eyes, in the way he said, "You have to decide who to trust!", and what Miss Celeste's screams were telling them that were enough for Wates to let it pass – at least for the time being.

So it was that Ulysses, Wates, Selby, Crichton and Nimrod, following his master from their breached cell, had rushed to the rescue, while Lady Denning and Constance Pennyroyal had remained where they were, finding the reserves of energy from somewhere to see to the captain, while John Schafer and the purser restrained the duplicitous Cheng.

Forced to follow those curving corridors still left intact they had soon found themselves inside a musty-smelling archive, filled with tumbled shelves and filing cabinets. A Babbage unit stood in one corner of the room but it did not look like it could be in any kind of working order; a film of algal slime covering much of it, and eating away a number of the files stored here, having spread to the cataloguing shelves.

"I told you! I discharged my weapon during the confusion of the Kraken's attack," Carcharodon protested. "We were descending a ramp into another of these godforsaken labs, still searching for Horsley when the attack came."

"Well, it certainly looks like you found him," Ulysses couldn't help throwing in.

"Scaffolding came crashing down," Carcharodon went on, as if he hadn't caught Ulysses' interjection, "and Celeste let go of my ruddy chair again. Went arse over tit, *again*, which I don't mind saying I'm getting more than a little sick of."

Ulysses gave the magnate's beleaguered PA's shoulders another comforting squeeze. She was even more of a mess than she had been before, dust having been added to her generally dishevelled appearance.

"Gun went off in my hands! By the time Celeste had pulled herself out of the wreckage I had already managed to right my chair myself. And then we came face to face with that," he said, pointing at the dead Major's skewered body. Carcharodon's complexion was pale, his eyes ringed grey with tiredness. A large purple bruise was blossoming on the left side of his face, an oozing graze above it. He did not look at all well, but was it as a result of shock or fear that his guilty little secret had been found out?

"And besides, who are you to accuse me?" he snarled, finding some of his old fire again.

"I don't remember accusing you," Ulysses said with icy calm.

"Well, no, but you as good as said so with your meaningful looks and that ruddy waggling eyebrow thing of yours. Well, I'll not stand for it!"

"I didn't think you stood for anything anymore."

"And since when did you go from being prime suspect to judge and jury?"

"I would say since someone else was murdered whilst Nimrod and I were happily tucked up inside our little make-do cell. Wouldn't you?"

"He does have a point, sir," Selby butted in.

Carcharodon could think of nothing to say in reply to that, so he merely sat in his chair quietly fuming to himself.

"So what now?" Wates asked, showing Ulysses the deference he would have normally reserved for Captain Mc-Cormack, obviously quite happy now to look to him for leadership in their steadily worsening situation.

Ulysses didn't answer Wates' question but instead appeared to have become distracted by the contents of the room in which they now found themselves.

Lying discarded on top of a filing cabinet, amidst reams of data printouts, were two dusty, sepia-toned photographs. The first was only small, five inches by four, and was a picture of a child, a young girl. She couldn't have been more than about six years old, Ulysses judged. She was wearing a pretty pinafore dress and had ribbons tied in her long fair hair. She was beaming at the camera, holding her dolly in one hand.

He recognised two things within the photograph, the doll and the room in which the picture had obviously been taken. It was the central chamber of the complex in which they had found the mummified corpse.

The second photograph was larger and formal in style. It showed a team of people arrayed in two rows, those in front seated. This picture had also been taken with the central lab-dome as its backdrop. Ulysses could tell from the uniforms and lab-coats that this was a record of members of the military-scientific team that must have worked here in the past. Chances were that it was their belongings that were now washing around the partially flooded corridors of the collapsing base. There were no children in this photograph, although there were a number of severe faces that Ulysses recognised.

Seated in the front row was a younger version of Jonah Carcharodon and he was still an invalid even then. He looked older than the rest, but there was less grey in his hair, his face less jowly, his eyes brighter. The second person he recognised in the front row was Professor Maxwell Crichton, his round spectacles and spiky hair unmistakeable. Seated directly next to him was an attractive woman, with her hair arranged in a bun on top of her head. Ulysses was taken aback by her beauty – she had been quite a looker in her day – but there was no mistaking her either, now having spent so long with her in such close company. It was Lady Josephine Denning. And next to her was seated the army-formal figure of Major Marmaduke Horsley.

There were two others remaining in the front row of the photograph. He did not recognise either the emaciated man with the walking stick, who looked like he had already been old when the picture was taken, or the significantly younger, bearded fellow. But there was still one other, among the nameless scientists, mechanics and naval personnel – standing at the end of the row behind the seated dignitaries – whose striking appearance stunned Ulysses to the core. The last person he had expected to see amongst the group in the photograph was Hercules Quicksilver, his own father.

Ulysses stared at the image in disbelief, only dimly aware of the discussions of the others taking place around him. He turned the picture over in his hands. Written on the back in a languid copperplate hand were the words:

Project Leviathan, February 1972.

Ulysses turned slowly to the professor who was still staring dumbstruck at the dead Major.

"Professor Crichton," he said, holding up the picture. "What is this? What is Project Leviathan?"

Crichton turned his eyes from Horsley's glassy stare and Ulysses could see that, behind the round lenses of his glasses, the man's eyes were glistening wetly. He opened his mouth to speak but before he managed to get a word out, his bottom lip quivering, he fell to his knees, as his body became subsumed by gut-wrenching sobs.

"God forgive us!" he spluttered, just as he had done upon encountering the body in the chair. The old, spineless professor had returned, his tougher, more resolute alter ego gone.

It was uncomfortable to hear a man making such a womanly sound, sniffing noisily between sobs, snot running from his nose, tears streaming down his face. But after all that had happened – incarceration, assault by deadly sea monster, attempted coup – Ulysses' patience had reached the end of its tether.

The dandy strode up to the downcast man, grabbed him by the lapels of his ruined suit and hauled him to his feet.

"Oh, for God's sake, pull yourself together, man! What is Project Leviathan? Tell me, Professor!"

With shaking hands, Crichton pulled his hip flask from his pocket – that old familiar, spirit-sapping crutch – unscrewed the cap and took a gulping swig. As the warming alcohol coursed through him, the professor seemed to find some of that lost resolve again.

Bringing his sobbing back under control, he took the photograph from Ulysses' hands.

"I thought I would never hear the name of that god-forsaken project ever again," he said, still catching his breath, wiping the mucus and tears from his face. "We all swore never to speak of it."

Rather than badger the professor with more questions – no matter how desperately he might want the answers to them – Ulysses gave him room to make his confession.

"We all swore never to speak of it again," Crichton repeated himself.

"They why speak of it now?" It was Carcharodon who was now attempting to derail the professor's confessional.

"Do not interrupt!" Ulysses barked.

Realising that he was dealing with a man on the edge,

Carcharodon fell silent.

"Go on, Professor."

"We believed our intentions to be honourable. It was all for the greater good of the Empire. To create bio-mechanical constructs, weapon-creatures to protect Magna Britannia's interests at sea. But in reality it was an act of the greatest hubris against God and nature. I can't even tell you about the experiments the German exiles were said to be carrying out on live human specimens."

The professor looked close to emotional collapse again. He paused and took a deep breath.

"But we were all equally to blame. We all had our roles within this blasphemous exercise. Carcharodon's company provided the ships to transport everything here, Umbridge Industries built the base itself." He paused, and pointed at the emaciated elderly man in the photograph. "That's Josiah Umbridge there."

"And he was the one prevented from coming on this trip due to ill health?" Ulysses asked rhetorically, putting all the pieces of the puzzle together.

"He sent that fellow Sylvester in his place, yes." Crichton resumed his story. "Lady Denning and myself were brought in because of our expertise in the fields of marine biology and evolutionary biology to help Seziermesser and his team of Frankenstein Corps exiles here," he pointed at a white-coated, also bespectacled, haughty looking scientist, "to create the hybrid-vivisects themselves."

"Hybrid-vivisects?" Ulysses couldn't help interrupting at hearing this.

"The Kraken, if you prefer. The amalgam of the Architeuthis Dux with genetic material from a number of other marine creatures, so that it might exhibit the properties of those species. There are the obvious accoutrements, of course, of the electric eel, crustacean armour and the melanocetus jaws, but other creatures had their parts to play as well. For example, the prototype also had grafted into its genetic matrix the attributes of Asterias Rubens, the common starfish, and anemones. It can regenerate damaged limbs, even re-grow other parts of its body, allowing it to recover from significant injury, given time."

Ulysses felt like he was sitting in on one of Professor Crichton's lectures. For a brief moment he caught a glimpse of the scientist at his most relaxed, talking about that which interested him the most – his work.

"Professor, you said they were bio-mechanical constructs," Ulysses said intrigued, trying to get to the heart of the matter.

"Well, yes. We needed some way of controlling them after all and marrying the mechanical to the biological made them even more effective and resistant to damage. Felix Lamprey, this man here," – he pointed at a young, bearded man – "designed both the creatures' internal endo-skeletons, including the mechadendrite tentacle cores, and also programmed the Babbage-unit adapted nervous systems. That was our way of controlling them. He was an undisputed genius. Until he lost it."

"Where did you collect your monstrous specimens from in the first place?"

"From the trench, of course. That was where Horsley came in," Crichton said melancholically, nodding at the still skewered Major. No one had thought to take the body down with everything else that was going on. "Big game hunter, wasn't he? He provided the expertise by which to hunt and trap the colossal squid living down there."

Ulysses paused. There was one last thing he wanted to know about, more so than Felix Lamprey's implied mental instability.

"Professor," he began cautiously. "Did you know my father?"

"Oh yes. We all knew Hercules Quicksilver."

"Then what part did he have to play in Project Leviathan?"

Crichton took another pull on his flask before answering. There couldn't be much left in the silvered container now.

"I believe his title was that of Observer. He was the face of the Empire down here in these damned abyssal depths."

"And what did you mean by Lamprey losing it? What happened to him?"

The professor suddenly froze and tensed, his face becoming a contorted gargoyle grimace.

"Professor?"

Crichton's body tensed again involuntarily and he fell, pole-axed, onto the floor with a painfully loud clang. The others surrounded him in a moment but there was nothing any of them could do. The professor was fitting, joints seizing, hands contorted into paralytic claws, spittle foaming from between vice-tight jaws.

"Professor!" Ulysses shouted helplessly. Just as the old sod had started to give him some idea of what might be going on, this happened. Could it be something other than coincidence?

"What's wrong with him?" Carcharodon squealed, his face pale as ever.

"He's suffering a seizure," Wates said. "It's like he's having a stroke,"

"I've seen this sort of thing before," Nimrod revealed.

"Go on," Ulysses encouraged.

"The introduction of certain neuro-toxins to the human nervous system can have such an effect."

"Which toxins?"

"Those naturally produced by some animals to help protect them against attack from larger predators. Sea-urchin venom, for one."

"But he hasn't come into contact with anything like that since we've been stuck down here," Selby said. "Has he? I mean there's not a mark on him to say that he has, is there?"

Ulysses picked up the hip flask from where the thrashing Crichton had dropped it. He sniffed at the open neck of the container. There was the heady aroma of alcohol and... something else.

"He didn't have to have been stung. He could have ingested it."

Renewed looks of horror spread throughout the group.

"Our killer has been busy."

The fitting Crichton's body tensed one last time and then his muscles relaxed and he lay motionless on the cold hard floor, his eyes wide open, the flicker of life within them faded. Nimrod felt for a pulse.

"The professor is dead."

"I see it now," Ulysses said, in a tone of wonder, as if he was experiencing an epiphany of sorts. "Carcharodon, what was the outcome of Project Leviathan? Why have I never heard of it? Why did everyone involved swear never to speak of it again?"

The shipping magnate met Ulysses' intense stare with one of his own. "I do not see how raking over something that happened a quarter of a century ago is going to be of relevance to our situation now."

"What? You can't be serious!"

"You heard what Crichton said. We swore."

"And look where that's got us! This has all been planned from the start only I couldn't see it. But now I have one more piece of the puzzle in my hands. Someone has tried to lure as many members of Project Leviathan here as they can and is now bumping them off one by one."

"I do not wish to discuss this matter any further."

"What sordid little secrets are you so determined to keep hidden?"

"I do not wish to discuss it!"

"Well we better had start discussing it, because unless I find out what's going on here, people are going to continue to die, Carcharodon!" Ulysses bellowed. "And you could be next!"

CHAPTER TWENTY-ONE

Lamprey's Legacy

Ulysses Quicksilver stormed back into the sub-dock anteroom, shoving a scowling Jonah Carcharodon in his chair before him.

"Horsley's dead," he announced, "Crichton's dead and you, Lady Denning and Carcharodon, are the only surviving members of Project Leviathan left on this base. You're the only ones left and this stubborn old fool," he roared into the cowed Carcharodon's ear, "refuses to tell me what happened to the project. Would you be so good as to tell me what the hell's going on before we all die here?"

"Mr Quicksilver? What do you mean?"

"Know anything about poisons, do you, your ladyship? Specifically neuro-toxins synthesised by certain sea creatures to defend themselves from potential predators?"

"Well, yes, I do," the older woman admitted, wrong-footed by Ulysses' bizarre tangential line of questioning, shocked by both his approach and the revelation that two of her erstwhile colleagues were dead. "In my work as a marine biologist."

"Care to elaborate?"

"Well, there are various species that employ such a method of defence, sea urchins, sea snakes and the like. Many of them produce toxins powerful enough to kill a man. But I don't understand. What are you getting at?"

"Professor Crichton just died of a neuro-toxin induced stroke," Ulysses revealed, with all the lurid panache of a Grand Guignol theatrical compere.

"Oh my God," Lady Denning gasped, covering her mouth in horror, as did a number of others around the room.

"I know all about Project Leviathan, Lady Denning. I know that you were here, twenty-five years ago, part of the team that created the monster that's been hounding us ever since our, as yet, unknown saboteur sent the *Neptune* plummeting to this watery hell. There's no point trying to deny it. Tell me, what happened to Felix Lamprey?"

"You've already seen for yourself," the marine biologist stated coldly.

"What? Enough riddles, Lady Denning. I want the truth, plain and simple. Tell me now! Tell us all!"

"In the chair, in the central chamber. I was not there at the end, but it couldn't have been anyone else. Of that I am sure. Felix Lamprey is the mummified corpse in the chair."

Ulysses called to mind the macabre discovery sat in the massive chair contraption in the central laboratory chamber, the curious helm upon the desiccated corpse's skull, the bullet hole in the middle of its forehead. Another piece of the puzzle was slotting into place.

"There's more you're still not telling me!" Ulysses snapped. "Tell me everything!"

"If you know of Project Leviathan, then you know of the auspices under which we all worked," she began. "We all had parts to play, that is true, but it was Lamprey who made everything work together. He was the genius who managed to programme a semi-organic entity to do as it was commanded. And not only that, he was able to use all of his technical know-how to cram all of the control mechanisms inside a helmet that transferred the controller's commands to the creature at virtually the speed of thought. He was undoubtedly a genius when it came to thinking machines and artificial cognisances. But then his daughter arrived."

"His daughter?" Ulysses thought of the photograph he had found in the archive.

"Little Marie," Lady Denning said, tears glistening at the corners of her eyes.

"How did her arrival change things?"

"I suppose, to put it simply, Lamprey had an attack of conscience. He had been so bound up in his work here at Marianas Base, determined to find a solution to every problem, driven by the question of could it be done, that he had never stopped to think whether it *should* be done. I suppose not many of us did. And if we had, then the question was always answered with the same platitude, 'For the greater good of Magna Britannia'. We had the security of the Empire in mind when we set about creating that beast out there."

Her words trailed off, as if she were reconsidering now her own attitudes towards the matter, or as if she were living in the moment of the memory.

"So what happened?" Ulysses pressed.

"His wife and little Marie were coming for a scheduled visit when their ship was attacked."

"Attacked?"

"We were told in strictest confidence that it had been the Chinese but there were those among us, Lamprey included, who suspected that the truth was something much worse. Rumour had it, that one of the test subjects had gone rogue during a field test. Some claimed that the beast attacked and sank the ship, mistaking it for a viable hostile target before it self-destructed. There were a handful of survivors, Marie amongst them, left bobbing on the surface in their lifeboats to be picked up by the Royal Navy rescue teams, but Lamprey's wife – little Marie's mother – she didn't make it.

"Her father now her sole guardian, Marie came to live with him here, at the base. It wasn't normal practice but then these were exceptional circumstances, and Lamprey was one of the senior members of the team.

"I suppose seeing her face, day in, day out, reminded him of what his work had cost them both. Lamprey's grief and overriding sense of guilt slowly wore away at his sanity until he went over the edge, and by that point it was too late to do anything to stop him.

"To his credit, he had tried to warn us," she said, a distant look in her tear-misted eyes. "He did try to persuade the others to abandon the project but, of course, our secret masters back in Whitehall wouldn't listen. And so he initiated the destruction of the base by the Kraken, using the control helm he had developed."

Lady Denning halted in her narrative, an icy silence following her words as all those listening considered the implications of what she had told them.

The sense of everything he had witnessed since arriving at Marianas Base was all becoming so much clearer now to Ulysses, like a smog lifting from the polluted streets of Londinium Maximum. The damage he had seen visited upon the base all made sense now too. The state of disarray in which they had found the place, as if it had been abandoned in a hurry, because it had.

"So, I take it, when the onslaught began that full evacuation procedures were initiated."

"Exactly so, Mr Quicksilver. Some died. Most escaped alive."

"And what happened to Lamprey?"

"I told you, I was one of the first to be evacuated. From what we have seen here tonight, I'd say someone managed to put an end to Lamprey before he was able to initiate the ultimate destruction of the facility. With, what we believed to be, the total destruction of Marianas Base, the project was deemed a failure and officially 'forgotten about' by those that had plotted it all from the start."

Ulysses considered the possibilities for a moment.

"And what happened to the girl, Marie?"

"That's the most tragic part of the whole affair. Such a young life, snuffed out."

"She was killed by the Kraken? Or by whoever did for her father?"

"I don't know," Lady Denning admitted angrily. "Her body never turned up. She was classified as missing, presumed dead, just like her father."

"And now history's repeating itself," Ulysses said.

"Yes," Lady Denning agreed. "It has a nasty habit of doing that."

A tremor rumbled through the base, this time lasting longer than any that had shaken the facility so far.

"Well, I know what we need to do now," Ulysses said confidently.

"And what is that, sir?" Nimrod enquired.

"We evacuate again. We take the *Ahab* or the *Nemo* and we get out of here before the beast brings this place down on all our heads."

"You can't be serious!" the purser blustered, obviously terrified at the prospect. His world had been shaken to the core when his commanding officer had been injured. Any nerve he might have once had had now deserted him.

"And what else are we supposed to do? Wait here until we either drown or end up as the next course on the Kraken's banquet?"

"But we can't go out there, against that, in those!" the purser was ranting, in danger of losing any semblance of rational behaviour altogether. "We don't have any means of fending it off."

"He's got a point," Selby added, speaking up for the first time in a long time. "The bloody thing's damn well near indestructible anyway; it's armoured and it can regenerate parts of itself."

"So what do you suggest?" Ulysses threw back. An uncomfortable silence returned.

"Quicksilver's right. There's no other way." It was Captain McCormack who broke the silence, his words laced with teeth-gritting groans. "Get out now, while you still can."

"But what about the captain?" Lady Denning asked, indicating her patient.

"Oh. Yes," Ulysses stumbled, blindsided. "How is he?"

"Not good," the captain gasped, wincing with the effort of answering for himself. His voice was thick with saliva and he coughed, bubbles of blood bursting on his lips.

It was only then that Ulysses realised that the doctor's body had been moved.

"Where's Ogilvy?"

"There," Schafer said, pointing to a space behind one of the curved iron buttresses that supported the internal structure of the dome. Ulysses could just see the top half of the doctor's body around the end of a strongbox, his face and torso covered by his own jacket.

"Oh. Did he say anything else before he died?"

"Oh yes," the purser replied. "Kept going on about how it wasn't his fault, how they had used his own weaknesses against him to ensnare him. He was delusional at the end, but it seems as though he thought Agent Cheng was going to take him in for the part he had played in an opium smuggling ring."

Ulysses was suddenly sharply reminded of the initial

reason for him joining the *Neptune's* maiden round-the-world voyage, to track down the source of the supposed smuggling ring. That was before the murder of Glenda Finch, before the act of sabotage upon the sub-liner, before the Kraken. It was strange to think now that this hadn't all been about the Kraken, the murders and the sinking of the *Neptune* right from the start.

"He might have been a washed-up narcotic-addled fool, but he didn't deserve that!" Lady Denning cried, directing her bile at Cheng, where he sat handcuffed to another of the pillar-buttresses.

Ulysses turned and, with purposeful steps, approached the defeated Chinese agent. "And what do you have to say for yourself?"

Cheng looked up at him with hooded eyes but said nothing.

"You weren't lying when you confessed to being a double agent, were you? Only I didn't realise that you were a turncoat to such a duplicitous degree, working for the Chinese Empire, making your Magna Britannian bosses believe you were on their side, leaking them secrets, only to use the information you gained in return to get back in with your slanty-eyed masters back in Beijing!

"But tell me something," Ulysses said, drawing even closer now to Cheng's sourly scowling face. "All this," he indicated the dome around them, "Project Leviathan. It was all going on a quarter of a century ago. Why now? What put you on to the possible existence of this place?"

Cheng took a deep breath and then, apparently deciding that confession was good for the soul after all, began. "There's been rumours of monsters in and around the Marianas Trench for as long as seafarers have plied these waters but in more recent years unexplained disappearances seemed to have been on the increase. Occasionally we would even find evidence, remains from the aftermath of such attacks. And then a long range scouting patrol turned up a survivor of just such an attack.

"He'd been in the water for days, drifting on a sundered piece of hull, and was suffering from the effects of exposure as well as dehydration. It's a wonder that something else didn't snap him up before we found him. Didn't last long either, but long enough to tell us that he had been part of the crew of a tramp steamer, six days out from Shanghai. He told us what had happened, what he had witnessed. He had no reason to lie.

"As you like to put it, Mr Quicksilver, all the pieces of the puzzle fitted then. We knew the beast that had taken the *Venture* for what it really was, a bio-mechanical weapon, engineered during the long cold war that has been fought between our nations for decades. But then I suspect you know this already."

"And if your government could steal the technology that had been created by Project Leviathan, they could then put it to use themselves, perhaps even take control of the creature."

"Precisely, Mr Quicksilver."

"And the homing beacon you triggered. It all makes sense now!" Ulysses exclaimed. "That's what brought your allies here in their sub only for them to be wiped out by the one thing they were after, because the same signal that drew them here also worked on the cogitator part of the Kraken's brain. It must have driven it insane, and brought it here as surely as it summoned your yellow brethren."

The dome shook once more, another tremor, like the presaging of a deadly seaquake.

"It's time we were gone," Selby stated bluntly.

"But if you all go now, and the true killer is one of you," Cheng suddenly piped up, a cruel smile of smug satisfaction on his lips, "don't you risk taking the murderer with you?"

"Don't think you're getting out of this that easily, Cheng," Ulysses spat. "You're coming with us."

The smug look vanished from the Chinaman's face in an instant.

"Everyone's in this together. It's in everyone's best interests to help us get out of this alive. I've said it before: our killer's not the suicidal type. This is revenge, pure and simple. They want everyone involved with Project Leviathan to suffer, for a reason, and to know about it. They'll not be able to get out of here without the rest of us. At least this way, we buy ourselves a little more time.

"So, back to the dock. John, Mr Wates, can you bring the captain with you? Nimrod, bring Cheng. And Mr Selby, if you would be so kind as to lead the way?"

"Well the *Ahab* and the *Nemo* are both still seaworthy and ready to go when we are. But there's a problem," the chief engineer confessed.

"There's enough fuel for our journey to the surface, isn't there?" Captain McCormack managed, from where he hung limply between John Schafer and Mr Wates.

"The subs aren't the problem –" Selby started to explain.

"So what is?" Carcharodon bellowed before Selby managed to complete his explanation.

"It's this place. The base. Some automated failsafe or other's kicked in. Must have been after that thing out there commenced its attack. The whole place is on lockdown."

Ulysses looked from Lady Denning to Jonah Carcharodon, the latter now with his assistant back to pushing his chair.

"The same thing must have happened last time, twenty-five years ago, when Lamprey tried to bring an end to everything."

"Yes!" Carcharodon snapped. "What's your point, Quicksilver?"

"So how did everyone get away that time?"

"I remember now," Lady Denning said, a growing sense of excitement colouring her words. "The lockdown was overridden. The correct access codes were entered and the pressure gates opened." Her face fell almost as quickly as her tone had brightened.

"Do you know those codes now?" Ulysses asked, already knowing the answer.

"I never knew them, I'm afraid, Mr Quicksilver."

"And you?" he asked Carcharodon.

"I was privy to them then, yes. But you don't expect me to remember them now, do you? It was twenty-five years ago, for God's sake!"

"Then we're stuck here," Ulysses said with cold finality.

"No, wait. There may still be a way," Lady Denning dared. "Lamprey designed and programmed the supporting cognisances used to control the bio-weapons, as well as the cogitator systems that operated the base – that are *still* operating the base – the logic engines which were the precursors of the Neptune AI."

"Of course!" Carcharodon shrieked in excitement. "If we could somehow link up the Neptune AI to the base's core cogitator systems – the ship's still out there, isn't it after all? – we could use it to crack the codes for us using a simple repeating algorithm."

"But how do we do that?" John Schafer said.

"I can answer that one," Captain McCormack coughed, his breath rattling in his chest. "One man, in a pressure suit could exit through an airlock – they all have manual overrides – return to the *Neptune*, find the AI chamber and initiate a link with Marianas Base."

All eyes looked back towards the entrance to the dive chamber where the motionless pressure suit still stood, where Ulysses had abandoned it.

"Well done, McCormack, that sounds like a capital idea. And I do believe I'm just the man for the job!" Ulysses said, a daredevil glint in his eye. "What do you say, captain?"

But Captain McCormack said nothing. For captain McCormack was already dead.

CHAPTER TWENTY-TWO

Ghost Ship

"Wish me luck then, old boy," Ulysses' voice crackled from speakers built into the exterior of the pressure suit, just beneath the bulbous fishbowl helmet.

"Good luck, sir," Nimrod offered obligingly, and Ulysses squeezed himself through the hatch into the airlock.

The solid circular door closed behind him with a clang and through the external comm-relay Ulysses heard the locking clamps shunk into place. The dull, droning siren that signalled that the airlock had been activated began to sound and the huge suit was bathed in a slowly circling amber light.

Using the techniques he had learnt during his time with the Monks of Shangri-La to keep his nerves at bay, with a pang of regret Ulysses recalled the last time he had heard the sound, and was reminded of the old woman's terrified face caught in that same orange light.

Having decided that Captain McCormack's dying piece of advice to them was the only way any of them were going to get out of Marianas Base alive, and having made sure that Cheng was now securely handcuffed to a roof support – John Schafer keeping a gun on him at all times – Nimrod, Selby and the indefatigable Mr Wates had accompanied Ulysses towards the airlock. As Nimrod had helped him back into the cockpit position of the hulking pressure suit, the engineer and the *Neptune* officer made sure that the suit's internal oxygen supply was hooked up properly and working efficiently, providing Ulysses with breathable air at the appropriate pressure.

The outer door of the airlock was shut using the manual controls inside the chamber and, once the water had been pumped out, air pumped in and pressures equalised, Selby opened the inner door again.

Ulysses swept his gaze around the small chamber, having to turn the huge suit from the waist to be able to take it all in from his cabin position, macabre curiosity getting the better of him. Of course there was no trace of Miss Birkin left inside the airlock now.

Since Whilomena Birkin had died, the first member of the party to lose their life since arriving at the Marianas Base, another eight people had lost their lives in that accursed place. Thor Haugland, the engineers Swann and Clements, Dr Samuel Ogilvy, Captain Connor McCormack, Major Marmaduke Horsley and Professor Maxwell Crichton. Four of them had died at Harry Cheng's hands alone, thanks to his deadly marksmanship. But four had died at the hands of the mysterious Marianas murderer. He sincerely doubted that Cheng and the Marianas murderer were one and the same. As far as he knew, Ulysses was leaving the rest of them behind with the killer in their midst.

He didn't like it, but he didn't see that he had any choice. If he didn't risk life and limb himself, then none of them would be getting out of Marianas Base alive. And he would rather be out there, trying to do something about it, than be one of those waiting behind, trapped like a caged animal, putting his future well-being into the hands of another. There weren't many he trusted with that responsibility.

But then perhaps the murderer wasn't one among their party at all. Perhaps there really had been a stowaway who had somehow escaped the *Neptune* with them, hidden on one of the submersibles, and who was now lurking within the passageways of Marianas Base, biding their time, picking off the members of the team that had worked together on Project Leviathan one at a time. But it was highly unlikely, Ulysses reasoned.

The alarm still sounding, amber hazard lights whirling like miniature lighthouse beams, vents opened and water began to flood the chamber. The outer door creaked open, the two halves of the opening hatch looking like blunt-toothed metal jaws. But was he escaping the hungry maw or entering into it, freely and willingly? Ulysses wondered as he took his first lolloping strides out into the abyssal depths beyond.

Adrenalin was rushing through his bloodstream with every pounding heartbeat, the excitement, trepidation and urgency of the moment all working together so that Ulysses' mind and body were operating at their maximum fight-or-flight-heightened potential.

He was aware of an ominous creaking sound with every step he took, just like those unsettling noises that had formed an almost constant background soundscape when he had been inside the Marianas Base with the others. But there he had quickly become used to blocking it out, so that after a short time he didn't notice it at all. He wasn't sure if the same would prove true now, as those same sounds reminded him that all that was stopping the mass of water all around him from crushing him flat as a pancake was the armoured suit.

From where he sat, harnessed within the cockpit, Ulysses' arms and legs reached into the armoured limbs of the suit, any movements he made magnified by the machine so that the monstrous appendages moved as if they were extensions of his own arms and legs. He could also drive the suit using controls in front of him in the cockpit.

So now, as he moved his legs inside the body of the pressure suit, so the mechanical legs of the contraption strode forwards, carrying Ulysses along the edge of the trench towards the place where the wreck of the *Neptune* still lay precariously balanced.

Cooped up inside the *Nemo* as the small submersible had chugged towards Marianas Base from the *Neptune*, the distance between the two locations had seemed long enough. But now Ulysses realised how quickly that journey had passed in comparison.

The prone shape of the *Neptune* lay ahead of him, still a good hundred yards away, teetering at the brink of the bottomless abyss. He could see that it had moved again since the refugees had escaped the flooding wreck. It now appeared to be resting more on its keel again, caught in a wide fissure in the crumbling sea-cliff beneath it, so that it had more or less righted itself. However, with such dramatic shifts taking place, Ulysses wondered how long he would have before the drowned sub-liner took its final voyage to the bottom of the Marianas Trench. He pressed on: there was no time to lose.

Each slow step kicked up silt from the rocky bed underfoot. He had not realised how slow progress was going to be, but he couldn't make the massive exo-skeleton move any more quickly had he wanted to. With a sudden cold pang of fear he remembered the Kraken. Dull booms carried by the dense water around him, and relayed to him both by the suit and its external pick-up mikes, told him that the monster was still labouring away at the devastated facility.

Intrigued, he dared to pause in his advance and *bodily* turn back to look for himself. His first anxious thought was how little distance he seemed to have covered on his *route* march across the seabed. The second was how huge and terrible the Kraken was. Its sheer size alone was threatening enough but its primal, aggressive temperament and appalling strength, married to a primitive determination, made it ten times worse. As Ulysses watched, the squid-beast tugged at a piece of the base's superstructure that had come free of its pile-driven moorings and cast it away, letting it tumble slowly into the hungry trench beyond the spur where the facility sheltered.

Turning back to the *Neptune* he plodded *ever* onwards, skirting the edge of the abyss, heading for the sunken liner, not daring to look back *again*. After all, it was now or never. Either he would make it in time or the Kraken would do for him first, and he was not about to encourage the latter by dallying here any longer.

And then, at last, he was standing in the shadow of the massive super liner. To see such a magnificent vessel brought low like this, made Ulysses fear the Kraken even more. That something could bring down so vast a ship was almost incomprehensible. Worse things really did happen at sea.

Ulysses entered the *Neptune* through a vast hull rift, giving him access to the bilges and engineering decks. It was dark inside the ship and there wasn't anywhere left within the vessel that wasn't flooded, at least not as far as his penetration of the ship revealed. In places damage caused by the Kraken's attack and the action of the sea working on the beleaguered superstructure had created further obstacles for him to overcome. Fortunately the servo-hydraulics of the suit increased his strength tenfold, allowing him to pull huge iron stairways out of his path and wrench open bolted hatch doors.

The lights projecting from the helm chased away the bizarre creatures that called these abyssal depths home, and which had already begun to colonise the dead wreck, dining upon the choicest morsels of the brand new banquet the sinking of the *Neptune* had provided for them. Slithering albino ragworms, skittering near-translucent shrimps and warty, black-skinned fish, every one of them as ugly as sin.

The pressure suit having effectively doubled his size, Ulysses could only just squeeze down some of the corridors at these lower levels, making his journey even more challenging. The other factor which made his expedition all the more arduous were the bodies. He had seen death in all its myriad forms more times than he cared to remember, but that didn't make it any easier, seeing the bloated, bulging-eyed corpses that had become trapped within the buckled passageways; crew, passengers, men and women, even children. The place had become a veritable ghost ship.

He also passed the occasional droid-automaton, the drudges non-operational now, the seawater and dreadful hydrostatic pressures having done for their delicate internal workings. But he continued to make steady progress as he negotiated the tortured passageways of the flooded wreck nonetheless, using the cutaway deck plans of the ship located at regular intervals to help check his progress, until he finally made it to the heart of the vessel.

Forcing open the doors bearing the *Neptune's* trident crest, Ulysses pushed through the space between them and entered the AI chamber. Having seen what the sea had done for the ship's automata crew, he only hoped that the significantly more complicated Babbage systems of the AI were better shielded and, as a result, still operational, otherwise they were all doomed.

Apart from obviously being entirely flooded and in utter darkness, Ulysses seeing everything through a particle-suffused murk of chill sea-water, illuminated only by his suit lights, the chamber did not look significantly different to the one and only time Ulysses had been here before.

The green-topped desk stood in the centre of the room before him, although the chair that was normally tucked in behind the control console was floating against the ceiling above him. Ulysses considered the keyboard of the Babbage terminal and then considered the massive pincer claw and Gatling harpoon gun gauntlet of his right hand. This wasn't going to be easy.

Carefully he manoeuvred the gauntlet hand over the control console and depressed the button recessed into the top of the desk. Ulysses held his breath, hoping against hope, not only that the artificial intelligence was still operational but also that the input terminal was also working.

He thought he heard a faint bleep and then, with a definite click, the cover on the opposite wall slid open, the screen humming into life.

"Thank God for that," Ulysses said to himself as he let out a pent-up heartfelt sigh. "Or should that be, thank Neptune?"

The start-up image of the trident logo on a calm blue sea glowed into life, bathing the room in ghostly white light. The artificial waves appeared to ripple in the current swirling within the chamber with Ulysses' every movement, magnified by the hulking diving suit.

A prompt appeared on the screen.

USER:

The Purser had hopefully provided him with all the information he needed – codenames, passwords and the like. Slowly he entered the late captain's name, keying in each letter with careful movements of the massive gauntlet's index finger.

Another prompt appeared.

PASSWORD:

Ulysses could see that this was going to be slow progress, typing with one finger.

There was a jolt and Ulysses had to steady himself. The ship had moved again. Not very much, but enough to emphasise the point that he didn't have long. And here he was having to type like an imbecilic child.

All he had to do was initiate the link and set the AI's systems to cracking the codes that would open the sub-dock doors and free those still trapped inside the base. But, there was so much more he wanted to do before he had to quit the ship. He had been given unprecedented access to the Neptune AI and all the secrets it contained.

His suspicions about what was going on were stronger than ever now, the possible identity of the culprit at the forefront of his mind. And he hoped that the AI would be able to help him uncover the last pieces of the complex puzzle this mystery had become, and confirm the psychopath's identity.

After all, some still unidentified saboteur had used the Neptune itself to initiate the first phase of the sub-liner's destruction. And what was it that Glenda Finch had been trying to tease from the data files of the all-knowing AI?

He entered the last letters of the captain's password and then hit the enter key.

The synthesised voice of the artificial intelligence came to him in a buzz of static, relayed through the intercom speakers built into the helm.

"Hello, Captain McCormack," the AI said in a softly

spoken voice that would be forever England. "It is good to hear from you again."

With careful, patient movements, with the ship creaking and shivering around him, Ulysses set to work.

The ship groaned and shifted once more, the complaining sounds of metal under stress the *Neptune's* death rattle. The hull fissure was before him now. With pounding steps, moving as quickly as the bulky suit would allow, Ulysses powered towards the breach.

And then he was through. He dropped back down to the seabed, only a matter of feet from the precipitous edge of the black maw of the trench, his landing causing impact craters to appear in the silt and sand beneath the heavy weighted boots. Without pausing for a moment's thought, Ulysses kept moving forwards, towards the devastated domes, visible as no more than shadow-shapes in the murk, barely lit from inside. He was abruptly aware of how bright his own suit's spotlights must appear in the torpid darkness. But then, such feelings of conspicuousness and inferiority compared with what awaited him out there in the abyss could not crush the growing sense of excitement and euphoria welling up inside him.

He had risked life and limb but it had all been worth it, he thought with a burgeoning sense of elation. Not only had he been able to initiate the required link to the Marianas Base, and thereby hopefully help save the lives of those trapped inside, he had also been able to wheedle the other information he had wanted from the inner enigmatic workings of the Neptune's Babbage brain.

He had accessed the AI's log and had it confirmed for him that someone – and chances were it had been Glenda

Finch, using another's identity – had accessed files about the Carcharodon Shipping Company's accounts, just as McCormack had told those at the briefing after her death that now seemed like weeks ago, but which in reality must only have been the less than forty-eight hours before. More importantly, he also knew that whoever it was that had initiated the sabotage sub-routine had logged on as 'Father'.

These were indisputable facts, facts that would help him uncover the true villain of this tragedy, the one responsible for the deaths of so many, not only those murdered in the last few hours, but the thousands who had died when the *Neptune* went down.

He felt the seismic tremor of the sea-bed moving uncomfortably beneath him, like some great whale disturbed from its rest. He stumbled, not daring to stop and look back, knowing that time had run out for the *Neptune* at last. He ran on, at least he moved at what approximated to a run, hampered as he was by the grinding servos of the suit. It had been constructed for diver-engineers to work at static points outside the safety of the scientific facility. It had not been designed to win races.

He kept on, pushing the suit as hard as he dared. There was no telling how the ship might go. It might even swing round, slam into him and carry him over the edge with it. So he kept moving forwards, at the same time angling his course so that he was moving further and further away from the edge of the precipice, hearing the scraping of the ship as it grated across the sea-bed, the metal of its hull groaning in protest. Ulysses only hoped that the AI cracked the codes before the link was lost and the ship pitched into the crushing depths.

Then the cacophonous noise of the sliding vessel subsided and ceased, and so did the seismic juddering Ulysses felt through the heavy feet of the suit. Was the sub-liner gone? Had it plummeted over the edge and was it, even now, sinking to its final resting place, far beyond the reach of man?

Ulysses stopped and swung the suit round. The *Neptune* was still there, although in an even more precarious position than it had been before. It was lying along the edge of the abyss now, fully one third of its length suspended over the impossible drop.

He heard a crack as loud as a thunderclap, as if some colossus had broken a giant stone egg against a submerged mountain peak. Alarm bells rang inside his head as blood turned to ice in his veins. He had to keep moving.

The suit pounding across the seabed, ever carrying him towards the beleaguered base, Ulysses saw the fissure appear to his left and race away ahead of him. Rock shifted beneath him, slid sideways, dropping the section of seabed across which he was moving by several feet. His pulse thumped in his chest and in his brain. It seemed undoable now, impossible, but when had that ever stopped him?

An entire shelf of rock at the edge of the precipice had splintered free of the rest of the sea-bed, giving way under the weight and movement of the shifting sub-liner and weakened by the explosive destruction of the vessel's engines.

With a roar like pebbles being ground on a beach by the surf, only a hundred times louder, the cliff gave way, boulders the size of houses tumbling into the hungry darkness, taking Ulysses, helpless now, trapped inside the pressure suit, with it, down into the unfathomable depths of the Marianas Trench.

CHAPTER TWENTY-THREE

The Belly of the Beast

As the heavy suit dropped like a stone, plunging Ulysses into the untold depths on his back, watching the trench wall slide past, the lip of the precipice disappearing from view, he found himself wishing that he had fitted a grappling hook extension before embarking on his mission. Ulysses wondered how long he had before the ever-increasing hydrostatic pressures crushed the suit, and his body locked inside.

Now he came to think about it, there was a painful building pressure in his ears. Straining to peer through the bubble of the helm he was certain he saw a depression forming in the casing of the suit's left forearm. A rainbow of fairy lights began to blink on and off across the instrument panel in front of him. A discordant tinny beeping sounded in his ear.

A wave of nauseous panic washed through him and he wondered how many more seconds he had before the reinforced glass in front of his face cracked. With an audible pop, a spotlight imploded, the beam projecting into the gloom from his left shoulder snapping off.

Everything about the suit flashing him hazard indicators and blaring sirens in his ears, Ulysses' own sixth sense screamed loudest of all. But he could see nothing; there was no sign of any approaching threat. At least, not from above.

There was a metallic crunch as something closed around him and suddenly he was hurtling upwards. The trench wall raced past as if Ulysses were riding an express elevator to the surface. Straining his neck to see every which way he could out of the helmet dome, through the myriad porthole windows Ulysses saw saw-edged teeth, each the size of a man's hand, row upon row of them rolling back into the massive jaw clenched around the suit. He saw pink flesh, his remaining spot-beam revealing flapping gills and a pitch-black cavernous gullet.

Ulysses could hear a cracking, creaking sound, suggesting that the enclosing jaws were trying to close even tighter. The pressure suit had resisted the terrible forces that tons of water pressure per square inch had worked on it, and was now resisting the crushing forces being applied by the massive shark's jaws. But Ulysses couldn't be certain how long the suit could hold out. After all, he had seen with his own eyes what a Megalodon had done to the bio-mechanically engineered marvel that was the Kraken. The huge fish had, like as not, been surprised to find what it had considered to be a tasty morsel dropping into its abyssal home was then more resistant to its attentions than it had expected, but that sense of surprise wouldn't last for long.

Activate weapon systems, Ulysses told himself, his own imperative helping him to focus his mind on the matter in hand.

With his right hand he pulled hard on the trigger lever built into the suit's right arm. At once the Gatling-style harpoon gun opened up. Short, barbed quarrels tore through the flesh of the monster's jaw, shredding its gills, leaving ragged white flesh in its wake, black blood trailing from the savage wounds Ulysses had dealt the prehistoric fish.

The Megalodon's jaws were enormous, but Ulysses, encased inside the equally impressive pressure suit, was much bigger than a normal man. The giant looked like it could swallow even a Great White whole, but the dandy adventurer was something else. Ulysses fought hard.

A vast shadow passed across his field of view, his remaining spotlight illuminating a circle of grey-green underbelly as the form soared passed.

There was another abrupt lurch, this time as the Megalodon's speeding progress slowed, and another, jolting Ulysses hard within his harness. If it hadn't been for the restraining straps, Ulysses would surely have brained himself against the reinforced glass and steel in front of his face.

The shark's jaws spasmed, opening again, and Ulysses dropped from the huge mouth.

He could see the ruins of Marianas Base directly below him now, the devastated outer domes, the fractured tunnels, the dim lights of the still intact central hub. The Megalodon's attack had carried him right over the facility.

Ulysses dropped feet first, the leaden weights in his boots drawing him back down towards the seabed. It looked like he was going to land within the man-made canyon of rusted steel between two bulkhead domes, all that was left of another gutted laboratory-cum-weapons-testing facility, a mere hundred yards from the airlock access. Lady Luck, or the god of the sea, was certainly smiling on him now.

He was moving before he even touched down on the solid seabed beneath him. That now seemingly ever-present dull throb of his subconscious warning him flared again and, instinctively, Ulysses turned.

He saw the severed head of the Megalodon, jaws open wide, its black pearlescent eyes bulging, dropping through the water.

Above it he saw a demon's maw of even more terribly

distended jaws crunch down on the rest of its huge forty-foot long body, devouring it in three economic mouthfuls.

He saw an ensnaring net of boneless arms pull back around the squid's mantle, fanning out around the hideous alien head of the beast, ready to strike, as the dead head of the giant shark bumped against a spar of sheered metal.

"There's always a bigger fish," Ulysses muttered.

Not waiting to see what the Kraken would do next, Ulysses turned and, with thudding steps, pounded towards the relative shelter of the dome wall in front of him. In his mind's eye he could see the creature behind him, as it readied to strike, hooked tentacles whipping forwards, ready to send a thousand volts of electricity through his body, cooking him inside the armoured suit. The thought spurred Ulysses onwards.

He felt the whoosh of the water surging around him, saw the shadow above him, caught a flicker of a tentacle paddle sweeping past him, and then was hurled forwards by the rippling watery shockwave of the monster colliding with something solid, something that was not Ulysses in the pressure suit.

On his hands and knees now, Ulysses risked looking behind him again. An unalloyed whoop of joy broke from his lips as, in his adrenalin-heightened state, he saw the Kraken trying to untangle itself from the skeletal ribs of the ruins, the outer limits of which Ulysses had passed beneath before the monster could seize him.

"The one that got away!" he laughed, punching the wall with the balled fist of his harpooning arm in delight. The open outer pressure gate of the airlock was within reach.

The blaring siren died, the amber light stopped spinning, and, locking clamps disengaged, Ulysses was able to open the airlock door in front of him. Easing himself through the round hatch, he stepped back inside the Marianas Base, his feet clanging hollowly on the steel-mesh decking.

He was feeling suitably pleased with himself. Not only had he had an encounter with both a Megalodon and the Kraken and lived to tell the tale, he had freed those left inside the facility from Lamprey's legacy and he knew who the murderer was! From this moment on, Jonah Carcharodon was a man with a price on his head.

Ulysses was convinced that it was he who was responsible for the murders. The information ferreted away within the Neptune's Babbage data banks had provided him with the missing link that now made sense of the mystery. The billionaire's shipping line was in trouble, suffering serious financial difficulties. The building of the *Neptune*, which had wiped out Carcharodon's personal fortune, had been a last ditch attempt to improve the company's portfolio and raise the value of its stock again. But construction costs and running costs, with this project more than any other as it had turned out, far outstripped the income that could be derived from selling berths on the cruise-liner. Ulysses supposed that Carcharodon had planned to sink the *Neptune* and claim on the insurance. With the ship lost to the Marianas Trench there would have been no way for anyone to effectively check up on his claim. But discovering that Glenda Finch was onto his fraudulent little scheme, and the subsequent intervention of the Kraken, and then believing Miss Birkin was onto him as well, he had had to ensure that there were no other survivors to contradict his story. Glenda's initial attempt at investigative journalism had turned Jonah Carcharodon into a desperate man, driving him to become a murderer. And who would have thought it of an old man confined to a wheelchair? Who but Ulysses Quicksilver?

But such epithets of self-satisfaction were put to the back of his mind as two facts regarding the reality of the current situation pressed in upon him.

Firstly, Ulysses had expected to be greeted by at least some of the team who had seen him off, Nimrod at least. But there was no one. A nauseous feeling began to creep into his gut, knotting his intestines with the cold, clenching claw of horrified realisation. Had he been wrong to leave his manservant behind, alone? But what else could he have done? There had been no other way of reversing the lock down.

And secondly, there was the countdown.

"T minus nine minutes and counting," the voice of Neptune boomed from speakers set into the roof cavity of the dome-chamber, the voice that had sounded so soft-spoken and gentle when he had heard it in the quiet of the AI chamber now sounded as ominous and echoingly thunderous as might the strident wave-crashing voice of the God of the Deep himself.

But what concerned Ulysses more than the booming presence of the Neptune AI within the Marianas Base, was the fact that he didn't know what it was counting down to.

And then Ulysses noticed a third change that must have occurred within the last hour when he wasn't there. The already dim lights were dimmer than ever before and flickering fitfully. Power relay cables hung from the ceiling like streamers and he wondered what other destruction had been wrought by the Kraken in his absence. He could only hope now that he was not too late, that the Neptune AI would complete its task and crack the necessary codes before the damage wrought by the monster finally overwhelmed the facility and proved the end of them all.

"T minus eight minutes and counting," Neptune spoke again, the coldly detached voice crashing from the steel walls like the sound of the trench shelf collapsing into darkness.

Ulysses turned towards the access way leading to the sub-dock.

Then Neptune spoke again. "Decryption complete. Access codes accepted. Lockdown reprieved. Target achieved. You may now exit Marianas Base at your leisure, Captain McCormack. I wish you a safe and pleasant journey."

Ulysses' momentarily renewed feeling of triumph – that he hadn't been too late after all – was quickly replaced by feelings of confusion and equally compounded feelings of unease.

"T minus seven minutes and counting," Neptune boomed, increasing Ulysses' fears.

If the AI hadn't been counting down to the completion of the task he had set in the guise of the late captain, then what was it counting down to?

Ulysses stomped into the dock, his weighted footsteps clanging from the hard floor. The scene that greeted him rooted him to the spot, leaving him wrestling with a near-overwhelming mix of emotions: feelings of horror, guilt, fear and despair.

By the light of a swinging electric lamp, dislodged from its mounting in the vaulted roof of the dock space and penduluming now back and forth at the end of a length of rubberised cabling, he saw –

– Lady Josephine Denning dead, body stiff as a board,

eyes wide open, too much of the whites showing, pupils contracted to pin-pricks, the test tentacle they had found back in the abominable lab lying on the deck beside her, shrivelled and charred, its attached energy source discharged –

– John Schafer, spread-eagled beneath a fallen pillar, groaning as he tried to shift the metal beam from on top of him –

– Nimrod, unmoving, unconscious, a puddle of blood oozing from his scalp –

– Agent Harry Cheng struggling to free himself, pulling at the loops of his handcuffs, rubbing his wrists raw until they bled, trying to use his freely running blood to help lubricate the manacles and allow him to escape –

– two more bodies, this time those of Wates and the purser, bobbing on the surface of the disturbed pressure gate pool, facedown, both of them having been shot –

– bubbles rising to the surface of the choppy waves in the wake of the passing of the *Ahab* as the submersible sank beneath the water and powered out through the blossoming pressure gate and free of the Marianas Base, leaving the rest of them behind, to their fate.

CHAPTER TWENTY-FOUR

Sins of the Father

"T minus six minutes and counting."

The continuing countdown shook Ulysses from the stunned stupor that had momentarily overcome him. He had been on the verge of being overwhelmed as the shock he felt on seeing the scene of death, devastation and despair before him took hold. To have battled against all the odds to lift the lockdown – risking life and limb aboard the doomed *Neptune*, having to contend with first an attack by a giant prehistoric shark and then confront the Kraken – and to discover it had all been for naught had almost been too much for his exhausted mind to bear. To find Lady Denning murdered and both Nimrod and Schafer apparently left for dead, with the *Ahab* steaming away with, he had to assume, Carcharodon holding Constance, Selby and his poor PA Miss Celeste hostage. What had it all been for if they were to die here now? But he wasn't about to let that happen!

Now, suddenly the passage of time seemed hyper-real to him, as if his strange extrasensory perception was working in a new way, time slowing to accommodate everything that needed to be accomplished in what felt like, on the other hand, no time at all. He could almost feel the individual seconds ticking by.

He activated the controls within the suit again and strode forwards.

In the hulking pressure suit, the armoured exo-skeleton dented and gouged from the attentions of the sea and the monsters that dwelt within it, Ulysses Quicksilver strode across the dock, armoured boots clanging against the metal floor.

"T minus five minutes and counting."

He reached the spot where Schafer lay pinned beneath the fallen pillar, the young man struggling to free himself, desperation writ large across his sweating, contorted features.

Ulysses paused for only a split second to look again at Nimrod's unconscious form lying nearby. Then he reached for the steel beam. Catching the pillar in the pincer-claw of the suit, the notched clasping pads gripping, the metal of the beam crumpling fractionally as they did so, he heaved. The pillar shifted and Schafer groaned, with relief at being freed at such a crucial juncture and with pain, as the injuries he had sustained flared.

Wincing, Schafer struggled to work himself free.

Grasping the other end of the length of steel with the automated right gauntlet hand, Ulysses strained again, heaving on the controls inside the cockpit, as his protective suit struggled to move the beam out of the way. With the beam moved safely away from Schafer, Ulysses let it drop. The steel crashed onto the decking with a resounding clang, bouncing once with the force of its fall.

Ulysses tried to kneel down beside Schafer to help him, but the bulky suit hampered him. The injured Schafer stared at Ulysses through the glass discs of the sturdy helmet dome, the look in his eyes one of hopelessness and intense personal desolation.

"How badly hurt are you?" Ulysses asked.

"I've been better," Schafer replied. "My left leg hurts to buggery but I suppose I'm lucky."

"It could have been worse." Ulysses agreed.

"Although right now, apart from the fact I could be dead already, I can hardly see how it could be worse."

The young man's love of his life was gone and Ulysses knew there was no way that she could have left willingly, after everything else that could have torn them apart during their descent into disaster having failed to do so.

He didn't need to ask what had happened, or where Constance had gone. The answers to such questions wouldn't speed a resolution to their desperate situation and there would be time later, if there was to be a later, if they made it out of there.

Ulysses needed Schafer with him; he needed every able bodied man to play his part, if those left behind by the escaping *Ahab* were going to get out of this alive.

"T minus four minutes and counting."

"John, stay with me. We're going to get Constance back!" Ulysses declared. "But, right now, I need you to see to Nimrod. I need you to tell me the old boy's going to be all right."

Schafer just stared at Ulysses, his face wracked with a mixture of shock and disbelief, fear and grief. He looked like he was about to breakdown and lose all control.

"Come on, John!" Ulysses bawled. "Is he breathing? Does he have a pulse? Is he going to live?"

Schafer blinked as if only just seeing Nimrod lying there for the first time. With tentative fingers he felt for a pulse at the old retainer's throat.

"I-I can feel something. There is a pulse. He's still breathing."

"Destruction imminent. Total destruction of this facility will occur in three minutes. This is your three-minute warning. Evacuate now."

Another seismic rumble juddered through the decking beneath Ulysses' feet.

He swallowed hard. Somehow, someone had initiated a self-destruct sequence that would totally obliterate what was left of the Marianas base. But how? And why now?

He judged that their not-so mysterious killer was to blame, from everything he saw around him. The reason was clear: destroy the evidence, stop anyone – but Ulysses in particular – from coming after him. His calculating mind working nineteen to the dozen he began to see how it had been achieved as well.

In all their time within the facility, they had seen evidence of great difference engines, cogitator banks, analytical calculating machines and Babbage-unit terminals. The macabre chair device had been hooked up to a whole pile of the things. And yet, not once had he seen any of the thinking machines in an operational state. He had assumed that the systems were all dead, but of course he had now received evidence to the contrary. And there was the fact that he had been able to establish a link with the base at all. How stupid could he have been? If it had not been for the restrictive bracings of the suit, Ulysses would have kicked himself.

With Ulysses having established the connection between the Neptune AI and the Marianas Base's cogitator network, waking the sleeping machineries after a quarter of a century's dormancy, someone still within the Marianas Base had utilised the very same link with the sub-liner to terrible effect. They had effectively used the state-of-the-art artificial intelligence to activate long dormant systems, to bring about the destruction of the Marianas Base.

For a moment Ulysses wondered whether the ghost of Felix Lamprey had somehow lived on in the link, everything that made him who he was – his thoughts, his memories, desires, beliefs, disillusionments even – retained within the precision engineered clockwork guts of the chair's difference engine, waiting to be woken when someone turned it on again. Was it possible that perhaps Lamprey was not truly dead at all, those marvellous machineries somehow keeping his mind alive inside the withered husk of his body?

But Ulysses dismissed such hokum as impossible. Surely it wasn't feasible, not after twenty-five lonely years, and it certainly hadn't been a lifeless husk of a man that had done for Miss Birkin, Haugland, the Major or Professor Crichton.

He could only guess at why Felix Lamprey had not used the same method to wipe all trace of the base from the bottom of the ocean. He supposed that, having decided to use the Kraken to bring about the demise of its creators, having strapped himself into the chair, he could not then access the base's difference engines to do anything else, having committed himself. Perhaps access to the difference engines he needed had been compromised. Perhaps there were too many who could have done something to countermand his instructions and prevent the cogitators from making the final countdown, thereby denying him the option of initiating the self-destruct sequence. Ulysses imagined that paranoia had caused the base's architects to include such a system, if the Marianas facility had been erected at the height of the cold war that had been waged between Magna Britannia and its imperial Chinese rival, in case it was in danger of falling into enemy hands. In all likelihood, Lamprey may well have hoped to make his own escape from Marianas before the Kraken wrought too great a level of damage, giving him the precious minutes to get away himself.

However, now, at this allotted time, at this allotted hour, someone had activated that which had being lying dormant within the very foundations of the base, far, far below the ocean waves. Someone insane enough, with their own escape route already planned had used the link to their own advantage, to ensure that any and all loose ends were finally tied up for good.

With a weak groan, Ulysses' faithful manservant, never one to shirk his responsibilities or be accused of dereliction of his duty, stirred at Schafer's touch.

Ulysses felt a surge of relief pass through every fibre of his being. "I knew you wouldn't let me down, old chap," he said quietly, as Schafer helped Nimrod into a sitting position, seeing what he could do for the cut on his head. After all, every able-bodied man would have to play his part, if any of them were going to escape from the base with their lives.

And talking of able-bodied men...

Still encased within the pressure suit, Ulysses cut an imposing figure as he strode towards Cheng's place of confinement.

Harry Cheng physically withered before him, recoiling as much as was possible, given his state of bondage, until Ulysses slammed to an abrupt halt a few feet from him.

For a moment they regarded each other, Ulysses seeing Cheng through the panels of thick glass in the portholes of his helmet, a cowering wretch who had tried to seize control and take over but who had failed, now looking like he was convinced that his time had come.

"T minus two minutes and counting," came the monotonously cheerful voice of the Neptune AI as the countdown continued to echo from the walls of the dock.

Ulysses raised the massive, pincer arm of the mechanised suit above his head.

"Mr Quicksilver, have mercy. I beg your most humble apologies for my impolite actions earlier. It was not my wish that anyone lose their life."

Not a word issued from the speakers of the suit. The

heavy claw hung there, motionless in mid-air.

Cheng pulled back as far as he could, exposing the links of the cuffs against the bare metal of the pillar to which he had been chained. There could be no doubt now that he believed Ulysses was going to finish him.

The claw swept down, describing a slow scything arc. There was the sound of impact, the shearing scream of metal on metal, the jingling of shattered links raining down on the deck, and Harry Cheng tumbled backwards onto the floor.

He sat up, looking at Ulysses with equal parts amazement and elated relief, distractedly rubbing at his bloodied wrists.

"Don't make me regret doing that," Ulysses' voice boomed from within the suit.

Cheng scrambled to his feet. Then, body straight, he bowed low. "I am your humble servant," he said.

"So, Nimrod, you think you can pilot this?"

Easing himself into one of the padded leather seats, Ulysses' loyal aide did his best to make himself comfortable, dabbing at the open wound on his head again with his no longer pristine handkerchief.

"Yes, sir. It shouldn't be too difficult."

"It certainly won't be if I take the co-pilot's seat," Cheng offered, smiling weakly and climbing into the seat next to him.

There was a moment's awkward silence. Nimrod looked back to where his master stood, squeezed into the cabin of the *Nemo*, still encased inside the massive pressure suit. Ulysses said nothing.

"Very well, sir," Nimrod said graciously, his aquiline

features not betraying any emotion whatsoever. "That would be most kind."

"Take us out then, Nimrod," Ulysses commanded, as John Schafer buckled himself into a seat behind the pilots' position.

"As you wish, sir."

Slowly the *Nemo* powered up, its propeller chopping the water noisily behind it, and then, ballast tanks filling, it sank below the unsettled waters of the sub-dock and glided towards the open pressure gate. And then they were through.

Leaving Marianas Base behind – a strange, haunted place that had on first impressions appeared to be a place of sanctuary – the *Nemo* powered after the *Ahab*, already a good hundred yards ahead of their position.

"It's now or never, Nimrod," Ulysses stated soberly, observing the distant shape of the vessel chugging away from them. "We have to catch up with that sub."

"And then what?" Schafer asked.

Ulysses fixed the young man with a thoughtful look through a side port in the helmet dome.

"Don't worry, I'll think of something."

"Sir, I hope you don't mind me asking," Nimrod said. "But you do know what you're doing, don't you?"

"Oh, you know me, Nimrod. I'm making this up as we go along."

"Very well, sir. It is as I suspected."

Seeing the horrified expression on Schafer's face, Ulysses laid the gauntlet hand of the suit gently upon the young man's shoulder.

"Don't worry, old chap," his voice crackled from the suit speakers. "We'll reunite you with your precious Constance soon enough."

"And what of the Kraken?" It was Cheng who threatened to jinx their enterprise with his talk of the sea monster.

Ulysses turned awkwardly in his suit so that he could see beyond the viewing port at the rear of the Nemo's passenger pod. The Marianas Base was already a shrinking conglomeration of broken domes, like cracked open eggs, overshadowed by the cliff-spur above it. And there, amidst the twisted spars and shattered structures the squid-beast wrestled with a stubbornly resisting hull section, caught up in its own frenzied assault, as if it was determined to bring an end to the place that had spawned it, nature using this most unnatural of tools to eradicate what had been begun here twenty-five years before.

"As I said, Cheng, it's now or never. So let's make the most of now, shall we?"

"T minus one minute and counting," the sober English voice resounded around the empty dock, but there was no one left alive to hear it.

"Fifty seconds," the AI told the corpse of Lady Josephine Denning, rigor mortis having locked her body into the pose that electrocution by mecha-tentacle arm had forced upon it.

"Forty seconds," it announced to the floating bodies belonging to the two crewmen of the Neptune, the purser and Mr Wates, gunned down as they had tried to fulfil their obligations to those they had helped save from drowning.

"Thirty seconds," it addressed the dead Captain Connor 'Mac' McCormack, hands still clasped to the ugly wound in his belly, the late Dr Ogilvy and the deceased engineers Swann and Clements, left behind in the dive preparation chamber.

"Twenty seconds," the voice boomed from the intercom panel in the Marianas archive, where Professor Maxwell Crichton lay, his face locked in a grimace of perpetual agony, the venom having done its work with deadly efficiency.

"Ten seconds," the voice of Neptune boomed from speakers in the workshop-cum-operating theatre, its continuing echoes sounding like the slamming of airlock hatches, Thor Haugland's hanging body swinging in its chains as the sub-seismic shuddering increased in intensity.

Nine.

Major Marmaduke Horsley, head hung low on his chest, the harpoon shaft still pinning his body tight to the chamber wall, stared with sadness into oblivion, a glassy expression in his never closing eyes.

Eight.

The mummified body of Felix Lamprey smiled its rictus grin with good reason now, knowing that the insane genius' final master plan would come to fruition at last, after so long a hiatus.

Seven.

Six.

Five.

Four.

Framed within the rear view porthole of the Nemo, the detonation that enveloped the Marianas Base seemed like such a little thing. Nothing really to write home about, Ulysses thought.

But nervous anticipation did set his heart racing again as he saw the Kraken disappear within the expanding sphere of light that suddenly brought stark luminescence to the abyssal night.

Had the abomination been destroyed, caught up within the sphere of destruction, which came like the wrath of the God of the Sea claiming its own?

Tears obscuring her vision, mucus running thickly from her nose and into her mouth, she pulled hard at the life-pod hatch. A blubbering moan of despair issued from between her quivering lips, from deep inside her – so heart-rending a sound from one so young – at last, all her weight hanging off the door handle, she felt the clamp depress in her hands and with a slow gasp of compressed air and the creak of complaining hinges, she pulled the hatch open.

She clambered into the bathysphere capsule with ease, pulling the hatch shut again behind her, young muscles straining as she activated the locking clamps, sealing the pod tight.

In a moment of near panic she tried to make sense of the instrument panel above her head, all winking lights, dials and switches. But then she saw what her father had always told her to look for, on those occasions when he had re-minded her of the safety protocols active within Marianas Base.

She slammed her open palm against a large red button and then collapsed back into the padded seat behind her, trembling fingers attempting to secure the harness straps over her shoulders and across her waist, as the warning siren blared its discordant wail, alerting the bathysphere's pas-senger that it was about to blast free of the base, a sinister crimson light filling the pod with its hellish glow.

She tensed in her seat, eyes squeezed tight shut, teeth

gritted in terror, desperate hands clutching for the doll that wasn't there, her ever faithful companion who could have seen her through this and made her feel better, but whom she had been forced to leave behind, just like her beloved father.

And then, announced by a deafening *clunk-chsssss*, the locking clamps blew, hurling the bathysphere away from the facility, the tiny escape capsule soaring upwards through the miasmal darkness, heading for the surface and safety thousands of feet above, the child howling in anguish, knowing that she would never see her father again.

He was inside the airlock now, the huge suit barely fitting inside the conning tower airlock of the submersible. The *Nemo* was closing on the *Ahab* at last, the smaller sub apparently the faster of the two.

Ulysses waited, with bated breath, his heart thumping hard against his ribs, every sense heightened by the rush of adrenalin pulsing through his body.

The crackle of static interference that presaged the activation of the radio pick-up in his helm was followed by the measured tones of his manservant's voice.

"We are closing, sir. *Nemo* will be in range in three, two, one. *Ahab* in range. It's now or never, sir."

"Now or never," Ulysses whispered, his mouth suddenly dry, his tongue sticking to the roof of his mouth.

"Good luck, sir."

Ulysses punched the emergency eject and the airlock blasted open in a torrent of bubbles and swirling seawater. The abominable pressures working on the craft at these depths sucked out the air, the pressure suit and Ulysses with it.

CHAPTER TWENTY-FIVE

Sea Change

Bubbles of escaping air blinding him, the hull of the *Ahab* nothing but a blur in the whirling confusion of light from the one remaining suit spot and the surrounding hungry darkness of the deep, Ulysses flung out the left arm of the suit. As the pincer touched the second sub, he pulled hard on the closing mechanism built into the arm, the effort of his exertions jarring his shoulder just as much as if it had been his own arm that had grabbed hold of the speeding vessel. The pincer teeth seized a protrusion on the outside of the *Ahab* and snapped shut, biting into the fin they had captured.

For one heart-stopping moment, the two subs touched, the collision barely more than a kiss but one which still sent the two craft reeling away from one another, the *Ahab* spinning on its axis. Ulysses clung on for dear life, but he needn't have worried; the vice-like grip of the steel lobster claw held fast. However, this didn't stop the suited Ulysses from being thrown against the hull of the sub, rebounding with a metallic thud that left him feeling nauseous and disorientated.

He reached out with his other arm, the gauntlet-hand taking hold of another protruding part of the vessel. Heaving on that hand as well, he was able to bring himself under control again. He was now flat against the hull of the *Ahab*, facedown, cinched tight to the curved surface, a tail fin in one pincer and a maintenance ladder rung held tight within his right gauntlet-fist.

To his right he could see a porthole, yellow sodium light

washing out of it. He was so close that he could almost see inside the sub, but he wasn't quite close enough.

His curiosity frustrated, instead Ulysses focused on his primary task, that of reaching the *Ahab's* lateral airlock access. Hand over cautious hand he pulled himself along the side of the submersible, first releasing the pincer and then, when that was securely clamped around another handhold, loosening the grip of the suit's over-large robot hand.

And all the while the *Ahab* continued powering through the water, heading inexorably for the surface, forcing Ulysses to battle the drag of the slipstream, which tugged horribly at the unstreamlined pressure suit.

Slowly but surely he traversed the exterior of the *Ahab*, the convoluted construction of the hull providing him with plenty of handholds with which to heave himself up, until eventually he came alongside the entrance to the vessel's airlock.

Where those who had made the journey to Marianas Base from the incapacitated *Neptune* on board the *Nemo* had had to exit through the conning tower airlock – as Ulysses had just done again himself – when they had surfaced in the pressure dock pool, Carcharodon's cronies aboard his private submersible had been able to stride out through the lateral dock and down a gangplank to the deck below.

Ulysses found himself alongside that same hatchway now and, grabbing hold of the door's opening mechanism cranked the manual override. With a shunk the door opened and Ulysses pulled the massive bulk of his suit inside, manually sealing the airlock again from inside.

He realised that one of the things he did not have working for him, given this approach, was the element of surprise. Those on board the *Ahab* already knew that

the *Nemo* was on their tail, the two, thankfully un-
armed, submersibles having already scraped together.
They would also have heard Ulysses' clanking progress
as he struggled up the side of the craft and would now
be listening to him operating the airlock. But he did have
something else on his side. He was, of course, encased
inside an armoured suit that made him twice as tall as
any other man, and ten times as strong, a suit that had
resisted the horrendous pressures exerted upon it down
in the ocean depths as well as the attentions of a fully
grown Megalodon.

It wouldn't be a matter of what Carcharodon could
do to him now that would be the problem, but what he
might do to his hostages in desperation, as he stared into
the gaping jaws of defeat.

With the hiss and suck of water being drawn out of the
chamber, the air inside the airlock equalised with that inside the craft, allowing the inner door to be opened. Spinning the wheel-handle with a flick of his wrist, readying
himself – his breathing slow, his heart racing – Ulysses
opened the hatch.

He took in the scene that greeted him inside the cabin
of the *Ahab* in a second. Constance Pennyroyal was huddled in a corner, tied up and gagged. Her eyes widened
first in shock at seeing the bulky mass of the deep sea
diving suit crammed into the airlock and then brightened
noticeably on seeing who it was inside.

At the other end of the cabin, Chief Engineer Selby
stood at the controls, being forced to pilot the vessel with
a gun to his head; a gun, which was held in the wobbling
hand of Miss Celeste. Next to her, Jonah Carcharodon sat
hunched within his wheelchair, his back to Ulysses.

"Quicksilver? Is that you?" Carcharodon challenged.

"Miss Celeste," Ulysses said, speaking through the intercom of the suit. "Put the gun down. It's going to be all right."

"So it is you. I thought so," said Carcharodon, weariness evident in his voice. "Who else would it be?"

"I'm sorry, Mr Quicksilver," the PA said in a quavering voice, "but I can't do that."

"Whatever hold Carcharodon has over you, it's finished. I know what he's done. It's over now. He can't hurt you anymore. I won't let him."

"But, Mr Quicksilver, it would appear you have made a terrible mistake."

Taking the gun off Selby, Miss Celeste turned, spinning Carcharodon's chair around with her free hand at the same time – in which Ulysses now saw she was also holding a moth-eaten rag-doll – and trained her weapon on Ulysses, for all the good bullets would do against the abyss-resistant armour. A look of surprise flickered across her face as she took in the imposing figure of the dandy adventurer sheathed within the massive pressure suit, but only for a moment. A second later, it was replaced by a cruel frown, a dark expression which filled Ulysses with a sense of unaccustomed foreboding.

The passing look of surprise on Miss Celeste's face was nothing compared to the shock which possessed Ulysses' features on coming face-to-face with the ageing shipping magnate once more.

He was wearing a bright yellow, yet deflated lifejacket, tied tight around his neck and waist. The pockets, pouches and ripped open inflation chambers had been loaded with sticks of dynamite, the same explosives the escapees had found in their search of the divers' prep chamber. The cobbled together bomb-jacket was packed with enough dynamite to obliterate the Ahab and all on board. Twists of wire protruded from the explosives, connecting them to a black box in Carcharodon's lap, on the front of which was a dialled timer.

"You've been busy," was all Ulysses could think to say.

"Oh, he doesn't know the half of it, does he, Madeleine?" Miss Celeste said, addressing the doll in her hand. The doll she had rescued from the base. The doll Ulysses had seen in a flaking sepia-tint in the hands of –

"The little girl," he said in wonder. "The child in the photograph."

"You recognise me then?"

"Now that you mention it, yes, I do see a resemblance. Your father was Felix Lamprey."

"Little Marie Lamprey?" Carcharodon uttered in disbelief.

"Yes, you doddering old fool." She hissed. "All this time, right under your nose. And you never knew. And not so little now, nor so helpless! The cuckoo in the nest."

"More like the viper in the nest," Ulysses said quietly to himself.

"Well, I..." Carcharodon blustered.

"What? Assumed that I was dead like my father, left behind for the sea to claim? Didn't give me a second thought? Never wondered what happened to that little girl you all left behind? Didn't care what had happened to her? Is that what you're trying to say?"

Ulysses had never heard the young woman say so much during all time they had spent together.

"It all makes sense now," Ulysses said.

"Oh, does it?" she snapped. "I'm so pleased. It took you long enough though, didn't it, Mr Consulting Detective? Had to see it for yourself before you would readily believe it, didn't you? We had to show him, didn't we, Madeleine?" The doll said nothing. "Well perhaps you can explain how I can make sense of it all, tell me why they killed my father and left an innocent little girl behind to die, a sacrifice to the beast, just like my mother, because I don't understand it!"

Ulysses stared deep into her eyes. If the eyes were the windows to the soul, then the soul he could see reflected in these particular orbs was a damaged, tarnished thing. She was wild now, any semblance of the mousey deference she had managed to maintain for so long entirely gone. They were now seeing her true face. The quiet, patient, ever-tolerant, uncomplaining, subservient Miss Celeste had vanished, to be replaced by the wrathful, vengeful, violent and unpredictable Marie Lamprey. And where Miss Celeste had seemed like a perfectly rational and reasonable individual, her alter ego was utterly mad.

The slightest of movements distracted Ulysses for a split second. In that moment his eyes jerked a fraction of an inch, and refocused on the figure of Selby, but only for a moment. But that was all it took for Ulysses to inadvertently betray the engineer.

Marie Lamprey, her own psychotic stare transfixing Ulysses' eyes, as much as his were locked on hers, saw the miniscule change.

She spun round as Selby heroically moved to stop her. There was the concussive retort of a pistol firing and a spray of red, grey and white splashed the viewing port beyond the pilot's position, as a soup of blood, brains and skull plastered the inside of the reinforced cockpit. Selby collapsed, looking like a puppet that had had its strings cut.

Constance gave a muffled scream from behind her gag and even Ulysses, who had seen far too much mindless violence in his life, gave an involuntary cry of shock. But despite that, the second Marie Lamprey moved against

Selby, Ulysses took a long step forward in the massive suit.

And then the gun was back on him.

"Don't come another step closer," the insane young woman warned him, "or you know what I'll do."

"That? Against that suit of armour?" Carcharodon pooh-poohed, unable to stop himself, having got away with treating people like inferior beings all his life. "Don't be ridic –"

Carcharodon was silenced by Marie bringing the butt of the gun down hard on the back of his head. The old man gasped in pain, his head dropping onto his chest.

"Shut up, you senile imbecile!" she snapped. "I mean it, I'll start the countdown on that bomb you're wearing. And once it's started, there's no stopping it."

"Why?" Carcharodon slurred, unable to take in everything that had happened in so short a space of time, desperate for some reason to be given to rationalise the irrational.

"Why?" she shrieked. "You want to know why? After all this time, only now do you wonder why all this had to happen? Why you all had to die? Isn't it obvious?"

"Revenge," Ulysses stated bluntly, "pure and simple. It usually is."

"And what's that supposed to mean?" Marie railed, turning on Ulysses. "Don't think for one second that there was anything usual about what happened. Everything happened for a reason, the most important reason of all: for my father's good name! I couldn't have him remembered as a psychopath or worse, forgotten about!"

"Oh no, I can see that. The name of Lamprey is going to be remembered for a very long time," Ulysses said. "You've certainly made sure of that. You'll be infamous after what you've done, but it still won't be your father that people remember, not when the name of Marie Lamprey is plastered across the headlines of broadsheets across the Empire."

"Why, you!" she spluttered, reaching for the timer dial on the hastily-constructed device.

"I understand why you believed Carcharodon here, Lady Denning, the Major and Professor Crichton had to die," he went on. Marie's hand froze, hovering over the dial.

"You do?" Carcharodon bristled.

"The Professor practically gave the game away himself. He actually told us what your motivation for committing this series of cold-blooded crimes was. You wanted revenge on all those you saw as being responsible for your father's death, for driving him to do what he did, once they had turned their backs on him. The other leading figures of the Leviathan project. You even planned to ensnare Josiah Umbridge, the industrialist, in your little trap; only he didn't take the bait. He sent that wretch Sylvester in his stead.

"And it was thanks to you that all the right people just happened to be on board ship for the *Neptune's* maiden voyage, wasn't it?"

Marie Lamprey said nothing but continued to fix Ulysses with her disturbing wild-eyed stare.

"Your own employer's confession should have given you away long ago."

"What confession?" Carcharodon groused, one hand clamped to the rising bump on the back of his head.

"It was over dinner, that first time at the captain's table. You said yourself, Jonah, it hadn't been down to you that any of us had been invited on board for the inaugural round-the-world cruise. You told me that your PA had sent out all the personal invitations. You said that she did everything for you. That way she could make sure that she had everybody here who she needed, or at least that's what you had hoped for," he said, turning back to Marie. "But as we've already established, Umbridge escaped the end you doubtless had cooked up for him, by dint of being at death's door already and being too unwell to travel.

"You must have been plotting this for years," Ulysses went on, only now, as he reasoned through all the salient points, realising the scale of Miss Celeste's – or rather Marie Lamprey's – audaciously planned act of vengeance. "What probably started out as a backlash against the injustice of a world that had taken both your parents from you, fuelled by grief and a dozen other childish insecurities gradually – perhaps inevitably – became an obsession until the desire for revenge was your whole raison d'être. There was nothing left but the desire to be revenged on those you saw as being responsible for Felix Lamprey's death. Quite simply, your obsession drove you mad.

"It must have taken you years to work yourself into a position from where you could put your plan into action, to satisfy your sick irrational need for retribution."

"Don't say that!" Marie screeched.

"What? That you're sick, Marie?" Ulysses reasoned calmly. "But it's the truth. You are: terribly sick."

"They were the ones who were sick, weren't they, Madeleine," she sobbed, tears suddenly streaming down her face, "leaving a child to die having already done away with her father?"

"Ruthless, yes, but sick? I would like to be able to agree with you, but I'm not so sure. Whereas you, my dear, are one hundred per cent certifiably a fruitcake!"

"Stop it!" she screamed. "Stop saying that!" She pushed

the muzzle of the gun hard against Carcharodon's head.

"So I suppose it was you who sabotaged the ship as well," Ulysses went on, managing to stay sounding calm, although he didn't feel in anyway calm on the inside. "But how did you manage that, I wonder?"

"You mean you haven't worked that out yet?"

"I thought I had," Ulysses confessed. "But I'm afraid I had this wretch Carcharodon here down as the culprit of our little morality play."

Carcharodon looked up at Ulysses, indignation blazing in his bleary unfocused eyes.

"I saw the log," Ulysses explained. "I know that the person who initiated the sabotage routine buried within the AI's memory core used the ident 'Father' to access the system, and I'm afraid I took that to be you, Jonah. I thought it was an insurance job." He paused as realisation struck. "Oh, yes. Oh, of course. If only I had seen it before. Lady Denning told us all we needed to know about the identity of the one the AI referred to as 'Father'."

"Then I take it I'm exonerated, cleared of all charges?" Carcharodon asked. "For all the good it will do me."

"Lady Denning told us that Lamprey – Felix Lamprey I mean – designed the difference engines that maintained the life support systems for Marianas Base. She also said that these more rudimentary systems were the forerunners of the significantly more complex artificial intelligence created for the *Neptune*. Its father, as far as the AI was concerned, wasn't you, Carcharodon, but Lamprey, the creator of the original AI template. Oh yes, very clever."

Still the quivering woman returned his stare, fire in her eyes, like the hellfire surely crisping her soul even now, in light of what she had done.

"And I'm guessing you used a combination of your cogitator skills and the privileged information you had access to as Carcharodon's personal assistant to sneak into the AI chamber at a time that suited you, access Neptune and activate the programme you must have implanted inside its memory core probably months before."

"Very good, Mr Quicksilver. He thinks he's so clever, doesn't he, Madeleine? But it doesn't matter now, does it? He's still too late to stop us, isn't he?"

"All right Miss Celeste, or Miss Lamprey, or however it is you like to be known nowadays, I understand why, by your twisted logic, Carcharodon and all his cronies from Project Leviathan were doomed to die. But tell me, why did the others have to die? Why did you kill Glenda Finch?

"Even now, after all we've shown him, all we've told him, he can't see it, can he, Madeleine?"

The tenuous grasp Marie Lamprey had on reality was steadily slipping away.

"No, wait, I see now. I've just given you the reason myself, haven't I? The AI chamber. You planned to set your scheme in motion almost twenty-four hours earlier, that night after the Blackjack marathon at the Casino. But on that occasion you were seen, or at least you thought you were. Of course. Being so bound up in your own scheme, with your own psychotic need for revenge, you were always paranoid about anyone else finding out what you were up to and putting a stop to things before you were done. You must have met Glenda as she was leaving the AI, after she had been doing a little digging of her own into the Carcharodon's finances. And you couldn't risk arousing her suspicions about you as well, could you?"

"Everything had been worked out down to the finest detail. I couldn't let a snooping strumpet like her ruin everything for me before I had even begun."

"But you didn't stop there, did you? You couldn't, not after Miss Birkin revealed that she'd seen the murderer with Glenda, the poor old biddy. What was it the Major said about her? Oh yes, always looking for a conspiracy behind everything. If only she'd known. If only she'd kept her mouth shut!

"Only she hadn't seen you at all, had she? She saw me, escorting Glenda back to my room after the Blackjack game. She didn't need to die, not even by the standards of your twisted logic. And of course, having killed Miss Birkin you had to keep on eliminating all of those who might have overheard her conversation with the captain.

"She wasn't a threat to you, but then you couldn't have known that until later, after Captain McCormack accused me of your crimes! And while people were busy thinking it was me, and added to that when Cheng tried to carry out his ill-timed little coup, it gave you all the distraction you needed to keep killing, hunting down the doomed members of Project Leviathan one by one, making sure they all paid for what they had done to your father. What they had done to you. You even bought yourself some more time by faking that attack on Carcharodon and yourself, when your attack on the Captain failed.

"And each of them died in a manner befitting the part they played in the creation of the Kraken. Horsley the big game hunter, skewered like a shish kebab by a harpoon, Crichton the evolutionary biologist poisoned with a lethally evolved neuro-toxin, Denning the marine biologist, electrocuted with a prototype cybernetic tentacle that she had helped to create. And now you've turned Carcharodon into some kind of living bomb.

"So, what I'm thinking now, having reached something of an impasse, is – where do we go from here?"

"We're not going anywhere," Marie Lamprey said coldly.

Reaching behind her with her free hand, she lifted something from the control console, something Ulysses had failed to notice, so preoccupied had he been with the goings on between Marie, Carcharodon and himself, although he realised now that he had seen it before – they all had, only the last time it was being worn by a dead man.

Carefully, Marie placed the metal-banded helmet on top of her head. The coloured light-emitting diodes that covered its surface were blinking on and off like fairy lights. The wires that trailed from the crown had been bound together into one thick cable which, in turn, had been plugged into the console.

"You were busy while I was away, weren't you? Well, they do say the Devil makes work for idle hands."

Marie said nothing, but continued to press the barrel of her gun roughly against her employer's temple, staring ahead of her at Ulysses. There was something about the look in her eyes that suggested she was seeing something else, that wasn't there with them inside the submersible.

"I'm guessing you're as much a whiz with computers as your father was. It looks like you've also inherited his tendency towards mental instability," Ulysses added. "But what, precisely, are you planning on doing with that, Marie?"

A slow smile spread across the haggard young woman's lips, and at that moment it scared Ulysses far more than the gaping grin of the Megalodon that had tried to make a meal of him.

"Why, don't you know? This is how I'm going break this stalemate we've got ourselves into. This is how I finally put paid to the last of the masterminds behind

Project Leviathan, behind my father's murder, and the son of the government representative who allowed such a scheme to continue. All in one easy stroke."

Knowing he had nothing to lose by doing so, Ulysses turned and peered out through the viewing port at the rear of the cabin.

There was something moving out there in the night-blue darkness.

The cold chill of fear slithered down his spine and made itself at home in his gut, turning his bowels to ice water.

He had hoped against hope that they had seen the last of it, that it had been destroyed along with Marianas Base. But deep down he always knew that such a result would simply be too good to be true.

He could see it more clearly now as it slid through the water after the two craft, chasing them to the surface, its grasping arms reaching out ahead of it.

And now Ulysses could see the injuries it had sustained, the damage it had suffered, caught up in the death throes of the dying facility. It had lost parts of several of its arms, sheared metal showing amidst the torn flesh. There were also whole areas where its pallid underbelly, and even pieces of its armoured shell, had been torn asunder to reveal its endo-skeleton beneath. And yet, despite having suffered such extensive damage, the Kraken still looked more than capable of taking down both the Ahab and the Nemo.

Ulysses turned back to face Marie. She looked very peculiar with the bulbous metal helmet covering her head down to her eyes, almost comical.

"I was wrong in my assumptions about the value the killer placed on their own life."

"What do you mean?" Marie asked, Ulysses having got her attention, piquing her own sense of the curious.

"You would willingly sacrifice yourself to see us all dead."

"With my father's killers brought to justice, my life has no further purpose. This has been my life's work. With it completed, there is no reason for me to keep on living."

"Why? Why? Why?"

Ulysses was slightly surprised when he realised that Carcharodon was sobbing as he repeated the same word over and over through his tears. The man who he had known to show hardly any emotion, other than anger or annoyance, was crying like a baby.

"What do you mean, why?" Marie shrieked, lifting the gun from the old man's head only to bring it down hard again against his skull a second time. "Haven't you been listening? He never listens, does he, Madeleine?" She was screaming now, her words a screeching banshee wail. "Don't you understand? You have to understand why you have to die! He has to, doesn't he, Madeleine, otherwise it's all been for nothing." Tears were streaming down her face again, mucus running from her nose.

"I understand. I understand why I have to die," Carcharodon struggled on, gasping for breath from the pain of the blows to his head. "I drove you to this. I understand that. But why did the others have to die?"

Now it was Marie Lamprey's who suddenly didn't understand. "What?" she said, her voice suddenly quiet. Ulysses thought he preferred it when she had been screaming.

"It was me. It was me who killed your father."

"What?"

"It was me. I shot him."

Marie's attention was now fully on the old man, slumped forward in his wheelchair at her side. He suddenly looked so very small and frail as he quietly confessed his sins, the two of them, employer and psychotic employee, master and servant, frozen in that moment of time in some weird parody of priestly absolution.

Ulysses readied himself. He could feel the moment coming when he would be able to bring this matter to its resolution.

"You killed my father?" Marie stammered, suddenly the uncertain, insecure Miss Celeste surfacing again.

"Yes. And there is another crime of which I am guilty. In doing so I helped create another monster, and this time I'm going to face up to my responsibilities and do away with it!"

With that, Carcharodon flicked the switch on top of the timer in his lap.

With a whirring hum the hand began to turn, the needle on the dial hastening away the seconds until the moment when the bomb would detonate.

"What have you done?" Marie screamed levelling the gun at Carcharodon again, holding the weapon tightly with both shaking hands.

The old man looked her straight in the eye and said with chilling calmness, "I'm bringing an end to this impasse."

The woman pulled the trigger. Ulysses heard the sharp crack of the gunshot even as he saw Jonah Carcharodon's head disintegrate in a spray of blood and bone.

It was now or never. Ulysses took a bounding step forwards. Still screaming, Marie grabbed Carcharodon's wheelchair by its handles and pushed it into his path, the old man's body lolling forwards as she did so.

Catching the chair in the huge gauntlet fist and the pincer-claw, Ulysses pushed back. Caught between the arms of the chair, Marie Lamprey stumbled backwards, the helmet falling from her head. Unbalanced she fell against the chair, skewing it sideways, before she toppled over, falling into the still open airlock.

The timer continued to spin round, speeding towards inescapable oblivion. Ulysses could still hear it over the muffled screams of the bound Constance Pennyroyal.

Without a second thought, Ulysses pushed the dead Carcharodon, in his invalid's chair, in after Marie and punched the control panel beside the airlock. With a satisfying shunk, and the hiss of altering air pressures, the inner door shut. Sirens sounded. Lights flashed. Marie Lamprey's face screamed at Ulysses through the small window in the airlock door. But there was nothing that could be done, not now.

With a sudden violent rush of escaping air the dead Carcharodon and the still living Miss Celeste were jettisoned from the airlock. The *Ahab* hurtled onwards, thanks to Selby's last act before he had died, the engineer having switched on the submersible's autopilot.

Ulysses turned his attention back to the rear viewing port. He could see the Kraken even closer now, grasping limbs outstretched, hideous jaws angling open. And he could see Carcharodon's chair sinking towards it, falling in slow motion through the churning water. And he could see Marie Lamprey kicking against the currents, arms flailing, as if trying to swim free, mouth open wide, silvered bubbles of air escaping her lungs in one last defiant scream, wide staring eyes, piercing Ulysses' own, staring straight into his soul, chilling him to the core.

The first thing she thought as she peered up through the porthole above her was how blue the sky was. She had almost forgotten, she had been dwelling down there in the ocean depths for so long. Seeing it now she could almost believe that what had happened down there, so far below, had been nothing more than a bad dream.

Only it hadn't been a dream. It had been a nightmare, and one from which she would never – could never – wake up.

The bathysphere bobbed on the rolling waves, making her feel a little queasy. She had stopped crying now, her tears spent, but the pain was still there, an aching hole in her heart, a hole that she knew time could never hope to heal.

She peered up again through the porthole. There were seabirds now, wheeling over the ocean under the porcelain sky, and something else, an iron hull, streaked red with rust, plying its way through the water towards her.

The vessel bumped against the side of the pod with a resounding clang. The bathysphere bell rang again, tolling an arrhythmic tattoo as it knocked repeatedly against the hull of the ship. A death-knell for those lost to her, far, far below the ocean waves.

She could see a ladder now – rungs black with pitch, crusted white with salt – and a man descending it. Ropes slapped against her small round window on the world and she could hear the shouts of sailors as the pod was secured to the side of the ship.

At last a face appeared at the glass above her. It was lined and weather-beaten, having something of a doting aged relative about it that comforted her. And then a kind smile spread across the crab apple features as twinkling eyes caught sight of the little girl inside.

"It's a child," she heard him say, his voice muffled. "A little girl, for God's sake."

Strong hands worked the hatch handle on the outside of the escape capsule and the sailor pulled it open, letting out the musty, stale smell of fear and letting in the rich aromas of brine, fish guts and stale tobacco. It was a heady mix of scents which, in that instance smelt like heavenly perfume to the terrified little girl.

A calloused hand reached into the pod.

"Come on, my little sparrow," the sailor said warmly, his voice thick with the apple orchard accents of the West Country. "Let's be having you."

Tentatively she reached up, putting her small, soft white hand into her liberator's meaty paw. His fingers closed around hers firmly and, in a trice, he had hauled her through the open hatch out of the musty pod.

"Well, well, well. What do we have here?" came a voice from among those crowded at the deck rail above them.

"What's your name, little sparrow?" the kindly sailor asked.

"M-Marie," she stammered, her mind reeling as she tried to take everything in.

"Marie?" the sailor repeated.

"Marie," she said again.

She listened now to the murmurings of the crew on deck. "What's she doing out here, all alone?" someone was saying.

"Who'd abandon a child like that, in the middle of the Pacific Ocean?" asked another.

"Marie, did she say?" said a third. "Would that be Marie Celeste then?"

She looked up, trying to find the face in the crowd, the face of the man who had named her.

Marie Celeste, she thought. She liked the sound of that name. She wondered what sort of a life Marie Celeste would have had so far. With a name like that she had probably had a much happier life than little Marie Lamprey had had to endure until this time.

Yes, Marie Celeste. She liked the sound of that.

And then, jaws agape, the Kraken swallowed them – chair, Carcharodon, Celeste and all. The massive jaws hinged shut and, for a moment, Ulysses thought that the creature was slowing, pulling back, satisfied at last. But it was not to be.

With a flick of its tail the monster powered forwards again, closing on the *Ahab* once more.

This is it, Ulysses thought. This is the end. There's nowhere left to run now, no aces left to play.

The suckered tentacles reached for the sub, the vessel's autopilot still directing it straight up towards the surface, that hideous angler-fish mouth opening once again, the grotesque limpid jelly-saucer eyes locked on its new prey.

And then the bomb detonated.

The beast's stomach swelled violently, distending horribly. Ulysses could almost believe that there was a look of startled surprise in the leviathan's eyes. And then there was fire in the water, fire and an expanding ball of concussive force.

The Kraken underwent one last appalling transformation as its body – grey-green flesh, cybernetic endo-skeleton, waving tentacles, and crustacean armour plating – was ripped apart by the explosion, destroying it utterly from the inside out.

Marie Lamprey, Jonah Carcharodon and the Kraken were gone. For good.

EPILOGUE

Britannia Rules the Waves

The *Ahab* surfaced first, closely followed by the *Nemo*. Within moments, Ulysses was standing in the open air on top of the *Ahab*, drawing in great lungfuls of salt sea air, relishing the freshness of it, delighting in the warmth of the sun beating down on his face. The pressure suit stood unoccupied within the sub. In his hand he held his bloodstone-tipped cane once more, having recovered it from Marie Lamprey's stash that she had carried on board the *Ahab*.

Constance Pennyroyal huddled next to him, anxiously watching the *Nemo* for signs of her beloved fiancé. Her patience was rewarded a moment later when Nimrod popped the hatch of the *Nemo's* conning tower, the equally anxious John Schafer emerging after him. Without even a pause for thought, Schafer took a swan dive off the top of the sub into the Pacific and, with confident strokes, covered the stretch of choppy water between the two vessels to be reunited with his sweetheart once more.

As the elated crying couple renewed their promises of love, Ulysses and Nimrod made use of hawsers to pull the two tubs together.

"Where's Cheng?" Ulysses asked, as he offered his man-servant a hand.

"I took the liberty of securing him below, sir," Nimrod said, with a hint of satisfaction in his usually impassive voice.

"Well done, old boy. Good thinking."

Nimrod looked exhausted and unwell. The trials they had all been through, and the wound he had suffered during the Kraken's final attack on the base, were taking their toll, now that the adrenalin rush of the chase and their escape from the beast had passed.

"That was a close call there," Ulysses said, flashing his loyal family retainer a wicked grin, "I don't mind telling you, I thought we were all done for that time."

"I had faith in you, sir," Nimrod said, struggling to maintain his mask of professional detachment.

"Thank you, Nimrod."

"So, am I to take it that the Marianas killer has been brought to book, sir? They have been made to pay for their crimes?"

"Oh yes, there's no doubt about that," Ulysses said, a wry smile on his lips. "Remind me, Nimrod, when we get back to civilisation to send a letter of condolence to Jonah Carcharodon's family."

"Really, sir?"

"Really, Nimrod."

"And what about Miss Celeste's family? Will you be sending them a letter of condolence as well, sir? Or flowers perhaps."

"I don't think so," Ulysses replied, his face suddenly hard as stone.

There was the roar and chop of a propeller starting up, and the water behind the stern of the *Nemo* became a churning spume of white froth. The tiny sub slid forwards, pulling the ropes holding it to the *Ahab* taut, for a moment even dipping the nose of the larger vessel, before, with a sharp crack, they snapped.

"Nimrod, what did you secure Mr Cheng to, I wonder?" the dandy said, his features relaxing again.

"I do apologise, sir," *Nimrod* said, his rigidly maintained façade of indifference suddenly crumbling, his face flushing in embarrassment, "there really wasn't very much else to secure him to. Should we pursue, sir?"

"I don't think so, Nimrod. I don't know about you, old chap, but I've had quite enough of breakneck pursuits for one day. Haven't you? I think we can leave him to his own fate now. After all, he's going to have to face the wrath of his superiors, and I'm sure that whatever they have in mind for him will be much worse than anything our government would dare to implement against an agent of the Chinese Empire. I'm not sure our new Prime Minister is ruthless enough."

"So, if I might be so bold, sir, what now?"

"Now, Nimrod? Now we just have to wait for the Royal Navy to pick us up. We're broadcasting on all bands a general distress call so it shouldn't take too long. A day or two at most."

"Very good, sir."

"And seeing as how the young couple are so bound up in each other, that just leaves you and me, Nimrod."

"Yes, sir."

Ulysses was quiet for a moment as he gazed out over the Pacific, nothing but sea and sky to the horizon in every direction. It was a beautifully calm day, but something was still troubling him, deep down.

"Nimrod," he said after several minutes' silent thought, "there's been something I've been meaning to ask you."

"Go on, sir. You know you can ask me anything."

"Very well then." Ulysses paused again and took a death breath before continuing. "What did you know of my father's involvement in Project Leviathan?"

Far, far below the surface, beneath the spot where the *Ahab* bobbed like a twig on the roiling surface of the Pacific, past the wreck of the *Neptune* and beyond the ravaged remains of the ruined base, beyond the hunting grounds of the Megalodons, deeper even inside the haunted depths of the Marianas Trench, something stirred.

Woken by the seismic disturbances that had followed both the destruction of the *Neptune* and the undersea facility, drawn for a time by the distant signal that had briefly been projected into the abyss, it rose now from those same untold depths. Disturbed from its slumber of ages, active once more, its original programming rebooting, it rose from its resting place within the trench, a gnawing ache deep within its massive gut.

The giant sharks sensed its approach and fled before it, but in moments all were devoured whole.

It swept past the ruined domes of the devastated Marianas base, something like memory recalling its connection with that obscene place, that was now just another watery grave.

It glided over the teetering liner, the backwash of its passing sending the greatest submersible liner the world had ever seen over the edge, to be claimed by the hungry abyss at last.

It pushed on through the sinking cloud of flesh and metal debris, pausing for a moment to taste a few particles, its augmented mind attempting to reconstruct what had happened, what threats it might encounter itself.

Hunger like nothing it had ever known seizing the primitive, instinctive, unadapted portion of its mind, it continued to rise, seeking the surface.

And at its passing, a sturdy sheet of paper, a blueprint plan not yet turned to mush by the water flew and flapped in its wake, on it a schematic image of a bioweapon twice the size of the Kraken, far more lethally equipped to hunt and kill, and a coded designation: Project Leviathan – 002.

Canst thou draw out leviathan with an hook? Or his tongue with a cord which thou lettest down?... Canst thou fill his skin with barbed irons? Or his head with fish spears? Lay thine hand upon him, remember the battle, do no more.

(*Job*, ch.1 v.1)

THE END

Jonathan Green lives and works in West London. Well known for his contributions to the Fighting Fantasy range of adventure gamebooks, as well as his novels set within Games Workshop's worlds of *Warhammer* and *Warhammer 40,000*, he has written for such diverse properties as *Sonic the Hedgehog* and *Doctor Who*. To date, his books have been translated into French, Hungarian, Italian, Polish, Portuguese and Spanish. The co-creator of the world of Pax Britannia, *Leviathan Rising* is his second novel for Abaddon Books.

Now read the exclusive new novella...

PAX BRITANNIA

VANISHING POINT

JONATHAN GREEN

Abaddon
Books

WWW.ABADDONBOOKS.COM

~ October 1997 ~

I – THE HAUNTING OF HARDEWICK HALL

Hardewick Hall was definitely haunted, of that there could be no doubt. Madam Garside had declared it was so within only a matter of minutes of entering the crumbling Gothic pile, her nose wrinkling as she was confronted by an atmosphere heavy with beeswax polish and camphor. A séance had to be held, she had informed Emilia, to discover why the spirits were restless. That way they could then discover which ghosts it was that were troubling her and lay those spirits to rest, although Emilia was sure she knew who it was who was trapped within the house, unable to escape to eternal rest in paradise. And of course Madame Garside decreed that the séance had to take place on the night of All Hallows' Eve, which was auspicious for such an undertaking, when the veil between the worlds was at its thinnest and spirits might more freely cross from the other side, into the land of the living.

So it was that on the evening of the 31st October 1997, as dusk was drawing on under a sky bruised purple-black with the promise of a coming storm, a group of disparate individuals gathered at the brooding manse in Warwickshire, at the personal invitation of Emilia Oddfellow, daughter of the late Alexander Oddfellow, scientist, inventor and eccentric.

Seven of them were to take part in the séance itself, with Madam Garside taking the lead, but of course such honoured guests could not be expected to attend without bringing their own staff too.

Emilia Oddfellow paused before the doors to the Library

where Caruthers had gathered her guests to await the arrival of the lady of the house.

Lady of the house, she thought. That was a term that would still take some getting used to. Her father had been gone these last three months, but still she couldn't quite believe it, perhaps because of the manner of his passing.

She paused to adjust the cameo brooch that had once been her mother's, pinned at the collar of her high-buttoned mourning dress. Her hands were shaking: she blushed in embarrassment at herself. Then, taking a few controlled breaths to compose herself, she pushed open the doors and stepped into the Library to greet her guests.

All eyes turned to look at her. She in turn scanned the faces around the room, her heart quickening in excited anticipation as she searched for one face in particular.

Four men awaited her, their own servants in attendance with them. To her left, sitting in a large, leather-upholstered armchair – which needed to be large to contain his corpulent bulk – was her honoured guest, Herr Sigmund Faustus. He was dressed in the manner of a country gent, wearing a tweed three piece suit. Standing stiffly beside his chair was his personal aide. He was staring at her expectantly, making no effort to hide the fact, his right eye bulging from behind the lens of a monocle, while his left eye was scrunched almost entirely shut.

Emilia moved on in her observations.

Trying to look casual, leaning an elbow on the mantelpiece above the fire smouldering in the grate, was a handsome, athletically lean man, his dark hair slicked back with lacquer, nonchalantly balancing a cigarette holder between thumb and the first finger of his left hand. On seeing Emilia, a brief smile rested for a moment upon his otherwise dourly aloof countenance. Emilia felt her spirits lift, but his delightfully welcome face wasn't the one she had been hoping for in particular.

The two remaining gentlemen were standing either side of a partially-unfolded card table between the library's two velvet-draped windows that looked out onto the croquet lawn. On becoming aware of her entering the room, the two of them stopped fiddling with the curious device standing on the table and looked up. Mr Smythe, the taller of the two, had a pinched and pale face, and wore round wire-framed spectacles. His companion, Mr Wentworth, was an unattractive specimen, stooped as if his spine was malformed with a feeble growth of spiky whiskers on his upper lip, the pathetic moustache only serving to make him look like some kind of rodent.

Both had attempted to dress smartly for the occasion, although Emilia rather suspected that their stained and moth-eaten suits were what amounted to their Sunday best.

She quickly scanned the room, hoping against hope that she had missed something the first time. Then her heart dropped; he had not come.

"Good evening, gentlemen," she said, doing her best to hide her obvious disappointment. "Have you all been introduced?"

"Herr Dashwood, kindly – how do you say? – did the honourables," the corpulent foreign gentleman replied. His voice was higher than might have been expected, with a fluting tone, curiously at odds with his guttural native accent.

"Thank you, Daniel," she said, addressing the young man at the fireplace, who dismissed the need to be thanked with a wave of his cigarette holder, and then turned back to the German. "Herr Faustus," she said, clasping her hands together in front of her, to prevent herself from nervously fidgeting while she spoke. "Thank you so much for coming such a long way to be here."

"Not at all, my dear," Faustus replied, tapping the arm of his chair with a finger, as if to emphasise the point he was making.

"You were always so generous in your support of my father's work. He spoke very well of you."

"The late lamented Prince Consort was not the only German philanthropist with a desire to help the people of the British Empire, my dear." He spoke to her as if he were an affectionate, although not altogether heterosexual, uncle. "And besides I had a – how do you say? – a vested interest in his work. It shames me greatly that the very project I was funding might have brought about his untimely end."

Emilia's throat went taught – to hear it put so bluntly like that, even after three months – and she swallowed hard.

"If there is anything I can do – anything at all – you only need to ask," Faustus added.

"You are too kind," Emilia replied, blinking away the moisture collecting at the corners of her eyes. "You have done more than enough, already."

She turned to the curious-looking pair at the card table, and their equally curious device.

"And thanks to you both, Mr Smythe. Mr Wentworth." She looked at the machine, all polished teak, glass dials and gnarled brass knobs. It looked not unlike the bastard offspring of a wireless radio set and an ornate clock. "You really think this machine will help?"

"We certainly hope so, Miss Oddfellow," Smythe replied, an excited, slightly manic smile suddenly seizing control of his pinched features. "We still need to carry out a final calibration of the device," he said, a hand straying back to the dials with which he had been fiddling when Emilia entered the room, "but we are highly confident of success."

"Confident of success," the weasely Wentworth parroted.

The library's wall-lights suddenly flickered and dimmed. All eyes were drawn anxiously to the humming lamps and Emilia's heart missed a beat. A moment later, full power was restored.

"I... I'm very pleased to hear it," Emilia said, feeling that someone needed to say something to dispel the growing sense of unease, but her words didn't seem to make any difference. "I am told that Madam Garside has almost finished her preparations and that we shall soon be able to begin. Please help yourselves to another drink in the meantime."

Her duties as a hostess dispensed with for the moment, Emilia moved swiftly across the room to the dashing Dashwood at the fireplace.

"Daniel, how delightful to see you," she said, clasping the young man's hands in her own. "I am so glad you're here."

"I wouldn't have missed this for the world," he beamed back at her, giving her a wink. He paused, looking around the room. "Any sign of you-know-who?"

"No, not yet," Emilia said, her carefully composed mask of togetherness wilting for a second, threatening to reveal her true feelings.

"Come on, chin up. I hate to say it, cuz, I really do, but... Well, I told you so."

"Yes. Yes, you did, dear Daniel, and I should have listened to you. He's obviously not coming."

"He could have at least replied to your invitation."

"I'm sure he's been very busy. I think I read that he'd

been involved in that Carcharodon debacle."

"That was months ago," her cousin chided, good-naturedly. "Stop making excuses for him, Em. He was always letting you down before, and now he's gone and let you down again."

Someone coughed politely behind her.

"Um, excuse me, Miss Oddfellow, but if your guests are all assembled, Madam Garside is ready for you now."

Emilia turned to see the medium's assistant, Renfield, standing behind her. She hadn't heard him approach.

"What? Oh yes, of course," she sighed, feeling her shoulders sag as disappointment deflated her. "We're ready. Caruthers will just have to join in to make up numbers," she said pragmatically, lowering her voice so that only Dashwood heard what she had to say.

She moved to cross the hall to the study where the séance was to take place. "This way, please."

Emilia paused in the hallway – her guests filing past her, led by the moon-faced Renfield into the mahogany-panelled study – and looked longingly in the direction of the front door.

And then she heard it; the faint purr of an engine and the grinding crunch of tyres on the gravel drive at the front of the house.

A moment later the sound of the engine died. A door slammed and leather soles were heard trotting up on the steps to the front door. The strident jangling of the doorbell made everyone pause and look round then, and sent Emilia chasing along the corridor, reaching the door before the hobbling Caruthers could get anywhere near it.

She flung it open.

"Not too late, am I?" Ulysses Quicksilver asked, flashing Emilia a rakish grin.

"Oh, Ulysses, I thought you weren't coming!" Emilia chided, grabbing him and pulling him close to plant a kiss on his cheek.

"You wouldn't believe the traffic coming out of London tonight," he said, pulling away from her. Behind him, his manservant, Nimrod, was extricating his master's luggage from the boot of a Mark IV Rolls Royce Silver Phantom.

Clasping her hands in his Ulysses looked deeply into Emilia's eyes, his expression suddenly serious. "I was so sorry to hear of your loss," he said. "His passing is a great loss to us all."

"Thank you," she said, returning his intense stare.

"How are you?"

"All the better for seeing you," Emilia said, and pulled him close again. There was a moment's silence between the two of them, which said more than words ever could, and then they parted, as if suddenly remembering that they had company.

"Ah, Dashwood," Ulysses said, catching sight of the darkly dressed individual at the other end of the hall. "How long's it been?"

"Not long enough," the other replied, that same aloof glower on his face.

"Well, I'd like to be able to say that it's good to see you again, but..."

"The feeling's mutual," Dashwood said, a false smile contorting his facial muscles for a moment.

"Not now, Daniel," Emilia said with forceful calm.

"But he can't just walk back into your life like this and carry on as if nothing happened."

"Daniel, please."

"Your concern for your cousin is very sweet, Dashwood, but I'm sure Miss Oddfellow can stick up for herself. At least she could when she and I were better acquainted," Ulysses said, flashing her that rakish grin. "Black suits you, by the way."

"Now come along, Ulysses, everyone's waiting. This way."

II – PARLOUR TRICKS

With everyone seated at the circular table that had been set up in the late Alexander Oddfellow's study expressly for the purpose, the séance began.

"Spirits, can you hear me?" Madam Garside called, her eyes tight shut, her head held high. "I beseech you, dark watchers from beyond the veil, hear my plea, and answer."

Ulysses Quicksilver opened one eye and took in the faces of his fellow attendees. Madam Garside sat at the head of the table, a glass and walnut bookcase behind her, her palms flat on the table cloth in front of her. Her bony fingers were adorned with ostentatious rings but Ulysses seriously doubted that any of them were of any real value, the precious stones set within were no more than cunningly cut-glass copies. Her dress was as vulgar as her jewellery, and about her shoulders was draped a shawl, embroidered with silver stars and crescent moons. But the piece which set it all off for Ulysses was the turban she had seen fit to place on top of her head. The green silk from which it had been wound was fastened together with an apparently gold and lapis lazuli scarab beetle brooch, like those cheap knock-offs sold in their thousands to tourists visiting the Nile kingdom every year. She was certainly keeping her options open with such an array of cosmological symbols.

In the ruddy light of the shuttered Bedouin lamp she had placed on the table in front of her, her overly made-up face took on an appropriately hellish quality.

"Spirits, heed the call of one who knows you, answer the petition of Madam Garside."

Ulysses couldn't stop himself from smirking at hearing

that, and snorted as he tried to suppress a laugh. He then had to loudly clear his throat to try to cover up his inappropriate reaction.

One eye suddenly flicked open and fixed on Ulysses. "Spirits!" she said again, her entreaty louder this time, as she tried to bring the séance back under control.

But it didn't change the fact that, as far as Ulysses was concerned, the whole thing was no more than an embarrassing charade.

To the phoney mystic's left sat Daniel Dashwood, hands flat on the table also – as had been dictated for all of them by Madam Garside – eyes closed and head erect, cigarette holder clenched between his teeth. The lazy blue tobacco smoke coiled upwards to join the clouds of incense fugging the room.

Beside Dashwood was Emilia, her eyes screwed tight shut, an expression of earnest desperation knotting her usually soft features. Ulysses seat was next to hers.

He noticed that his former sweetheart had taken to wearing her straw blonde hair plaited into a tight bun at the back of her head. The girl he had once known had worn it down, like a cascade of gold. That same girl would never have been seen dead in a stiff black mourning gown buttoned to the neck. Time and its cruel predations had changed her, he thought. And a broken heart might have had its part to play too, he considered ruefully.

She was so close he could almost touch her, the little fingers of their hands inches apart. The sarcastic smile left his lips, and at that moment he wanted nothing more than to grab hold of her, take her away from this morbid shadow play which was wringing a bitter grief from her.

Instead he turned his attention to the man to his left. Smythe was paying about as much attention to proceedings as Ulysses was himself. He was absorbed in fiddling with his machine. As he played with the knobs and dials on the front panel, the two short aerials that sprouted from the top rotated independently about a hemispherical gimble and the crackle of radio interference came from speakers at either end of the device.

It was a ghost detector, or so Smythe had told him as they had taken their seats at the table. All the fiddling was necessary to focus the signal apparently projected by all supernatural entities, thereby allowing the machine to read the presence of ghosts. Next to him sat his fellow parapsychologist Wentworth, who flicked switches and adjusted dials on his side of the machine from time to time.

Despite being an obvious fraud, as far as Ulysses was concerned, he had to give Madam Garside her due. It was testament to her level of concentration that she was able to keep up the pretence of communing with the souls of the departed with the constant background disturbance of Smythe and Wentworth's box of tricks.

Next around the table, and someone who was trying desperately hard to concentrate, despite the distraction of the apparition manifestation meter, was the rotund Faustus. Eyes closed, his mouth was slightly agape, as if in wonder.

And that completed the circle of seven.

"Spirits of the netherworld, if you can hear me, send me a sign."

The gathered séance-goers variously held their breath in expectation or struggled to keep a straight face. Smythe and Wentworth continued to tinker with their gizmo.

They waited, but if the spirits were there they were not in a talkative mood this particular evening.

Madam Garside stretched out her hands again and

decried: "Spirits, I invoke you, by Osiris, by Hades and by Samhain. I command you, answer me!" Her voice had become a savage growl of barely suppressed fury.

An unearthly quiet fell upon the room and Ulysses became aware of the muffled pitter-patter of rain from behind the thick velvet drapes drawn across the one window in the study.

And then, the expectant hush was sharply broken by a loud knock on wood. Emilia gasped and jumped in her seat while Faustus let out a girlish cry of alarm. Ulysses looked at Dashwood, but he remained unmoved, chin in the air, eyes calmly closed.

"Thank you, spirits. Now, you watchers from the shadow world, answer me clearly. Can you hear me?"

The knock came again. In the muted red light of the room Ulysses looked for the medium's assistant but he was nowhere to be seen. He knew that there was some manner of trickery at work here, and Renfield was certainly up to his neck in it.

"Are you ready and willing to answer my questions?"

Again, the knock.

"Very well," Madam Garside said, with the commanding tone of one who believes themselves to be in authority, "who is it that haunts this place, who is lost and cannot find their way to the other side?"

The two parapsychologists made another adjustment to their machine and it began to emit a high-pitched whine, accompanied by a cockroach-like clicking.

"What is that?" Ulysses hissed, leaning towards the fiddling Smythe.

"Just white noise," the investigator whispered back.

"Bit like her over there then."

The lights flickered. Madam Garside broke off suddenly, opened her eyes momentarily to glance around the room and then, finding Ulysses boldly meeting her gaze, shut them again.

"Dwellers in darkness, if you can hear me, give us a sign."

As Ulysses watched the Bedouin lamp began to rise slowly into the air above the table as, with a fizzing hum, that almost seemed in tune with the noise being made by the strange machine on the table, the lights in the room faded until only a feint dirty glow remained inside each buzzing bulb.

They all heard the mournful voice, despite its eerie distortion, as it came to them through the loud speakers of the wireless box. "Emmiilliiaa!"

Emilia cried out in alarm and gasps came from those around the table. Ulysses looked to the startled woman who returned his gaze imploringly, eyes open now, glistening with tears. "Father!"

"Emmiillliiaa," the voice came again and all looked to the parapsychologists' device.

"Mein gott!" Faustus whispered.

Smythe immediately began twiddling knobs and flicking switches again, in an attempt to fine-tune the signal.

"Come on, man," Dashwood said, although more demanding than encouraging in tone.

"Emilia!" came the plaintive cry, more clearly still.

"Oh, Father! Father?" she returned the call, looking desperately around the room, searching the air above her, as if hoping to see her father as well as hear his voice. "Can you hear me?"

"Emilia? Can you hear me?" the ethereal voice echoed her words. It was becoming chopped with interference.

"Come on, man! Get it back!" Dashwood snarled.

"I'm trying," Smythe threw back, "but the storm's

interfering with the signal!"

"Interference," Wentworth added pointlessly.

"Just white noise, eh?" Ulysses muttered darkly, one questioning eyebrow raised.

More concerned by the distressed state of Emilia than the miraculous signal apparently being picked up by the ghost detector, Ulysses looked past her, seeing the strange reaction of the medium, Madam Garside. She was sitting in her chair, staring straight ahead of her, eyes bulging from their sockets, her face slack with an expression of horror, her mouth hanging open.

Ulysses followed her horrified gaze to the far side of the study. Another strangled gasp from Emilia told him that she had done the same and could see what he was seeing. Unbelievable as it might seem, an eerie luminescence was beginning to suffuse the darkened room with its own unearthly light. As Ulysses watched, the light began to take on shape and form. The spectral image was that of a man, of that there could be no doubt. Smythe made another adjustment.

"Emilia..." came the broken voice again, still being heard through the machine. "...ere... the sphere..."

"What was that he said?" Dashwood snapped.

"...ere... the sphere... sphe..."

Ulysses strained to make sense of the unearthly message, but the signal was breaking up and the task was made all the more difficult by another dreadful moaning that now pervaded the study.

"For God's sake, woman," Dashwood turned on Madam Garside, "shut up!"

"Father!" Emilia all but screamed, for if there had ever been any doubt before, there could be none now. The apparition of Alexander Oddfellow had materialized before their very eyes, standing half inside his own book-strewn desk, as if it wasn't there.

"Well, that's a turn up for the books," Ulysses muttered under his breath.

The late Alexander Oddfellow reached towards his daughter and cried her name once more. "Emi..lia... pher.. the sph..ere..."

"Fear the sphere? What's that supposed to mean?" Dashwood exclaimed, in irritation.

The phantasmal image flickered, washed as if with static, and then blinked out of existence, leaving the room in almost utter darkness. The lights on Smythe and Wentworth's machine had winked out too and the falling pitch of the device's power cell running dry could be heard emanating from the speakers.

"What happened?" Dashwood demanded.

"It's no good," Smythe admitted, giving the machine a thump of annoyance. "It's dead."

"Dead," Wentworth echoed, emotionlessly.

"That's not all that's dead," Ulysses said, his tone demanding the attention of all present. All eyes turned to him and thence, from him, to the medium.

Madam Garside sat stock still in her chair, her mouth still agape, her skin white and waxy, glassy eyes bulging from her head, the light of life that should have shone behind them snuffed out.

Ulysses studied the body with clinical interest. So that's what someone looks like when they've been scared to death, he thought.

III – THE LATE GLADYS GARSIDE

Madam Garside was dead, there was no doubt about it. Ulysses had felt for a pulse as had his manservant Nimrod. Consensus of opinion was that her heart had given out on witnessing the appearance of the apparition of Alexander Oddfellow. It had shocked everyone, although they had all reacted in different ways.

Emilia was understandably distressed, and Ulysses had done his best to comfort her. However, he himself had been surprised by something else altogether: he was surprised that the parapsychologists' machine had seemingly worked so well.

Dashwood appeared angry more than anything else, seemingly frustrated that they had lost the phantom Oddfellow so soon after managing to make his ghost materialize before them. Smythe's reaction was one of frustration, with Wentworth seeming to follow where his partner led, as ever.

Sigmund Faustus had retired to the library looking as white as the corpse he had left behind in the study and, once there, poured himself a large scotch. Having downed it, he poured another straight away.

By the time he was onto his third, the philanthropist had calmed down enough for Ulysses to leave Emilia in his care, whilst the dandy returned to the scene of the visitation, and the stiffening body in the study.

Smythe and Wentworth were still there, taking apart their contraption – Ulysses supposed to change its battery – able to see quite clearly now that the lights in the room had returned to normal. And so was Nimrod, standing behind another of the chairs, pulled out now from the table, with Madam Garside's sagging flunkey slouched within it, the butler's hand resting firmly on his shoulder, in case he should get any foolish ideas.

"Tell me about the medium Madam Garside," Ulysses said sternly.

Renfield had revealed himself when he burst from behind the curtains in horror at hearing of his mistress's death, dropping the fishing line with the Bedouin lamp attached in the process. Any theatrical pretension he might have had before was gone now. Sidney Renfield had gone to pieces as soon as he realised Madam Garside really was dead.

He looked up at Ulysses with red-rimmed eyes, cheeks wet with tears of panic and fear.

"She wasn't one, a real medium I mean, but then I think you've worked that out for yourself, haven't you?" he blubbed.

"So she was a con artist. After Miss Oddfellow's inheritance was she?"

"No."

"Then what? All this tonight; was she doing that simply out of the goodness of her heart?"

"No, of course not."

"Then Miss Oddfellow was paying her for her services."

Renfield nodded, dabbing at his eyes with a balled up handkerchief.

"How many séances were there to be? How many tarot readings to help get Emilia's life back on track? What does an exorcism cost these days anyway?"

"I don't know. There'd only been two meetings before today, the second to set up the séance," Renfield said, confessing all he knew. "Gladys had never seen a ghost in all her life, of course. At least, not until... until..." Unable to continue he broke down, sobbing his heart out.

"Until tonight, and the shock killed her." Ulysses finished bluntly. "Didn't see that coming, did she?"

He paced the floor in front of the shaking Renfield as if deep in thought.

"I take it you've heard of karma, Mr Renfield? Well, I'd say that the late Gladys Garside got what was coming to her. How many other poor unfortunate souls – grieving widows and orphans the lot I'm sure – have you conned over the years? I think the authorities would like to hear about what you've been up to, don't you? Well you can contemplate your fate while the rest of us get to the bottom of what's been going on around here."

Turning from the wretched Renfield, Ulysses circled the table to where the two ghost hunting boffins were tinkering with their startlingly effective box of tricks.

"Gentlemen," he said. "How's it going?"

Smythe looked up in irritation while Wentworth continued to take out the screws that held the back plate of the machine in place.

"It's the battery," he confessed, not telling Ulysses anything he hadn't already worked out for himself.

"The battery," Wentworth agreed.

"Can you replace it?"

"We can. But it will take a few minutes."

"A few minutes, then you can have another go," Ulysses said enthusiastically, a devilish grin back on his face.

"Really? You want us to try again?" Smythe said, unable to hide the amazement from his voice.

"Indeed," said Ulysses. "It worked, didn't it?"

"Well, the device was designed to detect the presence of paranormal anomalies but..."

"I'm intrigued by the apparent connection between your gizmo here and the appearance of Oddfellow's ghost," Ulysses explained, without giving the pondering Smythe a chance to finish, a note of glee in his voice. "Like I say, I want you to do whatever's necessary to get that machine ready to have another go."

IV – WHITE NOISE

"We're ready when you are, Mr Quicksilver," Smythe announced, sticking his head around the door of the library.

"Ready for what?" Dashwood asked, suspicious and yet intrigued.

"To try again," Ulysses stated, as if that much was obvious.

"Who died and put you in charge?" Dashwood challenged as Ulysses followed Smythe out of the library, but Ulysses did not deign to offer a reply.

Ulysses re-entered Oddfellow's study after the parapsychologist. The machine was there on the table, reassembled with a new battery cell installed, Wentworth waiting patiently for his partner. The late Gladys Garside had been moved to another room at Ulysses' request.

"Well, I'm here now, aren't I? Don't wait any longer. Start it up!"

Smythe and Wentworth went through their well-practised routine and, as soon as the machine hummed into life, Ulysses could hear a high-pitched drone coming from the box. Then the clicking commenced and Smythe began frantically tuning the device once more.

Without looking round, Ulysses sensed the presence of the other house guests at the door to the study. The electric lamps flickered, their luminescence failing yet again. He heard gasps behind him but kept his attention focused on the machine sat in the middle of the table.

Thunder rumbled ominously beyond the walls of the gothic pile.

This time it was only a matter of moments before the clicking tone warped into recognisable speech.

"Emilia?" came the haunting voice. "Can you hear me? Anyone?"

"We can hear you, Oddfellow," Ulysses spoke up excitedly. Smythe continued to focus the signal the ghost detector was receiving from God alone knew where.

A sphere of luminescence glowed into life within the study again, this time above the table. It swelled, flickered and dulled, becoming the spectre of Alexander Oddfellow once more, everything below the waist sunk into and through the table.

"Oh, father, it really is you!"

Ulysses spun round startled. So intently focused had he been on the reappearance of the ghost, he had not realised that Emilia had joined the group of curious onlookers at the door.

The ghost seemed to reach imploringly towards the young woman but the voice coming from the box had become unintelligible static again. The wall lamps glowed into life and, in contrast, the ethereal image of Emilia's late father dulled.

"Father? What is it?" she asked, pushing past Ulysses into the study.

The fading ghost's lips moved in desperate articulation but nothing of what it was trying to say could be heard.

"Ulysses do something, please. I have to know what he's trying to tell me," Emilia gasped.

"Smythe, what's the matter?" the dandy demanded, looking past Emilia, but placing a reassuring hand on her arm. "Why is the image fading? Don't tell me the battery's dead already."

"We're losing the signal," Smythe explained. "The more we try to boost it, the more power it drains from the cell. It's like it's moving out of range."

And then, as Ulysses was looking through Oddfellow's

blurring body at the two ghost hunters, the spectre moved, as if making for the door. Then it was gone.

"Quick!" Ulysses exclaimed. "Oddfellow's leading us somewhere!"

Smythe and Wentworth looked at one another in bewilderment, then at Ulysses.

"Well, come on!" Ulysses exclaimed frustratedly, as he leapt for the door, sending the gaggle of gasping onlookers into a scurrying retreat. "We mustn't lose it."

Smythe and Wentworth looked at one another blankly again.

"For a couple of boffins capable of creating such a device, you really can be quite stupid, can't you? Pick up your box of tricks and follow me!"

Cottoning on at last they did as he commanded, Wentworth lugging the heavy metal box in his arms whilst Smythe awkwardly attempted to focus the signal the ghost detector was receiving.

Out in the passageway, the static whooshing from the speakers became a clear tone again and the ghost of Alexander Oddfellow materialized a few yards from them. It seemed to Ulysses that the apparition was looking through him as it beckoned with one hand. It then turned and moved off along the corridor.

"Keep up!" Ulysses darted a glance back at the encumbered parapsychologists. Emilia was at his side, the rest of the curious party following after Smythe and Wentworth.

At the foot of the polished staircase opposite the front door of the house, the ghost turned, following a narrow tiled passageway that ran alongside the stairs. At its end, Ulysses could see an archway, leading under the stairs themselves.

"Where's he taking us?" he asked Emilia as they kept

pace with the ghost.

"The cellar," she said, her voice no more than a whisper.

Ducking under the archway, Ulysses found himself at the top of a draughty flight of steps that led down into the damp and cold of Hardewick Hall's cellars. At the bottom of the staircase, the unearthly luminescence of the apparition illuminated a padlocked door. The ghost gave them a melancholic look and placed a hand on the lock.

A shaded wall light behind Ulysses fizzed and faded, then flared magnesium bright. Smythe cursed. There was a fizzing crack, and a burst of sparks erupted from the box of tricks. With an audible pop the detector shorted out and the entrance to the cellar was plunged into darkness as the apparition vanished.

Ulysses swore, punching the plaster beside him. "I really thought we had it then," he said.

He looked at Emilia. The sadness in her eyes was heartbreaking. He looked back at the door, making out the padlock in the gloom, now he knew where to look, the after-image of the apparition remaining as a grey smudge on his retina for a moment until he blinked it away.

"Why's this door padlocked?" he asked. "What's down there?"

"My father's lab," Emilia said plainly, her voice dulled with sorrow. "I've kept it locked since his death."

"Well I think it's about time it was unlocked again, don't you?"

V – FEAR THE SPHERE

The doddering Caruthers came with a key, the padlock was removed and, with a confident gesture, Ulysses flung open the door.

The party followed in Ulysses' wake as he led the way, with wary steps, into the darkened cellar. A moment later the gloom was banished as someone managed to switch on the lights. Electric bulbs fizzed into life, illuminating patches of the brick-built cellar, revealing intriguing silhouettes and the hint of unfathomable pieces of equipment, until Alexander Oddfellow's laboratory was revealed in all its glory. The distant grumbling of the storm could be heard, even here.

Between archways of crumbling brick a space the size of a ballroom was filled with the inventor's forgotten, half-finished contraptions, masterpieces in the making left to rust and gather dust in the musty gloom.

Amidst all the cluttered workbenches and abandoned mechanisms, on the far side of the cellar, against a wall all by itself, a waxy tarpaulin lay draped almost haphazardly over something that Ulysses could see was large and roughly spherical.

"And what do we have here?" he asked aloud, approaching the tarpaulin, the excitement of discovery flashing in his eyes. Emilia and her guests followed in a timid, yet morbidly fascinated, huddle.

Boldly he grabbed hold of a corner of the covering, making ready to tug it free.

"Wait! Stop!"

Ulysses was so surprised to hear Emilia utter the command that he immediately halted. "Why, Emilia? What's under here?"

"Don't you understand? This was where it happened. This was where he died." She cast her gaze at the ground, as tears welled in her eyes. "Under there is the sphere; the project he was working on when he died."

"When you believe he died," Ulysses corrected.

"What's that supposed to mean?" Emilia challenged, melancholic sorrow suddenly becoming the anger of the grieving, raging at the injustice of it all.

"Hey, steady on, Quicksilver!" added Dashwood, coming to his cousin's defence.

"I know this is hard for you," Ulysses said, dropping the tarpaulin and taking a step towards Emilia, clasping her shaking arms with his strong comforting hands, "but all along it has been assumed that Alexander Oddfellow died here, working on his latest project, and yet his body was never found."

"There were witnesses, Quicksilver, you fool. My uncle wasn't alone when the last test run of the device backfired. They saw the explosion. He was atomised – I'm sorry, Em, really I am – but he must have been. There can be no other explanation."

"There, you've said it yourself. These witnesses of yours saw a disappearance. They did not necessarily witness Alexander Oddfellow's death."

"Then, if he's not dead, where is he?" Emilia demanded.

"That's what I plan to find out." For a moment Ulysses and Emilia just looked at each other.

"You know, Em," Dashwood said, interrupting their unspoken conversation, "I think Quicksilver might be onto something here."

"Really?" Emilia said in surprise.

"Really?" echoed Ulysses. "You've changed your tune."

"Yes, I think you might actually have something there, old boy." There wasn't even an undercurrent of sarcasm to Dashwood's words. "Tug away."

With a dramatic flourish, Ulysses took hold of the tarpaulin and pulled it free.

As tall as a man and half that again, supported on a claw-footed base, stood the concentric rings of a gyroscope. The broken rings described a void in the shape of a sphere at the heart of the machine. Thick vulcanised rubber sheathed bundles of wires trailed from the strange device to the control panel of a logic engine.

Smythe and Wentworth both immediately approached the machine, placing their own useless device on the floor, running excited hands over the control levers and dials, unable to hide their boyish delight.

"So, Quicksilver," Dashwood said, "what's your theory?"

"What?"

"I was too hasty before. Tell us what you think happened."

"Yes, Herr Quicksilver," Sigmund Faustus joined the discussion, "go on. I would like to hear more about your theories myself. I am intrigued to learn how my learned friend Herr Oddfellow might have survived the accident, and where he went."

Emilia stared at Ulysses in bewilderment, looking like she had been knocked for six.

"Well," Ulysses paused, giving himself time to formulate how he was going to back up his hunch, having been caught off guard by Dashwood's dramatic change of heart towards him. "To be honest, I have no idea what it is that Oddfellow was working on when he vanished, but I am certain that this device, this sphere, was right there at the heart of it. For a start, has anyone else noticed that this thing is still on?"

Everyone looked towards the curious contraption again, and in the silence they all heard the electrical hum coming from the weird mechanical workings. Dusty yellow light glowed behind the glass dials of the controlling logic engine.

"Erstaunlich!"

"That's a good point," Ulysses mused aloud, turning to the German. "Herr Faustus, could you tell us what Oddfellow was working on?"

"I wish that I could," the philanthropist sighed, his expression one of open disappointment. "I am afraid I was only his sponsor, not his confidante."

"Really? You would fund an operation like this," Ulysses said, taking in the contraption with a sweep of his arm, "without having any idea of what he was attempting to do?"

Others among the party were considering the German philanthropist now, Dashwood frowning at him, as if he were trying to read his emotions and judge whether Faustus was telling the truth or not.

"I am a philanthropist, Herr Quicksilver," Faustus replied curtly. "You know what that means? I act – how do you say? – with benevolence towards my fellow men. I do not choose to judge them. I knew enough about Herr Oddfellow's successes in the past to know that it was worth sponsoring his latest project. His word was good enough for me."

His eyes still narrowed in suspicion, Ulysses turned to Emilia. "Can you shed any light on this mystery?"

"What? No. Father was always very secretive about his work."

"But you're his daughter. Surely he would have confided in you?"

"I didn't like to pry," Emilia said, surprised and affronted by Ulysses' challenge. "What are you trying to say?"

"I just find it incredible that nobody here – people who were close enough to your old man that they should be invited to a séance held in the wake of his supposed passing – has any idea what this machine is for, particularly when it's still running three months after it supposedly killed its creator!"

"That might explain the power drains and flickering lights around the house," Smythe threw in, as if someone might be interested to hear his theory.

"Power drains. Lights," Wentworth repeated.

"Then where do you suggest we go from here?" Emilia challenged Ulysses, her voice only one step away from becoming a scream.

"We run it up to speed again and see what it does!" he said, a manic gleam in his eye.

"You can't be serious?" Emilia rebuked him instantly. "Didn't you hear my father's warning? His last words to us were 'fear the sphere'."

"If that was what he was saying. There was a lot of distortion."

"He was warning us away because that was what killed him."

"Supposedly killed him, you mean," Ulysses corrected her.

"What?"

"That has yet to be proven."

"Oh, for pity's sake!" Emilia shrieked. "You're impossible! You haven't changed one bit!"

"I'm sorry, was I supposed to? Only I didn't think I was your problem anymore."

Faustus coughed politely, diverting everyone's attention onto him. "Herr Quicksilver, I think you should listen to

Miss Oddfellow. I would also warn against that course of action."

"You would, would you?" Ulysses' voice was almost a snarl as he turned on the quivering German. "And why is that, I wonder?"

"Simply because it was working on that machine that killed Herr Oddfellow as our hostess here was having pains to point out."

"I ask you again, Herr Faustus, what you know about the operation of this machine?"

"And I have already answered that question. Nothing!"

"Gentlemen. Gentlemen, please." It was the usually aloof Dashwood who interrupted the bickering this time, his soothing calm pouring oil on troubled waters. "We're not going to get any closer to solving this mystery if we don't do something."

He looked from the fuming Emilia to the furious Ulysses to the shaken Faustus and back to his flush-faced cousin.

"I have it," he said, an unaccustomed smile brightening his face. "Let's put it to a vote." He glanced round the cellar-cum-laboratory, performing a quick head count. "There are six of us who I would say are eligible to vote," he said, ignoring the servants. "So come on, all those in favour of running the machine up to speed?"

Ulysses confidently put up his hand straight away, although he continued to eye Dashwood with as much suspicion as he had Faustus. Dashwood also raised his hand, as did the two boffins Smythe and Wentworth, managing to tear their attention away from the wonderful machine for a moment.

"Is that everyone? All right, then. All those against."

Emilia defiantly stuck her own hand in the air, Faustus following her example, although rather more tentatively.

"Right you are then," Ulysses said sourly. "Let's get this thing going."

In light of their intensive analysis of the control console, with the excited assistance of both Ulysses and Dashwood, Smythe and Wentworth set about reactivating the sphere.

Emilia retreated almost as far as the cellar door, as if in defiance of the decision taken by the others to power up the machine, but not quite able to leave them entirely to it by themselves. Her father's patron joined her, putting a flabby arm around her slight shoulders to comfort her, but he too was unable to tear his eyes from what Ulysses and the others were doing.

Dials were adjusted, levers cranked and switches thrown. The broken metal circles of the gyroscope began to rotate, slowly at first and then, as the machine drew more power, faster and faster. The spinning rings began to sing, a harmonic whirring hum rising in intensity as the rings hurtled quicker and quicker.

The cellar lights began to pulse and fade as the machine pulled more energy from the house's generator.

In the near darkness of the dusty laboratory, the sphere at the heart of the machine could be seen, delineated by the whirling strands of light, a solid ball of darkness beneath.

Static electricity charged the air. The device was acting like some huge Vander Graf generator. As he stared into the heart of the gyroscope Ulysses could feel every hair on his head stand on end. A glance around the cellar revealed the same had happened to everyone else, making them all look as terrified as many of them were surely feeling. But Ulysses felt only the adrenalin rush of excitement.

He glanced at the control panel next to him. One switch

– large and gleaming brass – remained to be thrown. Ulysses seized the handle.

"Well, here goes nothing!" he announced, somewhat recklessly, and flipped the switch.

VI – THE GHOST IN THE MACHINE

A fuzzy ball of light glowed into life, like a blown ember, at the heart of the void-sphere. It rapidly began to take on a recognisable shape as Alexander Oddfellow materialized, suspended within the spinning gyroscope.

He appeared more solid than on either of the two previous occasions when he had manifested within the house. Looking through the whirling barrier of light, squinting as if he was struggling to focus through the distortion, he fixed his gaze on Ulysses and Ulysses saw a glimmer of recognition there.

"Ulysses Quicksilver," Oddfellow's voice wafted to him as if he were speaking to the dandy from another room. "What are you doing here?"

"Oddfellow," Ulysses said. "What is this thing? You've caused no end of problems, disappearing like that. There are questions that need answering."

"You can hear me?"

"I can hear you."

"Then listen carefully. I do not know how long we've got. I've been trapped here for... it feels like... I don't know how long."

"Where?"

"Within this damnable machine; inside this wretched containment field," Ulysses heard Oddfellow's strained words a split second after he saw them form on his lips. It was as if image and sound were fractionally out of sync.

"What was it designed to do?"

"What you see before you is the experimental prototype of Oddfellow's Matter Transmitting Device."

"A teleport?"

"That's what it was supposed to be, only something

catastrophic occurred." Oddfellow seemed to peer past Ulysses, taking in the others gathered within the cellar-lab, before adding, "A spanner in the works, you might say."

"So where did it teleport you to?"

"Nowhere. Limbo? I don't know. All I do know is that I'm still trapped within it. If the power were to fail, I don't know what would happen; where I might end up. I rather suspect my component atoms would be spread across the ether, never to be reunited."

"Well, Smythe was right, it does explain the power drains and the problem with the lights," Ulysses said, half to himself as he tried to make sense of what the unreal Oddfellow was telling him. "But if you're trapped in there, how come you appeared to us during the séance? And how did you lead us here in this incorporeal form?"

"I have wondered the same thing myself," the floating Oddfellow admitted. "I can only presume that some other device was used to focus my signal and project me to those locations in this wretched form. But I don't know of such a device."

"I can help you there," Ulysses exclaimed excitedly, "Smythe and Wentworth's Patent Paranormal Anomaly Detector! That crazy gizmo of theirs must have inadvertently focused the signal." The lights in the cellar dimmed still further and bulbs on the panel of the sphere's control console flickered and faded. "But I rather suspect that we do not have much time. Just wait there. Don't go anywhere," Ulysses instructed the hovering ghost.

The dandy turned to the two technical whizzes working the logic engine next to him.

"This thing requires massive reserves of energy," Smythe said, looking anxious. He and Wentworth had been listening in on Ulysses' communion with the dead.

"Massive reserves."

"It's soon going to drain everything the house generators have got, and then it will conk out again."

"Never mind that," Ulysses snapped dismissively. "If you could couple your detector to the sphere, do you think you could lock onto Oddfellow's signal again, but this time extract it from the device?"

Smythe stared intently at Ulysses from behind his spectacles, the dying lights of the control panel dancing on the lenses. "It might be possible."

"Then do it," Ulysses commanded.

"But this thing's using up a great deal of power as it is," Smythe countered. "I don't think we'll be able to keep it running like this for much longer."

"We don't have time to think. Just do it."

Without another word, and only a nod to his partner, Smythe did as Ulysses commanded and the two parapsychologists set to work.

And it was then that the machine died. With a gut-wrenching sound of rapid deceleration that set a numbing chill in Ulysses' stomach, the whirling rings slowed, the last Christmas tree lights of the control panel winking out one by one.

Smythe's hypothesis had been all to accurate; running the sphere up to speed had drained Hardewick Hall's power supply, killing the generator.

The rings stopped spinning and the cocoon of light they made evaporated into shadow. The ghostly image of Alexander Oddfellow faded into oblivion too, and the cellar was plunged into total darkness. There were startled gasps from the gathered guests.

"Damn!" Ulysses swore. "Just as we were getting somewhere."

"If this is going to work, we're going to need another

source of power," Smythe said his voice loud in the hushed darkness.

"Indeed," Ulysses growled. "But from where?"

Somewhere, far above the crumbling pile, thunder rumbled and lightning bathed the entire estate in a flickering flash of monochrome light.

The storm had broken.

VII – PHASE SHIFT

"Are you quite sure this is a good idea, sir?" Nimrod asked, leaning far out of the garret window, a bulky length of vulcanised rubber-sheathed cable in his hands.

"Don't fuss, old chap," Ulysses chastised his manservant as he danced along the apex of the rain-slicked roof tiles. "It makes you sound like Nanny Fitzgerald. We've been in worse scrapes than this."

"Yes, but you've never been out in the open, practically the highest thing in the vicinity of a thunderstorm with a trunk of copper wire in your hands before, as far as I am aware, sir," Nimrod replied, pointedly.

With a last, half-slipping lunge, Ulysses grabbed hold of the chimney stack and gave an audible sigh of relief.

"There. Made it," he called back over the drumming of the rain. "Should have this fixed up in a jiffy."

Wiping the rain from his eyes with the back of a hand, Ulysses set about the task of securing the cable to Hardewick Hall's lightning conductor. Three floors below in the cellar, Smythe and Wentworth were busily attaching their ghost detecting gizmo to Oddfellow's teleportation sphere, by candlelight. After the generator had failed, Smythe informed Ulysses that they had discovered that the machine's own reserve battery had retained enough energy to keep the sphere running on standby, as it had done for the last three months, and so still retained the teleport-trapped scientist's scrambled signal, but would only be able to do so for an hour at most. Time was once again of the essence.

"There, I'm done!" Ulysses called back to Nimrod as the downpour strengthened.

"Pardon, sir?" his manservant called back, his master's

words subsumed by a booming thunderclap.

"Never mind. I'm coming do– "

The flash of prescience struck a split second before the storm did. Sizzling white light exploded around the rooftop and Ulysses felt its heat as he went skidding down the rain-slicked tiles. The garret window shot past and he flung out his right hand, hoping to catch hold of the guttering. His fingertips brushed the mossy lip of a drainpipe and then he was over. His fall was sharply arrested by Nimrod's grasping hand.

Ulysses winced in pain as his shoulder jarred, antagonising the old injury, but despite the white-hot lances of lightning that felt like they were flaring along his arm, Ulysses still managed a knotted smile as he looked up into the aquiline features of his loyal manservant, now leaning bodily out of the attic room window above him. He hung there for a moment, the rain steaming from his clothes in the aftermath of the searing lightning strike. Above him the conductor crackled with the last vestiges of storm-born electricity.

"Told you there was nothing to worry about, Nimrod," he grinned and then gasped as his shoulder pulled again.

"Quite, sir."

"I know they say lightning never strikes twice," Ulysses managed through gritted teeth, "but under the circumstances I wouldn't like to tempt fate, so, when you're ready, if you wouldn't mind reeling me back in, as it were?"

A matter of minutes later, back in the basement laboratory, the sphere was running up to speed again.

The vibrating hum of the whirling rings filled the space with its organ-resonating force, the feeble light cast by candles stuck into the necks of empty wine bottles suffused by the lurid glowing shell of light at the centre of the gyroscopic machine. Everyone's hair stood on end like weird halos around their heads.

"Is it working?" Ulysses asked, sprinting over to join the boffins at the control panel. Wentworth was monitoring the sphere while Smythe was concentrating on the dials and switches adorning the front of his own device, now resting on the logic engine console in front of him.

"Let's see, shall we?"

Ulysses watched with baited breath, the ion charged hairs on his head streaming out around his scalp. As before, the image of the struggling Oddfellow appeared within the coruscating ball of light. It began to gain in opacity and colour, as if the old man were solidifying out of the ether in front of them, the incorporeal becoming corporeal again.

Whatever was happening to the aged inventor, it seemed to be hurting him.

"Father!" Emilia cried out as Oddfellow's features knotted in agony, strangely out-of-sync moans of pain wafting to them through the distorting containment field conjured by the machine.

And then, there he was, solid flesh and blood once more – although he looked pale and drawn – wearing the same clothes he had the day he disappeared, shirt sleeves rolled up, an untied bow tie loose about his neck.

"We've got him!" Smythe exulted.

"Got 'im!" Wentworth echoed.

"By Jove, they've done it," Daniel Dashwood gasped.

Tears running in tiny rivulets down her face, Emilia ran to her father as the circling concentric rings ground to a halt and the cellar was left lit only by the wax-dripping tapers. There was a distinct smell of burnt ozone and singed eyebrows.

"Emilia," the shaking scientist said weakly, his clothes and skin wet with perspiration, and took a faltering step out of the bounds of the matter transmitter. And then he collapsed, unconscious, into his daughters outstretched arms.

VIII – DEAL WITH THE DEVIL

"How's he doing?" Ulysses asked, observing the wan figure lying swamped beneath the sheets and blankets of his own bed.

"All right, I suppose, all things considered," said Emilia as she gently mopped the old man's brow with a flannel. "Anything's an improvement on being dead."

"You've got a point there. And how are you doing?"

Emilia took a moment to answer. "Better," she said simply.

In the soft candlelight of the bedchamber she looked more tired, more overwrought, more resolved, more noble and more beautiful than he had ever seen her.

"I'll leave you two alone," Ulysses said, suddenly feeling like he was intruding.

"No," Emilia said sharply, her voice loud in the pervading stillness of the room. "Stay. Please?"

The old man suddenly stirred under the covers and murmured something.

"What's that, father?" Emilia asked, putting her ear close to his mouth.

"Is he here?" the old man asked again.

"Who?"

"Quicksilver," Oddfellow managed before his efforts to speak gave way to a phlegm-ridden bout of coughing.

"Yes, Ulysses is here."

Half opening rheum-encrusted eyes, Oddfellow turned his head on his pillow to look at Ulysses. A hand appeared from beneath the covers and the old man beckoned him over.

"Hello, old chap," Ulysses said as he approached the bed. "How are you feeling?"

"Never mind that." Oddfellow sounded irritated. "I must speak with you alone."

"Father?" Emilia asked, surprised.

"Please leave us, my dear."

Emilia looked like she was about to protest, tears glistening at the corners of her eyes again. Then she thought better of it. "Very well." She sounded hurt. "I'll be out in the corridor if you need me."

"Understood," Ulysses said, feeling her pain but also keen to hear whatever it was that Oddfellow wanted to share with him.

"What is it, old chap?" Ulysses asked, as soon as he heard the door close softly behind Emilia.

"You know me of old, Quicksilver." Ulysses nodded. "And I know you. I know for example that you're not entirely the dandy playboy you make yourself out to be," he went on. "I know of your government connections, whereas, I believe, Emilia does not know how involved you are with the defence of the realm of Magna Britannia."

"I think you're right," Ulysses confessed. "It was that secrecy that drove a wedge between us in the past."

"But now is not the time to tell her either," Oddfellow warned. "There is still action that must be taken to bring this matter to an end," he wheezed and then coughing consumed him again.

"But it's over, isn't it?" Ulysses pressed.

"Would that it were," the old man managed. "Would that it were. You now know what that thing in the basement is," he growled bitterly.

"Yes, it's incredible – an experimental teleportation device. It's an incredible feat of scientific invention, Oddfellow." Ulysses gushed.

"It was slow progress at first, but then I got myself a sponsor and, with the necessary financial backing, I was really starting to get somewhere. But then certain things came to my attention – nothing major, just niggling doubts – and I began to suspect that, how shall I put this?" He broke off to cough again.

"Go on," Ulysses urged impatiently.

"Well, that certain malign agencies had taken an interest in what I was doing and were funding the project, intent on getting their hands on the fruits of my labours. You know the accident that trapped me inside the transmat's containment field?"

"Of course."

"Well, it wasn't entirely an accident."

"You were set-up? A booby-trap?"

"Something like that. I believe it was the work of..." Oddfellow paused, lowering his voice to a whisper, even though there was no one else present to hear. "An agent of the Nazis."

"Really?" Ulysses was incredulous. He knew that the Nazis were still an underground power in Europe, with their hooks in other parts of the world too, but he hadn't had anything to do with them himself within the British Isles.

"You must believe me!" Oddfellow pressed, his plea loud again. "Because if I'm right, now that I am free of the sphere, it won't be long before they make their move."

"Who is this agent?"

"I don't know – that's the trouble. They could be here, right now, in this house!" He sounded desperate now, close to panicking. "But they cannot be allowed to get their hands on my machine. I got as far as destroying all of my notes associated with the project and was preparing to destroy the machine itself when that so-called 'accident' occurred."

Ulysses fixed Oddfellow with a penetrating stare, the

pieces of the puzzle finally beginning to make sense. "What do you want me to do?" he asked, with cold purpose.

"You must destroy the sphere, so that no-one can ever use it as a weapon or to further any evil plan for dominion."

Ulysses didn't need to be told twice. He trusted the old man, and if he had decided that the machine was a danger to the safety of the realm, and needed to be destroyed, that was the course of action that had to be taken.

Outside the room he met Emilia pacing the corridor. "Stay with him, he told her, "and keep the door locked."

Ignoring her protestations and questions, Ulysses raced downstairs to find everyone else gathered in the library.

Something close to precognition sent an icy chill down his spine and turned his skin to gooseflesh even before he saw Sigmund Faustus, sitting in the same leather-upholstered armchair from earlier that evening. Fingers steepled in front of his face, he announced solemnly, "Mr Quicksilver, it would appear that you have walked into – how do you say? – something of a situation."

IX – VANISHING POINT

"Oddfellow truly made a deal with the Devil when he fell in with you, didn't he Faustus?" Ulysses riled, his body tensing, ready to deal with whatever the alleged German philanthropist might have in store for him.

"Oh, but you are mistaken," the bloated Faustus railed in response, his double chins wobbling in indignation.

A bark of cruel laughter from the corner of the library caused Ulysses to snap his head round in surprise.

"Not as quick as you thought, are you, Quicksilver?" Dashwood sneered as he emerged from the shadows, the gun in his hand trained on Ulysses.

Ulysses considered his own pistol, feeling the weight of it in the holster under his arm, but he kept his hands down by his sides. Now was not the time to go for his own weapon; Dashwood would shoot first and ask questions later, he was sure of it.

He hurriedly scanned the room. From left to right around the library, either seated or standing in anxious anticipation were the parapsychologist Wentworth, Sigmund Faustus, his aide, Ulysses' own manservant Nimrod, the quaking, all-but-forgotten Renfield, Smythe, Caruthers and then the pistol-wielding Daniel Dashwood.

"But Herr Faustus really hit the nail on the head there. This is what you might call something of a situation."

With a barely perceptible nod to Ulysses Nimrod suddenly leapt at Dashwood, more agilely than his slicked back grey hair and apparent age might suggest. But before he could reach the traitorous gentleman, and before Ulysses could make the most of Nimrod's diversion, Smythe, standing between Nimrod and Dashwood, sprung into life himself and floored the manservant with a vicious punch to the face.

In his shadowy life before finding a position as Ulysses' father's butler and manservant, Nimrod had, for a time, held something of a reputation as a bare-knuckle prize-fighter, but Smythe's attack had been entirely unexpected.

Dashwood's aim didn't waiver for a second. His eyes still fixed upon Ulysses, he gave another bark of harsh laughter and tensed his finger on the trigger.

"I believe you've met my colleagues – partners-in-crime, as it were – Mr Smythe and Mr Wentworth."

Ulysses said nothing but merely continued to watch Dashwood, hardly daring to blink in case he missed the one moment of opportunity he needed.

"Very useful they are too," the gloating Dashwood went on. "Particularly when it comes to cobbling together a containment field focusing device from what little I was able to salvage from my rather ingenious uncle's notes. They're also dab hands at setting up little 'accidents', shall we say.

"Although, of course, they might not have been so hasty to arrange one in particular if they had realised that uncle had already made moves to stop anyone following in his footsteps. But now we have both the inventor and his invention intact, thanks in part to you, Quicksilver, so what need have we now of cremated blueprints?"

Obviously already considering himself victorious, the arrogantly boastful Dashwood saw no reason to keep any element of his schemes secret any longer. He had revealed to Ulysses the how and the why, certain that there was nothing that the dandy could do to stop him. And, unfortunately with Nimrod out of action, he appeared to be right.

"All that remains is for me to tie up a few loose ends."

Dashwood's finger tightened still further on the trigger, easing the mechanism back, the barrel of the gun aimed directly at Ulysses' chest.

With a wailing cry, the flabby Faustus launched himself out of his chair with surprising speed. Startled, Dashwood turned, amazement writ large across his face, as the fat German barrelled into him.

The discharge of the gun was loud in the close confines of the library. Faustus gave a grunt, as if winded, and tumbled forwards onto Dashwood. It was the opportunity Ulysses had been hoping for. He went for Wentworth and sent him smashing to the floor with a well-aimed blow to the stomach, which he followed up with a double-handed blow to the back of the neck.

There was an audible crunch and Ulysses look round as Smythe cried out. Nimrod had had his revenge. Smythe lay howling, curled in a ball on the floor as blood poured from his broken nose.

Dashwood lay motionless, beneath the bulk of Oddfellow's sponsor.

"Nimrod, with me!" Ulysses shouted. "We haven't a moment to lose!"

Ulysses leading the way, the two of them raced back down the cellar steps and into the abandoned laboratory once more.

The sphere squatted there on its claw-footed stand, the machinery glowing faintly with what little power remained in its storm-charged reserve batteries, a malevolent presence in the candle-pierced gloom of the cellar.

The last time it had been activated, to effect the release of the imprisoned Oddfellow from its containment field, had drained the potential energy released by the lightning strike but no-one had thought to actually turn it off afterwards.

"We have to destroy this thing," Ulysses said, finding himself suddenly in awe of the machine.

"I do not mean to sound impertinent, sir," Nimrod said, "but how do you suggest we do that?"

Ulysses scanned the control panels of the device and the stilled rings. "There must be a way to overload it. Sabotage its controls or something."

"But overload it with what?"

"Ahh..." Ulysses was suddenly caught out. The generator was still down. "Don't worry, I'll think of something."

Ulysses hastened over to the control panel, frantic eyes searching for a solution. Then preternatural awareness flared inside his skull and he flung himself down behind the logic engine.

The retort of the pistol was dulled by the damp stone acoustics of the cellar. There was a second crack as the bullet spanged off the control console, shattering a glass dial. A second shot rang out and Ulysses heard it smack into the gyroscope itself.

He dared a glance around the edge of his sturdy shelter. The three scoundrels stood at the bottom of the steps. Smythe had a bloody handkerchief clamped to his nose while both Wentworth and Dashwood were gasping for breath, having been badly winded. But Ulysses couldn't see Nimrod. He had doubtless taken cover when he heard the felons dashing down the steps into the cellar.

However, Ulysses couldn't let their presence halt his mission. It was all the more important now that he destroyed the sphere and stopped the traitorous Dashwood and his lackeys getting their hands on it.

Grasping the thick trunking that connected the control panel to the machine he gave a sharp tug. He heard a tearing metal sound and felt something give at the other end of the cable. Teeth gritted he heaved again and was rewarded by a spray of sparks as a bundle of wires came away from the back of the gyroscopic frame. But other cables still connected the sphere to the logic engine, in some unnatural imitation of the umbilical cord connecting an unborn infant to its mother's womb.

As Ulysses reached for another bundle of wires, another flash of prescience sent him scrabbling away, shuffling backwards on his backside, heels kicking against the floor of the cellar.

Dashwood saw Ulysses as he emerged from behind the sheltering cover of the control console and drew his aim on the dandy once more. Distant thunder rumbled over Hardewick Hall.

"Now I've got you," Dashwood snarled.

Scintillating electric blue light exploded throughout the laboratory as the broken rings of the sphere began to spin again. Dashwood threw a hand up over his eyes against the retina-searing glare.

"Lightning never strikes twice, my arse!" Ulysses exclaimed delightedly to himself as he ran for cover.

Eyes narrowed to slits against the brilliant light pouring from the spinning sphere, Dashwood dropped his shielding hand and searched for his target beyond the edges of the coruscating glare, where the shadows appeared even darker now in contrast to the blinding whiteness. But there was no sign of Ulysses.

"God's teeth!" he swore. Smythe and Wentworth looked at him in confusion. "Turn that thing off!" he commanded, waggling his gun at the machine.

Not wanting to risk the wrath of their employer any further, his lackeys moved cautiously towards the now sparking control console of the matter transmitter.

The machine wasn't running as it had been before. Whether it was as a result of something Ulysses had done to sabotage the sphere, or thanks to one of Dashwood's poorly-aimed shots in the dark, something was most definitely wrong with Oddfellow's invention.

There was something feral and untamed about the arcs of lightning zigzagging between the crazily orbiting rings.

"Hurry up!" Dashwood bellowed, hastening Smythe and Wentworth over to the console with another wave of his pistol.

And that was when Nimrod struck. He caught Dashwood firmly between the shoulder blades with the wine bottle, smashing it across his back and sending him reeling. As the villain stumbled forwards, Ulysses made his move. He flung himself out of the shadows and, catching both Smythe and Wentworth around the side of the head, brought their skulls together sharply.

Smythe reeled sideways, a silent expression of pain on his face. Wentworth slumped onto the control panel, stunned. As he slid down the front of the console, he fumbled for purchase with a flailing hand and caught hold of a large, gleaming brass switch, and pulled.

Ulysses leapt from the control platform, sprinting past the bewildered Dashwood, covering the cellar with long strides, as the sphere activated one last time. There was a sound like a thunderclap, deafening within the cellar. Blinding white light flooded the lab, burning Ulysses' eyes even though they were closed. It was as if they had been caught at the very heart of a violent electrical storm, where the turbulent skies birthed their lightning progeny.

His ears hurt, his eyes hurt, his skin felt like it was on fire.

And then the light was gone, leaving glaring after-images on his abused eyeballs, and the acrid stink of obliterated ozone in its wake.

Ulysses fought to open his eyes despite the pain. He could see nothing. The exposed skin of his hands and face stung.

He cast his gaze around the cellar, blinking all the time, and then he saw Nimrod through the gloom. His faithful retainer's eyes were watering and his exposed skin looked like he was suffering from a bad case of sunburn.

And then Ulysses realised something; he could see Nimrod, he could see the workbenches of the lab behind him, he could see the cloud of smoke left by the lightning explosion. He looked around the cellar space again, hardly able to believe the what he was seeing, or rather, what he wasn't seeing. The reason he had seen nothing when he first opened his eyes, beyond the shadows sliding over his tortured corneas was because there had been nothing to see.

Caught within the matter transmitter's zone of influence, Dashwood, Smythe and Wentworth were gone. And so was the sphere. All of them had disappeared – villains, sphere, logic engine, all – teleported to God alone knew where.

Considering how Oddfellow's machine had failed before, Ulysses wondered darkly whether their final destination had been anywhere within the physical realm at all.

"Won't you stay, just for a little while?" Emilia beseeched him, practically on the verge of begging. "We have so much to catch up on." She found herself absent-mindedly stroking the material of his waistcoat.

Ulysses noticed that she was wearing her hair down, loose about her shoulders. He put a hand to her chin and raised her head, gazing into her darkly-lidded eyes. The day had dawned bright and clear, the storm having blown itself out in the night. The cold crystal blue sky of the first day of November was now reflected in those dark eyes of hers.

He could have lost himself in those limpid pools at that moment, he thought, but he had to be strong. The way fate and personal preference had dictated how he live his life was no life for a delicate flower like Emilia Oddfellow.

"I'm afraid there are matters awaiting my attention back in London," he said in all honesty, without actually giving away any pertinent details.

"I mourned you once," she said, "when *The Times* reported you lost over the Himalayas. Just as I mourned my father. But now I have you both back. I do not want to mourn you again."

"Which is why I must go," Ulysses stated flatly. "Go to your father now. Be with him. He needs you."

"Don't you need me, Ulysses?" she asked. He looked away to where a sunburnt Nimrod was loading his luggage back into the boot of the Silver Phantom.

Ulysses turned back to her and, a forced smile on his face, said: "It's been a pleasure, as always."

"Oh, I see. It's like that." Now it was Emilia's turn to look away. "So are we to live parallel lives now," she challenged, "never to meet again?"

Ulysses said nothing, but gazed out at the mist rising from the croquet lawn.

"Well, thank you for all you've done," Emilia said, suddenly prim. "Good day to you, Mr Quicksilver. I hope you have a safe journey back to London."

"Good day, Miss Oddfellow."

Feeling lonelier at that moment than he had in a long time, turning his back on Emilia and Hardewick Hall, Ulysses Quicksilver descended the steps to the gravel drive.

Two other vehicles were waiting in the cold crisp morning. A team of horses and adapted carriage sent by the local constabulary were taking Madam Garside's body to the morgue and the broken Renfield for further questioning. The second vehicle was a private ambulance. A pair of medical orderlies was lifting a stretcher-bound Sigmund Faustus into the back, his young aide looking on anxiously. The German still looked pale, unsurprisingly, but at least he was still alive.

"I meant to thank you, and apologise," Ulysses said holding up a hand to the stretcher-bearers to wait as he humbly approached the prone philanthropist. "I was wrong to accuse you. What you did was incredibly brave."

The German smiled weakly. "I was foolish and incredibly lucky, Herr Quicksilver. You, on the other hand, saved the day."

"I couldn't have done it without you," Ulysses admitted.

"Very well then, if you insist, I will – how do you say it? – take my share of the blame." He held Ulysses' gaze for a moment, suddenly serious. "Your father, Hercules, would have been proud of you."

An unsettling chill began to gnaw away within his gut at Faustus' mention of his father, as the injured man was loaded into the ambulance. Ulysses had not realised that Oddfellow's mysterious benefactor had known his father. What else didn't he know, he wondered.

There was a tug on his arm and before he really knew

what was going on, Emilia was there in front of him her scent heady in his nostrils, her lips crushed against his. And at that moment their parallel lives seemed to converge and all his doubts and conflicting emotions vanished.

THE END

Ulysees Quicksilver will return in *Human Nature*.
Coming December 2008!